RISE OF THE ATLANTEANS

DESTINY FOUND

T.A. FORLENZA

SOULSTONE PUBLISHING

Like a new-writer noob, I neglected to dedicate my first novel, Hidden Destiny, to the people that mattered the most to me.

To my best friend and wife, and my two amazing children, you are the drive that pushes me to explore this world. Thank you for believing in me. I love you all more than the mulletverse.

To Ali, thanks for helping a brother out. These would all still be collecting dust without you.

To my diehard Atlanteans out there, stay frosty. Atlantis awaits.

SOUNDTRACK

Like the previous novel, this one also has a soundtrack that readers can listen to while they read. The adventures in Atlantis stem more from just the writ word on the page; the ideas came to me first as I listened raptly to the instrumental scores of my favorite movies. I would blissfully daydream in the middle of other, newer music, this world slowly unraveling before my mind's eye.

It is here that I hope to share this with you. Listen or not; the way is open to you. If you find the need to hear what I hear, then read aloud this book as you play the music where noted. Hopefully, this will uplift you as it uplifted me.

Look for this soundtrack on Spotify by searching "Rise of the Atlanteans: Destiny Found".

"Dawn" from Dark Before Dawn by Breaking Benjamin
"Leeloominai" from The Fifth Element Soundtrack by Eric Serra
"We are here" from the Unbroken Soundtrack by Alexandre Desplat

"Bedding Down" from the Atlantis: The Lost Empire Soundtrack by James Newton Howard

"Merida's Home" from the Brave Soundtrack by Patrick Doyle

"Fire" from Feng Shui: Music for Balanced Living by Daniel May

"Death Strikes Deathstryke" from the X2: X-Men United Soundtrack by John Ottman

"Saving Buckbeak" from the Harry Potter and the Prisoner of Azkaban Soundtrack by John Williams

"Protect Life" from The Fifth Element Soundtrack by Eric Serra

"Bedtime Story" from The Day After Tomorrow Soundtrack by Harald Kloser

"Royal Pursuit" from Frozen Soundtrack by Christophe Beck

"Zombie Spike" from The Dawn of the Dead Soundtrack by Tyler Bates

"The League of Extraordinary Gentlemen - Medoly" from Score It! (KMN Score Remix) by Trevor Jones

"Concerning Hobbits" from The Lord of the Rings: The Fellowship of the Ring Soundtrack by Howard Shore

"Farewell" from the Terminator: Salvation Soundtrack by Danny Elfman

"Finding Faith" from the X2: X-Men United Soundtrack by John Ottman

"Platform Nine-and-Three-Quarters and the Journey to Hogwarts" from the Harry Potter and the Sorcerer's Stone Soundtrack by John Williams

"The Drive toParis" from The Bourne Identity Soundtrack by John Powell

"Antarctica" from the Aliens vs Predator soundtrack by Harald Kloser

"Slaves to Rome" from the Gladiator Soundtrack by Hans Zimmer

"Arrival at Aslan's How" from The Chronicles of Narnia: Prince Caspian Soundtrack by Harry Gregson-Williams

"Sacred Pool of Tears" from the Kung Fu Panda Soundtrack by Hans Zimmer and John Powell

"Uncharted Territory" from the Edge of Tomorrow Soundtrack by Christophe Beck

"The High Council Meeting and Qui-Gon's Funeral" from the Star Wars: The Phantom Menace Soundtrack by John Williams

"Tala Returns" from the Moana Soundtrack by Mark Mancina

"There are Witches Among us / The Bank / The Niffler from the Fantastic Beasts and Where to Find Them Soundtrack by James Newton Howard

"The Return of the King" from the Lord of the Rings: The Return of the King Soundtrack by Howard Shore

"I Claim your Sun" from the Transformers: Revenge of the Fallen Soundtrack by Steve Jablonsky

"Maester" from the Game of Thrones: Season 6 Soundtrack by Ramin Djawadi

"The Human Spirit" from the Day After Tomorrow Soundtrack by Harald Kloser

"Tap into your Mind" from A Wrinkle in Time Soundtrack by Ramin Djawadi

"History of the World" from the Alien vs Predator Soundtrack by Harald Kloser

"War" from the Avatar Soundtrack by James Horner

"Treebeard" from the Lord of the Rings: The Two Towers Soundtrack by Howard Shore

"Welcome to the Moors" from the Maleficent Soundtrack by James Newton Howard

"Hero's Theme" from the Justice League Soundtrack by Danny Elfman

"My Watch had Ended" from the Game of Thrones: Season 6 Soundtrack by Ramin Djawadi

"Specter of the Goblin" from the Spider-Man Soundtrack by Peter Anthony

"Hinx" from the Spectre Soundtrack by Thomas Newman

Jabulqa
Sophiel
River Phlegethon
Pyphlegethon
The Vigrid Plain
River
Thulr River
Nidavellir
Zion
Olam Haba
Bravalla Plain
Mimir
The Miyul
Ischin Bay
Nisir
Forest
Urdarrbrunn
Mi
Akhirati Fields
Shambhala
Jabulsa
Midgard
Lamayin Forest
Pure Land (Jodo)
Jarnvi
Urgyen
Bohdi Forest
City of Brass
Idavollr
(Agartha)
Sodom
Gammorrah
Ny
orest
Chayula Forest
Geb
Niflhang River
Atlantis
Eridanus River
Edjo (The Darkness)
Tuamutef

CONTENTS

RECAP

("Dawn" from Dark Before Dawn by Breaking Benjamin)

Brett Dourdon, a United States Marine, almost died after his camp in the Middle East was attacked by mortars. Instead, a fiendish man arrived to bring him back from the brink of death. Unbeknownst to Brett, the fiendish man, known then as the Outlaw, needed to keep Brett alive in order to fulfill his own devilish plan. His return from the dead strangely bestowed upon Brett abilities that put him far above his peers; abilities that intimidated even him.

Not long after, Brett was reassigned to Camp Pendleton, California. While there, the Outlaw assumed the persona of a fellow Marine, subtly guiding Brett's every action. In control of an entire naval fleet, the Outlaw steered Brett towards the destination where both their destinies would be fulfilled.

On the way to the island of Tahiti, the Outlaw and Brett made an uncomfortable contact. Using fiendish magic to drain Brett's ability, the power doubled back on Brett. In a dark vision, Brett saw the name "Andrew" scribbled over and over. Calling the name out to the Outlaw, Brett came to understand that it was his true name.

On Tahiti, Brett came face to face with love at first sight. Ke'eli, a beautiful woman of Polynesian descent, unlocked something else inside Brett that saw both partners able to do amazing things. Separated by Andrew the Outlaw, who revealed his true demonic form to the couple to steal their power, the couple awoke far away from each other. The very Daemon Hunters he sought to free captured Andrew, unsuccessful in his attempt on Brett and Ke'eli. The Daemon Hunters seized Andrew and returned him to the Otherworld, his devilish home.

Seeking each other out again, Ke'eli found Brett just as he was about to destroy the West Coast in a tidal wave of water. Easing his depression, the two found safety in their budding abilities, exorcising the demon that had entered Brett's mind. Andrew also found allies, his "Ring," which he had grown up with. With their aid and them in tow, Andrew returned to the light of the Upperworld to continue his quest.

Returning to a time where Ke'eli was pregnant with a child, Andrew knew not to try his siphon again. He was aware of three other potential "soulbounds" that he could instead seek and absorb power from, using his Ring to aid him.

After thirteen years and several other failed attempts, Andrew decided it was time to return to Brett and his budding family. Drawing him onto an airplane alone, Andrew was successful in beginning the siphoning process. In doing so, he unlocked a mental barrier erected in Brett's mind, keeping him from attaining higher power. With that barrier down, Brett struck back out at Andrew and his Ring. In a last-ditch attempt to steal the power for his own, Andrew miscast a *Wish* spell, thrusting Brett into an alternate reality.

Brett, in this alternate dimension, came to fully understand the powers he possessed, as Andrew inadvertently wished for Brett Titanes, Brett's true name. In returning to his own reality, Brett included three others with one additional stowaway.

Andrew, Ring in tow, made for a full attack on Brett's home. At the same time, a group of Atlantean "Seekers" sought to steal Brett's child, Drake, back to their home in Atlantis, thinking he was a powerful psychic. Instead, the Atlanteans returned with the entire family, leaving Andrew empty-handed once again.

PROLOGUE

("Leeloominai" from The Fifth Element Soundtrack by Eric Serra)

The serpent-like woman slithered along the bare, rocky walls of the cave, which had been its home for the last several thousand years. Though calling it a cave would insult other caves, this hovel beneath the earth had been dug out and remodeled so many times, the serpentine creature found it hard to remember what it looked like in the beginning.

She moved as fast as her scales could, answering the call of one other who lived there with her, together in their statue-filled fortress of solitude. They had been working together so long, the thought of this urgent call had her fearing the worst, yet also the best.

She turned a corner into one large, well-lit chamber, finding the man who had sent the urgent summons. His back was to her, his gaze down at a stone sarcophagus. She could see in the torchlight his hands caressing the statue inlaid upon the structure's lid, whispering softly. He stroked it gently, lifting his head as she drew near.

"Is it time?" The woman whispered, her slithering quietly on the ground.

The man rotated to face her, her body drawing near as she stroked his face. His long gray hair hung low over his face, concealing much of the scraggly beard he had stopped grooming long ago. His gray robes were blacker and browner from the dirt and soot of the self-imposed exile he had forced upon himself in the cave with her. But his physique was still nothing short of athletic perfection for a man of his advanced age.

Snakes for hair slithered back from the woman's scalp to reveal her beautiful, yellow-tinged face, which looked up tearfully into the man's eyes. Her long, snake-like tail wrapped them together in a tight embrace, his hands reaching up the small of her back. One of those hands came forth to wipe a tear from her eye, cupping her cheek to bring her close for a kiss.

"My dearest Stheno, you do not know how much you have meant to me over these many thousand years." The man spoke, his words caressing her as much as his hands. "I have felt the return of the amulet just now. I cannot tell who holds it, but for it to reappear in the midst of the country worries yet excites me."

"Which means you must leave me, no?" She lowered her head into the man's chest, hugging him closer.

"I must learn who possesses my rhomb and get it back if it's not who I think it is. We've been preparing for this for so long, I'm not sure I can go through with it."

The snakes from the top of the medusa's head slithered through the clumpy tangles of the man's hair as he laid his head on hers.

"You know, there was a time when I couldn't stand your hair doing that. Now I fear I'll miss it more than anything." He whispered to her, pulling her face up to his.

Fighting through the tears, she smiled at the joke. Her hair shot forward suddenly, snake tongues all striking out at the man's face all at once, licking him incessantly.

Like being tickled by a thousand feathers at once, the man moved his head back and wriggled his nose, wiping his face.

Stheno giggled up at him, her tail unwrapping from their entwined bodies. Using it to project her body higher into the air, her face was now level with his.

"Be strong, my love. You have been here for me in my darkest times. You have led me towards a path that I wouldn't have discovered without you, and now I understand that my destiny is forever linked with yours."

"Only you know, and my secret will be buried with you. If I should fail…"

The gorgon cut off the man's words with her fingertips.

"If this means what you think, there is no way you can fail. The prophecy will come true one way or another, and you can't fight that. This venture has been a thousand-thousand years in the making, and you have prepared as much as you can. Your absence will leave me lonely, though I will have treasured this time I have had with you."

As she whispered the encouragements, her face inched ever so closer to his.

"I will miss your wisdom and company, but most of all, your gentle kiss."

With that, the two wrapped their arms around each other and shared their deep and passionate love.

Stopping to breathe from their kiss, the man inhaled sharply, his eyes opening wide.

"I have had another memory, Stheno. They come quicker now that time has finally almost caught up with me."

Smiling through the interruption in what could be her last moments with her thousand-year lover, Stheno backed away slowly, pulling the man with her, hand in hand.

"Then let us begin. If time is catching up to the present, then we will have to hurry. It's time for you to embrace the destiny of being the King you have always been."

Nodding, he let her lead him away from the sarcophagus, through the many tunnels in the cave network.

As they walked, he took in the surroundings he had known for so long. Other gorgons were hard at work, some chiseling away at giant stone structures while others drew blood from one another to house in small glass vials. They, unlike Stheno, walked on two legs but still exhibited the snake-like hair and greenish-yellow skin of their kin.

At one junction, the couple came across two oddities in the serpentine lair.

"Artaxle, it is time." The King addressed a short, green-skinned goblin. The goblin turned to face the speaker, bowing low as he removed a large, exquisite black hat. Artaxle wore a series of daggers along his beltline and across a bandolier on his chest, which he subconsciously fiddled with as he looked back at Stheno. His black leather armor seemed almost to absorb the ambient light in the room, its matte black finish showing no reflection or glare, no matter the angle of his body.

Standing next to the goblin was a tall human clad in flowing red robes. He, too, bowed before the couple. Gripping a staff in one hand and an open spell book in the other, the man's black hair and goatee with just a hint of gray in it was groomed meticulously.

"Tal Dor, I cannot thank you enough for the sacrifice you are about to make. All has been explained to you?" The King grasped Tal Dor's shoulder in reassurance.

"Yes, my King, though I do fear for my well-being in the interim. Thou art assured that no harm shall befall my unprotected form?"

The King smiled, squeezing Tal Dor's shoulder.

"Trust me, son, we have been doing this for many years."

The King winced as he said the words, Stheno squeezing his hand tightly to bring him comfort.

"Your reply has me worried, my Lord."

"No, no, it's not that. It's just... I've had a lot on my mind as of late. Trust me, *Tal Dor*, your form will be protected from all harm. What will be like seconds for you could be years for us."

"Very well then, if it is to protect our people, then I will gladly make the sacrifice. Thank you for giving me this honor, my King."

"Thank *you*, Tal Dor. Please, follow the gorgons into the adjoining chamber and take your place. We will have you transported back to Laputa as soon as the ritual is complete."

Bowing low again, Tal Dor strode swiftly into a large room with arcane glyphs set into the flooring. In the center of a large dais, he brought the open book up to chest height and raised his staff high into the air, appearing as he might, as if he were posing for something.

The King could hear the magic chanting as the doors slowly closed before him.

"One more for the army, my King." Artaxle said as the trio continued their walk to another room.

"An army I hope we will never have to use, my old friend." The King grumbled to the goblin.

"Yet you say it is time. If that is so, then war may already be upon our doorstep." The goblin nodded his head up at the taller human.

Entering their final destination, the King stood within another circle of arcane glyphs, their outline glowing blue as he stepped across them.

Stheno moved up beside him, wrapping her arms around him tightly.

"If I delay any longer, I will not wish to leave. I must go now before something happens to the rhomb." The King squeezed the gorgon back, bringing her face up to his for a last kiss.

"I know, my dearest. You can't blame a girl for wanting to spend a few more minutes with the man she has come to love over so long a time, can you?"

"No, I cannot blame you. There is a part of me that wishes I could stay. But if this is what I think it is..."

"You do not have to worry, my love. Our relationship has been... *different*, but no less special than that of the others you love. If you recover your rhombus amulet and it is not in the possession of whom you think, then return to me and we will put into motion your return to the Olde World, as we planned. As you said, 'it is time'."

Smiling, the King reached down and kissed the gorgon again, long and hard.

Pulling away from him, Stheno avoided his gaze as she wiped another tear from her eye.

"Artaxle, my senses can only get me so close to the rhomb. Use your connections to find out what you can about who has just recently arrived in the country and where they are going. I will contact you shortly."

Bowing low, Artaxle moved off towards the physical entrance to the cave network, going up a series of ramps filled with statues of all kinds of different people. Before he left, he bowed again and kissed the hand of a goblin statue near the top of the ramp.

"I know what you are thinking, Stheno. Artaxle is a good man and will protect me, trust in that."

"He is a goblin, my love. He protects his best interests."

"You were once so shunned, were you not? And look at you now, the vision of beauty and wisdom. You and the children have become a necessity here that I could never have foreseen."

The King winced again as he said the words and even began to tear up as a sudden thought struck him.

"I must go, my dearest Stheno! The memories are returning so quickly, I cannot bear it!"

Stheno could see the distress on the man's face and knew there was nothing she could do or say to stop him leaving.

Backing away far enough so that he could impart the magic of the gateway where he stood, she blew him a kiss goodbye.

"Take care of him, my dear Stheno! If this happens the way I think, you will soon have visitors. They will all be confused and will need your guidance!"

The King blew a kiss back to her before waving his arm across his midsection, palm downwards. As he did, the runes on the ground flared to life, rising around his body.

Smiling over at her, he nodded once more before closing his eyes and fist, saying aloud "Tailerra".

In a flash, his body disappeared; the runes slowly drifting back to normal.

Stheno stood there staring, tears coming unbidden.

Moving from the teleportation room, she returned to the stone sarcophagus where they had met earlier.

Slowly, she made her way to see the upward face of the thing.

As she lay her eyes on the relief sculpture upon it, she smiled, stroking its face, and leaning down to kiss its stone mouth.

The sculpture was an amazing replica of the King, down to the tiniest detail.

A sizzling sound from the sculpture brought Stheno out of her reverie.

Where her tears struck the statue, the stone transformed. One drop hit the statue's cheek, and at once the gray gave way to a pink, fleshy color.

"No! It is too soon!"

Stheno wiped away the tear from the statue's face, focusing her gaze intently on the spot it had been. Her once-green eyes became a deep black, devoid of any other color. The flesh-colored area started to slowly turn gray, like the stone about it, as Stheno let out a gasp of air as if the effort was immense.

Wiping away any other tears from her face, she used the sleeve of her gown to ensure that there weren't any other tears on the statue as her eyes returned to their natural green.

Breathing a sigh of sad relief, Stheno looked down at the statue once more.

"Go forth, my King. Go forth and find your child."

CHAPTER ONE

ATLANTIS FOUND

("We are here" from the Unbroken Soundtrack by Alexandre Desplat)

Brett tried to take it all in stride. He had just ridden through a magic gateway in his living room wall to a hidden world thousands of miles away. Not just him; his wife and two kids as well. The five... *people*, if he could call them that, tried to reassure him and his family that they were safe from the *other* people who had also stormed into his house, apparently intent on killing him.

Those other six Brett was intimately familiar with and needed no reassurances that they were up to no good.

But now, the dragon-woman, an elf with magic literally on his sleeve, a half-robot gnome, a hulking... *hulk* and a bald human who could read thoughts were trying to tell the family that they had intended to help them and that they were safe from the others who tried to assault them. A fact they hammered home by saying there was no possible way the 'devils' could find them here, where they currently were.

It hadn't started out so casually calm as it was now. Initially, the elf threw bubbles of force around himself and Ke'eli, keeping them from their children. It was only the raging inferno that was the combination of his fire-wielding son and air-whisking daughter that pushed the boundaries of formalities out the window. The bald human had convinced the elf to 'pop' the bubbles, and father and mother went right back on the offensive.

How Brett felt at the time concerning his family helped to distract him from the raging waterfall of memories that was still assaulting his senses. He knew to be in the here and now but couldn't help twitch at the corners of his eyes as he took in his surroundings. Surroundings that seemed strangely familiar. Not just the waving grasses in the field they were in, but the color and smell of the place.

He could see a white wall at the limits of his vision, rising high into the air and turning a mix of purple and blue. The sun was rising far to what he guessed was the east, and it was strangely metallic looking and seemed smaller than what he was accustomed to. This place they were in was definitely not one known on the planet Earth; at least one that he was aware of.

The conversation went sour not long after they were freed. Not only had Andrew the devil broken in with his five cronies to assault Brett's family, so hadn't the five in front of them. Before they could get any genuine explanation, Brett angrily demanded to know why these creatures had come for him and his family in the night, saviors or not.

Quickly, and with less formality than Brett was used to, the human explained they were a team of 'Seekers', whose sole job was to find special people around the world. Special people like Brett and his family. When the human mentioned 'finding' special people, Brett observed that all five nervously turned their gaze to Drake. That earned Brett's ire once again. Brett somehow knew what they had intended to do; to steal Drake and escape with him.

Palms up and pleading for mercy, the human further explained that it was a gift and a curse to be a part of this team. Psychic children were all over the globe, and if their abilities were left unchecked, they could become evil tyrants and despots. Worse still, he mentioned that the fiends they had encountered previously in their home could also sense these children and possess them. As terrible as it was, the Seeker's job was to protect the children by bringing them to this otherworldly place, raise them to control their abilities and keep them far away from the evil entities in the wider world. This otherworldly place that was then explained to them as being the lost continent from antiquity, Atlantis.

It was a strange revelation then that calmed the family at the mention of Atlantis. The same Atlantis that had apparently disappeared thousands of years prior but had in actuality just upped and moved from the Atlantic Ocean down to the World Ocean at the South Pole.

The anxiety somewhat quelled by this point, exhaustion finally set in. Though the family was asleep, and it was dark when they left, the rising sun grated on their nerves. The Seekers too had been up most of the day and night packing their things and preparing for this mission. As Brett slumped down to the ground to sit and breathe, it became the call that it was okay for everyone else to do the same.

Still keeping their distance, the four other Seekers came to sit near their apparent leader, who the family overheard from the others was called "Mason". Ke'eli and the children also came to be close to their father, all releasing an almost simultaneous exhalation of nervousness.

Conversation at that point began in earnest.

"Thank you for finally seeing reason, my friend." Mason started, strangely smiling throughout the entire transaction. A smile that went up into his eyes, which had also become teary. Brett thought it strange how much this guy seemed to resonate with his family, and to what lengths he went to protect them.

"No problem. I hope it doesn't bother any of you much, but we need to know..." Brett responded, looking at each of the other Seekers slowly.

"Why my friends do not appear human?" Mason replied. The family as one shuffled about as they remained seated on the ground. Yes, it was one thing to be talking to a bald guy with tattoos on his head. It was another to see a giant lizard with wings sitting cross-legged across from you.

"Well, before we delve any further into the pleasantries of our station or where we are, please, let us introduce ourselves." Mason waved to the other seated around him.

("Bedding Down" from the Atlantis: The Lost Empire Soundtrack by James Newton Howard)

The one with the pointed ears stood first, whisking away any grass or brambles that remained on his long, dark cloak. The family watched and noted, though, that he didn't physically *touch* his cloak; a strange energy preempted his fingers, cleaning the cloak for him.

Though they had just seen a lot of it a moment prior, the obvious ability of 'magic' still awed them, as minor a cantrip as it was.

Tipping his head slightly, the cloaked magic user introduced himself.

"I am Tumidus Deincepius Certusi filius Porros nepos Aelfi tribu Invenio Cupitorius Olympos."

Before he could even continue, small giggles erupted from the children sitting on either side of their parents.

Though Brett fought down his own urge to smile, he looked over to the children and put on an air of authority. Ke'Eli, much more akin to exotic names, nodded slowly, but also peeked out of the corner of her eyes towards the children.

The act not lost on Tumidus, he huffed and ruffled his cloak, but continued on, a small scowl on the edges of his down-turned lips.

"As I was saying, I am second in command of this Seeker group Kapha and excel in the arts of Agrius Augurium. Sorcery to those of you who are unfamiliar with the term. I am he who used the Art to bring us forthwith to our home, as you so obviously noted in the previous moments. It is I…"

"Okay okay there big-cloak," the small mechanical man slowly said, standing as well. "I think ye done did 'em all in when you said yer name! Ay, I've been with ye for many a year, and I dinna even know your entire name! Let the kiddos breathe."

Tumidus, at first exasperated that he was so rudely interrupted, realized that the family did not have the slightest hint as to what he was talking about, and looking quickly from the gnome to the family, acquiesced by again tipping his head and sitting to the ground.

"Aye, now that *that's* done," the gnome started, hiking up his britches, "ye all can just call him Tumidus. He be what ye call an 'elf'. Aye, like the ones ye read about in your fantasy stories, 'cept he be about 10 times bigger than the wee ones you might think about flitting about on little butterfly wings."

The gnome looked over at Tumidus, smiling and winking. Not one to be output, Tumidus' voice peeked up to emphasize that fact.

"Ah yes, but there are those of us around who are of that ability and stature!"

Looking to talk about magic and elves again, the gnome coughed slightly and looked down his eyebrows at the elf. Though the elf was sitting, and the gnome was standing, they were both on equal level eye-to-eye. The elf caught the hint.

"As I were sayin'," the gnome continued, "he be an elf and I be a gnome. Aye, some people look at me sorcerous friend Tumidus there and then look at me and think we right ought to be related! Maybe I just be a smaller version of an elf!"

The gnome looked at the family quizzically to see if they would react. After several seconds with no reaction, he continued, laughing in a high-pitched metallic tone.

"Ha! If'n he be so lucky as to be related to me! Aye, before I get started on me own name, just know that we all look different, but on the inside, we're all still as human as ye be there before us. Long time ago, when we were all upright, hairy apes, we was changed to what ye see 'fore ye now. But we all bleed red and can bare children with any other person in Atlantis."

The scaled woman huffed loudly, smoke coming from her nostrils at the gnome's proclamation. The gnome didn't look back at her but could sense the act and just nervously shrugged his shoulders, continuing.

"So, I be Pwyll O'Feoil, but ye can call me just Pwyll. I see ye lookin' at me robotic legs and wondering what I be. Though I be a gnome, me and me other cousins the dwarves like to make use o' machines. My people like 'em so much, we put 'em in our bodies! Not by choice most o' the time; guess that's what happens when a stick o' explosives goes off in yer pants!"

The gnome again metallically guffawed at the family, shaking the pouches about his beltline. He laughed even louder when he noticed Ke'Eli pulling the children just a little further away from the gnome, catching on to the hint.

Wiping a tear from his eye, Pwyll looked around at the others of his group. Nodding his head back and forth toward the big hulking creature who was now laying down on the ground looking up to the sky, Pwyll looked over to the dragon-woman who finally turned her head back towards the group.

"Aye lass, looks like yer up. The orc's probably asleep and I'll leave the best for last." Winking over at Mason, Pwyll sat back down, facing the family and leaning back on his hands.

All the family's ears perked up when Pwyll mentioned it was time for the dragon woman to talk.

Sensing that all eyes were on her, the woman made no move to stand or speak. As the seconds ticked by, she seemed lost in contemplation, looking down at her hands which sat in her lap. The bottom of her scaly legs that rested on the grass started to turn a dark green, blending in with her surroundings.

Drake was the one to break the tension.

"Awesome fire-breathing dragon lady with wings that kicks butt is a long name too!"

Mason began to inch his way up before a slight cuckold escaped her lips. The corner of her scaly lips curled up in what the family could only call a smile before her head rose as well.

"I am Xunshi Xinzang. I am a scaleborn monk of the Green Lotus. My tribe is that of the Xia. You may call me Zang."

Nodding her head ever so slightly, her gaze settled on Drake before returning off to the distant horizon.

"Keb Umhlaba. Earthmaw clan. Orc."

The orc remained laying on his back, yelling up into the air his name. The family could see him raking the dirt with his fingers like a child might. When he said nothing else, Brett nodded his head and smirked, looking finally over at Mason.

"Well, that would leave me!" Standing and brushing some of the grass and dirt off his brown robes, he bowed deeply to the family.

"My name is Mason Clemens, a name to which was partly given to me when I was also found in the wider world and brought here. I belong to the human Mystic Enclave and, as you all are intimately familiar with now, I have control over aspects of the mind. I too was brought here from Germany over 200 years ago."

At the mention of being over 200 years old, the family looked at each other, obviously not believing the very young-looking man before them. Before they could ask questions, Mason continued.

"Yes, I know you have many questions about Atlantis. Time seems to work differently here, much like being inside the event horizon of a black hole. Within the confines of this shielded country, for every one day that passes here, two have passed in the Olde World, which is what we refer to as the greater world beyond. Time also seems to slow even more the closer you get to the capital of our country, where the great Soulstone pyramid resides. It is this construct that has gifted us both our unusual abilities and our different forms you see before you."

"So, this is the lost *continent* of Atlantis? The one that was supposedly in the middle of the Atlantic Ocean? Or was that all a trick to fool everyone?" Ke'eli asked, obviously trying hard to believe everything she was seeing and hearing.

"Aye lass, this be the continent whole." Pwyll began. "We upped and moved it about 13 and a half thousand years ago usin' magic and science. Chalked her right down the middle 'tween Africa and South America. Why d'ye think there's a big ole gash in the middle of the waters 'twixt them?"

The Mid-Atlantic Ridge, thought Brett.

He somehow knew what they were talking about, as if he were taught about these events. The lost continent of Atlantis was Antarctica, moved by some mystical power combined with technology down to the South Pole. Not only had the place moved, but the entire civilization that also lay beneath the ice had existed at least the last 42,000 years.

All the stories of ancient civilizations that had existed thousands of years *before* the current timeline were true. Brett had read about the existence of other human-based advanced civilizations from Hancock's "Chariot of the Gods", but thought that if anything, it would be cities that lay in the ocean or that sand or sea had swept away. Here was a group of obviously non-human people telling him that a *very* advanced society had existed since the end of the last Ice Age and that it spawned the whole globe.

It was strange that Brett did not seem surprised. A nagging inclination to read books about other worlds and civilizations had always tugged at his conscious, which is why he subscribed to Hancock and other strange interpretations.

Ke'eli and the children, on the other hand, were in shock.

Tumidus, recognizing that the family was still in their night-clothes, gave them additional clothing from a bag the size of a woman's purse, but that could hold a lot more than it let on as he reached his entire arm into the thing. They were dressing themselves as they pondered the revelation.

"An entire civilization, *under* the ice?" Ke'eli asked, incredulously.

"For the last several thousand years or so, yes. And outside the ice for at least 30,000 years before that." Mason replied. He could not hide his smile as he spoke. These were the ones spoken of in prophecy. The ones that would return to bring about a new age of Atlantis. And most importantly, two of the four were females.

Mason's monastic sanctuary forbade women from entering, citing another ancient prophecy that a female mystic would bring about the destruction of Atlantis and the world. None of his sect worried, because the crystals they wore around their necks allowed them to sense mystics in the world, which always led them to males. No legitimate female psychic had ever been discovered. Until now.

And not only one psychic female, but two; and related! Mason explained to the family that not only could they control their respective elements; they could control minds if they wanted to. This was how Ke'eli could calm the nerves of her hot-tempered son. This was how Brett could levitate the water. He could levitate the water not because he was attuned to it, but because he was telekinetic.

Brett thought back on the inherent abilities each of his family had. Deep down, Brett had come to terms with his ability to control water. He also found that he could move things with his mind, which at first, he thought was because they had water in them. *Everything has water in it, doesn't it?* He would think to himself. In time, he realized he could move things devoid of water.

Ke'eli was the most empathic in the group. She could read people's emotions like a page in a book. She could also hear what other people thought, much like she could hear what the surrounding plants were whispering. Her connection to the Earth was what they thought had caused it, but once it developed past plants, they knew better.

Kelly was the natural healer. She could control the air, yes, but she could also use that same energy to instill life and healing in things that astounded the parents. She could close her eyes and check where an injury might grow, using her abilities like Reiki to calm the nerves and increase the blood flow. *Fruit of my loins,* Brett would say, thinking she had some connection to the water as well. She could motivate the body to do things one normally could not do.

Which left Drake. Obviously, the fiery tempest inside him was burning to get out. But the energy inside him was not the only thing that burned. His thirst for knowledge was insatiable. Technology was his specialty. He could create Lego machines that used their own power sources to move with no instruction at all. He could program his parent's phones with apps and software that even a learned coder had issue with. One of the greatest gifts he had gotten was the Java edition of Minecraft, which allowed him to create his own mods to the game. A techno-savant for sure.

"So, you guys go out into the world and steal other people's kids to bring them here? And they never get to see a girl? Or fall in love? Or have children?" Kelly retorted heatedly, understanding the implications of an all-male society, even at the tender age of thirteen.

"Like I explained, the mystic power of a child, if allowed to grow unchecked, can cause havoc the likes none of you have ever seen. There are less-powerful psychic people out there. The fortune tellers you see at carnivals or the palm readers in New Orleans. They are nothing compared to what an untrained psychic can do if allowed to grow without control. We help the world by helping these children." Mason explained again.

"Look at Drake. He is the first pyrokinetic human child *in our known history*. Look at what he can do at only eleven years old. Imagine what he could do if not taught how to control his powers. He could roast a city if he wanted to, over a dispute about the smallest thing."

"But that's not why I am interested in all four of you. Your coming was foretold thousands of years ago, from the original Four. They saved Atlantis, moving the entire continent thousands of miles from the middle of the Atlantic Ocean, down to where we are now. They were mythical all over the world. All the stories about heroes of old were about them. They influenced this country so much that when we set back out after the Great Deluge, those stories went with our ancestors, who re-told them to the budding civilizations of man who had survived the great flood. We taught them how to survive, and in those stories, we passed on the legacy of our own saviors."

"But your people *caused* the worldwide devastation. These 'Four' were the ones that destroyed the world! They don't sound much like heroes to me." Ke'eli veritably growled her response. The idea of being stuck on an island, under a dome, covered in ice, did not sit well with her, no matter how large the continent was.

Tumidus spoke up now, growing increasingly interested in the intellectual debate. "The Four *saved* the entire world. When the Armies of Man had grown beyond bounds, they began to decimate the world. With spiritual fiends of Hell incorporating themselves into the minds of them as well, it made them even more fearless, reckless, and bloodthirsty. They wrought havoc and destruction across the entire world, and they had their sights set on Atlantis."

Brett and Ke'eli had asked the most questions concerning the fel-creatures that had broken into their home. Though they were loath to speak about it, the Seeker team relented and told the family about demons and devils and how they had infiltrated the world. Spawning from some location in Northern Europe, fiends had always been a staple enemy to the civilizations of humankind. Physical embodiments of chaos and evil, fiends' sole purpose seemed to be the destruction of humans, and they cherished the act of slaying mortals.

In time, it became known by the ancient progenitors of Atlantis that once a fiend was slain, its spirit endured. The creatures were not native to this reality and being separated from their home dimension caused their eternal spiritual essence to wander once they were killed. This enhanced the supernatural superstitions of being 'possessed by the Devil', because, in essence, humans *were*.

The fiends had possessed enough human beings 12,000 years prior to induce them to set sail for the island of Atlantis to lay siege to it. These 'enslaved' mortals, as those possessed came to be known, were strong and persistent, driven on by fiendish fervor. It was this massive attack that spurned the world-ending event that went down in the annals of history as the destruction of Atlantis and the Great Deluge that washed away the broken remains of the previous world.

The robotic gnome, Pwyll, wanting to add his own two cents, continued. "Aye, Atlantis had the technology then to destroy the whole durned world if'n they wanted to. We knew the demons would just return and the whole Gods-forsaken thing would start over again! The Four changed that, eh? They threw in a natural disaster or twenty of epic proportions and made sure it stuck well in the minds of the remainin' humans, makin' it look like Atlantis was destroyed in the process. So far so good, in'it?"

Xinzang, finally breaking her contemplative silence, then continued with a growl as well. "We protect the world from the demons that still infiltrate it. But we cannot do that alone. Mason's, and our, mission is to find mystic-born children to not only continue the human legacy on Atlantis but also to train and prepare battle-worthy mystics to aid us in our eternal war with the denizens of Hell. They have remained unaware of Atlantis thus far, but these monsters still wage a mental incursion on the hapless survivors, who have, to this day, flourished. The humans of the world are naught but mental meat to these beasts. All the evil. All the perverted wickedness in the world is because of these fiends. Man is born free of will. A child knows no evil. But evil finds them and turns them against each other. If we could truly rid the world of this menace, you would find an era of unprecedented peace."

"The Age of Aquarius." Mason smiled as he said it.

Brett and Ke'eli could not help but laugh at the proclamation. They had heard of 'Ages', and especially in the song from the 60s.

They were the only ones laughing.

Tumidus, who had remained quiet and distant until then, rose from the little campsite the group had created in the spot they had arrived in to convince the family. The *Four*, or so Mason believed.

But Tumidus had an undeniable trait: knowledge couldn't be overlooked. When it came down to educating someone about the history of Atlantis, or even the world, the elf was the best at it.

"You laugh, humans, but the measure of our time is divided into the Great Ages. As the Earth spins about, each astrological sign takes its turn, being dominant over the others. Your own kind have devolved into questions about when the next Age would begin. Some say it has, others say not for two hundred years. They guess it is somewhere between every two thousand years. The correct way to measure the change of the Age is by a major event. We entered the Age of Pisces 2016 years ago, which your kind labels the birth of Jesus Christ. In actuality, it was the Mandate that Atlanteans remain on the Continent. Before then, our people traveled the world in disguise and at will. Since the Mandate, we need special permission to leave and are 'monitored' almost constantly. The Ancile Shield that protects our home had become an invulnerable bubble that now kept us in."

Ke'eli looked over at the elf at the mention of Jesus.

"So, Jesus wasn't born then?"

Tumidus sneered.

"Yes human, Jesus Christ was born then. He was what we call an 'Avatar'; an Old Atlantean born outside the Continent. He was a human with the abilities to heal like the halflings do. He led a group much like the *True* Elders did to free the world from this sin and these fiends. And look at how you treated him. But please, do not get me started on *that*."

Tumidus rose and strolled further from the group, anger rising.

"What's a 'True Elder', and why do you say it with such reverence?"

Ke'eli could tell she touched on a nerve. She had noted the inflection in the elf's voice as he mentioned it, which, along with the empathic adoration he had at its mention, made her think he liked them over something else.

Tumidus turned back around, looking back at his fellow Seekers.

They all knew how he felt about the 'leaders' of his country, and how outspoken he was of them.

Mason put up a hand towards Tumidus, showing that he should continue. Tumidus turned back to address the family again.

"The True Elders are the original leaders of Atlantis, the Founders of our great country. There were ten in total, and they are ever-living. They are replaced in their stead at certain intervals by others who *aspire*, unsuccessfully, I might add, to live up to their illustrious name. None who sit on the seat of the named Elders now have done so much as dwindle away at our resources and bicker amongst each other."

Ke'eli felt intrigued.

"So, they are the rulers of Atlantis? Why don't the True Elders just come back and take over if they're 'ever-living'?"

"Because, my dear, the True Elders have been missing or asleep for over a thousand years. Imagine, being an immortal, alive for over 40,000 years. Wouldn't you like a break occasionally from the monotony of the world, especially of politics? The political upheaval you have in your own country is not as far-off as what you might expect here. Except here, we are a variety of different races, *stuck* under an ice-shield, having been forced to go from the most advanced technology you have ever, or will ever see, to barbarians over night! All because of these devilish fiends, like the ones who were in your very home!"

Mason could tell that Tumidus was getting worked up. Approaching his friend, he put up a calming hand, saying that it was enough for now.

"What's a 'Soulstone Pyramid'?" Kelly asked, hoping to help in averting any more discussion on the topic.

"Ah lass," Pwyll replied to the curious little girl, "the Soulstone Pyramid is an ancient and curious device at the center o' our land. It was founded by the True Elders over 40,000 years ago and is what gives us our abilities. None knows truly what it is, only that it's one o' the most beautiful, if not *the* most beautiful, thing in the world. It lights up the night with a magnificent beam out o' the top o' it that creates the shield that protects our entire land. Bein' close to it supplies energy to power our devices that is clean and non-harmful. Aye, she connects to the baby pyramids we built out o' Deepstone around the whole o' the land, creating a miniature leyline system akin to that o' the Earth's. With it, we can travel using gravity faster than anything, communicate with each other easy-peasy and even control the weather!"

Kelly's eyes lit up. The possibilities immediately intrigued her.

"Is that why the monsters, the 'fiends' or whatever you called them, want it so bad?"

"Aye lass, the fiends want nothin' but to destroy the world, bit by human bit. They come here whole, but we tends to kill them good when we see 'em. But they're no from *this* universe, you know? They come here one way or another, and when they die, their spirits canno' return to the Hells which spawned em. It's a weird, spiritual thing that has ta do with souls and the like, but the gist of it is, they're stuck here in our universe. Since they are, and they're might powerful to boot, they inhabit the bodies of men. It's like being possessed by a ghost, and the ghosts are getting stronger and more brazen, like the fiends that attacked ye in yer own home!"

Surprisingly, the least outspoken of the five, Keb spoke up to fill in the sudden gap of awkward silence, gritting through the pain still in his body. "The earth, in pain. Man, destroys. Man take more than man need. But man, not man. Man being eaten by hate. By fear. By evil. You know. You feel. We cannot be free until man is free." Looking at Ke'eli as he finished, Keb leaned down to the earth, patting it with his hand.

"But there's magic and stuff here, right?" Drake asked. "Why can't you guys just cast a spell and get rid of all these bad guys?"

All eyes turned back to Tumidus then. He had calmed himself quickly, and at the mention of magic, his pointy ears were back in the conversation. There were two things that could get him talking. History, and his forte; magic.

"My boy, magic is a wonderful and valuable tool. But it is not the answer to everything. We are capable of some amazing things, but though almost anything is possible, everything is not always probable. We have limits to the things that we can do, and because we have to work in secrecy, our methods are... *limited.*"

"One of the greatest gifts the Soulstone has provided are these." Lifting the necklace from under his shirt, Tumidus marveled at his emerald-green gemstone. "They are called rhombs and are the life energy of the entire country, capable of amazing things. But even they have their limitations, and Atlantis is the only place where they are found."

"Please, I understand you are scared and confused, and have been taken from your homes most horribly." Mason pled again. "But I promise it is for the best intentions that we teach all four of you how to control your abilities. What you do with it, then, is up to you."

"Mason, we must take them to the Council. They must know that they are here." Tumidus said matter-of-factly.

Mason bowed his head. "Yes, I know Tumidus."

"What's the 'Council'?" Brett asked, wary about this decision already.

Tumidus, already past the excited delirium of talking about the Elders, took up the challenge of reciting a history lesson again. "There are twelve different districts in our country. The respective Tribe of our ancestors oversees each district. When you think of a Tribe, think of a race of people who, tens of thousands of years ago, were all human. Through unique events involving the Soulstone, a transformation occurred, changing them to become the mythical creatures you might have read about in stories."

"Like a great clock, each number is a dividing line between the Tribes and their territories, with the Soulstone as the centerpiece. For instance, at 12 o'clock are the dwarves, deep in their mountains. Going clockwise at 1 o'clock, you then have the gnomes, like Pwyll, great inventors. The elves, like me, come next at 2, experts in the magical arts. Then, the goblinoids at 3, artisans of magic creations and secretive rogues. The spirit-speakers at 4, orcs like Keb, roam the countryside at one with the elements and our ancestors. Though they are not an original tribe, the aquarians at 5 o'clock exist in the seas to the south, masters of magical music and connections to our old allies in the Pacific. Neighboring them are the barbaric hordes of the beast-born at 6, violent and reckless like the humans they once were, but worthy fighters. Also, not a Tribe, the undead at 7 o'clock reside in the Dark Plains."

"Wait. 'Undead'? Like, back-from-the-dead?" Brett asked, fear in his voice. He looked to Ke'eli's knowing eyes, their memories from 15 years prior flooding into their forethoughts. "Are they bad guys? Do you all even have any bad guys here? Like these barbaric beast-born guys?"

"We have our own challenges," Tumidus continued, "But no, most of the undead are hard-working and valuable to our society. There are some, though, who return from the dead, the shock of which drives them insane. They roam the continent, striking out at any living creature in retribution. Some people even create them using foul necromantic magic out of the greed of our people and mercilessly control them."

Tumidus scowled at Mason then, the look not lost on the enraptured crowd.

"As I was saying, next are the scalehide like Xinzang at 8 o'clock, who live in the majestic mountains of Kunlun. To the West at 9 are the skin-walkers, feral creatures who can turn into beasts. North of them, at 10, are the humans like Mason, hidden away in their enclave. There are other humans down in the south near the beast-born, but they are what we call "Untouched". You would consider them very akin to the original Native Americans of South America. The halflings at 11 o'clock live north of the humans, healers and clerics of the ancient ways."

"Another group who does not belong to any one Tribe are the humans who had found love in the arms of other races, creating an off-shoot race of their mixed heritage called chimeras. It is most often through humans and elves that half-elves are born, though there are other mixed breed creatures like half-orcs and such. Their home is just north of Atlantis in Midgard. Last of all are the mechanical golems. Creations of the gnomes who have grown in sentience to carve out a niche all their own, they still live in the capital of Atlantis."

"All about this land are the fantastic and mythical creatures of legend. Monsters to some, magnificent beasts, and friends to others. Most of our society congregates in the main cities. The wilds are left undisturbed, as nature intended. But each Tribe has rule over its territory, and a de facto 'ruler'. The major capital of Atlantis is the neutral meeting ground, where the tribal leaders meet to relegate matters for the betterment of the whole. That is where the Council sits, and where the ultimate decision on what to do with you will be made."

"What to 'do' with us? What the hell does that mean? *You* guys brought us here." Brett, calm until that point, raised his ire once again.

"Be calm, friend." Mason began. "The Council must know of your arrival. Never have we turned away any who have found Atlantis of their own will, nor any stowaways who have returned from a trip into the Olde World. They have to be met with, to tell them that there are rogues in our territories and to give you a chance to speak with them."

Ke'eli and Brett exchanged nervous glances. They knew that there was nowhere else to go. The group had told them as much. The magic shield that protected this place also kept magic from being used to send people outside it from functioning effectively. People had to travel the old-fashioned way; by seaborne ship.

Not only that, but they were in a strange and fantastic country that no one in the world had ever seen! If Mason was right, and their family had powers that needed to be harnessed, wouldn't it be wisest if they had the best teachers in the world who utterly understood it?

All these knowing thoughts passed in a heartbeat between the two lovers, but they knew they needed to talk it over with their children.

"Can you give us a second?" Brett looked to the group, huddling his family closer to him and further from the group.

Mason bowed his head, showing for them to take as much time as they needed.

Pulling the family in close, Brett dropped to one knee to be level with his children. Ke'eli also kneeled beside him, her gaze intent on the reactions of her children.

Brett could not even get a word out before both children leaped to hug them close.

"I want to stay." Kelly whispered in her father's one ear.

"Me too." Drake whispered in the other.

Pulling the children away, Brett and Ke'eli cupped their faces.

Ke'eli did not have to be psychic to know what Brett was thinking.

"This is a strange new world. I know we were working on how special you were before we left. Are you sure you guys are up to this?" Ke'eli, ever empathic in measuring the reactions of her children, watched for any sign of concern. All she saw, though, was excitement.

"Of course," she started, looking to Brett, "you guys are excited to go to the grocery store! What's a whole new hidden continent full of magic creatures and wizard-stuff got compared to that!"

Ke'eli smiled as she looked over at Brett. Yes, this could be an adventure for the family.

Ke'eli's smile faded though as she looked over at Mason. A flash of some sort of vision filled her mind, then of another tall and bald man, talking to Mason in his mind. Though Mason's head was not moving or acknowledging the conversation, she could see almost a spiritual overlay of Mason nodding mentally as he received some sort of instruction.

"Babe, you okay?" Brett's intrusion pulled Ke'eli from her mental reverie.

Snapping out of it, she looked back over at Brett and forced another smile.

Brett finished the decision by standing up and looking back at Mason and their entourage.

"Ok. We're in."

Chapter Two

PHOENIX FIRE

("Merida's Home" from the Brave Soundtrack by Patrick Doyle)

The group set off at once. Mason had his bearings and knew where they were, explaining to the family as best he could. Most of the continent still belonged to Mother Nature. People constructed cities where they deemed necessary, mostly along ley lines and their nexuses.

The ley lines, like lines of powerful energy, connected across the continent to pyramids that lay along the outer perimeter. There were six pyramids besides the Soulstone pyramid in the center; four of which were still home to many of the people of Atlantis.

The connection these powerful structures had on each other made flight and fast travel capable. Made from rock called Deepstone, the pyramids absorbed latent energy from the land and also received much of it from the Soulstone pyramid itself. The Soulstone pyramid directed its powerful energies up into the sky, creating the protective dome shield by connecting it with the outlying "Childe" pyramids. Direct lines from each pyramid created the ley lines, which Atlanteans used to travel back and forth. The pyramids also absorbed, amplified and re-directed emotional energies, much like the Soulstone did as well.

The people who made the Childe pyramids their home also protected their powerful structures. Two pyramids were lost in the battles that the country seemed to be constantly in the throes of, surprising Brett and the family. Despite being segregated from the rest of the world, it still seemed evident that skirmishes and disagreements followed humankind wherever they went. In this place, magic had the power to turn a hero into a villain in the blink of an eye, amplifying things tenfold.

Dragons, undead, fiends, monsters, wizards; even the Elder Gods, at one point, all had to be dealt with destructively, to keep the safety and sanctity of Atlantis whole.

Additionally, the actual country of Atlantis self-proclaimed itself as the protector of the entire world, redirecting any errant magic portals opened up anywhere else in the world outside the shield to a random location here under their dome. Special teams of Portal-Hunters constantly scoured the land, able to sense when portals opened up near them.

Which was why Mason tried to hide the Seekers and family as much as he could from prying eyes. Normally, Portal-Hunters would receive an alert about a Seeker team's return to the country and would come to their aid. Mason had not wanted that conclusion, and actively worked to re-direct their efforts, even having Tumidus open up other gateways further away from the family to keep the Hunters off their trail.

Either way, the expected travel along the ley lines to the capital excited the family. The talk of the other pyramids confused them, but they could not get much more information from Mason other than the basics.

The south pyramid, known as Herald's Gate, became lost when the first fiendish attacks reached Atlantis 12,000 years ago. It was called the Red Gate and was formerly the entrance to the entire countryside from the South, when the continent was still in the North Atlantic Ocean. It had absorbed the death-throes of thousands of fiendish creatures and now radiated an aura of chaos and evil, warded from access by the most powerful of Atlantis' protectors.

The pyramid that Xinzang's people protected in the deeper parts of their mountainous home in the Southwest of the continent was called the Peachtree Pyramid for its orange-colored radiance. Not unused to the surprises they had been experiencing almost continuously since they arrived, the family just nodded their heads when Xinzang told them that the city there was called Kunlun; only the most secretive and mystical place that none could ever find in the world, now for obvious reason. Only scaleborn were permitted within its vaulted halls, where the most powerful monks trained and communed with the spirits of their ancestors.

The scaleborn were very neutral in all dealings, following the natural ways of life and balance more than any of their cousin Atlanteans. Color betrayed their ethical and moral alignments. The darker scaled draconians were more chaotic and eviler while the lighter, metallic ones were more lawful and good. White-scaled draconians were the most untrusted; they could assume the color of any other scaleborn and were shunned in most societies. Some of the most influential people to lead their kind, though, had been those who abhorred the light of 'goodness' and who could make the drastic and sometimes needed decisions to keep their fellows alive and thriving. Though they all still followed the proclaimed law of the land, their morals were still walking the line between good and evil.

The next pyramid the group of Seekers talked about was also one other that had been lost to forces outside of their control. Nearest to their present location, the Kalapa Pyramid in the Northwest of the country was formerly the home of the human mystics of Atlantis. Mason had not wanted to talk much about the place, considering he had never been there before, so Tumidus took up the challenge for him. Tumidus, always the one to push boundaries, talked about the place accusingly, as if Mason, being a human, made the fall of the pyramid his fault.

The "Plagued Pyramid" as it was called now, emitted a strange yellow color from its peak. Tumidus explained it was because of the strange experiments the humans had conducted when they lived there that caused it to be overtaken by alien-like aberrations from nightmare. What he could only describe as chthonic-type monsters, Tumidus shuddered at the recollection of the place while Mason seemed detracted and distant, knowing that his ancestors had been the ones to unleash the creatures into Atlantis.

Not the least bit concerned, Mason reassured the family that none of the aberrations ever made their way further than the darkened husk of the countryside, content to reign in the pyramid's place. The creature's presence gave the pyramid a very evil aura, leading to it being left alone.

Changing the topic quickly, Mason spoke next about the magnificent Emerald Pyramid in the North, home to the dwarves. Not as confined as the scaleborn in the south, the dwarves allowed certain people to visit the place, but most often times by invite only. This pyramid too lay nestled in the mountains of the Godheim Range. The ancestral home of the dwarves, it was called Asgard in their native tongue and had a green hue to it, most often attributed to the many gemstones the dwarves mined from the mountains surrounding it.

Brett and the family went wide-eyed once again as they realized the implications of what Mason was saying. They knew now that each 'Tribe' represented some mythical aspect of history, but it all still seemed so surreal. The dwarves that were spoken about in the ancient Nordic poems were not background players; they were the Asgardians themselves.

The dwarves, mostly, kept to themselves and adhered to their own code of conduct that did not always see eye-to-eye with the rest of Atlantis. They were all very good-hearted to their cores, but had traditions all their own that did not mesh as well with what one might call 'the law'.

Tumidus perked up to describe the next pyramid, one that he seemed to be intimately familiar with. Another of the few that did not permit outsiders to enter, the Sapphire Pyramid in the country's northeast belonged to the elves and the elves only. The surrounding city, called Thule, catered to all kinds of sorcery and was apparently the stuff of dreams. The pyramid emitted a strange energy into the countryside, affecting elves there more strongly with physical changes than other Atlanteans, hence the stories of elves looking different in various ways.

Either way, Tumidus beamed at the idea of visiting the place again. One could only spend so much time within the vicinity of the chaotic construct before being changed into something totally unrecognizable. While some welcomed the prospect, others only visited once upon their lifetimes before settling somewhere else.

The last pyramid seemed the most humanized of all the others and was welcome to all Atlanteans. Originally in the land of the orcs, goblins had taken over the place several thousand years ago, much to the displeasure of the original owners. The shamans of the orcish people considered the pyramid an ancestral and special place, but they did not do much around it except for making pilgrimages and dedications to it.

Called the Sister Pyramid, it most resembled that of the Soulstone Pyramid itself. While the Soulstone was a shimmering translucent violet color, the Sister Pyramid emanated a deep purple color. The goblins did not think it should go to waste as an ancestral site for the orcs, considering that around the perimeter of all pyramids, energy could still be harnessed and used to power electronic devices.

What became a spiritual home one day became the center of debauchery and excess the next. Mason could only compare the city that sprung up around the pyramid, called Alaka, as that of an Atlantean version of Las Vegas. Controlled chaos reigned within its confines, all upheld by the local decree of the goblin rulers who had displaced the orcs. It could remain because of the increasing population of Atlantis who needed places for its people to live.

Which brought about the concept of surviving under the dome of ice that both protected and entrapped the people of Atlantis. Ke'eli was having the hardest time accepting the idea, convinced that it would damage people's psyches. Mason reassured her that the people accepted it, though there were still pockets of others who yearned to return to the Olde World. Xinzang was loudest of those proponents, agreeing with Ke'eli that it was unnatural to not see the genuine stars.

Regardless, Mason explained to the family as they continued their trek across the countryside how the People, as they came to be called, survived. Crops for food were aided by druid skinwalkers, who could speak to the plants to make them grow bigger and faster, thus not needing the overuse of farmland.

Trees felled to make homes were re-grown, again with the help of the druids. Also, the stone worked by the dwarves was the sturdiest in the world, able to make towering skyscrapers. As Mason explained it, Atlantis was super-advanced in the past but had to stymy its technology to keep a smaller energy footprint in the world, lest the fiends sense it. That was the one primary goal of the monsters; to seek Atlantis and take its power for their own gain.

As a result, their technology went overnight from flying cars and crystal magic to using tamed animals and torches once again. Only near the main pyramid in the center of the continent and its six children pyramids around the perimeter was higher technology allowed. And this only because it used the power of the pyramids to function.

Long ago, researchers discovered the fiends were attracted to power and could almost smell it. They credited that power to the Soulstone, the other pyramids, and the actual people. Atlanteans could perform amazing feats of both arcane and divine magics, create groundbreaking technological devices, harness the power of their spiritual chi, and even communicate with the dead, but the authorities had to closely monitor and control them. Too much power could become a magnet for fiends, which would destroy everything the Atlanteans had fought to both build and hide away.

Which was why they concealed themselves in the World Sea at the bottom of the world, surrounded by ice.

In the end, Atlantis was still many years more advanced than the rest of the outside world. Phones were unnecessary for them because each person received a crystal shard called a rhomb, which allowed telepathic communication with anyone else who was willing, regardless of distance. Mason described it like having a cell phone, credit card, GPS tracker and identification all in one.

People still used vehicles, although they were not as damaging as the ones outside the dome. Thousands of years ago, they harnessed gravity, allowing most transportation to float above the ground without destroying it. Hover trains were used to conduct long-distance travel along the ley lines, as it could get you to another receiving tower in less than an hour.

Even with all the technology, though, the group resorted to walking. Mason and Tumidus both agreed that it would be too dangerous to summon a vehicle or mount to retrieve them, as there would obviously be questions asked that the Seekers were not ready to answer.

Pwyll, with his technical acumen, showed the family a holographic map of the entire country. Teleportation *out* of the country was verily impossible, and teleportation into it was very chaotic. The family was told that the bubble around Atlantis harnessed all the other errant gateways of the world to its borders. If any conjurer of skill in the Olde World could decipher how to open a gateway anywhere, it would automatically deposit them in a random location somewhere in Atlantis instead.

The holograph showed them they were on the northwestern expanse of land, near to a large body of water called Lake Apsu and in between the Rivers Phirat and Pyshon. Pwyll relegated to the group that the territory was that of the halflings, who were peace-loving and carefree. Mostly healers, the halflings kept to their temples and church-cities along the lake, each named after an angelic version of the planets in our solar system. The closest to the west would have been the city Sophiel but going to it would have been pointless because there was only overland travel there, and not the gravitronic railways they were looking for. It being the largest city next to the capital of Zion, rescue most likely would have come from there.

They found themselves fortunate that they arrived on dry land. Had they cast their teleportation spell and rushed in quicker than they did, they could have found themselves over water or some other inhospitable place. The family received a warning about some of the more exotic locales of Atlantis, which were created in the throes of errant magic gone awry, or the culmination of chaos that had erupted after the original True Elders had 'lost their way'. All about the 'continent', as they called it, were regions of strange happenings and areas that were deemed off-limits.

One such location was near to where they had arrived, which unfortunately had the family's ears perking. Not far to the north was a place called Archon's Hollow, a semi-permeant rift to the 'higher realms.' Rifts were one-way gateways to other realities, except only the energy of the plane issued forth. Occasionally, on days or nights of extreme influence, a material object or creature might appear, but these were rare, and the site was always under observation.

This was where the angels of myth had originated from. Magnificent creatures, several had appeared over the thousands of years, some to come aid the Atlanteans, some to force Atlantis over to their militaristic viewpoint of the cosmos.

Either way, the area that the rift encompassed became suffused with energy from that plane, transmuting much of it to golden and silver versions of the original. Trees lustered bronze in the artificial daylight while the grass became literal blades of gold. The water that flowed through the area took on a silver sheen as the radiance of it literally glowed.

As excited as the family was to see this new exotic world, their entourage pressed the importance of getting them to the capital as quickly as possible. They would avoid the main roads, blanket their rhombs from any outside contact, and maintain secrecy until their leaders could be made aware of their discovery.

Three days of hard walking, during which the group learned to start trusting each other slowly. It was not even until the second night that the family sat with their new guides, though there was not much talking done, as badly as Mason had wanted to. Drake found it easiest to speak to the others, of which he took a particular liking to the scalehide woman, Xinzang.

Though there were so many questions about the place they were in, Brett confided in his wife and children first, making a Plan B in case this one didn't pan out. The knowledge of where they were and where they were going had Brett splitting at the seams. Memories stirred in him as he watched the group of Seekers go about their daily and nightly routines.

He had caught some small snippets of conversation, learning that each had their own homes to return to on the outskirts of the continent. How they could travel so quickly from one side of the country to the other still baf-fled Brett, but only because he thought it was so familiar.

Finally opening to conversation, it was Kelly who had inquired of Mason how long it was going to be before they found civilization. Several times already on the trip, the group had come across beasts that were larger than they who looked like they were hungry for humanoid flesh. Thankfully, the size of their group outweighed the curious hunger of the creatures that stalked the edge of the fire-light.

In finally opening to Kelly, Mason had confided in her that each Tribe had a "Trade Capital", which allowed all other races entry into. They also had a "Tribal Home", which was another city deep inside its territory that only those of the Tribe were allowed access to.

The railway in Zion would grant them travel east to the city of Nidavellir, the Trade Capital of the dwarves, which would then get them south to Atlantis. Mason estimated they would be there by noon of the next day.

As scary as some creatures they saw were, the sights that the family of four saw were amazing. They followed the edges of Lake Apsu, the largest freshwater lake in the world, along its northern border east towards the city. Monstrous aquatic creatures, comparable to Nessie, lapped in the cool waters of the lake, hazarding a glance at the group as they paused to refresh themselves. Other creatures that also drank from the lake appeared to be giant armored beasts that Tumidus mentioned were called "Land-sharks" and who normally just basked in the sun.

They received a warning that, despite its appearance of safety, they were in wild lands and had to be on their guard. Using magic to enter Atlantis not only put you in a random location in the country, but also drew curious creatures who could sense magic in your direction.

At one point, the group slowed as they approached what looked to be a road heading the same direction they were.

"Malak's Path." Xinzang said, landing lightly among the group.

"Did you see anyone along the road, my friend?" Mason asked, concern in his voice. There was a reason the group had avoided the road and the small city west of Zion; they did not want curious onlookers seeing them traveling with two human women.

Granted, Mason had said that they could explain their presence by being half-elves with more human looks, but it would be easier if they encountered less trouble along the way.

"No, I saw none on the road, but I did not travel far. You know as well as I that the Seraphim have not traveled this way in some time, their being so involved in the battle to the west."

"I do, which is why I worry about being on the road. None know the threats that might have risen up in the Seraphim's absence."

Almost to stress his point, a guttural roar echoed out across the grassy plains.

Mason looked back at the family, all now wearing looks of concern.

"Let us rest here. Xinzang, you have returned from your patrol. Regain your strength so that we may once again ensure the way is clear." Mason smiled as he showed the group should join him off the side of the road for an afternoon break.

Xinzang answered the unspoken question as the family sat down to eat bread and jelly conjured out of thin air by Tumidus. Though it was not the tastiest thing they had ever had, they enjoyed the fact that they were eating 'magical' food.

"We should arrive at Zion in the early morning tomorrow, board a vessel to Atlantis, and be there by noon. The Council will be in session until the late afternoon, so we should have plenty of time for proper introductions."

Mason smiled as he relayed the information.

Watching the children nibble on the magic biscuits, Xinzang let out a low growl. She had refused any food offered since the party had returned, and now she fought the urge to complain.

Mason, noticing the complaint anyway, looked over at her with annoyance.

"I agree with your decision to stay off the road, Mason. I, however, do *not* agree that I should not hunt for us and bring in a proper meal. The children are skinny and small and should eat meat to gain strength."

Xinzang looked at the two children and cackled as she said the last, which made the children unsure whether or not it was a joke.

Drake, as interested as he was in eating his magic biscuit for the fifth time, could not help but notice that the "drag-on-lady" as he liked to call her, sat alone.

("Fire" from Feng Shui: Music for Balanced Living by Daniel May)

"Can you really breathe fire?"

Xinzang jumped out of her scales as she realized Drake had somehow snuck his way over to sit right next to her. She realized he had been asleep when the attack in his home occurred, and that it was her flame that had awoken him and the family.

In response to his question, or at the fact that he had frightened her, she exhaled a puff of red flame from her nostrils.

Drake looked at her with eyes wide.

"Wow! Do all dragon-people breathe fire?"

His innocence at the question and the fact that he placed his hand on her scaly knee had Xinzang taken aback. She looked from Mason to Tumidus, then over to the child's parents to wave away the question but found that all were as eagerly intent to hear the answer as he was.

Huffing out a puff of smoke, Xinzang turned to address the boy, trying not to growl too much.

"No, hatchling. All 'dragon-people' do not breathe fire. Nor can they fly. We are called the scalehide and we each have a talent that may be different to others. Some are more like dragons in that they are fearsome and feral, while others have wings, like me. All can bring up the acids from our bowels to spew at our enemies, while some still can breathe fire, gas, and even lightning."

Without even knowing it, Xinzang had the attention of the entire group.

"She doesn't normally like to talk about her people or her past." Whispered Mason to the parents. "She has been a Seeker longer than any of us and has a troubled history."

Brett nodded as she continued.

"My people seek an eternal balance in the world. Some consider it heartless to allow evil to continue, but too much good can tip the scales in the opposite direction, perverting what some might consider 'good' to a skewed version of their own evil."

Drake was raptly paying attention, though his mind was full of a thousand questions.

"Why do you look like a dragon then? Why don't these other guys look different too? I mean, Keb is like a big pig, but you look totally different."

Laughing away the insult, Keb snorted.

"Keb look best. All others look different."

Ke'eli, who had been sitting close to Keb, nodded her head as well, patting Keb on the back. They had also begun to form a bond on the trip thus far, both being of the mind that the Earth was a living, breathing thing.

"I look the way I do hatchling, because we are closest to the ancient dragons who wander this country. My scales show who I am on the inside. No scalehide except the snow-skins can hide who they are. Our morality comes through by the color of our skins. The darker a dragon or scalehide's scales, the more evil in their heart. The more polished and brighter, the more good. Snow-skins, or white scalehide, are albinos and are very stealthy and sneaky at hiding their true affiliations."

"Coooooool. So, I'm not a genius or anything, but how can you fly? Your wings aren't that big, and you have pretty big muscles. Isn't it hard?"

The scalehide chuckled again.

"Well then hatchling, it is time for a lesson in chemistry!"

Drake screwed his face up into one of confusion as he looked back at his parents. Brett and Ke'eli caught on to what Xinzang was talking about, but the children had not.

"Are you familiar with a hot-air balloon?" she asked Drake.

Nodding, Drake cocked his head as he tried to figure it out. The hint was all he needed.

"Ohhhh! Because you can breathe fire, you can fly? Because fire makes you float?"

"Not necessarily young one. But the fire in my bowels does make it easier. If I exhale too much of the element, if becomes that much more difficult to take to the winds. Which reminds me. You would do well to train with the Flamespeakers. They could teach you much about how to control that inferno in you."

"Well, what about you? You can breathe fire. Can you teach me?"

The innocence of the question moved the scalehide. She locked eyes with Drake as she processed his request. His smile and big brown eyes glittered in the campfire's light.

Several seconds passed before a smile spread across the scalehide's face.

"Yes hatchling, I shall teach you some of the art of flame-speaking. But only if you promise not to use your power for ill. The flame is a powerful tool that can replenish the land, but also to destroy it. Do we have an agreeance?"

Eyes lit up at the realization that he would learn from a dragon-person, Drake nodded up and down even as his impossibly enormous smile got bigger.

"Very well hatchling. Your first lesson is this. Fire is the easiest of elements to mold from your mind, yet hardest to control. Yes, air is wispy, but it has no substance. Water flows but yearns to be free. Earth has substance, but no flow. Fire wants to be subdued, directed, and unleashed, which is where the control comes from."

Xinzang took the fake biscuit from Drake's hand and puffed a small flame into it, setting it alight.

"Look into the fire youngling. What is your favorite flying animal?"

Drake laughed.

"Well, that's easy. It's the phoenix!"

Xinzang looked to the boy quickly, cocking her head at him as she saw the reflection of the fire in his eyes. He remained enraptured by the flame as she pushed away a memory from what seemed like a lifetime ago. She realized then that the memory was not hers, nor could she understand it. She blinked as she fought back the strange intrusion.

"A phoenix?"

"Yeah! I know they're not real, but they're so cool!"

"Oh, my hatchling, they are definitely real."

Her statement pulled both her from her strange memory and Drake's gaze from the fire.

Shaking her head, she focused back on the lesson.

"Focus back on the fire. See the phoenix in its flames. Mold it with your mind, but do not lose control over it. Realize that if you do not maintain your concentration on it that it will fade."

Drake squinted his eyes into the fire. As he stared, one eyebrow arched as his eyes opened wider. Realizing that something was happening, he squinted his eyes again trying to keep his focus.

A loud pop from the biscuit startled everyone, as if they expected a fiery monster to leap out at them. Settling back into their relaxed positions, they all instead sucked in their breath as one as a tiny flaming bird poked its head out of its top, as if it were being born and the bread was its egg.

Chuckling, Xinzang admired the tiny bird as it fought to keep its balance on the now dwindling magic bread.

"Maintain your focus hatchling! It will bend to your will so long as your will is strong!"

Drake smiled as he watched the spectacle himself.

The bird started to flap its tiny wings, lifting into the air. The bread was its fuel, and it was burning it away quickly. It made a slow turn, making to float over to Drake.

Drake stood and put out his arm.

Brett and Ke'eli at once leaped to their feet.

"Bud, I don't know if that's a good idea!"

Picking up a waterskin, Brett uncorked its top, ready to call out the water from inside it to splash on the thing.

Xinzang stood as well, calming Brett down with a clawed hand.

"He is one with the fire. It will not harm him."

Brett looked to Ke'eli, and then back to the scalehide. He had already seen so much today and knew that his son was probably immune to it. The fear would not settle though.

His decision was made up for him.

The little bird floated down to land on Drake's outstretched arm. Like a raptor returning to its master, the bird folded its wings behind its back and casually sat there, waiting for further instructions.

If there could ever be a more alarming yet amazing sight to see, it was then if anyone were looking at Xinzang. Her lips parted wide to reveal a fang-filled smile that enveloped her entire face.

Drake looked to the bird perched on his arm as it grew smaller and smaller. He realized the bread as its fuel was dwindling to crumbs and it made him sad.

"It's going to die, isn't it?" he asked, forlornly.

"Yes, my hatchling. You have birthed it from the flame made by the bread. In time, you will learn how to use the very air around you as the only fuel you will ever need. With that, the things you create can take on a life of their own, if given the proper amount of power."

Drake's smile beamed up at Xinzang once again.

Petting the bird's fiery head with his other hand, Drake could feel the physicality of the creature. The fire did not hurt him, and the bird reacted in kind, tipping its head to his hand. Knowing the creature was nearing its end, Drake lowered and then raised his arm to the air. The bird took off into the wind, a tiny flaming beacon as it shrunk smaller and smaller. With a fizzle, the bird disappeared in a puff of smoke. In its path behind it, a stream of ash appeared. As the ash neared Drake, it began to solidify into a small, red object.

Drake opened his hand as the ashen object floated closer. In a blaze of fire, the ash lit back up and fully engulfed the object, turning it into a small red feather. Drake caught it gingerly.

"A gift from the fire elements! It may yet return young hatchling. You have done very well for your first lesson!"

Drake smiled up at the scalehide. If there was any way to make his day brighter, it was when he also realized something else.

"Hey! My name is Drake! That's kind of like short for dragon, right?"

His excitement made Xinzang smile again.

"Yes hatchling, Drake is much like dragon. And there are creatures called drakes we ride here in Atlantis."

"And your name is Xinzang right? I think I'll call you Xin from now on."

The smile immediately left the scalehide's face as she roared out.

"NO! You shall not call me..."

Xinzang growled as she realized that everyone's attention was suddenly on her. Even Drake was surprised and had taken a few steps back. It was then that she realized her claws were open and flexing, as if the name had brought about painful memories.

She looked over at Brett then, realizing something else.

Pwyll, who had been quiet this entire time, looked over at Xinzang and then back at Brett as well.

"Time..." he muttered, looking back at Xinzang.

She stood quickly, trying to understand the jumble of memories coming back to her.

"I apologize... I... do not be afraid hatchling. I..."

Turning away, she leaped up and out into the air.

Everyone looked at each other with confusion on their faces.

Pwyll addressed everyone's concerns.

"She was part of our old Seeker team who use'ta call her Xin. We ran into some trouble some 50 years or so ago. Aye, our team done met with some unfortunate circumstances during a mission that nearly cost us our lives. Dinnae be afraid, lad. Somethin' about her ole name musta triggered somethin' or other."

Brett cradled his son close, squeezing his own eyes shut at the painful memory of some event, locked away in his subconscious. It seemed so like what happened in his own home, yet so different.

CHAPTER THREE

A FIENDISH FIGHT

"Stupid human" thought Xinzang as she flew higher and higher still.

The cool wind of the Atlantis elevation chilled her to the core. The great Ra orb that imitated their sun had already settled in the west where it was becoming encased in its metallic orichalcum shell, rising again as the moon. As much as she loved flying in the day with the heat on her scales, the privacy of night was her favorite and she looked forward to the setting sun.

Xinzang growled to herself as she retracted her statement. She knew the boy meant no harm. She had grown to dislike the pain of being a Seeker recently. Her people were ones who embraced the natural order, and it did not seem natural that humans were being stolen in the night. She vowed to observe and report to her brethren, hoping to stop or at least change this gruesome task.

But the pain of the memory of 'Xin' was distant yet seemed so fresh now. She loved the name Xin and had welcomed it with her former Seeker group. All but she and Pwyll had gone separate ways and lost touch for some reason, yet she continued to be a Seeker. Why had it become such a nagging in her mind?

Oh, my poor helpless lizard.

The thought was not hers, and she could not fathom its speaker. As she flew, the blue sapphire crystal shard she wore as a pendant around her neck glowed softly.

I cannot see you, but I can sense you. You have returned with a new prodigy for the Mystic Sanctum. Yes, I can see the boy child now in your memory.

Xinzang's eyes became lucid, and her wings slowed to a glide as the mind intruded on her own. She fought against the mental insinuation, but found she was helpless against it. Her subconscious, still focusing solely on Drake, aided her then as the intruding mind in hers only saw him, and not the other three of the family.

Ah, I see he is immensely powerful! A pyrokinetic... remarkably interesting. I will have to spend some time with the boy myself. I have yet to taste the power of a true human flamespeaker. There is a group of my adherents not far to your north. You will take the boy there and hand him over to them. You will not interfere in the skirmish. Let them take the boy. You will return to the Seeker Enclave empty-handed, your allies deceased at the hands of roving monsters.

Xinzang could not help but nod as the mental command was placed inside her head. She had experienced these mental attacks before but had never remembered them. Her subliminal programming aided her again this time. Whoever, or *whatever*, was intruding in her mind seemed very cocky. They assumed the Seeker group had only the boy, and that they were bringing the sole child to the Seeker Enclave, as opposed to having the entire family brought right to the Elders themselves.

The blue sapphire stopped its glowing as Xinzang shook her clouded head.

Without even realizing it, she scolded Drake again, though he may had just saved the entire group from something she did not even know was happening.

"Silly boy."

("Death Strikes Deathstryke" from the X2: X-Men United Soundtrack by John Ottman)

"Drake, look who's back" Ke'eli whispered early the next morning.

Landing among them, Xinzang forced a weak smile at the sight of the family. She approached them all, head bowed, kneeling before Drake.

"I am sorry I frightened you, hatchling." She said. "How about you call me Zang instead?"

The great hug Drake gave her was all the recognition she needed. She smiled as she returned the hug.

"Alright, 'enough of the alligator tears' as they say in your home. Zion is just over the horizon!" Zang said as she stood up taller.

A slight tick from Zang made Ke'eli wince.

Zang continued. "But I must inform you, Mason, that there are people along the road to the east. I suggest a northerly route, less than half a mile from the edge of the road, to be safest. We travel east with the road on our right and we will be close enough to enter Zion by mid-afternoon."

"Very good, my friend. Who are these people on the road before us? Threats?"

Mason looked up at Zang as she looked down in confusion.

Ke'eli saw it again. Just the slightest tick in Zang's head movement. But it wasn't the physical act of her head moving, but the mental. Ke'eli focused more on the image of Zang.

Zang responded to Mason's probe.

"I do not recall. I did not get close enough to see, only that there were humanoids traveling. The sky is too clear. If I were to get too close, I might startle them into action."

Zang is lying, Ke'eli thought.

She wasn't sure how she could tell, but Ke'eli could see an image of Zang as she spoke that blurred itself to become an image superimposed on the other whenever she answered. The superimposed image looked like Zang, only fighting to say something or wincing in agony. The 'real' image was the one doing the talking.

Before she could say anything else, Mason had everyone on the move.

"Head north, my friends, just a quick jaunt through the taller grass. Then we will continue east with the road on our right."

Ke'eli went to the one person she could confide everything in.

"Brett, something is wrong with Xinzang. I think she's lying about something."

Unbeknownst to Ke'eli, Brett could sense something, too.

"Babe, I feel something weird. I feel like we are walking into a trap. I just... smell something off. It's weird."

Ke'eli stopped with her husband as the rest of the group pushed through into the higher grass.

"Let me try something on you. Stay still."

Ke'eli reached her hands up to the sides of Brett's head.

"Are you trying to do a Jean Grey again on me?" Brett laughed, trying to ease some of the worry.

Ke'eli squinted her eyes hard at Brett, a silent order to shut up.

Putting her hands to Brett's face as if to kiss him, she focused on his mind and what it was he was feeling.

Flashes of red light illuminated her inner mind. Dark, then light. A sudden heat. The sound of nails on a chalkboard making both cringe.

The two were so connected, it was on a molecular and spiritual level. Within seconds, Ke'eli could see what was ailing Brett.

"You're connected to him somehow." Ke'eli huffed out, breaking the connection.

Turning to catch up to the rest of the entourage, Ke'eli grabbed Brett's hand.

"Somehow, when Andrew siphoned out some of your power, I think you sucked something of him out, too. I could feel them in your mind. Fiends. Or maybe it has something to do with that cursed necklace. I don't know. All I know is that there's no darkness there; just something like a subconscious sense."

Brett looked at Ke'eli with the slightest bit of fear in his eyes.

"Should I let the super mind-melter take a look?"

Ke'eli looked ahead at Mason, who led from the front, pushing aside tall blades of brown grass.

Looking back over at Brett, she still saw the concern on his face.

Then she 'smelled' it, too.

Her connection with Brett was getting stronger. Both parents stopped, the strange smell and taste of sulfur in their nose and mouth.

"Stop!" both said at the same time.

Everyone stopped to look back at them.

They were now all in tall grasses that were at least five feet high, some others taller than that. The grass, while not tightly packed, was close enough to make moving through it difficult.

"What is it, my friends?" Mason asked, hands on his hips.

Ke'eli and Brett looked again at each other, each again smelling the air before them. Like they were following the smell of food, they inched their way forward before the rest of the team.

Ke'eli looked at Mason.

"Look in our minds, Mason. What is this we are sensing?"

Mason looked shocked. Looking from his allies to the family, he put on the best smile he could.

"My lady, I would never dare to look into the minds of the Four! I could trigger something in you that would render me limb from limb!"

"Well, that's always good to know that you won't be fishing around in there for something, but no, help us figure this out. We can't without your help."

Ke'eli grabbed Mason roughly by the tricep. Forgetting she had abnormal strength, she let go at once, but cocked her head to the side, expecting him to absolve.

Mason, rubbing his arm, nodded finally before letting out a deep sigh.

"Please don't lash out at me if I do this. There can be serious repercussions."

Ke'eli nodded, assuring Mason that she would not make his head implode.

Giving in, Mason closed his eyes and placed his hands on Ke'eli and Brett's foreheads. Within seconds, Mason exhaled deeply, letting go of the two parents. He opened his eyes quickly, whispering out orders to his team.

"Circle formation! Family at the center!"

With no hesitation, his Seeker team came around the family, forming a protective circle.

"Where is Xinzang?!" Mason growled.

Before he could answer, screams rent the air.

Strange creatures came at them from all angles, wielding short blades and daggers. They were a hodgepodge of different races, some halflings, some humans, and some dwarves. The one thing they all had in common were the horns that came out of their skulls to wrap around their heads.

Ke'eli could feel Brett tense up.

Though they were nothing near to what Andrew was, that these creatures resembled him so much made her cringe as well.

Despite being on the defensive, neither the Seekers nor the family were surprised. Immediately, Keb slammed his hand down into the ground, sending out a great shock-wave, flattening out the grass for twenty feet in every direction.

There appeared to be six of the creatures all around them.

"Tainted." Mason said, lowering his gaze as one came at him, readying its small sword.

But the attackers had lost the element of surprise, and without that, they knew they were outmatched.

Right away, five of them tried to turn around and run back into the higher grass.

One by one, the Seeker team struck the creatures down as they fled.

Tumidus sent six bolts of energy out at two of the creatures, felling them right away.

Pwyll threw a bottle of some liquid at one, where it struck the creature on its back. As the bottle broke, the creature's back armor sizzled where it hit. Acid ate away whatever protection the thing had, eating right into its skin, knocking it down, unmoving.

Mason locked eyes with the one that was about to attack, tipping his head to the side quickly. Mirroring his action, the one creature before him who had not turned to run yet made the same motion as Mason, yet much more extreme and forceful. His neck broken, the creature fell to the ground in a heap.

Which left two more of the things. One had made its way back into the taller grass before Ke'eli reached out her hand to stop it. She had only intended to create a wall of some sort to block his escape. What she made instead surprised her tremendously.

An obelisk of stone came shooting out of the ground before the running creature to hit him square in the face. A loud *crunch* echoed out as the thing's head came face to face with the rough stone, flying backward from the assault. Where the body landed, it did not move.

Which left one more creature.

This one was a dwarf, and it stood staring hard at the family. Its horns were larger than normal, and it even had a tint of red to its skin.

Brett stared hard back at the thing. He had intended to use some sort of dehydration attack against it, but he suddenly felt something else inside him.

The creature moved to attack; it being the only one to not run and hide.

Ke'eli watched as Brett focused on the thing. She knew what he was going to do, as they still seemed connected somehow.

What he did, though, shocked her.

He simply raised his hand, as if telling the thing to stop.

And it stopped.

The rest of the group looked on at the thing, expecting it to come forward to continue its apparent attack. They could see Brett with his hand raised.

"Good move Brett. Freeze the liquid in its veins to keep it from moving."

Mason thanked Brett as the rest of his entourage went to work dispatching the thing.

In short order, the last of the strange creatures was deceased.

Brett let out a heavy breath.

"What did you do?" Ke'eli whispered, cradling her husband as he seemed exhausted from the effort.

"I could see him. The *real* him, Ke'eli. That thing... was possessed."

Mason walked up to the family, ensuring them they were all safe.

"I have done a mental scan of the surrounding area and cannot detect any more humanoids, though I do sense something up ahead in a clearing. We are going to move there to recuperate."

Mason walked ahead with Keb, clearing the grass for them to continue.

"I thought there weren't any fiends in Atlantis!" Ke'eli yelled out at Mason.

Stopping slowly, Mason lowered his head. The rest of the entourage stopped as well, though they remained on the defensive.

Turning around with a fake smile on his face, Mason tried to sound reassuring.

"My lady, those were not fiends. As we mentioned thus far on our journey, there are certain gateways and rifts to other planes that are scattered all amongst the Country. Do you remember us regaling you with the history of the Sister Pyramid and the city of Alaka?"

Hugging their children close and averting their eyes from the scene they realized just played out in front of them, both parents nodded.

"Well, that pyramid is also accosted by energies from the infernal plane. Every rift has its opposite polarity in Atlantis, usually on the opposing side of the country. Where we are in the northwest near the angelic Archon's Hollow, to the southeast outside Alaka is the Devil's Claw; a place of otherworldly evil energy. The one place in the entire world, with a full contingent of our armed force stationed around its perimeter."

"So, fiends get in through this rift? And it's right next to your version of Las Vegas? No wonder it's so crazy there." Kelly asked, huffing at the absurdity of it all.

"No, my young friend." Tumidus corrected for her. "Any fiend that enters Atlantis is immediately captured or slain, its essence being destroyed by our radiant magics. Unfortunately, the permutating energy of the rift itself causes certain... *changes*, in people. Much like how I told you about the city of Thule and the magic there radically changing elves? The same can be said for any other rift in Atlantis. Energy that comes from these places changes us on a genetic level."

Brett just laughed as he came forward ahead of his family.

"So, then these rifts turn Atlanteans into devils? What the hell kind of sense does that make? And they can just wander about wherever they want? *Really?!*"

For not the first time on their long trip, Mason put his hands up to try to calm Brett.

"The Atlantean Guard stationed near these rifts aren't changed, like Tumidus and his elven kin."

Mason looked away from the family and back down to the ground before he continued. That he said it out loud showed that it was something people avoided.

"The Atlanteans aren't changed; their *children* are. And just because their children come out looking fiendish or angelic, or plant-like or more fey than others, does not mean that we should automatically assume that they have evil in their hearts, nor good, nor what-have-you. These were not fiends; they were plane-touched, and they were tainted by the blood in their veins; no more so than any power-mongering human might. It is well we put them to rest. But no, not fiends."

Mason made it a point to end the conversation by moving on through the grass, his comrades slowly filing in behind him. Keb stayed the longest, huffing and pushing aside the grass for the family to walk through.

"Some turn bad. Some turn good. Most not liked, like orcs. Keb feels bad for them."

Ke'eli smiled half-heartedly back to the big lumbering boulder, leading her and the family through the grass. She looked back at Brett, who just nodded his head and pinched his nose like he had a headache. She moved closer to him, keeping the children in front.

"Are you okay?" She asked, he still rubbing his nose and then his temples.

"I don't know. Babe, I didn't do what I wanted to do. I planned on stopping him by freezing the blood in his veins, but I felt something else when I focused on him. I could... *sense* something else inside him. Not some fiend-born plane-touched or whatever Mason was talking about. This seemed different. Like there was a fiend inside him."

"But that would mean there are fiends loose around inside Atlantis, which he seemed pretty adamant about there not being. They've been keeping this place a secret for tens of thousands of years. If even one fiend knew about this place, don't you think it would be pretty bad?"

"I don't know, love. I guess they were wrong. Let's go. I need to sit down somewhere." Brett replied.

Ke'eli grabbed Brett close, whispering to him the image of what she saw in one of the creature's minds and what they had intended to do to them. She knew he had sensed something; she had got a glimpse into their plan as well.

"They were going to kill us all..." she whispered to Brett, "all of us except Drake."

The dwarf creature's body twitched, as bodies often do after being slain. The fiend inside the dwarf's body could tell that the group had passed on, not daring to try to possess one of them. It twitched again as the evil essence inside it seeped out, seeking a creature to own and control.

The fiend had to get back to its master to report this news.

The floating essence found a rabbit around the scene where its latest symbiote was killed by the Seekers. This would suffice for now until it could find a more suitable host.

It had been taught. It knew who to seek, and to whom not. The 'tainted' were easy to control, already having a bit of the fiendish essence inside them. There were others in Atlantis the fiend could try to control, but this place was dangerous. It had been here for quite some time and was admonished that should its presence be known, no place in the infinite realms would it be safe.

Eternal destruction was the penalty.

So, the essence, known to others of its kind as Dwolok, forced the rabbit it rode along in to travel back west, towards safety.

It was inherent the Master be told what had occurred. It had sensed the man who reached out to stop it. The man had used some sort of power to stop the tainted right in its tracks. Not something that affected the body's blood like the others had thought; something that affected the fiend inside it.

This was bad.

Dwolok knew that forcing the rabbit against its will would kill it quicker than a slow bonding, but time was of the essence.

The Master must know.

("Saving Buckbeak" from the Harry Potter and the Prisoner of Azkaban Soundtrack by John Williams)

Keb pushed through the last of the tall grass into a wide clearing. He was on the defensive; tiger claws out and was ready to attack whatever was making the monstrous sounds he and the others had started to hear.

Behind him, Mason and the others entered the clearing as well. A small copse of trees had provided shelter from the midday sun, and beneath those trees were an assortment of creatures that had the family of four staring with wondering eyes.

Ahead of them, tied to a series of stakes, looked like three lions. It was not until the group got closer that they noticed the lions had wings... and that the front half of the 'lion' was that of a beautiful eagle. One immediately sensed the group and jumped to its feet, spinning around to face the interlopers as much as it could, being tied down with several ropes around its neck.

The thing was majestic. Having the hindquarters of a lion but the front head and legs of an eagle, the creature spread its wings wide, letting out a loud roar-like screech. Two others tried to rise to meet the intruders as well, moving to block a fourth, who remained down on the ground, covered in blood.

Everyone froze.

"They're called griffins."

Xinzang came around one tree, approaching the group.

Mason stalked towards her, obviously angry.

Before he could say anything, Xinzang answered the unspoken question.

"I had taken to the air. I could hear these creatures further ahead of us and I wanted to make sure they were not loose. I feared they might attack us if we stumbled into their nest. They are normally very docile, but not wild ones like these. I made it here, just as you engaged in battle. When I returned to the air, it appeared you had dispatched whatever foe had attacked you and were heading this way, anyway. I did not want to land within the grass for fear that you would think me another foe."

Mason scowled at the scalehide, turning his back on her.

"Let us return to the road. With our aerial reconnaissance unreliable, I would rather face common travelers than risk being stalked in the high grasses. Besides, these creatures would just as soon bite our faces off should we try to free them." Mason said as he backed away from Zang, returning the way he came.

But Kelly's interest was piqued.

"They're trapped! And one is hurt..." she said, moving closer to the creatures.

"Kelly... come away from them now. You don't know what they could do." Brett whispered harshly, hoping his doting daughter would listen.

Which, of course, she did not.

Slowly moving towards the creatures with her hands up, everyone could feel an air of calmness and serenity flow from her direction. The adults looked back at each other with confused glances.

"She's always wanted to be a healer. She dreams of being a doctor one day." Ke'eli mentioned to the others.

They all watched in rapt fascination as she drew closer to the first creature, who had now lowered its wings to see what this tiny person would do.

Brett crept up beside his daughter, just in case.

Ever so slowly, Kelly got closer and closer. Her hand was up, palm towards the thing's beak. And ever so slowly, the creature calmed its nerves and lowered its body closer to the ground. The other two took the hint from the rational leader as they too calmed themselves.

"There's an injured foal." Kelly said, without even seeing the baby itself. "It's with the mother over there. I think it's sick, though."

As the griffins calmed themselves down, Pwyll moved in to help.

"Keep 'em calm, girl. I'll help the wee babe."

Coming around the other side of the mother, Pwyll could see what Kelly meant. The foal's coat was purple, instead of brown or gold, like the surrounding others. It was breathing and seemed to twitch. It was not until Pwyll could see its head that he knew something was wrong with it.

The foal's face looked distorted, and its beak had fangs. The creature's eyes were blood red and a putrid slime oozed out of its ears.

Pwyll took out a small device, pushing buttons on its cover. He raised the device and seemed to scan the foal, looking at the screen for information.

"Me thinks he's been poisoned. Some sort of blood taint. The mother's got some kinnae arcane runes on her belly. The poor thing seems to have died during the childbirth. I smell somethin' evil lads."

Mason saw the concern in Pwyll's eyes. "Can you help it, Pwyll?"

"Aye, should be able to. Should be a normal affliction, easily cured." But the hesitation in his voice had everyone, even the family, looking at each other with worry.

Kelly, believing that the griffins understood they were there to help, moved away from the clear father toward the deceased mother of the foal.

She saw what Pwyll was doing and looked back down at the foal. As Pwyll worked with his equipment to create the proper antidote, Kelly focused more on the foal. She squinted her eyes as she tried to 'see' what was wrong with it from the inside. The effort brought her down to her knees.

Everyone rushed to her side as the griffins stomped the ground as well.

Through gasps for breath, she huffed out, "It won't work... It's not poison... It's a curse."

Pwyll looked up at Mason with his eyebrows raised.

"Ah, lassie, I had an idea it might be, but I wanted to make sure, ya know? I think the lass is right, though. The baby's been cursed somethin' wicked. I am no so sure I can heal him with what I got here now."

Mason looked at the others gathered around him, settling on Tumidus. Pwyll and Tumidus were the most educated on magic in their entourage, so he relied on their ability to guide him now.

"What say you, friends? What could have caused this?" Mason asked, pointedly at Tumidus.

In response, Tumidus shook his head, the answer obvious to him.

"The Tainted."

Brett, still coming to grips with whatever had just happened, had to know.

"So, wait, I thought you guys didn't have fiends here in Atlantis? How do these 'tainted' people curse animals? Those marks look pretty evil to me!"

Mason's eyes raised at the proclamation.

"Well, like I said earlier, we don't! We have plane-touched who are connected to the elements as Keb here is..."

Mason pointed to Keb, who nodded his tucked head.

"Keb special orc. Keb talk to rocks better than other orcs."

"Aye," Mason continued, "Keb is an orc, just as those things we fought were halflings and dwarves. Our proximity to the halfling region means there are more here than in other parts of Atlantis. That is all Brett. Nothing more. These were creatures that subsumed themselves with whatever evil they found in their blood for their own personal gain. Just because Alaka is on the opposite side of the Country from here, does not mean a halfling or dwarf Guardsman did not come into contact with the Claw's energies. Hells, it could have been two generations ago for all we know. Just because you're subjected to the rift's energies doesn't mean your next-born will be tainted."

"Are you sure people can't be changed or possessed by fiends coming from Alaka?" Ke'eli asked.

"No. There are many protections in place, headed by a very important team of human mystics that can detect when a true fiend enters through the rift. Just because the open rift from the Abyss is larger than others does not mean..."

Brett walked up to Mason, tired of the bull-crap.

"You *just* said there aren't fiends here, but there's a rift or whatever to the *Abyss*? Like, Hell? What the hell do you think comes from Hell?! You really think you can stop these things?!"

Mason tried to calm Brett down, nodding his head side to side.

Tumidus interjected for him, though.

"You wouldn't understand, *human*. Just because there are gateways to other dimensions on our continent, does not mean creatures come willy-nilly into our midst whenever they want. The rifts are more energy-like. People who come about them are affected by their energy. The beauty of Atlantis is that nothing can escape it. The surrounding shield is very particular about that. No other-worldly essences, in or out. Much like how we explained Archon's Hollow. The two are inexorably linked. Archon's Hollow appeared as a balance to the Devil's Claw near Alaka."

Mason scowled at Tumidus. Though he had gotten the point across, it was harsh. He continued, more calmly.

"Think of it this way, Brett. Atlantis serves as a focus for all other inter-dimensional travel *in the world.* If we were not here, then gateways to other dimensions, good or bad, could open anywhere else in the world. And believe me, many have tried. Because of the Pyramid at the center of our continent, all gateways from other places *must* come to Atlantis. Here, we have a fighting chance to keep the evil from spilling out into the rest of the world. Which is why we constantly fight to keep our numbers up. Which is also why we have become so good at it. Our country has been at the brink of war, protecting the rest of the world since its inception. And we relegate not only that protection to the people of this continent. Seekers are not the only ones who go out into the wider world. Any who do, though, are more thoroughly scanned and interrogated than you can possibly imagine."

Brett shook his head, all the information coming to his brain too much to bear.

"I can heal it."

The statement came not from Pwyll, but from Kelly, getting back to her feet.

"Like Hell you will!" Brett responded, returning to his daughter's side. "You don't know what that crap is, you don't know what it will do to you. You don't even know if you can! I love you baby girl, but I will not let you risk anything to help a baby... bird-lion."

"Dad, I can feel its pain. I already reached out to it and touched it in my head. If anything is going to happen to me, it's too late to stop it. I can fix him. Let me try."

Ke'eli walked up to Brett's side, there to back him up in whatever course he decided. He looked over at his wife, fear, and anxiety again in his eyes. She reached out to hold his hand.

"I'll back you up, whatever you decide. We are stronger together."

The revelation hit him like a brick. A memory stirred in Brett's subconscious. One of his wife holding his hand, telling him how much she loved him, even though he 'wasn't hers'. A memory of how powerful the family was, together.

"Like a battery..." Brett muttered.

Everyone looked at each other, confused, but Brett went on anyway.

"Kelly, let Pwyll heal the foal..." seeing the coming retort, he calmed her down with his hand. "Let him heal the foal, but you *help* him. Pwyll, she's like a battery. You can use her to increase the power of your healing, or whatever it is you do."

Pwyll looked from Brett to Kelly, his expression curious.

"Well, what de ye think, lassie? Think ye can give me a boost, then?"

Without hesitation, Kelly smiled up at her dad and walked over to stand next to Pwyll.

"What do I do, dad?"

Memories rushing in like a broken floodgate, Brett closed his eyes to process it all. He was not sure if it was because of the combat with the tainted dwarf, or just being in this place, but everything seemed to jumble about in his head constantly.

Brett knew he was going crazy, but he also knew that there was some modicum of control over the crazy. He just had to figure it out.

An image popped into his head. One of his daughter helping another woman who held on to Drake's hand. Drake's *lifeless* hand.

Brett sucked in his breath, looking over at his boy. But the memory was vague and foggy.

How could that even be *a memory?*

Brett thought back to it, trying to avoid the image of his son laying on the ground, unmoving. He watched as Kelly put her hand on this other woman's shoulder, focusing her energy into her.

Brett brought himself back into the present, if that was what this was.

"Just put your hand on his shoulder, close your eyes, and concentrate. Not too much... just enough to give him enough juice to do whatever it is he needs to do. Focus on the healing aspect of it."

Everyone exchanged nervous glances. Tumidus and Mason were used to the strange magical ability their people possessed, but they had never seen anyone use another person as a "battery."

Pwyll removed another device from his belt pouch, the one he had injected into Keb when they first vaulted through the gateway back into their home here. He pressed some buttons on its top, nodding his approval before looking back at Kelly.

"Ready girlie?"

"Let's do this." Kelly responded. Standing taller than the gnome, Kelly reached out her hand to place it on his shoulder, closing her eyes and bowing her head.

"Remember, not too much darlin'. Just think of reaching out with your mind and making the dark spots on the mare's coat evaporate, turning it brighter. Just breathe." Brett was watching his thirteen-year-old daughter very carefully.

"We've been through this baby-girl. Just see whatever it is in your mind that's hurting this thing, and lightly fix it." Ke'eli followed up, squeezing her husband's hand in worry.

("Protect Life" from The Fifth Element Soundtrack by Eric Serra)

Pwyll pointed his ray gun object at the mare, focusing on it. His eyes went wide as Kelly's eyes squeezed tighter. As she furrowed her brow, Pwyll felt the queue in his entire body as an energizing warmth filled him. Squeezing the trigger, a bright golden light shot out of the ray gun, striking the foal in the side.

The foal did not react, at least not like it probably would have if it had gotten shot by a ray gun thing. Instead, the golden light began to spread along its body, as if it were eating the purplish hue.

The other animals around the group stomped the ground as if they knew what was going on and they could feel the energy in the air. Though they seemed agitated, they did not pull on the ropes securing them to the ground. Instead, it almost looked like they were reinforcing the event.

As the healing golden hue spread across the creature, the purple gave way to a yellowish white color. Slowly, the energy crept across the body of the infant, cleansing the odd taint that affected it.

Finally, the golden energy reached the creature's head. Immediately, the thing changed. Looking painful at first, the group realized it was a calming energy that transfixed and repaired the pitiful thing. Bones popped and flesh melted away, revealing the proper form of the creature beneath.

Kelly could sense the creature's pain and bore down on it, washing it away with positive energy. She squeezed her eyes as everyone else's widened at the spectacle before them. Brett and Ke'eli held each other closely, amazed at what their young daughter could help do.

Finally, the light died away. Before them, covering the rest of its body with its wings, appeared the infant griffin, now with metallic golden-tinged fur.

Kelly opened her eyes with a wide smile on her face. Pwyll turned to face the girl.

Before anyone could say anything, Kelly crept towards the infant, placing her hand on its wing to pull it away so that she could see its face.

Blinking as if it were seeing the light for the first time, the infant foal looked up at Kelly and nudged its beak into her hand. Slowly, it pulled itself away from its deceased mother as it tried to stand.

Everyone stared anxiously as the baby stood on shaky legs. It appeared too difficult at first, but then another amazing thing happened. As they watched, the golden hue of the creature lit up and cascade down the thing's legs. Immediately, the legs stopped shaking, and the infant became stronger. Planting its feet firmly, the infant rose to its full height, leaning hard into Kelly's midsection to nudge her with affection.

"Ha ha ha! Thata-girl! Well dang lassie, you dinnae fail to surprise!" Pwyll harrumphed aloud.

"That's my girl." Brett came over to his daughter and wrapped her up in a tight embrace. Kelly's smile could not be bigger as the infant also leaned its body in affection against Brett as well.

"I did it, dad! Mom, did you see?" Kelly's exhilaration was not lost on just the humanoids standing around the animals. What was presumably the father griffin stopping its stomping and lay down on the ground, resting its head on its claws.

Kelly looked over at the other three creatures, frowning at her father.

Brett, not even waiting for any other word, walked over to the head griffin, approaching slowly.

The beast raised its head but did not stand up. It knew that without the human's help, it would be stuck here until it died.

Brett reached out his hand to the beast's neck where the rope had rubbed away parts of its skin. Gingerly, he loosened the noose around it and slid it off, one rope at a time. After the third rope was off the beast, it rose its head, testing to see if there were any other restrictions on its neck or body.

The griffin stood then, shaking its head side to side, happy to be free from the restraints. It walked up to Kelly and nudged her with his enormous beak. Everyone gasped at the action, knowing wild griffins to be hard to not only be around, but to touch as well.

The group released the other two griffins, both of whom stayed calm. The three rejoined the smaller newborn, nudging him with their beaks.

As if to signal that their time together had ended, the creatures began to move off into the tall grass.

The newborn stopped and looked back at Kelly, giving off a short screeching tweet before following its herd.

Brett and Ke'eli could not be happier.

"I think I'll name him... Gold Feather. How's that sound, dad?" Kelly asked, looking back up to her father.

"Sounds great, munchkin."

Mason, smiling still, broke the exuberance.

"It's time to go, my friends. We have much *more* to tell our Elders concerning this strange blight that affected the newborn and the presence of tainted so far from Alaka, especially those brazen enough to attack us! After the day's ordeals, I believe it is best to take a long rest and arrive tomorrow morning in Zion. We can rest near to here if you all are amenable to that."

The smile never leaving her face, Kelly followed her own herd, pausing long enough to look back at the way the griffins had gone.

"See you around Goldie!"

CHAPTER FOUR

MONSTERS OF ATLANTIS

The family and the Seekers decided it best to rest near to where they discovered the tied-up Griffins, but far enough that they would not be discovered if any of the camp's former cultists returned. A low fire, protected by the slow wind from the east by a small hill, gave the family what warmth they could.

One aspect the family from California could embrace, though still thought odd, was the dipping of the temperature as the country's artificial sun set in the west. Rising back up as a large blue orb, the 'chariot' that moved the thing still gave off a semblance of heat, otherwise Mason stated the entire country would freeze overnight.

Nevertheless, it was just cold enough to want to embrace each other, or put on extra layers of clothing, of which Tumidus seemed to have a plentiful amount of. Putting on longer hooded cloaks and robes of thick velvet, Brett and Ke'eli made sure the children were nice and cozy. At one point, Tumidus even offered to produce the sleeping tent that the Seekers had used to observe the family, but Brett waved it away, saying it was better to sleep out under Atlantis's stars, fake as they were.

("Bedtime Story" from The Day After Tomorrow Soundtrack by Harald Kloser)

Looking up then at the artificially starry expanse, Brett marveled at it.

"It's beautiful, no?" Mason asked from the other side of the firelight.

Brett looked down at the man, who just lay back with his hands behind his head, staring up into the dome above them.

"Thought you didn't read minds there, baldy?" Brett quipped. He knew he didn't need to; Brett had been staring up at the dome every night they had been there. Something deep inside Brett resurfaced when he lay down to sleep every night since coming back here. Something that came with the remembrance of always looking up at the tiny twinkling lights above him.

"Well, my friend, you know as well as I that I need not have to read minds to know that you feel something. You are transfixed by the sight. I had not wanted to broach the subject earlier, but with the children asleep and you still awake, I figured we could have a talk."

Brett looked down from the sky across the fire to the mystic, who had now rolled over to his side and was sitting upright. Ke'eli was close enough to Brett that she moved over and put her head in his lap, still always within an arm's length of the children.

"You wonder what makes the twinkling in the sky, don't you?" Mason asked.

Brett had an idea, but it was still hazy. Memories of him remembering what the stars looked like outside the dome made him always look up and daydream about being home when he was younger. That much had returned to him. Even being here, in these grasslands, made him remember things that seemed unreal. Wearing robes a lot like Mason's, being part of a group of boys who trained together, things that just didn't seem to make sense.

Shrugging, Ke'eli answered for him.

"Yes, he loves the sky. Since he's been here, he stays up half the night taking turns between watching the stars and watching the kids and I. What are they Mason?"

"Well milady, they are emanations of the Soulstone itself. Remember how I told you that the pyramid at the center of our country does some amazing things? Well, one thing it does is imbue certain gemstones with a portion of its power. We mentioned earlier that we call them our Rhombs, as they are rhomboid in dimension. Each one has a spectacular quality that makes it different from others."

"Take mine for example. I carry a white ulexite stone. It allows me to use a stronger form of telepathy than I would normally be able to, uniting all four of my fellow allies' minds together to perform our mission."

At the mention of telepathy, Mason looked pointedly at Ke'eli, eliciting the response he expected; she shuffled her shoulders up and averted his eyes.

Moving on, Mason tested his next hypothesis.

"You know when we were in your home, I was able to manipulate your body against your will. For that, I apologize again, but it was because I can also telekinetically move objects with my mind. An ability that has great utility, but that can also be used offensively and defensively."

At the mention of telekinesis, Mason made eye contact with Brett. But Brett did not react. Nodding his head slightly, Brett followed up with the point of their conversation.

"What does all that have to do with stars?"

Confused, but continuing nonetheless, Mason put his stone away.

"Well, my friend, the Soulstone enriches these gemstones to become more than they are. It does that by enhancing the ground beneath our feet, the stone in the mountains and in the depths of the sea, and the air all about and above us. Deepstone is the magical rock we gather from immensely pressurized areas, able to hold a magical charge indefinitely. Smaller snippets of power grow in certain parts of Atlantis where the energy is more directed. It is here that flowers and roots of magical gems are grown. The buds and seeds of these crystalline flowers are the shards we all possess."

"There are several more powerful versions of these stones. One of which we call Rubethyst. A red and purple concoction of gemstone, it is much like Deepstone because it holds a magical charge. These are very rare indeed."

At the mention of the purplish stone, Ke'eli held her hand to her chest. The stone that Brett had given to her to hold was very much the same sounding color as what Mason described. Even now, she could feel the power of it reverberating through her.

Brett could feel it too. Slowly and to not draw attention, he placed his hands on Ke'eli's shoulder, squeezing slightly. He hadn't told her because he didn't consider it necessary, but even with her wearing the pendant, he could feel its thrumming energy as well.

"Another of the rarer stones," Mason continued, "are what we like to call 'shooting stars'. They are gemstones that grow from the top of the dome and are very powerful indeed. It is too cold to get close enough to retrieve them, and dangerous to boot. But these stones do not need to be harvested from above. Occasionally, they will detach from the dome and fall of their own accord. When they do, they shoot across the sky, leaving a streak of light. As they grow, they also give off a small amount of light. Hence, the reason we have stars in the sky."

Brett looked up again. He knew somehow that it was more than that. The 'stars' seemed too close in appearance to what the true night sky looked like. It was almost as if the growing stars were purposefully placed by the Soulstone in specific spots to mimic the true night sky.

As if he were reading his thoughts, which he knew not to do, Mason smiled over at the couple.

"You wonder why they so closely resemble the true night sky, do you not?"

Brett looked down into Ke'eli's face, who looked up at him from the corner of her eye. A hint of a smile beckoned there, and Brett knew his façade was up. Both lovers had discussed late into the night the strangeness of the place around them, and yet how simple it all seemed. Almost artificial in nature.

"We had talked about it before, yes." Ke'eli again answered for him.

Mason was smiling his standard, casual smile. The same one he liked to wear so often since finding this family of four.

"Well, that is certainly an interesting conjecture! Some believe the Soulstone can see through the dome and into the true night sky and that it tries to imitate the stars there. I can tell you from experience being outside the dome that it does a splendid job of doing so. Most peculiar though, is that it imitates the sky over different places around the globe at different times. None have been able to ascertain why or how, but it is still beautiful, nonetheless."

Mason looked back up to emphasize his point. Even now, the twinkling of the shards in the night sky seemed to lull him into a sense of calmness and serenity. Putting his hands behind his head, he lay back down with a loud sigh.

Brett and Ke'eli looked up into the sky as well. Stroking her head, Brett thought to the memories that still seemed to not be his, but that were worming their way back into his consciousness.

They were in a small hilly area, blocking the light from their fire in every direction, but it still afforded an amazing view of the rest of the countryside. They could see the artificial moon rising in their southwest, creeping closer and closer to the center and back to the east of the continent. It imitated a waning crescent moon, which Brett remembered was also the same phase of the moon outside the dome.

Tumidus had informed them about the transition of the sun to the moon as well. He explained a vessel called the Chariot carried the artificial sun from east to west into the territory of the skinwalker tribe. As it did so as the sun, it was known as the Mandjet. Apparently, skinwalkers were the progenitors of ancient Egyptians, so they called the sun Ra in respect to their leader at the time, who helped to rein in the fiery tempest of its flame with his druidic magic. This tribe of half-human, half-animal people lived in the west and sacrificed a good portion of their land to house the flaming sun as it descended into their territory.

As it rose as the moon, though, it became known as the Menektet and took on an entirely unique form and function. Becoming enclosed in a massive orichalcum shield to contain the raging heat, an elven sorceress named Selene devised a way to still distribute the warmth across the continent without the glare of the light. Blue arcane runes lit up along its encasement, simulating the warm glow of Earth's sole satellite.

Brett looked up into the sky as Ke'eli rolled onto her back, her head still on his lap. Leaning back on his hands,

Brett just marveled at the strange beauty above and below him.

"Pretty, isn't it?" He asked Ke'eli without taking his eyes off the sight.

"As above, so below, right?" she asked, smiling. Catching on to the little quip, Brett smiled before looking down and kissing his wife.

A low rumbling sound interrupted their quiet reverie as Brett's lips quickly left hers. Both their eyes open wide, Brett and Ke'eli stood quickly to take in their surroundings.

Keb, too, rose from his light sleep, though no one else stirred.

Keb and Ke'eli had spent a little time together, talking about the elements and how to attune to them. Since they both felt the earth keenly, that was the one thing most often talked about. But this strange rumbling was not coming from the earth. It came from the sky.

All three looked back upwards into the starry night. Mason, catching on that they had stood up and were not muttering under their breath, rolled onto his haunches.

"What troubles you?" he asked.

That was when they saw it. A large silhouette of some massive object blotted out the stars above their heads. Flying from the southeast, it passed over them, heading further to the northwest. A creaking and rumbling sound echoed slightly from it, and Mason could just barely make it out.

"What..." Mason began, but Keb was already two steps ahead.

"Flying ship. Getting lower." He said, trying in vain to watch it go further into the horizon.

As if to punctuate the ship was in danger, a painful scream erupted into the night from its direction.

Everyone was awake now.

Chasing after it somewhat into the darkness, everyone who was now awake tried to adjust their eyes to the darker night.

A slight light came from the rear of the vessel, which was already a lot lower in the sky than it had been.

"It's on fire." Tumidus said, his eyes growing quite large in the dim light.

Ke'eli looked over at him, her own eyes wide.

"Well, we have to go help them, right?" Brett and Ke'eli looked from each other to the five Seekers who now stood around them. The children had woken up quickly and had come clinging to their parents' sides, the scream more than enough for them to be scared to their roots.

Mason looked at the other Seekers present. He knew it would be dangerous to let anyone else see the family. He tried to put on an air of neutrality.

"It is too dark, and we do not know where the ship will set down. It could be hours away and, with the lack of light, we will have no idea where to go."

Mason looked futilely down to the ground before turning back to head towards their camp.

"Bullshit." Brett said, hands on hips.

Everyone stopped then but said nothing.

"You spend weeks tracking people in the world to kidnap them, but you can't find a giant flying ship that crashes on the ground?"

Tumidus interjected, though he too seemed saddened by the fact they weren't going in search of it.

"It is a flying ship that does not use any kind of propellant to fuel its travel. If, and when, it crashes, we will most likely not even see a thing. It is folly to travel out in the night with no beacon or way to find it."

"But someone sounded hurt!" Ke'eli pleaded. "Can someone survive a flying ship crash like that? I don't know about you, but it seemed like they could use a hand."

Pwyll came up, padding Ke'eli's hand.

"Lass, with no way to find the ship, we'd be walking in the wrong direction goin' backwards all the way we been going forwards. True right, I think we all want to help, but it's no a place for children to be walking in the dark. We're still no out o' the woods yet."

Ke'eli and Brett looked from each other to everyone else around them. The children were the ones to put the nail in the coffin.

"So, we're just going to let them die?" Kelly asked.

"Alone, out in the middle of nowhere?" Drake followed up.

Ke'eli's eyes went wide.

"Wait. Keb, you said we can feel the earth, right? So, when this thing hits, we can feel where it landed, can't we?"

Keb nodded, but answered the unspoken question.

"We feel hit, but Keb can not feel after. One time hit and nothing after. Back in the dark."

But it was enough for Ke'eli. Dropping to all fours, she laid her head to the ground.

No one said a thing. Everyone slowly inched away from her as Keb tiptoed closer and laid down as well.

Several minutes passed where neither Keb nor Ke'eli moved or even seemed to breathe. Since they had seemed so determined, Mason instructed everyone else to start packing camp. They knew Zang might get a pinpoint from the air if they knew what direction to go in, but that was a hard maybe. The family seemed determined though, and the Seeker group wasn't about to quarrel with them, wanting to save some other Atlantean's lives.

Ke'eli storming into the camp had everyone perking up.

"We didn't hear it crash." She said, somewhat forlornly. Keb came in behind her, all toothy and tusky grin.

"But Mother spoke to Earth-lady. Told her where it is." Ke'eli's forlornness turned into a smile.

"I felt the aftershock. They're about five miles north-west of us. Let's go."

("Royal Pursuit" from Frozen Soundtrack by Christophe Beck)

The group set off at once. Though Ke'eli had felt what she determined to be the aftershock waves of the crash, she still wasn't entirely sure where they were. To speed them along on their travel, Tumidus cast a spell on the group, lengthening their strides. It would only last an hour, but it allowed them to gallop across the countryside.

"Why don't we do this all the time?!" Drake yelled from the top of his father's shoulders. The wind whipped through his hair as he held on for dear life. Though his father wasn't running *super* fast, it was still a bumpy ride, and they had been at it for quite some time.

Kelly held on to her mother's neck as tightly as she could as Ke'eli veritably carried her. Bigger than Drake but too big for her shoulders, Ke'eli decided, after some back and forth from her daughter, that she would just yoink her up and carry her like the babe she used to be. Being stronger than her husband, Ke'eli didn't mind it in the least.

The rest of the entourage either took advantage of the spell afforded by Tumidus or had ways of their own to traverse the terrain. Keb ran with no aid of the spell, though Ke'eli had bet that the earth spirits helped him along. Pwyll had robotic legs, and though he was smaller and slower than the rest, he did not need to stop to catch his breath as often as everyone else did.

Zang took to the sky and, with the aid of her nightvision, could monitor the group from above.

It wasn't long before she saw what she believed to be the wreckage of a ship not far in the distance. The hulking mass was mostly in one piece, but there was debris everywhere and a long streak of rutted earth showing the crash trajectory. She saw something else there, though, that gave her pause. Recognizing it for what it was, she made to find her companions and alert them as fast as she could.

The rest of the running group stumbled upon the beginnings of the rut in the ground as well.

"See?! We found it! Wasn't too hard!" Ke'eli exclaimed. Before she could dart off again to investigate, Mason put a hand to her shoulder.

"Now, we mustn't be too hasty, milady." He started, also holding Brett back in the darkness. "We don't know why the ship crashed. Someone was screaming as it passed us, which implies danger. I advise we approach with caution and be wary of whom we encounter. Ships going in this direction..." but Mason trailed off as a thought occurred to him.

"What about ships going in this direction?" Brett asked for him.

Lost in thought, Mason looked around, almost fearfully.

He didn't exactly answer the question though, instead seeking Pwyll and Keb.

"Where are we *exactly*, master gnome?" he asked, squatting down to be on eye level with Pwyll. "Keb, I need your senses. Please, join us."

"What the hell is going on, Mason? It's just a ship that crashed, right? You didn't seem this perturbed before we left." Brett rolled up to Mason's side, but turned around as another scream lit out into the night from the direction of the wreckage.

Everyone perked up at the sound, and instinctively, the Seekers made a defensive formation around the family.

"All eyes up." Mason started before turning back to Pwyll.

Pwyll, looking down at the wristwatch-type contraption he had on his hand, tapped the front of it and twisted it, revealing a small holographic display. Pinching his fingers together and spreading them apart, the display expanded into the air, showing a map of the entire continent.

A small series of dots blinked not far from the large lake that they were told they arrived near to. A city was also not too far away; what Brett assumed was the halfling capital they had been traveling to.

Mason stared at the holographic map, tracing where they had been and where they were now.

"Keb, verify this for me. Is the ship using its crystal shard array to travel towards Kalapa?"

But Keb was already two steps ahead. Laying his hand on the ground and looking into the distance, he seemed to mumble to himself. Grabbing a fistful of the dirt beneath his hand, Keb stood slowly.

Nodding his head once, it was all Mason needed to confirm his suspicions.

Still on the defensive, Brett just looked around at the people beside him.

"Hello? What shitstorm did we just walk in to? Why are you freaked out, Mason? And why are we not still all motivated to go help the people on the ship who are apparently still alive?"

Mason came closer to Brett and pulled Ke'eli closer to his side so that only they could hear him.

"If I am correct, then this ship was using its flying ability to go directly towards what was formerly the home of the human mystic people. The Yellow Childe Pyramid and the surrounding city of Kalapa were left to its own devices a very long time ago. There is not much that goes that way anymore, and we are right on the cusp of the lake. It would not make any sense for the ship to stop between here or any other city near this location. If they were going towards Kalapa, it could mean either of two things."

"One: they are shard hunters and are looking to harvest the flowering crystals I mentioned to you earlier, or two: they are of the Minoan Guild and are smuggling goods. Seeing as they were flying dark in the night and ran into some trouble precludes me to believe that they are of the latter. That does not bode well for us."

"And why not, pray tell?" Ke'eli asked, already anxious enough as it was seeing as she literally dragged her children here with her.

Mason looked from father to mother, then to the children.

He sighed as Zang landed among their group, rushing up to them with her claws upraised praying quiet.

Mason nodded his confirmation to her they were all indeed aware of what they were up against.

Whispering now, Mason looked back toward the wreckage he knew to be there.

"Because when I say they smuggle 'goods', I mean they smuggle dangerous creatures."

As if to stress the fact, the group heard a tremendous cackling roar, followed by another scream that cut off quickly and violently.

Already making to back away and pulling his children close, Brett whispered to everyone around him.

"So why the fuck aren't we leaving?"

But Ke'eli stopped him cold.

"We can't just leave these people to die, Brett, no matter what kind of monster they had with them."

But Brett was not having it.

"Kee, think of the kids." Pointedly, he looked back up to Mason. "Could you even handle something like this? You guys said you weren't normally prepared to do battle. We're not putting our kid's lives at risk because some smugglers got stupid and up and got killed by the things they were smuggling."

Zang was with them now and close enough to inform them of what she saw. One word was all she whispered that had the other four Seekers veritably trembling.

"Myrmidons."

Mason looked deep into Zang's eyes to confirm her suspicions.

"How can you be sure?" Mason asked, rubbing his hand across the top of his now sweaty bald head.

"I saw a large insectoid creature scrambling about the wreckage. There did not appear to be any of the flying variety, or I would probably already had been dead. I believe it to be the creatures..." but she trailed off as she looked sidelong at Brett and Ke'eli.

"Go on." Mason said, using the fear of the scaleborn to show them why it was ill-advised to continue to the wreck.

"One was already digging a hole and had a captive by its abdomen." She said, shaking her shoulders in revulsion.

"Okaayyyyy, so what the hell are these things, and why aren't we either running or burning the shit out of them?" Brett asked, looking towards the ship and squinting in the darkness.

Tumidus took over the conversation at that point.

"They are of elven make." He started. Mason sighed, turning from the group and reaching out with his mind powers to determine if there were indeed any other survivors.

"They were created long ago to fight fiends. They are a combination of what you might liken ants, bees and wasps to, though much larger. When they feed on fiendish energy, they grow larger and more fierce. We banished them to the far south of Atlantis, where there was still fiendish energy for them to feed on, hoping they would remain there."

Tumidus looked past Brett as well, hoping to not see one of the creatures.

But Brett was confused.

"If they're just big bugs, why don't we just go squash them?"

The incredulous look every one of the Seekers gave Brett shocked him, even in the dark.

"They don't just feed on fiends, Master Brett," Tumidus continued, "they also reproduce the same way many wasps do. They paralyze their prey, drag them to a hovel and lay eggs in and on them. When the eggs hatch, they eat their paralyzed surrogate... *while they are still alive.* Worse still, because of the magic of Atlantis, sometimes the eggs laid inside the prey do not hatch. Instead, they change the person on a genetic level."

Everyone was cringing now. Unconsciously, they were also slowly backing the way they came.

A loud buzzing sound came from the wreckage now, and loud clangs as if someone was swinging a bat at a metal door.

Mason turned back to the group, opening his eyes.

"There are still eleven survivors inside the ship. They have secured the main cabin doors, but there are four of the creatures, and they are trying to get inside to them. It appears as though two Myrmidons have taken captives and are digging a hovel for them now. We need to decide if we are to act or not. Regardless, the creatures will get our scents and track us even if we return to our camp. In all honesty, they should not be left to survive and expand."

Brett perked up. He knew his wife would not let these people die, smugglers or not.

"Well now boys and girls, I guess it's time to go stomp some bugs!"

As motivated as he tried to seem, the fact that he was whispering it and looking quickly at the surrounding team belayed his intense nervousness. Was anyone going to talk him out of it?

Ke'eli just smiled, though.

"Okay, so what's the plan?" she asked.

Mason waved his hand towards Tumidus, letting the expert on the bugs lead the plan of action.

"Well, we have the element of surprise. They are no more resistant to the elements than any other creature. We should definitely destroy them all, seeing as if even one survives, it could mature into a queen. Just be extra careful to not get stung by them."

"How long are you paralyzed for?" Kelly asked. She thought deep down that if these big bugs hurt or stung anyone, that she could suppress it.

Tumidus forced a smile.

"My dear, the sting may paralyze, but it may also lay an egg inside you."

Kelly slinked away from trying to be an adult and edged deeper inside the protective huddle that was her parents.

"Be warned; they have strong melee attacks and can spray acid from their maws. If you destroy one, its death will most likely fuel the rage of the others. Some of the older creatures can also shoot needle projectiles. Hopefully, we are only dealing with the weaker males here."

Brett and Ke'eli just looked at each other.

What had they gotten themselves in to?!

Another scream echoed out into the night. Another prisoner for the creatures.

"Okay, let's go." Brett started. "Stay low and stay together. Watch each other's back. Lay into whatever you see moves."

("Zombie Spike" from The Dawn of the Dead Soundtrack by Tyler Bates)

Each Seeker took their turn, activating or amplifying some magic they had on their person. Not the same situation as earlier with the plane-touched, who had almost surprised them. This was them prepping for war.

Keb turned to the children, looking to the parents for permission to cast an enchantment on them.

"Give them stronger skin." He whispered.

Nodding profusely, both parents watched in wonder as Keb brought the handful of dirt to each of the children's heads, sprinkling it lightly atop them. They couldn't see anything happening in the dark, but knew that Keb had protected them with his shaman magic.

Ke'eli hugged the big orc, as he continued to dust himself with the protection ward as well.

"Aye, don't ye be shooting out any of your durned flame all haphazard like. I'm about to become invisible and I'd hate to get roasted!" Pwyll looked pointedly at Tumidus, who just shrugged.

Mason moved to the parent's side to relay the plan as he too prepared for battle.

"Once we get closer, I will point out a section of the ship that has separated from the rest. Tumidus will use one of the more offensive spells he has to destroy that section with fire, which will also light up the area for us to see. If my senses are correct, a bug hole is near to where the wreckage is, so we should be able to save those trapped inside by the creatures."

Brett and Ke'eli brought their children in close, giving Mason the thumbs up.

"No heroics. You stay by us and hold our hands the entire time. Let the fighters do the work." Brett looked deep into his children's eyes in the dark, holding their faces with his palms.

Not a stranger to combat, even Brett was nervous. He had squashed plenty of normal sized bugs in the past, but never something that could bite back, let alone whisk him or his children away to grow eggs in.

With all the stealth they could muster, even the group moving into attack were stumbling in the darkness. They knew they had the advantage, if they could remain stealthy enough. Walking headlong into a battle with giant wasps, though, had the children veritably freaking out, five powerful Atlanteans protecting them or not.

"Dad! I heard something!" Drake exclaimed, hugging his father closely.

Sure enough, a loud buzzing sound heightened in intensity before more banging against the ship.

The clanging was too loud for Kelly and her sensibilities. Averse to loud noises of any kind, she grabbed the side of her head and covered her ears, letting go of her mother's hand.

"No no no... make it stop!" she wailed, furtively trying to keep quiet.

Ke'eli was there in an instant.

"Baby baby... it's okay, shhhhh... just hold my hand. We will stop the sound soon enough."

Zang, nervous at protecting the children, but strangely more towards Drake, came to their sides as well to warn them of their stealth, or lack thereof.

"Hatchlings, please be quiet. We must not alert..."

Zang's voice trailed off as she looked up towards the ship's hull.

The banging had stopped.

Mason, attuning himself into a precognitive state of battle, could sense that the creatures were aware of the group and that they were dashing towards them.

What the group could not have known was that in this precognitive state, Mason had connected them all on a telepathic level. He knew his group needed to get their attacks off first or fear the creatures stealing away with one of their number; most despairingly, one of the children.

Instantly, time seemed to slow for Mason. He could see snippets of the future and knew that three of the bugs were swarming towards them while one continued laying its egg-incubated victim.

His team moved into their preconceived methods of action, spurred by the mental push from Mason. Tumidus had cast his spell of fire several seconds earlier and was concentrating on maintaining it until told to release it by Mason. He could not see the broken piece of the hull as well as Zang could in the dark, but knew the general direction of the thing.

With the mental prodding of Mason, Tumidus reacted.

"Creare globus ignis!"

A small, pea-sized pellet of fire shot out of Tumidus' hand, swirling towards its intended target.

("The League of Extraordinary Gentlemen - Medoly" from Score It! (KMN Score Remix) by Trevor Jones)

Brett watched the thing sail off into the distance, wondering what the hell a tiny little flame the size of a marble was going to do to give them light.

Brett huffed under his breath, fear gnawing at him. Not for himself. No, he would die before anything happened to his family. But that was the rub. Here he was in the midst of a battle with his family beside him. Thoughts of fighting outside a pyramid with them beside him flittered into his consciousness again. He could see Ke'eli, or a version of her slightly older, erect a massive wall of earth and stone between him and Kelly while some robotic construct shot what looked like .50 caliber bullets at them.

The pea-sized flame hit the side of the ship's aft, interrupting his thoughts. An explosion rocked the hillside, blasting apart the wood and paneling, sucking the air from their immediate surroundings. Brett gasped in surprise, shocked that so little a thing could cause such devastation. The boom brought Kelly to her knees, Ke'eli cradling her. Drake looked on in sheer adulation. His excitement was short-lived; sure enough, the fire illuminated the night, showing the group what the monsters looked like.

As large as a horse, each creature reared up from the blast. Looking only vaguely like insects, they had dark orange carapaces that bordered on almost being black. Stripes in different striations marked their bodies, which

Brett concluded quickly separated them into different castes, just like ants.

Their jointed appendages skittered about, all six of the legs ending in sharp protrusions that looked like swords. The four legs on the thorax supported the body while the two front legs raised up, turning into giant scythes. The segmented part of their abdomen had the enormous stinger Tumidus warned them about. Even from here, Brett could see the debilitating poison dripping from the end of the vesical.

Mandibles so large they looked like they could sever a man's body in twain twitched towards the group of prey that the creatures now recognized in the light. Even from the distance they were at, Brett could hear the sizzle of acid as it dripped from the open mouths of the monsters.

Two of the insectoids were smaller than the third, it apparently leading the assault against the Seekers and the family. Even with the bare light from the exploded and now burning ship, Brett could make out the larger third creature inverted its tail upwards like a scorpion, pointing it at the group. Hadn't someone mentioned earlier that the bigger ones could shoot projectiles?

All three creature's antennae twitched in response to the explosion, all furtively reacting before they seemed to act as one to return to their hunt. As if they were speaking to each other, the two smaller creatures stalked forward towards the group while the larger one began to back into the relative safety of the darkness.

Surprisingly enough, Brett was the fastest of the entire group, wanting nothing more than to kill these bugs and get his family to safety. He recognized that the big one could probably shoot the projectiles and figured he should take that one down the quickest, since it looked like the thing was trying to hide from the light. Could these things see in the dark? Brett shivered at the thought again.

He still wasn't sure what he could do against these monsters, but ideas flooded his mind. Things he wasn't sure he could do, but that, for some reason, had been taught to him. Memories of being in another world surrounded by water and being able to do amazing things with it. But where was the water?

Brett smelled the air quickly. The fire burned not far away, but he could also hear and *taste* the liquid of whatever was left in the vessel. These smugglers flew around in this thing, but Brett guessed it wasn't much different from a ship at sea; they had to have some food and water somewhere?

Brett honed in on the pungent tang of potable water coming from a series of barrels in the main portion of the ship that remained undamaged. It was not too far away from either him or the larger creature.

Closing his eyes, Brett reached out with his mind and his hand, using the other hand to keep a hold of Drake. His fingertips felt moist suddenly, almost as if he could touch the water in the barrels. Trying his best to imagine protecting his family, he thought the best thing to do was to keep the big bug in the light so that everyone could take it down quickly.

Squeezing his fingers into a fist, he yanked backwards quickly. He felt a tug there, as if the water was resisting him, but it lasted only a second. A small wave of water rose from the ship, seeking the larger bug. Brett opened his eyes and saw the tiny stream of water, thinking it could do nothing against the sheer size of the beast. Anger welled up in him, reminded by the squeezing hand of the son by his side.

The ground began to shake as Brett furrowed his brow at the monster, even as the thing's barbed tail rose in response. Whether it aimed for Brett or someone else, he didn't care. He just knew that a dart that big entering someone's body could kill them, and no one was dying tonight on his shift.

As the ground continued to quake, a massive wall of water erupted from under Brett's feet in a line from him towards the monster, hitting one of the other creatures as well. 60 feet long and 5 feet wide, the water wall was immense and tidal, sheer forces of nature pulled from the water reserves underground. Surprised by the upswell of energy and knocked off his own footing, Brett could only back away with Drake as the water died away, his control broken.

The wave struck two of the three creatures, injuring them somewhat. He had hoped to pull the bigger one closer, and it looked like the thing stopped for just a second, but its greater strength prevailed as its sword-like limbs dug deep into the earth.

Brett growled aloud to no one in particular.

"Fuck. These things are strong!" he yelled to his entourage.

"Aye lad, but I see what yer tryin' to do!" Pwyll replied. "The big one is seeking to hide in the dark! Where ye goin' lass?!"

Pwyll laughed as he launched his signature bag of black goo at the larger creature. He had sneaked in closer to the thing, so the appearance of the flying bag and the gnome as well was a total surprise to the insects.

The bag splashed down into the area surrounding the larger insect, the goo immediately clinging to its legs. It seemed slowed, but still its superior strength won through. The goo would only slow it down for a moment.

Pwyll, realizing this, also realized that he was *way* too close to the monsters. Taking out another small vial, he put it to his lips and drank it down. Right away, his mechanical legs wound up, his speed almost doubled. Running back to the main squad of Seekers and the family, he let the more offensive types lead the way.

Fast beyond all belief, Brett sucked in his breath as he watched Zang leap into the fray. She whizzed past the first two creatures, also intent on keeping the larger one from hiding in the darkness.

Jumping over the larger insect, her wings opened wide to give her the altitude she needed to avoid the wandering stinger tail. Landing hard behind the monster, Zang went to work.

Striking an offensive pose by bringing her arms in close to her sides with her elbows bent at 90 degrees and her legs half squatting, she let loose the most feral roar any of the group had ever heard. Still using her wings to aid her, she leaped up into the air, bringing both of her fists down hard onto the head of the creature as it turned around to confront her.

Seeing the oncoming attack, the monster twitched its head to the side just as the first fist came in at it. Adjusting for the miss, Zang continued her aerial assault, her left fist coming in just as hard as her right.

The strike broke pieces of carapace away from the thing's head; the attack was so strong. Zang had funneled a portion of her own Ki into the strike to send shockwaves through her fist, not only trying to stun the creature but also knock it down.

The effect had everyone else cheering, but for the wrong reasons. The beast dropped to the ground as the fist dazed it, but it did not kill the thing. Granted, any other attacks against it would be easier, which Zang wasted no time in attempting.

Coming down from the air with her knee leading, Zang crunched her scaly appendage into the side of the thing's head again, causing a deluge of green blood to pour from the wound. Zang landed nimbly beside the Myrmidon as it swung a scythed leg out at her. Jumping back quickly, she regained her balance as Mason whispered into her mind.

"Let it be. My turn."

Standing back by the family, he had seen the intents of the rest of his group, recognizing them for the tactical ploys they were. Granted, the larger one was prone, but was still too close to the safety of the darkness for his comfort. Reaching out his hand much like Brett did, Mason needed no water to affect the power he used.

Squeezing his hand tighter, he yanked back suddenly on the prone body of the insect. Having never fought one of these creatures before, though, he too underestimated their strength. The same scythed leg that struck out at Zang came slamming down into the ground, furrowing a deep rut in the earth as it fought being dragged by Mason's telekinetic hand.

Mason squirmed as his mental strength fought out against the physical strength of the monster. Exhaling loudly, Mason opened his eyes, looking back at his Seeker team and the family, even more scared than he was before. This would not be easy.

Mason ended his look upon his friend, Tumidus. Looking back at the fray and where the relative distances of the enemies were, he looked back again at Tumidus.

"Do it. She will not be as affected."

Mason, angry determination replacing the fear he had before, looked back forward at the fray.

Each creature was within 20 feet of each other, including Zang. Mason knew what Tumidus could do, again, though the heat from the fire would most likely burn the scalehide in the midst. As leader of the group, his priority was keeping the family alive, and as much as it hurt him, that meant sacrificing his own team if he could protect the humans.

Tumidus recognized the act for what it was. Other sorcerers could imbue an ally with a shield of sorts to protect them from area of effect spells like the fireball he was about to cast, but he was not one of them. Quite the opposite; he intended to make it harder for the creatures to survive the assault.

Producing his arcane wand once again, he pointed it at the group of insects before him and muttered the words of power.

"Creare globus ignis maximus!"

Once again, as before, a small pea of fire arced out of his outstretched hand, flying fast towards the group.

This one seemed different for some reason. Evern from as far away as the group was, they could feel the intensity of the heat emanating from it.

The bugs seemed to sense it as well, but reacted much too slowly. If anything, one thing seemed entranced by the small bead of light, inching closer to it as it suddenly detonated in their midst.

The effect was twice as tremendous as the first. A blossoming ball of fire scorched the ground beneath it, instantly vaporizing the grass. The one creature who watched the ball approach was vaporized as well, its head exploding from the sudden burst of flame.

Both other creatures were also affected, though not as intensely as the first. The remaining smaller insect caught on fire, its strange, garbled chittering becoming a screaming.

Xinzang, recognizing that Tumidus was launching an enhanced version of his spell, dove for cover behind the hulking and prone mass of the larger myrmidon. Making it just in time, the flames licked above her head as the creature behind her was wracked by the heat.

Not quite defeated, the remaining two creatures squirmed about in an attempt to put the fires out. The death of the third released a cloud of burning spores and pheromones into the air, causing the others to flail about in a maddened and estranged state.

A *thump-thump-thump* was all the insects heard before the pulverizing mass that was Keb strode into their midst, his cat-like claws wailing away at the monsters. Keb, recognizing that the remaining smaller creature was bloodied and almost defeated, focused on it first. He then pointed at the larger creature and muttered something in Bantu at the ground beneath his feet.

Massive arms leading, Keb tore into the burning insect. Grabbing it with his left hand, Keb punched the thing in the face over and over as it finally stopped twitching and became still. Covered in green blood, Keb looked over to the other prone creature and growled out a challenge of combat in Bantu.

The ground beneath Keb's feet began to roil and churn, but he was unfazed. The disturbed earth continued, but spiraled closer to the last creature beside Zang. Suddenly, a gout of dirt erupted from the side of the last Myrmidon as a creature made of rock and stone appeared beside it. Slamming its rocky hands down into the side of the prone monster, the sharper ends of pointed stones pierced its hide, drawing more of the thing's lifeblood.

However, it refused to be defeated. The monstrous insect, screaming into the night, scrambled around in the sticky tar until it could gain its footing. Standing upright once again, the thing shook from the exultation of its fellow insects' demise.

Two immensely large front legs rose towards Zang, who was its closest enemy. The blades appeared as though they were about to strike down hard at her, but they were only a distraction as the tail lowered under the thing's body and a dripping poison dart fired towards the monk.

Recognizing the act for what it was at the last second, Zang was just barely able to deflect the missile, though the object still scraped along her forearm. Even that minute amount of damage was enough to introduce the debilitating poison into her system, though. Normally able to shrug off other poisons and diseases from her extensive training, this toxin was something altogether different.

Her eyes going wide, Zang realized the danger she was in as her entire body locked up. All this pain and paralyzation from just the nick of a dart?! She knew in her heart of hearts, though, that at least the children would not be taken and that she was a worthy sacrifice. She tried to look past the monster to the family to ensure they were safe, but her eyes opened even wider as tears flowed. Zang was sure that only she could see it as her eyes adjusted to the darkness behind the family.

The other Myrmidon that had been burying its prey had heard the death screams of its own and had come calling. It crept from the darkness into the midst of the family behind them, none of them aware. The thing looked like it was weighing its options, not as affected by the pheromones of its dead kin and still able to make logical decisions; logical for a giant insect.

Zang trembled as the thing focused its gaze on the smallest and easiest prey of the group: Drake.

Growling under her breath, the paralyzing effect of the poison had registered her unable to move or speak at all. She could only look on as the two immensely bladed legs of the creature came down to pierce her flesh.

Not able to resist the attack, both legs punctured her shoulders, lifting her up high. She knew that if the beast was in its right mind, it would probably run off to lay its eggs in her and be done with the fight, but the pheromones seemed to have made the beast want to stay and fight.

Zang grimaced at the pain she felt, but willed the specter of death away. She focused on her training, intent on protecting the boy.

Almost as if she relayed the thought to the child, Drake let out a gasp as he saw her be lifted into the air by the giant bug. Looking back to his father to get his help in saving Zang, Drake looked beyond his protector into the darkness and saw the other insect creeping up from behind. The Myrmidon didn't look normal to him; only an outline of dark blacks and light grays devoid of color, but he recognized the thing for what it was.

Letting out a yelp, he pointed at the monster. Anger at his friend Zang being attacked and, most likely, killed from what he could tell, Drake's yelp evolved into a scream of rage and denial.

Brett recognized the heat rising in his son's hand and looked back at what Drake was pointing at, but could see nothing in the dark. Something inside Brett told him to trust in his son, seeing as he also saw Zang get skewered by the beast, and nothing could distract Drake like another threat.

Fire sweltered in his son's hands, burning Brett. Another image came unbidden to Brett's mind again; that of his son on fire and blasting away at buildings and robots, leaving them molten slags of metal.

Brett knew that Drake probably couldn't do that now, but with his help, he might at least try. Moving behind his son, Brett put both hands on his shoulders and kneeled behind his son. Whispering in his ear, Brett encouraged the fire but instructed his son to direct it at the foe.

Almost immediately, Brett felt a coursing of energy evaporate from the insides of his chest to channel down his arms and into Drake.

Drake, in response, raised his hands to chest height as a gout of flame as hot as the sun came pouring forth.

That's when Brett saw what Drake was looking at. The flame shot out past the dim edge of light afforded by the fire of the ship to strike the fourth Myrmidon. Another of the larger variety, the attack surprised the creature, taking the fire directly to its face.

Its skin burned and popped, chittering screams erupting from it as well. But the flame did not slay the creature. Portions of its body melted away to nothing, falling to the ground as the flames continued to bite at it, but the monster kept coming.

Drake dropped his arms down to his sides, passing out from the exertion. Even Brett felt light-headed at the expenditure of energy it took to help fuel his son's fire. He looked up into Ke'eli's eyes pleadingly.

The creature now on fire, Ke'eli turned to face the monster lumbering into their defensive formation. She knew Zang needed help, but this monster was right on their front doorstep. Pushing Kelly back behind her, Ke'eli roared out at the monster, who had been focusing on her son, Drake.

"Not today, motherfucker!" she yelled, charging towards the flaming monster.

The surrounding earth seemed to sense her anger as each step she took towards the Myrmidon had dirt and stone flying in every direction. Ke'eli could feel the muscles in her arms swell as tears in her eyes blurred her vision.

She didn't care. She would hit this fucking thing and end this.

The Myrmidon skittered about on its flaming legs to face Ke'eli, not registering the determination and vitriol aimed at it.

It didn't have to register it for long.

Ke'eli went sailing through the air, her right hand leading.

One punch was all it took.

One punch, and the Myrmidon's head exploded from the impact.

Breathing heavily, Ke'eli whipped her hand out from the inside of the monster's brains, pushing the now still husk away from her as it toppled to the ground, motionless.

To make sure, Ke'eli kicked the thing for good measure, sinking her boot into the thing's insides once again.

Positive the thing was dead, she turned to run back to the rest of her family.

Kelly looked on in fear, but then admiration as her mother literally knocked the insect's head in. She felt remorse for the insects, who had probably been stolen away from their homes and brought here against their will, but she also realized that her friends and family were in danger.

No more so than Zang, who she could see from here dangled from the claws of the last Myrmidon standing. She had never tried to heal anyone before, and she realized with dismay that she probably couldn't from so far away. The thought did not deter her. She knew that if she didn't do something, Zang could die.

Kelly did the thing she did best; she fought against prevailing odds. Picked on in school for her odd ways, Kelly had always been socially awkward. She had unnatural intelligence about her. Everything that came at her only strengthened her. Any obstacle she encountered, she found a way around.

Reaching out through her tears to Zang, she tried to keep her alive. She focused on the massive weapons impaled in Zang's body, praying to make them go away somehow. Her own body reacted, suddenly feeling sharp pains in her shoulders. Instinctively reaching up to massage away the pain in her own body, Kelly realized maybe she could relay the sense of ease from her own pain into Zang.

Closing her eyes as the rest of her family had done to focus on their power, Kelly rubbed the aching pain in her shoulders, willing it away.

The effort exhausted her as well, but she could feel a slight sense of numbness wash over her pain. Not necessarily removing it; just easing it.

Zang, through her paralyzed state, felt the wounds in her shoulders slowly start to close. Though the scythes were still impaled in her body, the pain lessened some.

She looked on through teary and now bloodshot eyes as the entire entourage of hers came swarming over to aid her. The other three monsters had been vanquished, and it was only this badly damaged one with no sense of self-control left to deal with.

Though it felt like the creature was trying to rip her in half with its legs or bite her head off, it seemed distracted by the others coming up behind it to delay its tactics for just long enough.

Everyone acted as one.

Brett willed the blood to flow more quickly from the creature's body, watching in abject revulsion as it literally sprayed out in all directions. The creature shook about again on shaky legs, but still refused to die.

"Fuck! Why don't you just die!" Brett even yelled out in exasperation.

Pwyll ran up beside Brett, realizing that if they didn't do something soon, the creature would rip Zang in half.

Throwing a small orb towards Zang, Pwyll smiled in satisfaction as the projectile hit her, opening up its contents all over her scales. The nanobots spread to cover her body while also going into the talons belonging to the Myrmidon.

"Aye lad, here's hoping my little buddies have given our scaly friend there a bit of sanctuary from the beastie!"

Pwyll kept moving regardless towards the creature, intent on being there for Zang when the rest of his allies finished the thing off.

Zang saw this all transcend in fascination. She knew they might not make it in time, but felt relieved to see that Drake was going to be okay. Fighting four of the monsters in the dark with their poison was one thing; fighting one of them while it was injured was another.

Still, she felt an otherworldly determination to survive this to further protect the child. *Just the child?* She thought to herself. Of course not. She would protect the whole family. It was her way as a scaleborn.

The thought of having to endure to further protect the family brought her back to her senses. It was true. The wounds healed somewhat in her shoulders, but the monster's poison still paralyzed her.

Try as she might, she could not will her body to be her own again. The paralyzation continued as she prayed to her goddess she would survive this escapade.

Mason also recognized the perilous state they were in. He knew Tumidus was preparing another of the few offensive spells he had, risking nothing in the last assault. Keb and his earthen familiar were ready to storm the creature, yet the monster still had Zang in its clutches. He had to get her away from the beast.

Resolving to use the same tactic he had before but on Zang and not the Myrmidon, Mason moved his hand from the imaginary body he held in his grasp just a few inches until it rested upon Zang. Squeezing again, though not as tightly, he could feel pressure in his palms, showing he had what he sought.

She, like the creature, might normally try to resist the telekinetic pull of his mysticism, but not in her current state. Easily, he removed her from the monster's scything talons.

The beast sensed his intent and struggled to allow her to be removed. In its angered state, on fire and now with the benefit of Pwyll's spell working against it, the Myrmidon couldn't help but let go of its prey.

Zang flew horizontally backwards from the grasp of the talons, just into the edge of the darkness. Still paralyzed, she couldn't react or move; only gasp as the holes in her chest were opened to the air and the continued sting of the pain and poison flowed in her system.

Mason held her aloft, even raising her up in the air somewhat in case the monster pursued. But he needn't have worried.

Tumidus saw the opening he needed and acted. Ensuring his spell's success, an aura of purple energy coalesced around his form, warping the air. Brett worried as the elf's features distorted some, his ears growing just a tad bit longer.

The fireball, seeming to have worked perfectly before, was again Tumidus' spell of choice. Anxious at the idea of being used as a food source for the insect's burrowing prodigy, Tumidus wanted nothing more than to end this threat once and for all.

He knew that Keb's familiar was beside the monster, but also knew that the thing was spiritual and could be caused to return, once Keb had time to cast the ritual to bring it back. Zang was far enough away from the blast that she would not be affected, even in her paralyzed state.

Tumidus also couldn't help but smile as the raw magic flowed through his body. Wild and chaotic, he tapped into a reservoir of power that ensured his spell would make it harder for the creature to survive. By doing so, he had to test the boundaries of his people, the elves, but it was something he was accustomed to and knew that if the magic escaped his control, he could redirect it into himself to further alter his physicality.

Thankfully, the surge of wild magic did nothing drastic to him, short of lengthening his already long ears. The purple glow funneled itself into the growing energy of the fiery pea before him, highlighting it in amethyst.

"Creare globus ignis!" once again echoed out into the night. The flaming pea shot off towards the Myrmidon, striking the monster's side before blossoming out into a raging inferno of purple and red.

Bits and pieces of the monster flew everywhere, its side exposed to the air as the giant gap where its abdomen used to be vanished. Wavering about on shaky legs, the group exhaled as one as the monster finally dropped to the ground, unmoving.

The group moved as one, staying close together, even though they knew the threat was gone. Tumidus and Keb moved to each of the creatures themselves, ensuring they were deceased. The main point of the group was to get to Zang, by whichever route they thought was safest.

Pwyll arrived there first, his automated legs still moving quicker than everyone else's. Sliding to Zang's side, he fought to keep the worry from his voice.

"Aye, lass, time to get up now! Got a pint of healing here for ye to drink!"

Reaching into one of his automated bags, Pwyll produced a large bottle of red liquid. Supporting her head, Pwyll drizzled its contents into her mouth, ensuring she swallowed every drop.

Kelly and the rest of the family arrived shortly thereafter, kneeling beside the scaleborn. Kelly reached out and grabbed her limp hand, squeezing tightly as Drake kneeled on her other side, taking her other hand. Both children could feel a connection between each other, though Drake was on the verge of passing out again. Once Brett and Ke'eli arrived to be around them as well, their energy returned, and they regained their focus.

Kelly went right away, trying to focus on expelling the paralyzing poison in Zang's system. She could suddenly taste a metallic tang in her mouth, which she spit out to the side. As soon as she did so, Zang let out a gasp of air as her hands squeezed the children's back.

"Whoa whoa now lass, you're still healin'! Don't be getting all upset and moving around too much yet!" Pwyll veritably had to lean on Zang to keep her from getting up.

The family watched in awe as the wounds on her chest gradually closed, her breathing becoming more stable. Zang closed her eyes as she knew they were safe, her Team and the family surrounding her.

"The bugs are deceased? What of the rest of the crew?" She whispered out.

"The crew is gone." Mason exclaimed, coming over to stand with the rest of the team.

"While you were tending to her wounds, I reached out to find them. Turns out, once the bugs were distracted by us, this wayward group of smugglers took it upon themselves to flee for their own good. They have scattered to the four winds."

Brett laughed at the information.

"Did they leave the one that was buried? The guy with the..." Brett gagged slightly. "... um, the guy with the eggs in him?"

Mason smiled down at Brett.

"Ah, but they were ever the ones to salvage what they could! Their ally was impregnated with the eggs, which should hatch soon. What they lost in four adult Myrmidons, they gained in a clutch of newborns. I could not track them deeper into the darkness."

Brett stood quickly.

"Didn't you say it would be bad for these things to get out into the wild? Are they not *in the wild* now? Eggs or not, should we try to stop them?"

Mason sighed.

"They have split up to avoid any further chase in case we could not defeat the Myrmidons. I do not know which of the groups has the impregnated captive. It is dark, we are injured, and our energies are spent. I recommend we salvage what we can from the wreckage and try to identify who these smugglers were and relay that information to the Council once we finally arrive at the Capital."

Looking around to the rest of his team, the other Seekers all nodded in agreement.

Tumidus approached Mason, holding what looked like a small glob of yellow resin.

"This was all I could salvage from the beasts. It appears fire and royal jelly do not go well together!"

Mason held the small glob gingerly.

"What is that? Is that what I think it is?" Ke'eli asked, sniffing at the substance. She knew about most things in nature, and giant bug or not, she had an idea of what it could be, but was aghast at the idea of it.

Mason didn't have to read her mind to know.

"Yes, milady, this is royal jelly. In smaller amounts in bees, it is much like honey. Here in Atlantis, it is the one reason these creatures may live in the depths of the south desert seas. Royal jelly can replicate any other liquid substance we can make. It is an amazing tool, and intrepid adventurers make fortunes exploring the wastes of the south for hives to gather it."

Mason looked down at the still injured Zang, then back to the jelly in his hand.

Looking up at Tumidus, the elf sighed but nodded his head. This small amount of jelly could fetch them a small fortune if sold to the right people. But the elf knew what Mason intended and would not interfere.

Nodding, Mason kneeled beside Zang. Looking around at the family, he held the jelly in the palm of his hand.

"Pwyll just administered his strongest healing potion, but Zang remains injured enough that she may require more medical attention than we can provide."

As if to stress the point, Zang's wings twitched in pain, folding beneath her. She grimaced, letting go of the children's hands to hold her shoulders.

Mason wasted no additional time. Dipping the jelly into what was left of the potion Pwyll had pulled out of his bag, nothing happened at first. As they watched, though, the jelly took on a reddish appearance, matching that of the potion's original color. After only a few seconds, the jelly was now blood red.

Mason poured the thing back out into his hand, bringing it up into the firelight for all to see. It was the same color as the healing potion, though still jelly like.

Lowering it into Zang's mouth, she swallowed the thing whole, while nodding thanks to Mason.

"I am sure she would have been able to continue towards the Capitol without this, but our aerial advantage would be gone. This should heal her back to a semblance of normal." Mason explained to the family.

Right away, the remaining wounds on her shoulders and the slice on her forearm faded away. Breathing deeply again, she blinked hard. Sitting up on one elbow, she smiled meekly at the gathered group.

"I am well. Thank you for your sacrifice. I know that could have been used for much wiser things than just me, and…"

"Oh, stop it, will ye, ye big dumb lizard."

Pwyll laughed as he slapped his hand on her back.

Nodding at the gnome. Zang stood up and stretched.

"Very well, gnome. Shall we return to our interrupted rest? I believe a ship as this, damaged or not, should have a Captain's quarters with much better sleeping arrangements than being on the cold ground."

Brett smiled at the group.

"Yes, please."

CHAPTER FIVE

ZION

(“Concerning Hobbits” from The Lord of the Rings: The Fellowship of the Ring Soundtrack by Howard Shore)

Later the next day, they came to the outskirts of the magnificent city of Zion. Much like dwarves, this diminutive race of halflings was the same shape as humans, just of a shrunken sort. Many halfling adults were the height of human teenagers, and halfling teenagers were half again the height of Drake and Kelly.

The new visitors marveled at the beautiful city. Halflings worked with nature, building their homes in the hillsides, and sharing the bounties of the Earth.

Fields of green stretched as far as the eye could see, gardens of all kinds filling the spaces between each home. The landscape looked like a sea of grass, each small home a wave in the ocean. Halflings milled about, lazily tending to their farms and gardens, nonchalantly looking up at the traveling entourage.

The 'city' was hill after hill of large hovels, replete with a smattering of large wood buildings that looked sturdy but ramshackle at the same time. Mason assured the group that the bones of each building were buried deep in the earth, while the shell was more for purpose than for any cosmetic allure. Halflings did not dote on trying to impress others, content with doing what they could when they could.

The above-ground view of the city belayed the tremendous sights that rested beneath the earth. The halflings, healers of all types, hated to use any formerly living materials in their buildings. Instead, they dug underground like their dwarven cousins, living within the hills. Not as mired in the depths of the dirt as dwarves, halflings spent as much time outside as they did inside.

Either way, most of the short folk were smiling and laughing while they spoke with each other. The smell of food permeated the air, odors of all types intermixing to make a soup of mouth-watering flavor. Some halflings sat, their hairy feet propped up on benches while they smoked from long tobacco pipes.

Brett could not hold the question in anymore. "Why does everything seem so like Lord of the Rings around here?"

Mason laughed.

"We asked ourselves the same question for many, many years." he replied. "How could the rest of the world know so much about our culture, but so little?"

The group continued, walking past an open-air market where vendors displayed every imaginable type of food.

"We discovered recently, less than a couple hundred years, that it was all our fault. And when I say 'our', I mean the human mystics."

The other chaperones smirked and nodded their heads. Tumidus, always proud to show off, encouraged him to continue.

"Humans who are not of the Olmec Native Americans in Atlantis are all mystics, born of the outer 'Olde World' where you all were from. The children taken from the Olde World remember their homes and their families. We try our best to console them, which is why we prefer to find them when they are young, hoping it will be easier to forget. For many, though, because we are mystics, we recall our heritage."

"Because we have power over the mind, we forecast our dreams out into the wider world. We see this amazing and secret world of Atlantis, with the myriad races and creatures who dwell here, and we dream of them. Because we also dream of our homes, we inadvertently send our dreams out into the wider world. Everything we see here gets shot out like a laser beam into some unwilling or un-witting minds, usually those who had the greatest impacts on us, like our relatives."

The realization dawned on the group then. Ke'eli spoke up first.

"So, you're saying that everything that is fantasy-like in the rest of the world is based on your dreams that you send out into the world? Nothing is original?"

"No no no, not that at all!" Tumidus replied. "Think of what they do as a sort of catalyst. The idea or image of something might be remembered in a dream, but the impetus is whatever they wish up! You humans are very imaginative in your own right."

The timing could not have been better.

As Tumidus finished his sentence, the family stopped dead in their tracks. Not even forty feet away from them was what could only be called an 'alien'. Short and bald with gray skin and huge, bulbous eyes, the thing waddled toward them, raising a long-fingered hand in salute.

"You've contacted aliens?!" Brett exclaimed.

The escorts laughed, while the small creature that stopped in its tracks did not seem to find it funny.

The "alien" lowered its hand and spoke in what sounded like Latin to Tumidus. Tumidus, nodding solemnly, replied, waving his hand at the group.

"Iter nostrum nos amici novi, ut in clara civitate."

"We travel... friends... city." Drake spoke aloud.

All eyes turned to him then, surprised.

"What? I downloaded dad's Rosetta Stone thing and read up on some languages. Latin is pretty cool!"

Brett responded, the biggest and proudest smile on his face a man could have. "Boy, you never cease to amaze me. Good job!"

Tumidus waved his alien-friend goodbye, continuing the story about dreams.

"That 'alien' was the perfect example of what I was talking about. You humans see something you do not understand, and you make up an explanation for it. If you were to dream in a visual context only, your imaginations would fill the gaps."

"Your minds wouldn't be able to understand many other fantastic things we have here in Atlantis, let alone 'aliens'." Zang said as she poked Drake.

"Don't mind her." Mason continued. "Dragons and their kin are still the least understood of all creatures in Atlantis. What Tumidus was trying to get at is the dreams of our people, as they are broadcast out into the wider world, give the rest of humanity a simple and one-sided view of what goes on here. They then use that knowledge as an impetus to create amazing stories, people and places that simulate the real-world creatures and places here, under 'the dome'."

"That 'alien' you just saw was an elf, like Tumidus. Elves are one of the few races able to harness the amazing energy that you might call 'magic' in your world. Magic is a form of radiation that can be controlled to create wondrous things. It is a danger, but the potential is unlimited."

"The more an elf uses magic through their bodies, the more it changes them. Over time, without proper control or direction, the radiation can mutate the elf into something that looks like what you just saw. Many elves pour their magic into scrolls that can be cast without fear of it harming them, since the magic is infused in the components and ingredients, instead of it coming out of the elf." Tumidus smiled.

It was Mason's turn to smirk.

"Some elves turn to chaos and instead let the magic take control to wreak havoc on their surroundings, instead of on their bodies. Hence, Aelfsium."

Tumidus glared at Mason.

"Aelfsium sounds a lot like Elysium. Is that another dream-coincidence?" Brett asked, always curious to know more about history.

"Unfortunately, no." Tumidus continued, "Aelfsium was just lost in translation, but is a wonderfully magical place. What Mason refers to is the chaotic energies of the place that were inadvertently unleashed thousands of years ago. If you can handle it, the land of Aelfsium is very easily manipulated, very 'Heaven-like'. If you cannot handle it, it can be an extremely dangerous place. Not like Mason, the human has room to talk about unleashing catastrophes!"

Tumidus stopped the entourage as they neared the hover rail platform. His smile faded as he herded everyone together.

He whispered to the group, "It looks like you will all be privy to a private demonstration of some illusory magic!" He looked back over his shoulder, as did Mason and the others.

A small contingent of heavily armed soldiers was walking their way. Not purposefully, but close enough where they would pass by the group.

Tumidus continued speaking to the Four. "I am going to alter your form, Ke'eli, so that you look like a native race of Atlantis. The children are easily passed as halflings and you, Brett, can be a human, but your wife must be altered to protect her."

"What? Why? What's wrong with her?" Brett looked up over at the guards, evaluating their strengths and weaknesses.

"No, it's nothing. We will explain it to you shortly. Prepare yourself!" Tumidus whispered.

Closing his eyes, Tumidus reached his hands out to Ke'eli, waving over her head as if he were petting her.

"Mutata Specie."

Brett and the children looked on in amazement as Tumidus molded the features of Ke'eli. Barely able to hold out his snicker, he covered his mouth as he fought to keep it in.

"You have pointy ears, Kee!" Brett, for a United States Marine with all the bearing in the world, giggled like a little schoolgirl.

Sure enough, Ke'eli's face and body had reformed, growing slimmer, her already oval eyes canted slightly. Her ears grew longer and pointier, her hair becoming a dark hue of blue instead of black.

The children, already the size of halflings, were told to keep quiet and to keep their heads down. There was not much that needed to be done for them, but Tumidus hushed them with a look that meant they should say nothing if the guards approached them.

And sure enough, the guards veered in their direction.

"I have made you in the resemblance of my wilder relations, the Titan elves. They look more like your standard elf and shy from the use of magic. Just... say nothing!"

Tumidus looked over to Mason, nodding that they could continue their walk.

"They are the Atlantean Guard, like your Marine Corps, Brett." Mason explained.

"Trained in the many arts of combat, they defend the continent from the various threats that occasionally rise. They are also trained in the art of politics, for they are the continent's police force as well. They are not to be trifled with."

The group could see why.

A massive dragon-man, twice the size of Xinzang, marched at the forefront. Though he did not have wings like she did, his intimidating nature radiated from him like a wave. Scars marked his face, showing part of his fangs revealed from a torn lip.

("Farewell" from the Terminator: Salvation Soundtrack by Danny Elfman)

Behind him, even more intimidating to the family, was what Pwyll had called a "golem". A machine created by the gnomes, the pyramid at the center of Atlantis had somehow granted the robots sentience, and they had become the de facto protectors of the principal city.

The family was not ready for what they would look like, though. Without warning, Drake yelled out, "Ultron!" as he looked fearfully over at the group. Sure enough, the resemblance was uncanny. What appeared to be the menacing robot from the Avengers movie scanned the crowd, ready for anything. As if the red eyes and skull-like face were not enough, it was also carrying two giant swords magnetically attached to its back.

The family looked over to the rest of the crowd in the bazaar, expecting fear or for them to be intimidated. The exact opposite occurred, though. Halflings hailed the Guard, even coming over to them with food and drink. The robot seemed to smile somehow, as it waved away an offering of fruit. A halfling woman giggled as well, as she patted the thing on its arm.

Brett felt an upwelling of vigorous anger at the sight of the robot for some reason. An image flashed in his mind of a creature much like it, using a salvo of bullets, rockets, and lasers to shoot down a man on fire, flying around in the sky.

Subconsciously, Brett looked down at his son, Drake, his eyes brimming with tears. Something about the human torch he saw in his mind made him think of his son Drake and of what he was capable of again.

Could he do that one day? Brett thought. The image seemed so real; it made Brett feel like it was more a memory than just an image he thought up. His chest tightened at the emotional feeling he had, so he reached his hand out to bring his son closer to him.

The strange memory of Kelly healing Drake's lifeless body came back to his mind as well.

Feeling the solidarity of his son in his hands, Brett shook the thoughts away and refocused on the group approaching them. In a vain attempt to change his mental state, he joked about how the robot looked like the one and only Ultron.

"Well, smack my ass and call me Sally." Brett said, all eyes coming to him with bemused expressions.

Ke'eli elbowed him sharply in the ribs, giving him a look of disdain.

"What?! You can't tell me you expected *that*!" He laughed. The children had just gotten the opportunity to watch the movie before all this insanity happened, so the situation was convenient.

"Yes, unlike your police forces in the Olde World, ours here are highly respected and sought after for their protection." Mason said the obvious.

"Must be nice." Brett smear-smiled, a face that his wife had coined. Somewhere between a grimace and a frown, it was always a telltale sign Brett was sarcastic. He had known many of his former Marines who had gotten out of the Corps to explore employment as police officers. The climate for law enforcement was not the best, and Brett feared for his comrades.

The entourage of the Atlantean Guards continued through the market, almost making a beeline for Mason and his group.

Mason motioned for the group to follow him. "Quickly, this way. They will be curious to know why we are back without a new mystic child."

Ke'eli could not hold back the question, though, as they followed Mason close behind.

"How do they know who you are? Are you famous or something?"

Tumidus answered for Mason.

"Though we were all once human, since the Separation so long ago, there have been racial divides. Atlantis is a place of wonder, but it is not without its faults."

Keb huffed at the comment, adding his own words of wisdom.

"You all stubborn. Too much pride."

Mason, ashamed of the truth, continued.

("Finding Faith" from the X2: X-Men United Soundtrack by John Ottman)

"We refuse to share in the mutual knowledge that had aided us for thousands of years after we caused the Deluge. Our Tribes, or races if you will, went their separate ways, stubbornly keeping to themselves. Therefore, there are few humans who practice magic, or elves who can control the elements. The opportunity is there. The tribal Elders just refuse to open their minds to the possibilities."

"Some say it is because each race was destined to be a certain way, and to share it with the unlearned would be catastrophic." Xinzang growled the last bit, hitting on something the family was unaware of.

"Yes, there have been attempts in the past, but it was doomed to failure because the tribal Elders limited the interaction between the racial delegates. How is one supposed to learn if they are handicapped from the beginning?" Mason furrowed his brow at the stupidity of it all.

"So, elves are the only ones that can do magic?" Drake asked, who seemed extremely interested in the subject.

"In a sense, yes. But the half-breed elves can use magic uniquely. They read it from books, memorizing certain gestures and words. Elves have magic innately in their bodies. There are other races as well, who have a smattering of magical control. The gnomes and goblinoids use magic to enhance themselves and their devices. The aquarians have developed a kind of magical music in the cold, dark depths of the sea."

"So, what about everyone else? So Pwyll is simply good with a laser pointer?" Brett drew a smattering of laughter from the group as they ducked into a nearby alley.

The hover platform lay not too far off in the distance. The trepidation Brett felt surprised him. For some reason, the sight of the giant metal platform freaked him out, as if he had been on one before.

"Ah, not a'all my friend! You ain't seen none o' me magic because I ain't showed ye none! I'm what ye might call an artificer. I like to put me magic in me own contraptions. Ye ever seen one o' these?"

At that, he reached for a small pouch at his hip, reaching his arm all the way inside it up to his armpit, which was impossible for the size of the bag.

His big smile melted away into a strange, confused look.

"Actually, yeah, I've seen those bottomless bags a couple times. Don't care to remember much about them, though. Pretty cool though on you, buddy!"

Brett tried to ease the sudden terseness of the conversation. He had indeed seen the pouches before; just in Andrew's hands.

Mason continued, "Gnomes have millions of tiny nanobots in their blood that enable them to do amazing things. Truth be told, these nanobots are constantly in the surrounding air, and they can be instructed to heat, mend materials, or even explode."

"The halflings, on the other hand, thought for the longest time that they were the God's chosen, because they could heal the sick and bring down righteous fury from what they thought was the Heavens. What they later came to realize was that they had an intimate connection with the Primal Elders themselves that enabled them to do miraculous things. The dwarves garner their power from gems and metals imbued with the power of the Soulstone, helping them to forge great armor and weapons, becoming the first Atlantean Knights. Either way, our three sister races are capable of amazing feats of what you might also call magic."

"And what of my toothy and scaly new friends here?" Brett asked, eyeing Keb and Xinzang out of the corner of his eyes.

Zang answered the remark with a low growl. "I know the secret arts of yin and yang that would destroy your soul, were you ever to attempt to learn it, little man."

Mason huffed. "What she means is the scalehide are master monks. They can use their ki to do superhuman things. They are very sought after for their wisdom."

Mason smiled and bowed to Xinzang, hoping to ease her temper. Though the scalehide were quiet and contemplative in their monk-like demeanor, Xinzang had returned to a rather displeasing mood; one of which Mason was yet to understand.

"So that brings us to Growl. Or Grill? I'm sorry, big guy, I don't know your name. No hard feelings?" Brett offered his hand in acknowledgement.

Ke'eli answered for Keb, putting her arm around his large neck.

"His name is Keb, and he's almost as strong as your wife! You better watch out Brett. I like these enormous arms of his!"

Keb chuckled under his tusks. "You funny for humans. I speak to Earth, like your mate. My people speak to spirits and work with them. My spirit is elements, like you and water, boy like fire and girl like wind."

"Why is your English so broken? Is language segregated too?" Brett asked with all the sincerity he could, without trying to sound offensive.

Mason smiled, noting the pleasantries.

"Language was once all one, known as Atlantean. When the Soulstone Pyramid at the center of the continent split the people into different races, it also split the language. What was created was the root language for every other dialect in the world. Pwyll and Keb's accents are deeper because of their Tribal segregation from the rest of Atlantis. The gnomes mostly remain in their hills to the northeast, while the orcs are nomadic, roaming the plains to the southeast."

"We do not force them to learn a language they do not want to learn." Tumidus continued. "The languages we speak here are the root languages that have spread across the whole of the Olde World. As you saw earlier, my language is Italic, the root for Latin, Greek and Italian. Pwyll's is Celtic while Xinzang's is Chinese. Keb's is a form of Bantu."

"Wow, so you guys are pretty much a condensed version of the entire world. I'm surprised you all get along so well, even with the racial prejudices you all seem to have." Brett was testing the limits of his new companions, trying to get a rise out of at least one of them. He *had* been a trained counterintelligence Marine, and if there was one way to get the truth, it was through testing someone's loyalties to country.

Tumidus took the bait, which was what Brett figured.

"We do not have prejudices here. The Soulstone Pyramid helps us to find empathy in all things, big or small. It radiates a warming energy that not only powers our devices, but it also empowers our souls."

"And refreshes your magic." Mason slyly added.

Tumidus scowled at the man, but Mason continued.

"The Soulstone provides much, but it isn't unlimited. Natural boundaries block the empathic emanations that the pyramid gives off. We created the Childe Pyramids around the perimeter of the continent to enhance this energy, but found that they differed from the original Soulstone. Remember, these other pyramids were susceptible to empathic change. Therefore, the beast-born to the south and some orcs and goblinoids are evil. Not only is there is a large mountain chain that blocks the energy from the Soulstone from reaching them, but the pyramid to the south that was attacked by the Armies of Man transferred some of their chaotic and evil tendencies into it. The beast-born are some of the best fighters in the world, but they are of the barbaric lot. They shrug off injury like an elephant shrugs off a fly. Goblinoids are roguish and seemed more concerned with personal wealth sometimes than they do about anything else. As for the orcs..."

Mason looked over to Keb for his permission to continue, but found he did not need it.

"Orcs have Clans in Tribe. We honor battle and honor ancestors. Sometime, ancestors say fight. Sometime, we fight other orc. Sometime, we fight other Tribe. Many time, we keep to self."

"There was also a plan once, to create other pyramids around the world to act as relays for the Soulstone."

All eyes turned to Tumidus now, as he spoke.

"Groups of the Eleusinian Mysterie spread everywhere, teaching man how to build replicated pyramids, infused with crystals that could boost the power of the Soulstone. There was the hope that they could create a shield around the world, protecting and blessing everyone."

"But again, the greed of man won out. Maybe it was the fel-spawned demons and devils who coerced them in the end. Maybe it was their own sin. Either way, the pyramids were built, but man turned against the Atlanteans that had been sent to aid them. Where once the Atlantean emissaries were looked up to as saviors, they were instead feared and hunted."

"Let's not forget our role in that division, my friend. There were some of us who took the role of 'savior' a little too far, thinking that the Atlantean way was the only way." Mason continued.

"But I digress from your original question." Tumidus laughed. "We are recognized for exactly the opposite of everything I just told you. We are in a halfling city, a group of five of different Tribes heralding a human boy to our capital city. We are either a Seeker group, part of the Atlantean Guard or a band of mercenary adventurers, of which there are none too few of in the great country of Atlantis!"

"The Atlantean Guard would surely 'escort' us to the safety of the capital should they have recognized us. That, we would not like to do right now." Mason smiled as he continued to move the family along.

("Platform Nine-and-Three-Quarters and the Journey to Hogwarts" from the Harry Potter and the Sorcerer's Stone Soundtrack by John Williams)

The information was overwhelming. There were so many questions that they still wanted to ask, but the time for them to converse wore out. They were finally at the base of the platform, which was at least two hundred feet up.

"There is so much here, and so much to understand!" Ke'eli cried with excitement.

"We have been a force behind the scenes, trying to aid the human world for thousands of years. Thankfully, we have kept most of our secrets." Mason smiled as he ushered the family under the rail.

Brett stopped short as he saw the train. His heart began racing as he panicked and grabbed Ke'eli close to his side.

"I don't know about this." He said, his voice shaking.

"I assure you, Brett, this is the safest device in the entire country. If you are worried that there are no wires or supports of any kind, don't be. This runs on gravity technology, pulling it from one tower to another. The force to break that connection would have to be monumental. Let me tell you, there are entire cities that float off the Earth, supported only with gravitonic technology."

"Aye, been that way for thousands of years!" Pwyll interjected.

Pulling Ke'eli to the side, away from the group, Brett went on with his fears.

"Something about this thing. It's like a bad dream. I see us dangling from it like a bunch of leeches, and you're dangling way back, getting tossed around like a rag doll."

"What? Honey, we're going inside it." Ke'eli laughed as she stroked her husband's face.

Brett looked up at the train. She was right. Things were different. For some reason, Brett had the memory that he had to covertly ride this thing. From *underneath*.

"Okay, let's go. Sorry guys, was a little freaked out."

Brett looked around at what appeared to be the steel girders of the platform that supported the enormous rail above them. He did not see a way to get to the top, but saw a large square hole in the middle of the platform above them.

"So, how do we get up there?"

Mason smiled as he pulled everyone close to the middle of the ground beneath the platform, standing on a 10-foot-wide metal plate.

"Up please!" Mason said, as if he were talking to someone they could not see.

Suddenly, the entire group lifted off the ground into the air, hurtling upwards towards the platform.

The four family members grabbed each other closely, letting out screams as their feet left the ground.

Brett reached out to grab Mason.

"What the Hell?! A warning would have been nice!"

But Mason was laughing all the while.

"Watch your head!" he said, as they passed through the opening at the top.

The scene that appeared before them seemed all too unreal. Though the platform looked large from below, standing on it gave the impression that you were in a miniature city all together.

Stores were all along the middle of the platform, stacked on top of each other like shelves. Each was about a 15 x 15-foot square with a half-desk at the storefront's face, a greeter sitting and smiling behind it.

And, of course, there were no stairs.

Brett, Ke'eli and the children marveled at how 'customers' would stand on a metal plate and say a level, to levitate up to that level effortlessly. Once there, they could stand on a solid platform next to the store, or just float there.

"Holy guacamole. This is crazy!" Brett exclaimed.

Not only were there stores on the platform, but all kinds of buzzing activity. Trains were coming and going every couple of minutes. Many creatures were walking about, including half-animal types that the family had not yet seen.

"Is that a... werewolf?" Ke'eli asked, pushing her children behind her before realizing that anything went here in Atlantis.

"Ah, yes and no. Not in the lycanthropic sense that you might think, but yes, in the sense that he is half man, half wolf. At least, I don't think he's a lycanthrope. Those do exist and are a blight on the land. But, yes, I am sure he is not." Tumidus answered smugly.

A sodden smell hit their nostrils then, as the same were-wolf-man stopped to speak to a group of what could only be skeletons.

The family looked at each other, their eyes bigger and their jaws lower than they had been the entire time in Atlantis.

Drake broke the silence.

"Are those real skeletons?!"

Mason smiled at the boy, leaning down to whisper to him.

"They are the undead, yes. You have nothing to fear from them. You see how their eyes glow blue? That indicates intelligence. It is when their eyes glow red that you have cause to fear. And do not be mistaken my young friend, we do have many things to fear in Atlantis, which is why it is fortunate that we are so well protected. Now, shall we?"

Mason led the entourage to a rail that had just arrived.

A golem greeted them at the door.

"Destination?" it sighed, in what sounded like the most bored receptionist voice it could muster.

"All for Atlantis, Seeker credit please." Mason responded. At the same time, he removed his small white ulexite crystal from around his neck, which was scanned by some device the golem held.

A beep sounded from the golem.

"Do you currently possess the Seeked?"

Mason looked back at his entourage. He motioned for the golem to wait one moment as he asked Drake to step forward.

"As you can see here, this is the Seeked."

"Seeker credit is limited to 5 plus the Seeked."

Mason huffed as he turned back around.

"What's going on?" Brett asked Mason.

"I don't want to alert the golem that all *four* of you are the 'Seeked'. This crystal is a form of payment, much like your credit cards."

Mason straightened as Keb lumbered over to the golem, plunking down a shiny rock.

"This buy us train."

The golem looked down at the large ruby that he placed on its counter. For a robot, Brett could have sworn that its eye twinkled.

"Very well. Please be seated."

CHAPTER SIX

ATLANTIS RISES

**("The Drive to Paris" from The Bourne Identity
Soundtrack by John Powell)**

The hover train barreled across the countryside. Passing first over the grassy plains they had entered this world in, they transitioned to rocky hills.

"This is the land of our neighbors, the dwarves." Pwyll exclaimed.

The land was zipping by so fast it was hard to get one's bearing.

Ke'eli tried to get a good look at the ground beneath them but gave up after the first few minutes of crowding around other people.

She looked over at Keb, who strangely enough, sat by himself and to which no one else on the train would come near.

Finally, taking stock of the other members on-board, she noticed that there were two people with blue skin and fins on their arms, an assortment of gnomes and dwarves, and finally what looked like two human males, one wearing a golden breastplate and the other wearing dark blue robes. Ke'eli scrunched up her eyebrows as she noticed the male with the robes looking at her oddly.

Not thinking much of it, she moved to go sit next to Keb.

The man in the robes slid himself to stand between her and Keb, smiling as he did so.

"Why hello my fellow half-elf friend! So nice to see another of my kind traveling the great wide expanses of Atlantis!" he said, bowing ever so slightly.

"Um, hey fellow half-elf, nice to see you too!" Stumbling over the words, she made to move by him, but he moved again to intercept her.

"I say, what strange garb you wear! Are you of Titan blood? I am personally from Olympian stock, but I hold no qualm with my fellow half-bloods! And I see you carry no staff! Yet, I notice you imitate with magic to make your ears look longer."

Ke'eli was getting nervous. The last thing she wanted was for someone to recognize her as a human woman, since Tumidus and Mason had made such a stink of this so-called prophecy and whatnot.

Before she could respond, the man continued.

"Ah, I jest, my dear. I, too, use magic to hide my true nature. But that is what I do to belong in this wonderful place, no?"

Ke'eli had caught on to the sarcasm in his voice. She decided to probe him to understand why. Information from someone who might not tell you what you want to hear, like from the Seekers, could be helpful. With a little nudge from her mind, she probed his surface thoughts.

Ah... there it was.

"Yes, my friend. It is sad that we must hide who we are to belong." She continued for him.

Ke'eli had guessed right. His eyes lit up at the mention of having to 'hide'.

The half-elf frowned.

"Ah, to be accepted without question. To belong to the races that we call siblings, though be the bastard children of both. Is it too much to ask? Was it I who decided my father should seek love in the arms of an elf?"

Ke'eli could tell the half-elf was passionate about his heritage. Tears formed at the edges of his eyes.

"Oh, I am sorry, my lady! Look at me getting all worked up!" He wiped the moisture from his eyes before bowing low.

"I am called Sinat of the Copper Fields. I am originally from West Arcadia, but as I am sure you are aware, the village has still not regained its foundations. Where do you hail from?"

Ke'eli tried hard to think of something that sounded believable. The half-elf had mentioned that he was 'of the Copper Fields' and that he was originally from West Arcadia. Ke'eli also pieced together what little she knew of Greek mythology, linking the Olympian and Titan blood quip as a belief that they must have been two distinct groups that imitated the Olympian Gods of Greece, opposed to the Titans who fought against them.

Either way, she could not think of anything quick enough. Looking back to her husband, who watched her closely to make sure she was okay, she got a glimpse of all the thoughts going through his head.

He better not touch her.... Can't trust anyone here... Is he checking her out? ... She is the most beautiful thing in the world. Why wouldn't he?... Anniversary is coming up... Wonder if they have a summer solstice here... It is the month of...

"June... o. Juno. My name is Juno, I'm sorry, I was distracted. Juno of the Summer... Lands. Yes, that is my name. And yes, Titan-blooded."

The half-elf cocked his head at her confused admission.

Ke'eli looked into his eyes to see if there was any glimmer of recognition, but Sinat just smiled and bowed again.

"Well met, Lady Juno of the Summer Lands. I regret that I have not heard of your home before, but the Titan elves are so prone to seclusion and privacy. Happy am I that you have ventured out of your wooded sanctuary, but know that you have nothing to fear from the rest of your half-blood kin. I will not mock your smaller human-looking ears."

With a twist of his hand, he made his own ears appear longer as they stretched sideways out the side of his head.

Smiling now with six-inch ears, Sinat frowned as Tumidus stood up, approaching the pair. Sinat bowed towards Tumidus as he arrived, the smile gone but the politeness still present.

"Well met Elysian, I am Sinat of the..."

"I know who you are, half-blood. Leave my... apprentice alone." Tumidus glared at Sinat as he pulled Ke'eli away from him.

But Ke'eli's arm became uncomfortably stiff in Tumidus' grip and her body did not move. Ke'eli looked up at Tumidus with a firm look of conviction, letting the elf know she could handle herself.

Whispering in her ear, Tumidus growled, "He is an illusionist and can probably see through the image I made of your elven ears. It is not safe."

"I can take care of myself, *Master*." mocking him for calling her his apprentice. "Besides, I'm interested in why you hate his kind so much."

Ke'eli's reply had Tumidus' eyes wide.

"Oh yeah, I don't need to be psychic to hear the condescension in your voice. You might want to take your hand off me before I crush it."

Ke'eli began to press her bicep and tricep against her ribcage where Tumidus' fingers rested. Ke'eli knew from watching him that the sorcerer's somatic spell-casting ability relied on being able to use his skinny little fingers.

She smiled as he yanked his hand back quickly, shaking his wrist. Backpedaling, he glared at her as he made his way back to his seat.

Brett, meanwhile, stared and smiled.

Turning around to resume the conversation, she frowned at the fact that Sinat had returned to where he was standing before, avoiding her eye contact.

Walking up to him, she smiled again.

"I apologize for my... *Master's* intrusion. He thinks his pureblood position holds sway over me somehow."

But Sinat was hearing none of it.

"I understand Juno. Please, take no offence. I did not know you were apprenticed to be a... *Seeker.* It is a highly respected position and one I do not wish to hinder."

Sinat put such a strange emphasis on the Seeker title that Ke'eli could not help but want to press the issue, but she could also tell pushing that issue might cause Sinat to become more curious. So instead, she nodded and turned to continue towards Keb.

"I wish you well in your travels, Juno." Sinat said to her back, as he forced a smile.

Ke'eli forced the smile back as she sat down next to Keb.

Patting him on the back, he returned a genuine smile at her as she joined him. There was even more now to talk to the orc about.

"What is the deal with the half-blood thing, Keb? There are mixed races here, and what, the 'pure-bloods' don't like them?"

Ke'eli looked around at the other mix of races in the train car. The aquarians seemed so strange and foreign, but no one hesitated to get around them. Sure, the half-elves were close enough to the other groups to not be noticeably different, and Keb the orc was totally by himself. Ke'eli could not figure it out.

"Keb different. Keb orc, but Keb also special. Like little people fighting in halfling field, they special too. But evil special. Keb earth special. Good special."

Ke'eli nodded, knowing what he was talking about. The Plane-touched were Atlanteans who had ventured too close to an anomaly in Atlantis, their bodies absorbing some of that extra planar power and changing them.

Since broaching the subject, Ke'eli had discovered there were quite a few of these spatial rifts in reality scattered all about Atlantis. She knew that the shield that protected the continent also *forced* these rifts here, instead of out into the greater world.

Elemental tears were the most common, but there were apparently rifts to the Negative and Positive Energy planes, the Astral Plane, the Ethereal Plane, and many others. Her family and the Seeker group were told that they had arrived only a few hundred miles south from the rift to the Celestial Plane called Archon Hollow, which mirrored the fiendish rift a thousand miles distant near the city of Alaka, called the Devil's Claw.

"Always opposite sides of the continent," Mason had said, "and always spitting out nasties for us to handle."

So, Ke'eli was not as inclined to see one of these "celestials" that came from Archon Hollow as she thought. There would be time for that later, she was sure.

"Why don't people like you, Keb? Aren't you like a local hero?"

Ke'eli nudged the orc in the ribs to get him to open up, hoping the accolades would break the ice.

But Keb just shrugged.

"See half-elf with shiny armor?" he asked Ke'eli as she nodded.

"Atlantean Guard recruit. Very special. Keb just, special."

"So, you wanted to be in the Atlantean Guard, and they wouldn't let you join because you are plane-touched?"

"That too. Keb, orc. Even if just normal orc, Keb not clean enough. Even if Keb strong, not strong enough. Even if Keb talked good, Keb not talk good enough. Keb tried. Keb not allowed in. Orc skin light brown. Keb skin dark brown like dirt, but not matter. Keb orc."

So, there was a good amount of segregation here, even past the color of one's skin.

Ke'eli ground her jaw at the thought of it.

Apparently, there was nowhere for anyone to live a normal, peaceful life away from racism, segregation, jealousy, and hate. And here in Atlantis, not only was there an actual separation in species, but there was also still bigotry against the color of someone's skin.

The nerve.

Ke'eli had had her fair share of racism herself. Even her own family had ostracized her for trying to be a successful woman.

Ke'eli sighed to herself.

"If only there were a way to bring peace to the entire world." She muttered to Keb's shoulder.

A thousand miles away outside the protective Atlantean ice shield, frigid wind whipped about, freezing the air almost solid at the Casey Station, Antarctica. An over-snow bus pulled in, disembarking some much-needed supplies for the Australian scientists stationed there.

The warmer air inside the bus gushed out as the doors opened. Braving the cold to get to the supplies, several people rushed to get the boxes and containers on to sleds.

Six people exited the bus as well, bundled up in several layers of clothing to ward off the cold. Even under The Christmas Story-level amount of protective gear, several of the six still shivered, grumbling under their frozen breath.

("Antarctica" from the Aliens vs Predator soundtrack by Harald Kloser)

"This was not what I expected when I left the warmth of Hell, Shadowson."

The muttering came from one of the taller bundles of furs, his hands rubbing the outside of his arms in an attempt to add warmth. The pointed tip of a sword handle poked out from a bundle he hugged close under his armpits.

Two of the smaller bundles of clothing went quickly forward, grabbing up handfuls of snow to build into snowballs. Immediately, like children, they pelted each other.

"This is so much fun!" the female mumbled through her scarf.

"Won't be with no sun!" the male responded, getting hit in the face by snow.

"Enough!"

The tallest male exited the bus, barely wearing much more than a single layer of warm clothing. Despite his minimal clothing, he didn't appear to be cold. He looked down at the pair, scolding them.

Behind him, an equally tall woman came off the bus as well. Seeming much thicker in the midsection, she waddled through the snow, glaring back at the taller male.

"I agree Sigurd. Poland was one thing. This... this is something entirely different."

Andrew turned back to look at the female. He knew he needed her help the most for the upcoming challenge they would face.

"I know what I am doing, Brigid. Let me work so that we can finally rid ourselves of the frost."

The sixth member, the same size as the other two smaller ones, tiptoed out into the ice and at once began to convulse.

All around him watched in abject fascination.

They knew what was happening to him underneath the clothing, and they envied him for it.

As they watched, the jacket the thing was wearing expanded. A thick tuft of fur erupted from Pelles' wrist between the edge of his jacket and his glove, while the other clawed hand was out of sight.

It looked painful, but they knew that one of the special abilities Pelles had allowed him to acclimate to almost any environment. His grotesque features attested to the experimentation he went through to gain those abilities, and some were not sure the benefit was worth the cost.

Still, they were jealous now.

Standing up straight again, Pelles shook his head side to side to get his bearing.

"I apologize Master, I am ready now," he said, looking up at Andrew.

Nodding, Andrew waved Pelles over to him. Taking off a backpack, Pelles produced a large tome from its insides, one whose pages whipped in the winds as Andrew opened it.

Brigid looked about her surroundings, taking in the humans still unloading supplies.

How simple, she thought. Here were six strangers standing in the snow, doing Gods-knew what, and none of the other humanoids even paid them any mind.

Blind sheep, she continued. She knew what Andrew wanted her to do.

They had spoken at length after the failed incursion at the very home of Brett Dourdon, Brigid, almost leaving the Ring in futility.

She had been on the surface here, aiding the one she knew as Sigurd Shadowson for many years now, and each escapade the group had gone on had ended in utter failure. She knew his true name to be Andrew, but she also knew that the less who knew that, the better.

So, she stayed true to the course of her Ring-brother, but these excursions were getting old.

Of all the Soulless, she was the rarest. While Andrew had absorbed the essence of the more populous fiends in their home, she had gotten the luxury to go up against a celestial. And while Andrew could 'feed' regularly enough here in the Upperworld to keep his power, she could not. There were not as many creatures of celestial origin here as there might be in the place she had formerly called home. It had been... *difficult*... supporting her energy here.

She could feel her power decreasing.

So, it was only through this latest and last gambit she told Andrew... *Sigurd*... that she would remain.

He had gleaned information from Brett on the plane over the Devil's Triangle. Information that included the location of a very secret place. A place that had celestials.

Brigid looked back down at Andrew while he worked.

Reading an ancient script in his tome, he completed a ritual that would allow him to detect magic wherever he looked.

He stood up from the book as Pelles placed it back in the pack.

Brigid watched him closely.

No more tricks. No more games. I care for my Ringmates, but I cannot survive in this Upperworld for much longer.

She waited to see what Andrew would do.

One month, she told him. One month to complete this ordeal. She believed he had been truly destined for great-ness, but there was only so much she could do.

She would return to Tartarus and face the consequences if she had to. It was that or dwindle away to nothing. Thankfully, they had left the place most recently as its heroes, and not the Outlaws they had been years prior.

Andrew opened his eyes, taking off his protective gog-gles.

Brigid could see that his eyes now had a pearlescent glow to them, but nothing anyone not trained in the art of magick could understand.

Scanning the buildings and the people, Andrew walked towards the large construct they had learned was the "Red Shed".

Brigid and the rest of the Ring were on their guard. Andrew suspected their enemies were here and about, and Andrew would find them easily now.

Andrew looked at each human as they pulled the sled full of supplies towards another building called the Green Shed. Looking over at Brigid, he shook his head no; these were regular humans.

On they moved toward the primary structure.

Brigid reached back into the large bag she had on her back, feeling the familiar grip of her hammer there. It had been a gift from a celestial they did not have to kill, and she cherished it more than anything. She could will the thing to flare to life with a bright fire, and she longed to activate it now, if only to shed these cumbersome clothes and stretch her wings.

She knew to do that now would probably kill her, as the wind would shred her feathery limbs to pieces.

Still, it would be some warmth.

She approached the main door to the Red Shed; it covered entirely in ice. Looking back at Andrew for permission, he nodded, showing she could open the door.

Always prepared for battle, she brought the bag from her back to her left forearm, just in case. Gripping the door handle in her right hand, she twisted and yanked, sending flakes of ice and snow flying.

Inside was a staging area for gear, but no humans.

The six stalked in, unaware of what threat they could face and going only on the impulse of their leader, Andrew.

In the semi-warmer zone of the Red Shed, the group removed their more cumbersome clothing. They knew they would join in some sort of battle here; they went nowhere without killing someone or something.

Brigid unfurled her feathery wings, feeling good to finally extricate them from around her waist. Her hammer in hand, she willed the head of it to flame, just to supply a small measure of warmth.

"We must move. I can only see in this magical sense for a few more minutes," Andrew said, rushing his comrades.

Brigid nodded. Now that she could move more smoothly, she pushed on ahead more quickly.

The building had a basic layout. Long and rectangular, much of the work done near the center.

Making a beeline for the next area, Brigid halted the rest of the group with an upraised hand.

Andrew crept up beside her to look around the plastic sheathing into the room where the humans spoke. At least, they *appeared* to be human.

"Light Elves," Andrew whispered into Brigid's ear.

Her eyes raised at the proclamation. The group of scientists were human, but she knew that with the magic eyesight Andrew now had, he could detect magic on their bodies, which included magic intended to deceive by illusion. She had no reason to doubt Andrew's belief that the station was a front for an advanced civilization that hid under the ice here in Antarctica. But to be so blatant as to impersonate humans as well?

Andrew had reassured her it was because they wanted to make sure humankind would not discover their secret world, so they fabricated ice cores and evidence that the continent was one massive slab of frozen water.

The truth was, near to where they were standing was one of the main entries and exit ways to a world shrouded in secrecy. A world that Andrew was positive Brett had traveled to, his entire family in tow. A world he had seen in the memories of Brett when they had connected. A world Andrew would find and one where he would have his last words with Brett.

Brigid nodded back to the rest of the group.

They only needed one impersonator to interrogate.

With brutal efficiency, the Ring snuck into action. Taking the 'elven' human scientists by surprise, there was no hope of survival.

Conall and Pelles slipped in, keeping to the shadows and the larger bulk machines to slice and stab away at several of the elves in quick succession.

Frey fired off a series of arrows too quickly to prepare for, taking out another two.

Freyja assumed the form of a small rodent, infiltrating closest to the main console where two more elves sat, in case there were some forms of magic alarm they could sound and that she could avoid them activating.

Brigid stormed in her form and feathery wings, a confusing sight to a group of creatures who might have been accustomed to such a sight in their home. As expected, two of the elves stood, looking at each other, but neither taking any action. One even smiled.

Brigid did not endorse violent action for the sake of violence, but Andrew had assured her any survivors here would warn the land beneath their feet of their pending arrival, and that it would make things... *complicated.*

So Brigid only slightly grimaced as her hammer struck sideways, one elf's head crunching from the blow.

The other, whose eyes and face were full of smile, still stood there smiling, his body stiff, tears running down the side of his face. All the other elves save this one were dead.

"Only one," she reiterated to herself as she moved to the side.

Andrew crept up behind Brigid, his hand extended towards the lone surviving elf. As she moved aside, the elf caught sight of the fiendish man. The black chains slowly tightening around the elf, completely immobilized him, rendering even his facial expressions frozen.

Brigid stood resolute to the side as Andrew approached, he whispering into the elf's ear.

"You will tell me what I want to know, or you will die a slow and *very* painful death."

The hover train hummed to a slow stop, lights illuminating information on a screen and a light 'beep' waking any travelers who might have dozed off.

It was still only the first stop of two for the family and the Seekers, so they stood briefly to stretch their legs and look out over the amazing city.

"Ah, well then. This be Nidavellir." Pwyll waved everyone to one side of the train.

From out the window, they could see a vast city, all worked in magnificent stone. The group couldn't determine if the buildings were carved into the rock, or if they were just so well constructed that they appeared to be.

Parts of the city appeared to be carved into the very side of the earth, not much different from the city of Petra in Jordan. Where the columns rose to support the roofs of the voluminous city, they were instead carved to resemble giant-sized dwarves. Mimicking the great founders of old, the statues appeared very Viking-like, bearded figures full of strength. It appeared comical to the family, a giant city full of gigantic structures for such a diminutive race.

Further north in the distance lay the city proper, the hover-train platform being far enough away to require visitors to go through various checkpoints. The family could just make out the glittering of various gemstones and crystals embedded in parts of the chief city, the reflection from the artificial sun making them twinkle like stars.

Where the city ended further to the north, the plains leading up to the Godheim Mountains began. Even from here, they could see the immense mountain range, a slight green glow pulsing up into the sky from the pyramid placed there in Asgard, the dwarven capital.

A massive train attached to the ground lay waiting near the north end of the city, its cargo that of large rocks. The train itself looked more like a cargo ship than a locomotive, as dwarves ambled all along its side. The dwarves' major export was stone and gems, and the train appeared to be laden with both. Tracks continued as far as the eye could see into the plains.

Steam-operated vehicles traveled the length of the city, while some gravitonic cars hovered here and there.

"Why steam?" Drake asked. "I thought you guys were advanced?"

"Ah, well then ye wee smart one, the power o' the pyramids be fuel for some o' the vehicles. The energy that the pyramids put out is mighty large, but it be limited to just a short ways away from the pyramid itself. Think on yer' WiFi signal in yer home. It gets weaker the further ye get from yer modem, aye? Same here. We got ways o' harvesting some o' the energy, but the batteries need special metal or gems ta power, and they ain't as easy to get as they useta be back in my pa's, pa's day. So, the outlyin' cities use more traditional forms o' clean energy, like steam, hydropower, geothermal power and solar. No use dirtying up the place when we're trapped under the dome!"

Either way, everyone could tell that Pwyll was connected to this city and its inhabitants.

"He was born there, Pwyll was. His family all live there as engineers and artificers. They are immensely proud of him." Mason explained.

"So, some of the other races live outside their homes, like what, in Embassies?" Brett asked. He had some experience with Embassies, almost having to go to one as a Marine.

The memory of his life as a US Marine came floating back to the forefront of his mind then. He had just left all that behind, suddenly and dangerously. If the police had arrived after the little skirmish they had in his living room, they probably would have found Keb's blood and a lot of destruction.

Though he knew that life as a Marine was probably dead and gone now that he was here, the idea of his reputation still lingered. He had just gotten back from a "very traumatic event" when his plane crashed in the ocean outside Japan. Only one day back and the whole family mysteriously disappears? Questions would be asked, and he was sure he would be at the forefront of that suspicious line of queries.

A look over at Ke'eli reassured him as the thoughts took on a darker tone. Everyone they knew back in California, Brett's adopted family in Florida, Ke'eli's family in the Pacific; everyone would think that he did something evil to his family. Ke'eli's smile wore all that worry away. They would find a way to communicate with the family back home, if only to reassure them they were all okay.

"To answer your question, Brett," Mason began, interrupting Brett's troubled images, "yes, there are Embassies in each Trade Capital city for each other faction of Atlanteans. There are also headquarter buildings for each type of Guild and organization."

"What's a 'Guild'?" Drake asked. "I mean, I know about Guilds in video games and stuff, but it sounds serious here."

Mason smiled. Of the entire Seeker group, he was most familiar with video games. Being a human taken from the Olde World, he was always the most curious to experience the things he had considered lost whenever he left Atlantis.

"Oh, you mean like the game World of WarCraft?" Mason smiled as he asked Drake.

The responding grin and eye raise hit the mark Mason was aiming for.

"Waitaminute, are you reading my mind, Mason?! I thought you wouldn't do that!" Drake scowled as he considered the intrusion.

Laughing, Mason patted Drake down with his hands.

"No, my boy, I know all about video games. Though we don't have the wide range of delectable games as you do, I am still very aware of them. World of WarCraft looked very interesting to me, and I would have liked to have played if I had more time in the Olde World! I am very aware of the mechanics of the game. We have something very similar to it here in Atlantis, though all our games are held in a virtual world and do not require keyboards or other peripherals."

Drake was listening, open-mouthed and eyes wide. Even Kelly came over to listen, both children being very technology-invested.

"Our games are more of the intellectual type, and more often than not induce a lesson of learning as they are played. Pwyll could tell you more than I, as it is the gnomes who lead the charge in constructing and play testing! I just enjoy them because it reminds me of the humanity I came from."

Mason took on a more wistful look as he considered the statement. Did he really need to be reminded of the place from which he was taken? Where did *that* thought come from?

Without being able to consider it even more, Pwyll continued for him.

"Aye laddie, me n' my own make all kinds of games for Atlantean pleasure! I am no good at it as me kin, but aye, I been known to put on a headset before!"

"A headset?" Kelly asked, balking. She had held an aversion to putting things on her head for the longest time, an effect from the form of Autism she had. Very sensitive to certain tastes and textures, she avoided putting things on or near her ears and head, as she felt the pressure on her head to be too stressful. She had learned in time to push through it, but it was something she still did not enjoy.

Pwyll caught on to the trepidation.

"Aye lass, it be a headset you put on that covers your eyes and ears. Ye then log on to a virtual world, using your mind. It was a cooperative effort between Mason's types and me own. Most popular game ever! Had people flocking to the pyramids to play!"

"The game is a form of technology that harnesses the power of the pyramids in order to operate, so it doesn't work except near one of the structures, or in the capital." Mason continued. "It has had to be regulated as of late, for fear that too many Atlanteans have escaped reality and forego their normal duties! I believe your draconic friend has even found time to play, Drake!"

Drake smiled up at Xinzang as Mason called her out.

"Something else we have in common! I love playing video games!" Drake hopped in his seat at the excitement and hope that he would have time to play this strange new game.

"Yes hatchling," Xinzang said wistfully, "it is an amazing way to torture the masses with thoughts of freedom outside this dome, living a life under the true sun."

The blunt statement quelled the excitement of the children and had Mason frowning.

Seeing she had just squashed the hopes and dreams of the group, Xinzang attempted to relight the fervor.

"Guilds in the game, which is called Rise of the Atlanteans, by the way, are ordered together by familiarity, much as they are in reality. A Guild is a group of like-minded Atlanteans who, regardless of race or Tribe, endeavor to work together to create or provide a specific product or service."

"The Guilds in Rise are easier to be in because your race is changeable in the game, so you can be whomever you like. It was actually the game that spurred the real Guilds to open their doors to other Tribes. Some Guilds have always been open-armed, like the Thieves Guilds and Merchant Guilds, but some had very specific requirements."

"Aye, the developers usta have a lot more emphasis on the Guilds back in the day, but for some reason, they toned them down lately. Not sure why, but I dinna play the game, so I no really care, right-o?" Pwyll shrugged his shoulders at the thought.

"Personally, ye all look like damn zombies wearing that headset o' yours! And that's no insult to real zombies! I never no could tell what ye all liked so durned much about it. Ye live in Atlantis for the God's sakes! Get out and see the country for the love o' Pete!"

Pwyll laughed as he tried to make light of the mood as well, but he could tell the children were intrigued. Even Brett and Ke'eli, avid gamers themselves, looked wonderingly as they considered the options.

Mason wrapped up the conversation as more people boarded the hover train, it preparing to continue south to the Capital.

"To answer your first question, yes, there are major headquarters in many of all the cities that harbor the Guilds. Guilds can include everything from the very secretive types like the Depredators, who are tasked with returning to the Olde World to recover Atlantean artifacts, to the openly established Lamps, who are politician-types that aspire to be Tribal Elders one day and who work with the current Elders in their dealings. Most Embassies have a listing of what Guilds are present in each city and how that Tribe represents them."

A loud train horn interrupted any further conversation as the train doors closed and the vehicle slowly revved up. An entirely new group of people had boarded and sat much in the same way the first had; they to themselves, with only a few intermingling. The train was much more condensed this second time, as this one was heading to the Capital of the Country.

("Slaves to Rome" from the Gladiator Soundtrack by Hans Zimmer)

The train barreled forth again, speeding south through the countryside. This time, they passed over what looked like another city in the middle of a large forest.

"Midgard." Tumidus informed the family. Ashamed of his prior bout of superiority towards Ke'eli, he felt it his duty to explain why the half-elves were on the train previously, and why they debarked in Nidavellir.

"It is the city between the human home of Shambhala and the elven home of Aelfsium. When humans found love in the arms of the most beautiful of elves, the children they sired felt at odds in either of the cities. In time, the half-bl..." Tumidus stopped mid-sentence from the glare Ke'eli gave him, "I'm sorry, the *chimera*, as they prefer to be called, built their own city between the two along the ley line they share. Because it is in the dwarven territory, the bearded ones named it Midgard, in recognition of the midway point between the two cities. Just as many humans visit the city as there are half-elves, hoping to further find an acquaintance with the half-elven women who have grown to maturity there. The illusionist friend you made was probably heading there, as it was his home."

Ke'eli bowed her head to Tumidus, to show that she respected the attempt at an apology to her and his treatment to the half-elf. Smiling and bowing in return, Tumidus returned to his seat.

The woods below them stretched for miles in every direction. It was Kelly who first caught sight of the Stone Trees.

"What... are those?"

Tumidus turned in his seat to see her excitement and smiled as he realized his error in assuming the humans knew anything about Atlantis.

"Well, my lady, those are the Stone Trees. Do they not seem familiar to you?"

Massive mountain-like trees, the structures resembled that of stone mesas. Each of the three that Kelly could currently see stretched on for miles, one shorter than the other two, who looked to be as high as the height of their train.

The trees that surrounded them on all sides pointed to why they were not stone. Bark on the sides of the massive mesa-like tree was still brown and they could see other smaller trees sprouting from its top. The spirals on the inside of the top went on in a dizzying circle, ring after ring showing the extreme age of the severed tree.

"A most unfortunate circumstance. The trees had to be severed before Atlantis could move south out of the Atlantic Ocean. The shield that protects our home can only go two miles up, and these trees broached the top of that easily. Only one object..."

Tumidus stopped suddenly, a stern look and a cough from Mason telling him to stop talking.

Tumidus fumbled with his words, smiling through his slip-up.

But Ke'eli could see what Tumidus wanted to say in his mind.

Being around so many people and being able to really exploit their abilities had Ke'eli's power growing by the day. She tried to be like Mason and avoid actively looking into people's thoughts, but she found it was hard to. She didn't want to allow any secrets to pass between the group members until they were firmly established in this new place. They didn't trust their new allies, and here was a reason to question it.

A giant mountain came to the forefront of her thoughts. Not only a mountain, but one that capped the top of the shield and held some long-storied secret that only the most important people knew about. An escape.

Tumidus continued as best he could from the interruption.

"Yes, ahem, as I was saying, only one object was not leveled before the shield went up, and unfortunately, that object was severed by the shield, so we took all appropriate measures to ensure it did not happen again."

Tumidus tried to press the lie, and everyone bought into it except Brett and Ke'eli. Nodding in feigned understanding, Tumidus continued.

"We saved the massive seeds of those trees, and hope to one day bring them back to light outside the shield. Some of the smaller trees, like Yggdrasil, still survive to this day, though they number so few. Still, their majesty in form is one to behold and pay homage to."

"So, you're saying Yggdrasil, the 'World Tree', is real?" Brett cocked his head and rubbed his chin as he pondered the probable size of this tree.

"Oh yes sir, every Tribe has at least one World Tree in their territory, while some have more. The trees require an immense amount of nourishment, but the return investment is very much worth it." Tumidus smiled as finished.

Just as he was about to go on about the 'fruit' of each tree, Drake inhaled sharply as he looked out the front of the train.

He was the first to see their final destination.

Passing between a series of low mountains and one last Stone Tree, the grandeur of the capital city shone like a lighthouse in the depths of the dark sea. Their elevation and stopping point outside the north side of the city allowed a grand view of the entire Capital.

Like the descriptions of Plato thousands of years prior, the city layout was that of a massive circle separated into three rings. As one moved closer to the inner ring, it became more populated.

Skyscrapers to rival those of the tallest and grandest in Dubai lay scattered closer to the center, making it look like a condensed version of New York City, but with materials none of the family had ever seen.

One building looked like it was made from pure glass with no beams or supports. Another was stone, like a castle tower. Still, a third appeared to be made of clouds.

Technological marvels were everywhere. Flying cars, both made of metal and stone, zipped by the rail as the occupants waved at the passengers. Flying creatures from legend also were active, their wings flapping hard against the noonday sun, their passengers holding tight to the reins. Everything from the griffins the family met earlier, to half-bird, half-horse creatures, even to something that resembled a dragon with only two legs flapped about.

Looking up higher, the group could see giant balloons that seemed to rest near the top of the dome that protected the continent nearly two miles up.

The family could now also see a blue-tinted line that was at the top of the dome above them, stretching from east to west all the way to the horizons. More importantly, it appeared to have what looked like the sun beneath it. Since it was noon when they arrived, this sun lay directly above the city.

"Ah, perfect timing to see more clearly see Ra, our artificial sun." Mason began.

"Before we had to limit our technology, we used it to create nuclear fusion. Much of what you see outside the capital is solar powered by this device. We could only create one because of the immense amount of material needed to contain it. The orichalcum we told you about earlier is very rare, and Ra needed a large amount of it."

"Ah yes, orichalcum," Tumidus smiled. "The 'magic metal'. Not found anywhere else in the world. The Soulstone Pyramid at the center of our home randomly converts standard metals throughout the continent into a special golden-red material. This metal can hold a magical charge and is what a lot of our larger technological devices are composed of, at least to some degree. Exactly like the rubethyst and deepstone I mentioned."

From near the balloons, what looked like rain poured out over the city and surrounding area.

"Are they peeing up there?!" Drake exclaimed a little too loudly, laughing all the while.

The group looked around at the several other people who were present on the rail, worried that someone might take offense. Thankfully, everyone else was too focused on something else to mind.

"No, my young boy." Mason interjected before Tumidus could scold him. "There is a massive shield two miles up that protects the entire country from the millions of pounds of ice above our heads. If that shield were not there, we would all be crushed to nothing by the weight of it. But we also need water, air, and rain for our crops as well. There is one way to create a hole in the shield that allows some elements through."

"They are up there, using this method, to allow the sun to warm parts of the ice, which then falls to the ground as rain. This is also why the equatorial region of the continent is so much more populated with greenery and plant life than other parts. You shall learn more in time, my friend."

Though there were plenty of flying vehicles present, the city did not just seem to have technology bursting at the seams. Nature reserves of every kind were at regular intervals, besides what looked to be a theme park. Rides and other festivities at this theme park made Disney Land look like a series of electronic penny horse rides from the grocery store.

And between them, barely perceptible between the towering buildings, lay the Violet Pyramid; what Mason and Tumidus had otherwise referred to as the Soulstone. From its top center, which is what the group could barely make out, shot a purplish beam into the air, striking the shield two miles above to cascade down across the continent. Just the top of the pyramid itself was a beauty to behold. It glistened in the daylight like a giant prism, each side facing a cardinal direction. Everyone on board leaned against one side of the train, itching to see more.

Just looking at the thing instilled a sense of peace and happiness in all the occupants of the rail. Everyone smiled, shaking hands, and hugging as if they had gotten done with a church sermon and it was time to go.

The four family members had smiles that made Mason's all the bigger.

"Welcome to New Atlantis." he said proudly.

CHAPTER SEVEN

NEW ATLANTIS

("Arrival at Aslan's How" from The Chronicles of Narnia: Prince Caspian Soundtrack by Harry Gregson-Williams)

The rail slowed to a stop as it entered the station north of the city. From their vantage point, the group could not see the other railways, but were assured there were ones placed in the east, west and south that took travelers to some of the other major trade capitals.

The size of the city was massive. The only sincere appreciation they had of its grandeur was from above, on top of the railway system. As they levitated down to the bottom, they realized they were in the third circle of the massive city. They would have to make the rest of their way in either on foot, or by one of the other public transit systems the city had.

The family of four were still awestruck. Even at ground level, the design of the buildings and the sights they saw blew away any they had ever seen before. Because they were in the north section of the city, more of the architectural designs were dwarf-based. Many of the buildings were stone, with beautiful carvings all over.

Though there was a definite gothic feeling about the place, the strength and sheer weight of the area impressed everyone. Dwarves, halflings, and gnomes casually walked around the northernmost part of the city, talking, trading, and laughing.

Tumidus pulled everyone to the side again to renew his spell of disguise.

"Look, but do not touch. For if someone touches you, they will realize that it is a disguise and become suspicious, like your half-elf friend." Tumidus told Ke'eli as they continued.

"Why would anyone be suspicious? Isn't magic a common thing around here?" Drake asked, his curiosity in the arcane never wavering.

"We have our own enemies on this great continent. Shapeshifters, who can take on the appearance of anyone they like. Do you see those large bells?" Tumidus pointed out what looked to be an enormous dome topping a metallic pole.

Everyone nodded. He led the group to the pole, showing that they should reach out and touch it.

To their surprise, the pole vibrated under their fingers. The engravings on the sides of it shook in their hands, and they could all feel a low hum coming from the thing.

"There is no dongle in the bell. It is a sign that this is a Glamour Pole, created to ward away mimics. Strike it if you care."

And Drake, without hesitation, did just that.

A low *thum* went out from the pole then that to Drake's surprise, seemed to be hollow.

"What does it do? What's a mimic?" Drake asked, excitement barely held.

"Mimics are the Old Poseideans who live underground. When Atlantis made its way south, there was another country along the peninsula to the west, where a group of people lived in a country called Poseidia. When the shield came down to protect us, it did not include Poseidia, so it was assumed that they were lost to the sea. But they were resourceful. They were the ones who had dug the tunnels out for Atlantis that led all the way to the other side of the world, where the Muians and Lemurians lived. Many of their people lived underground, more comfortable there than in the sun's light."

Brett had to interrupt.

"Wait, did you say Muian and Lemurian? As in Mu and Lemuria? Those places are real too?"

Brett's children first looked at him with confusion, then back to Tumidus and Mason. Ke'eli, on the other hand, was remarkably familiar with the two mythological countries.

Mason continued the tale.

"Yes, Mu and Lemuria exist. They are older civilizations than Atlantis, and Atlantis has been around for 42,000 years! We used to trade with them via massively long tunnels, bored into the planet's crust above the Inner Ocean. They are also a civilization that survived by taking to the bowels of the Earth. A colony of them existed here when the Soulstone changed us, turning them into those who we now know as the Aquarians. The Aquarians became a cousin-race to the Muians and Lemurians, and communication continued at a snail's pace. That was until we created the Far-gate. It links our realm with theirs. It is one of the few places in the world where you can still get Deepstone, which is what we use to create magical things made of stone that last indefinitely."

Tumidus continued, "The Glamour Poles constantly vibrate at a frequency that Poseideans dislike, and which does not allow them to keep their shape shifted form. You see, Poseidia blames us for their country's destruction, even though many of them were spared not only by our warnings, late as they might have been, but also because they lived underground and avoided the initial tidal onslaught. Their underground domain included parts of Atlantis that were under the shield."

"It is a grudge that they have held on to for 12,000 years. And they strike back at us by constantly attacking us unprovoked and attempting to infiltrate the city to get at the Violet Pyramid, which is what they consider to be the prime offender. So, we have erected these poles, which do not allow them to get in past the city without someone knowing. Their true form is... recognizable."

"Well hell, I'd be pissed too if I were them! Guess you can't blame them though, huh? Has anyone tried reconciling with them?" Brett asked.

"There is only one person they would even bother to listen to, and he has not been seen in this country for some time. No, the Poseideans do not seem to want to negotiate. They continue to fight, hoping they will win." Mason sighed at the realization that there always was conflict and strife, no matter where one went. Despite their proximity to the Violet Pyramid, which seemed to inspire happiness in a mystical way, there were still bound to be downers.

"But I digress," Mason continued "we have a city to show off to you! If my comrades do not mind, I think it would be okay to take the long route. We are just in time for the daily Tai ji quan break, so I couldn't think of a better time to show off the many varied and amazing people of the city than now."

And with that, Mason moved over to a large vehicle that sat parked along the curb.

Drake had been eyeing it warily as the group had spoken, noticing that the thing had no wheels, yet looked like a large SUV. The outside was metallic and much more aerodynamic, like a plane hybrid. As Mason opened the door to it, Drake noticed the inside was exceptionally large and comfortable looking.

Drake, who had spent the last many days out on the road, desired nothing more than to finally sit on some soft chairs.

"Please, my friends, pile on in! You will find that there should be ample room for all nine of us!" Mason waved his comrades toward the vehicle.

One by one, each entered the contraption. With Xinzang though, she waved the invite away.

"I must see to my Elder, as I am sure most of you should as well." Flexing her wings, she looked back at the group.

Drake, who had taken a liking to the dragon-woman, frowned as she turned to leave. In their continued time together, Drake had learned more from Xinzang about how to control his fire and had learned more about actual dragons. The two had spent most of their time together experimenting with each other; she with her breath, and Drake with his fire-controlling abilities. The childish fear she was going to eat them all faded as quickly as the fear that had been in them at the first sight of her.

"Zang," Drake called her with her final permission, "please don't go. Aren't we going to swing by your place, anyway? How about we just go to the boss-man or woman or whatever, and then you all can go back to your homes? I like having you around. *All* of you."

Zang looked back at Drake sidelong, bowing her head. She also enjoyed her time with the young fire-starter and admitted to herself that she could protect the boy. Having a maternal instinct about her, she looked up to see Mason smiling at her. He shrugged his shoulders, knowing she was going to buckle.

"Very well, hatchling. Make room for a dragon!" she laughed as she leaped into the vehicle. As she did so, everyone else inside noticed that the inside of the seating area stretched just the slightest bit wider.

"Magic." Tumidus said, smiling. "For every person added to the inside, the room for others gets wider. This is a transport vehicle and is regularly available for others to… how would you say it, 'rent'?"

With that, Tumidus looked forward to Mason, saying that all were aboard and that he could continue with his tour.

Taking his crystal necklace off from around his neck, Mason placed the tip into a stone block near the front of the vehicle. It glowed purple for the slightest of seconds before everyone felt the vehicle rise into the air.

"Dad, we're flying!" Kelly said with excitement.

Brett looked outside the window with the slightest bit of apprehension. Ke'eli caught on to his look of concern.

"My love, you still worry about being in the air? Look, we rode the train with no problems, and we are now in the middle of the city. I am sure that this thing can't possibly go as fast as the train!"

Brett looked at his wife and tried to smile.

"I just... I don't know. I feel safer on the ground is all."

"Is everyone ready? Good." Mason turned his head back to his entourage as he put his hands on the rock next to his crystal.

Ke'eli grabbed Brett's hand and held it tight.

"Here we go!" Mason said as the vehicle lifted higher into the air. "Tumidus, if you would be so kind as to give the tour whilst I fly us?"

Tumidus, who was already sitting next to Mason, nodded his consent.

"My new friends, we entered the city from the north and are currently passing through the third circle. Here is where many of the people of Atlantis live. As you can see, there are parks, both natural and fabricated, to entertain the locals. The houses made to the specifications of the owner and built together with the community. Using a combination of magic and technology, we can create a fully furnished home in less than a few days and destroy it just as quickly.

"The third circle is protected and then bisected by the outer ring, which is a flowing canal that connects to the second circle."

As Tumidus spoke, the vehicle flew over a part of the wide canal that flowed south into the 'outer ring'. The body of water was massive and had boats of all kinds. Evenly spaced along the inside of the ring were piers that rivaled those of the largest docks Brett had ever seen. Ships that were just as large parked their hulls along the extensions, waiting for use.

Brett, analyzing the tactical capabilities of the place, saw naval vessels that not only floated in the water but also in the air. The fleet of battle-ready ships he saw was amazing. Some of the flying ships still used sails, while others had massive engines that caused giant propellers to spin. Even with his experience in the Marine Corps and being on ship as often as he was, Brett decided he did not prefer to go head-to-head in a naval battle with this country.

Continuing, bridges connected the third circle to the second, allowing both vehicular and foot traffic to cross, though most of everyone had a mechanical device or creature to ride upon. The bridges in this outermost ring were massive, wide enough for plenty of foot traffic to use, but high enough for the giant ships to get through.

The massive canal exited North from the city, where everyone was told it continued all the way to the dwarven Tribe in the Godheim Mountains.

Speeding over the outer ring, the vehicle began its voyage over the second land circle.

("Sacred Pool of Tears" from the Kung Fu Panda Soundtrack by Hans Zimmer and John Powell)

"The second circle is where the people of Atlantis work, train, and learn. It has the largest buildings in the world and covers all aspects, from military to philosophy to herbalism. Just like the spokes of a wheel and like the greater continent of Atlantis, each area specializes in a certain trade or form of education. The northern sections are relegated more for the educational aspects of our culture while the southern sections are more for trade and manufacturing."

The family could see a building that resembled the famous Chartres Cathedral in France, yet unfathomably larger. Pwyll smiled at the family's awe of the structure.

"Ah Blessed Be. That be the home of the Templars. Much like yer own Knights Templar from a time forgotten back in yer homeland! They be immensely proud dwarves and halflings mostly, specializing in the healing branch o' the Atlantean Guard. Ye'd be hard pressed to cross 'em in a fight though too!"

The family looked on, awe increasing as they went into the heart of Atlantis. Each individual area opened sights that seemed so out of place with each other, yet so seamless when looked at as a whole. The massive citadel-like church bordered another building that looked like a steampunk's fantasy come to life. A towering and thin building, resembling Big Ben with a massive clock at its center, it had other cylindrical objects floating around it, like an atom. Additionally, there appeared to be a red hand on the clock face, along with gears surrounding the outside of the main clock face with numbers on it.

Kelly was the first to recognize it for what it was.

"That's a clock, but it has displays for the day and the month too, doesn't it?"

Pwyll spoke up, pride in his voice at the astute young woman.

"Aye lass! Made by me own people! I dinnae know as much about it as me lad elf here, so I'll let him explain." He continued under his breath to Kelly, "I'm more of a toy-tinkerer than some clock-maker!" He finished with a wink and a nudge.

"Ah yes, Ms. Kelly, the center face tells the standard time in 12-hour increments. There is a third red hand there as well that tells what month number it is. The gears around the outside rotate around the clock face, indicating what day it is. Time works differently here than in the outside world, and we also measure it thus. Our months are only 15 days long, but we try to keep track of the days outside our world to maintain some sense of normalcy. The outside gear points to the day until the number 10, which is where it stops and another gear continues, completing the circuit again. This time, though, it stops at 11, showing that it is in the second group of 10 days. The third time would make it stop at 12, which is a complete month. Sometimes, we have an extra day thrown into our year, which would make the gear stop at 12 for that one day before starting again."

"We have so many ways to calculate the year that it is not normally something we put on display. If you were to get closer to the clock, you would see the year in every different culture's time-keeping method, including our own."

Kelly stared on in awe. She could see the clock from anywhere, even as they continued. Tumidus caught on to her confusion.

"The clock is also magical and can be seen from anywhere in the city, no matter what might block your vision. It might appear in a reflection, or in an entirely unique spot, but always where you can make out the time."

"Wait a minute... it's only been like 30 seconds, and the second-hand already moved!" Drake was the one to catch this minor error.

Tumidus laughed again.

"Like I said, my young friend, time works differently here. The Soulstone is technically a singularity, and we are on its even horizon. The entire continent is!"

The car shifted strongly to the right, Mason looking back at the group.

"Sorry! Got caught up in the conversation and almost hit our home-base!"

All eyes looked out at the giant rock that appeared before their eyes. Like a floating mountain, a massive castle lay perched atop it.

Mason continued on, "The floating building is known as the Seeker's Rock. One of the other many benefits to controlling gravity is the inclusion of floating structures. This landmass was raised many thousands of years ago and is attached to an anchor point beneath it. The building itself is the home of the Seekers, of which we five are a part of. We will report there after we have escorted you to the Elders."

As if jetting around in a flying car was not fascinating enough, the addition of a giant floating building finally set the children off their kilter. A series of 'woahs' and 'wow's' and 'oh my God dad, look at that!' finally echoed inside the vehicle.

"I'm honestly surprised it took them this long to get excited!" Brett laughed at his wife.

"Well, I think everything else they have seen until now kind of put them in shock! They are on overload status now." Ke'eli laughed back.

Continuing south into the city, the group could finally begin to see the massive Violet Pyramid in front of them. The thing was larger than the pyramids of Giza in size, shape, and grandeur, yet looked like a giant prism; perfectly smooth and glowing.

The image was fleeting as they entered the last ring of the city. Newer medium-sized buildings rose to block their gaze as they descended. Mason brought the vehicle down lower to show the family the first and final circle, but promised they would see the pyramid again soon.

"We are passing over the inner ring now and entering the first circle. This area is specifically for the many races of Atlantis and is considered their 'headquarters'. It is an area open to all, and much trade and work goes on between the many people at all times of the day. It is the area closest to the great pyramid and is the most calm and peaceful. You will see as we come closer to Paladices, the dwarven Institute of Martial Learning, directly ahead."

Below them, the people of Atlantis flowed out from their buildings, walking towards the center of the city.

"What are they doing?" Kelly asked, the gears in her mind churning.

Tumidus replied, "Every day at noon, everyone in Atlantis stops what they are doing and goes outside for two reasons: To pay tribute and respect to the great pyramid, and to complete a form of exercise known as Tai ji quan. Some people in the outer world do this as well, referring to it as Tai chi. It is a form of meditative exercise, helping the people of Atlantis to focus on the wonders of life and enjoy their time here on this Earth. It is also a time for one to get up and take a break from work!"

"Aye, don't ye be forgettin' the rechargin' of all our gadgets, lad!" Pwyll lowered one eyebrow in Tumidus' direction, showing he knew more than he let on.

"At high noon, yon fancy sun contraption in the sky be right above the Soulstone. Since she's an ultraviolet prism, each side magnifies the energy o' our sun, sending it off to the other pyramids. Makes for a pretty light show as well!"

As the family watched, thousands of people exited their giant buildings, heading to wide open areas facing the center of the city, directly towards the Soulstone. Mason kept to the outside perimeter of the buildings so that the family could take in the entire view. The pyramid was now fully in view. As if expecting their observance, the great Violet Pyramid glowed the slightest bit brighter.

Unexpectedly, the pyramid hummed as everyone could suddenly feel it in the vehicle. They looked out the windows and thought at first that there was something wrong with their ride. When they could feel it in their bones, they knew it was something powerful and external.

"The people of Atlantis sing to the Soulstone, and it sings back." Tumidus whispered, closing his eyes to feel the power.

Sure enough, the family could hear the singing of the people down below as each recalled words to some long-remembered song. Each movement of the Tai-ji quan mimicked a certain lyric or phrase and each echoed out across the square. The steps combined with the song infiltrated the minds and bodies of everyone there, feeling an even more impressive aura of happiness and love.

"It is in memoriam of the ancient and original language of Atlantis. High King Atlas was the only one to still know the words after the Awakening, and he reinstated it. It is magical, no?" Tumidus seemed the most influenced by the act, though everyone else in the car also sat still with their eyes closed, humming, or whispering the song themselves. All except Mason, who continued the tour as the song slowed.

Mason gave a slight cough as he continued flying the vehicle around the outskirts of the pyramid, which drew everyone else's attention.

"The Remembrance is done, and we still have a tour to finish giving! My friends, there are sights to see that would fill your entire lifetime. May I draw your attention *away* from the Soulstone to the next series of buildings? Tumidus, if you would be so kind?"

Finally, able to take his eyes away from the group below, Tumidus sat up straight in his chair and smiled at the family, who also pulled their eyes away from the windows to look at him. He looked back out the opposite side window and nodded.

"Ahem. Very well. The next building and group going clockwise around the pyramid would be the gnomes and their College of Magick Arts as Understood through Technology, called Artificy. Pwyll, I believe you spent an inordinate amount of time there?"

Pwyll smiled as he pointed out the contraptions and gizmos whirring all about the building. Gears spun and steampunk-looking automatons were everywhere, as were the gnomes themselves.

"I just realized, are they like little elves?" Kelly asked.

Mason laughed, expecting the sour look from Tumidus, who replied as quickly as he could.

"No, little one, they are not 'little elves.' The gnomes are purveyors in the sciences and technology, specializing in robotics and alchemical creations."

"But they look like smaller versions of elves," she said, sheepishly.

Trying his hardest to keep a smile on his face, Tumidus continued. "My dear, though they might *slightly* resemble elves, the connection is nil."

"Oh, stop it you big durned elf!" laughing from his belly, Pwyll interrupted. "Aye lassie, we're like little elves, though much more handsome! We use magic in a ways in some o' our contraptions to make 'em do amazing things. Though we look like the tall ones, we gets along better with the dwarves to the west. At least they let us in when the goin' gets tough, aye Tumidus?"

Obviously ashamed, Tumidus turned away to look out the window.

Mason, not having to use his abilities to sense the sudden seriousness in the vehicle, tried to explain to the newcomers.

"Child, each racial Tribe has specific things that separate it from the others. For many years, that separation cost us our familial ties, driving a wedge between our own known ancestries. We were all once human, through and through. The pyramid changed that, and though we live in an advanced society, some habits die hard."

"So, what you're saying is, you guys have it just as bad as we do out in the real world, what with racism and segregation." Ke'eli asked, having already gathered that from the interaction on the train with the half-elf. She reached out a hand to Brett as well, knowing that his mixed skin color caused more than one confrontation as well.

All five of the other species in the vehicle suddenly grew much more somber, looking away with downcast eyes.

"Mother right. Too much hate." Keb said, again speaking volumes of wisdom in the very few words he had said.

The air of excitement died down for the briefest of moments as realization dawned on them all. Nowhere in the world was there a place that was devoid of animosity or resentment, even directly next to a structure emanating the stuff of goodness. Positive vibes or not, some things you could not work out of the human DNA.

"What. Is. That." Drake's exclamation broke the silence.

Walking stiffly below them, standing thirty feet tall, was a massive man.

"It's a giant." Xinzang said matter-of-factly.

Drake looked back at her, furrowing his brows. Zang just chuckled at his expression, but continued.

"Giants are not humans and were not too affected by the Awakening. There was originally one race of giants who lived in the Olde World. They were feared and persecuted by the Armies of Man, many of them killed for not joining the bloodthirsty bands of humans. The ones that escaped sensed the Calling, traveling far and wide to arrive at the shores of Atlantis."

"They set up a city in the north which the dwarves came to call Jotunheim. Another city is in the south, called Hyperborea. The giants keep mostly to themselves, though some reached out to cooperate with the then-humans of Atlantis.

"After the Awakening, many of the giants found a certain aptitude in the distinct elements of the Earth. They came to also separate into groups, much like our Tribes, mimicking the altered humans who had also changed so drastically. They became the hill, stone, fire, frost, cloud, and storm giants, based on their characteristics and what they favored the most."

"The ones that still worked and traded with the Atlanteans were afforded certain privileges, including the construction of the Ordning, which is their great hall you see there before you. Unfortunately, many of the others, mostly the ones to the south, fell to in-fighting, believing that some were more destined for greatness than others were. They are a race that the Atlantean Guard constantly have to be wary of."

As the car flew by the giant, it was as if the thing could reach out and slap it if it wanted to. It eyed the occupants with a raised eyebrow, noting that the four humans were staring at it open-mouthed.

Tumidus began beaming suddenly, trying to pry the group's eyes away from the giant man.

"Aha! My friends, welcome to Sorcere, the Academy of Magic!" Tumidus pulled the family's arms, steering them forward of their vehicle.

Before them was the shiniest and most vaulted building the family had ever seen. With the magnificent stonework and masonry of ancient Greece combined with the power of fanciful magic, the building glowed with power. People walked up the side of the building with not a care in the world.

Elves below them practiced the Tai ji quan but included flares of their own form of magic into the air as they completed certain moves or hand gestures. One shot a stream of fire out of his palm while another sparkled electricity over her hair.

Not only that, but the people near the building also seemed to fly as effortlessly as they walked.

"The elves take their magic to heart. It permeates the very ground they walk on." Mason began. "As was mentioned before, it is actually a form of radiation that they can control. Too much of it, though, causes the mutations you saw back in Zion."

"But it is a beautiful thing, no?" Tumidus stared longingly at the building and its surrounding area, raising his hand to the glass window. His admiration for the place surpassed even that of the family who were seeing it for the first time.

"He has been gone too long. When elves leave the confines of Atlantis, their magic diminishes. Now that he is home, I am sure he is feeling much more refreshed." Xinzang cackled.

Tumidus turned away from the window with a wide grin on his face. Obviously happy to have seen his home again, he appeared content enough to continue the tour. Until he recalled the next area and its inhabitants. His look of serenity changed to that of disgust.

"Ah, well, ahem, yes. The next group of... 'Atlanteans' you will see are the goblinoids." He stuttered as well as he could. To his shame, the family leaped from their seats to see them.

"You mean, like real goblins? Like monsters? Like little gremlins and stuff? I LOVE gremlins!" Drake could hardly hold his excitement.

"Well, yes, child, they *are* gremlins. The lot of them." Tumidus replied with a look of disdain.

"Now now Tumidus," Mason scolded, "they are also remarkably close to cousins for you as well, are they not?"

Mason knew how to push his friend's buttons. It was true. The goblinoids were much like gnomes. Just *greener*.

Exasperated, Tumidus continued the tale to the waiting ears of the family.

"Yes, fine. Well, goblinoids are the greener, and some say meaner and greedier, versions of gnomes. They are of the same size and weight, and both carry a fondness for technology and mixing magic with science. Where gnomes enjoy automatons, the goblinoids enjoy the alchemical side of things, brewing strange concoctions and experimenting with the flesh."

Keb plopped down on the floor of the vehicle to prove the point.

"Keb have tattoo. Goblin make good ink." Sliding up his arm sleeve, he showed the group a wondrous tattoo of a large man holding a huge rock above his head.

"Ah yes, *tattoos*." Tumidus continued. "The goblinoids have secreted the knowledge to imbue certain types of ink with magic power. Take Keb's tattoo. When he wills it, though only for a short duration, he can increase his strength exponentially."

"Make Keb strong like bull." Keb emphasized the point, flexing his already large muscles.

"Almost as strong as Zang, eh Keb?" Xinzang laughed as she poked him in the ribs with her clawed toes.

"Dragon-lady strong," Keb smiled back at her as he took his seat, "but Keb squish like little lizard."

The two laughed at each other over the statement, drawing smiles from everyone else on board.

Tumidus again broke the mirth.

"Yes, I suppose goblins and gremlins have their uses. They are especially good at stealth and finance as well. Let us just say they have secreted many valuables at the behest of the Atlantean Elders."

"Some say they keep it right there at their Guild house, known as Rogal. Half home to the goblins, half bank; all trouble. But even we have things we want to keep secret and safe! And none can keep a secret or keep something secure, like a goblin." Mason nodded his head toward the non-descript building in the first ring, facing east from the pyramid.

"Right under everyone's noses."

"All this is so amazing! I can't believe how much is here under the ice!" Ke'eli exclaimed.

"Oh, my lady, we have barely touched the surface! Next, we have our good friend Keb's home-hovel, known as Shamas. As you can see, it is much like the halfling's building type. Very Earthy, very modest, yet very accommodating. Isn't that right Keb?" Tumidus nodded over to Keb.

Keb, though, just looked down at his people and smiled a tusk-filled smile.

The family laughed then, entertained by such a brute who could so easily break the façade of a monster-stereotype with nothing but a smile.

"Ah, along with the great orcs of the south, we have the beast-born."

"Oh, don't let Tumidus get you all roiled up. He is a fan of the barbarians." Mason quipped.

Sure enough, the vehicle flew close enough by a large rampart, spikes and plates protecting an even larger monster of a building.

"Why are there so many guards? Why aren't they doing the kung-fu stuff?" Drake asked innocently enough.

"They do NOT practice Gung-Fu!" Zang snapped back at once, resenting the act.

Drake sat back, startled by the outburst.

Calming herself down, she redirected her anger to Tumidus.

"This one would think that the barbarian horde would be the saviors of Atlantis if given the opportunity, even over his own kin."

"My lady, magic is finite. The beast-born can resist all kinds of seductions, including those of the fiends. They will away pain and fight beyond death. I do envy the power they have inherent in their bodies, able to call upon at a moment's notice."

"Wait, what? What are you all talking about?" Brett was inquisitive of these beast-born, remembering the episode of demons he and Ke'eli had experienced themselves. The mention of the things again brought back sharp memories.

Tumidus continued, "The beast-born are monstrous, yes, but they have a barbaric side to them they can control. They enter a sort of rage that allows them to shrug away injuries, both physical and mental."

"Yeah, but you mentioned them resisting fiends. If you don't have any fiends here, how do you know they can?" Brett pressed for more information.

"It is a long and storied fact, my friend. Beast-born, as barbaric as they are, are the closest to what we humans were in the beginning before any possessions tried to take root in our world. We, as roving bands of hunters and gatherers, were barbaric in the beginning and they mirror that reality. Their physical forms changed to more closely resemble the inner monsters, while their mentality mimicked the bestial nature inside. That baseness, though, protects them from hellish energy. And there are plenty of fiendish creatures in the Olde World."

Brett and Ke'eli looked at each other in alarm. Their joy at cruising around Atlantis suddenly and irrevocably ceased.

Mason caught the sudden change in the atmosphere and decided that at least half of the city would suffice.

"My friends, I think we have shown you enough of the city for now. Let us take this moment to see first-hand the people of Atlantis as they finish Tai ji quan. I am positive that after the Council has met you, they will relinquish preparations for your future here to me and we will continue the tour afterwards."

The children complained at the break, but Ke'eli and Brett both agreed. The vehicle became stifling at the remembrance again of the creatures they had battled against both at the beach, in their home and then again here in Atlantis, and neither wanted to brooch the subject in front of their children.

Parking the vehicle south of the Great Pyramid and outside the perimeter of the central circle, the entourage exited to the open-eyed stares of some people there. The illusion that had disguised Ke'eli had worn off, and they were now obviously a family of four very real, very non-Atlantean or Native American humans.

Mason realized this and at first feared that it would cause a commotion. Many of the native Atlanteans were still completing their Tai ji quan while some had already re-entered their workspaces or other buildings. He calmed though as he also realized they were parked near the beast-born, who did not practice Tai ji quan and thus, their area was mostly vacant.

The Senatus building lay directly to the south of the pyramid, parallel to one of the four sides. It also sat across from the large fortification described to the family not even a minute prior. Because the beast-born had no cause to practice an art that exemplified calm and peace, they were not as present as many others. These were the warriors of Atlantis, and they knew only battle.

That was not to say that there were none present at all. A large, green-skinned behemoth began to pointedly lumber over to the group, warts covering its sickly hide. Its mouth was full of broken and cragged teeth, saliva dripping down its chin.

"Troll." Mason whispered to the group, moving himself before the four humans.

Drake could not help himself, though. He had to see a real troll up front and personal! He squeezed his way beside Mason, even as Brett closed his hand down on his shoulder.

Brett was not afraid of the creature. In actuality, he thought the thing looked comical, like a puppet from Jim

Henson's movie The Labyrinth. It was gangly and sloppy, no clear weapon or armor of any kind. Just a large warty creature with cragged teeth.

Mason hailed the creature as it approached.

"Seeker business. Heading to the Senatus for review. Nothing to see here, friend."

("Uncharted Territory" from the Edge of Tomorrow Soundtrack by Christophe Beck)

But the creature did not stop. If anything, the beast increased its speed toward the entourage, oblivious to Mason.

Mason noticed the increase as well, looking back at his companions.

"They are known for being the more brutish of the brutes. Not much in the way of brains up there!"

But his concern was well-noted as he looked back at Xinzang.

She knew all too well the brutishness of trolls. She looked back to Brett as well, asking that he release Drake.

"Trust me," she said. "He will be of much use in frightening the beast."

"It's getting closer...." Tumidus whispered, he also preparing to protect the family.

"Little one, remember the fire-bird we practiced?"

Drake smiled as he looked up to his favorite friend, nodding an emphatic yes.

"I need you to concentrate and summon it. Toy with the troll. He will learn his place." Xinzang smiled as she finished, inhaling a bit to prepare the flame he would need.

Drake lowered his brow in determination, waiting for the cue.

The troll lumbered closer and closer. It was now within twenty feet, a slow and lumbering gallop. Its claws opened and closed, and it looked like the saliva was getting greater dripping out of its mouth. Mason glimpsed its thoughts; it was smart enough to recognize a human woman and her human daughter. Both things were highly illegal in Atlantis. Its one-track mind knew only one thing; they had to die.

"Breath of the Dragon!" Mason yelled.

Immediately, his team formed a reverse wedge formation, creating what looked like an arrow pointed away from the creature. Xinzang and Keb took up the points while Mason and Tumidus were one step behind and inside them. In the rear center stood Pwyll, his hands on a multitude of gadgets and gizmos, ready to wreak havoc or heal, the family was not sure.

As for the family, they stayed behind the wedge formation. All except Drake, who stepped to the direct center.

The troll was oblivious to the boy and focused on the women behind Pwyll.

"Now!" Xinzang yelled out, puffing out a small amount of fire from one nostril.

Drake focused on the flame, enlarging it, and giving it form.

The thing blossomed into a large and fiery bird, danger-ously beautiful to behold. The miniature phoenix's wing tips glowed orange as it flapped toward the troll.

Its effect was immediate. The troll could sense the crea-ture and feel its heat on his skin. His eyes bulged wide enough to almost fall out of his head as he stumbled back-wards away from the thing.

Drake made the phoenix flap and fly around the troll, stopping in front of it every so often to let loose a loud 'squawk' before continuing its parade.

The troll turned tail and ran as quickly as it could the other way.

Mason ushered the family towards the Senatus, looking back every so often to make sure no other beast-born was following.

Brett held out his hand for a high-five from his son.

"Good work buddy! That was awesome!" he exasperat-ed, to an equally proud 11-year-old.

Approaching the golem-guards, Mason made a symbol in his palm, showing a secret pass. The golems, who had seen the spectacle in the courtyard, let them pass, albeit warily.

"Well, that was fun! Phase 1: get the human family to the Tribal Elders; done." Mason felt relieved as he ushered them all into a private room.

"I'll be back," he said, turning to a curtained door.

"Famous last words," Brett said, as he sat down to close his eyes for a moment.

The family was dirty and tired, but appreciated the ac-commodations that the waiting room had to afford. The rest of the Seeker entourage remained behind with them, not only to ensure their safety but also because Mason was their leader and was the only one to request a formal audience with the acting Elders.

"Well, guess it's time to see what happens!" Brett exclaimed to the group.

The group sat on the edges of their seats, waiting patiently for a response.

CHAPTER EIGHT

THE ELDERS

A storm of shadows swirled down the dark corridor, causing the green-flaming torches to dance about in their sconces. The earthen cave had long ago been dug out, his people working like ants to connect tunnels, widen passageways and create living chambers. Even now, this far away from the central cavern, the shadow-creature could feel the energies of the pyramid structure there.

Its glowing red aura was a reminder to him of the prison that was his home. Though it had sustained him and his people, the price was high. Occasionally, the pyramid's inner hue would change, predicting the change that would come over it. An eternal siphon of energy, the pyramid drew its power from other planes of existence by opening gateways to those locations. Denizens of those other planes did not always appreciate an otherworldly construct draining power from it.

Not only did the pyramid drain energy from other realms, it did so to the people who lived about it. It had long ago been determined that the pyramid worked as a siphon of some sort, drawing light to it as energy. The red that resulted was actually the red of the infrared spectrum, which was not really light to the people who lived around it. Because of its siphoning aspect, it absorbed all light, including that of the color of the people's skin, resulting in everyone's pigmentation growing darker to a shade of gray.

He was not just some person, though. He was Belial the First, Chosen of the Bloodstone and King of the Otherworld. He was the first to draw the evil essence of a fiend into himself, making his skin turn a blood-red. He was the one who had communed with the pyramid itself, promising it energy in return for a power of a different sort.

The pyramid was a living, breathing construct. One that held a certain form of intelligence about it. The thing knew that to survive, it needed tendrils to reach further out into the wide expanse of its underground hovel. It also knew it was trapped here, but it didn't seem worried.

Instead, it cooperated with the other denizens of the home it had created. At first, thousands of years ago, the thing protected them from the onslaught of demons and devils that came flowing out of its insides. Yes, it was intelligent. It knew that to be controlled by those fiendish creatures meant a lifetime of servitude, and the pyramid was no one's slave.

A pact was made with the humanoids, who had come to its beck and call; the Soulless. They could hear its siren song from anywhere in the world, and they came to its aid against the incursion of monsters. The pact taught the Soulless how to kill fiends. Not just physically, but spiritually as well.

Belial had been the first. He, a leader in his own right, had founded the Bloodstone with his brother so many thousands of years prior. Contacting the pyramid, it communicated with him and offered its gifts. He had been the first to be provided a blood shard gemstone, connecting himself with the pyramid on a metaphysical level. But he needed to be tested.

The first pit fiend to come strolling out of the construct's insides still reverberated in his mind and heart to this day. A towering monster, Belial nearly died that day against the monster. But his gift from the Bloodstone allowed him to survive. No, more than survive; to endure.

And it was thus that Belial had taught the others how to siphon the energies of the extra-planar creatures that came through the ever-changing gateway of the Bloodstone. Those energies were also siphoned to the pyramid itself. The pyramid absorbed all light, leaving none. Originally, black as the blackest night his people's skin had become. But with absorbing the energies of other creatures, the blood shards had acted as conduits to the Bloodstone, the wearers much like the pyramid itself. They absorbed the energy for it, which caused them to exude the color of *all* light; white.

Over time, the Otherworld, as their home was called, allowed people of all skin colors. Those who did not embrace the form of Daemon hunting; trained in the art of drawing on the energies of creatures that came out of the

Bloodstone, came to have the darker skin the closer they lived to the pyramid. Those that kept their distance at the extreme edges of the homeland kept a lighter complexion.

Daemon hunters: they were another story.

Belial growled as he remembered the rest of the pact he made with the Bloodstone.

Not long after saving it from itself, the denizens of the Otherworld found that the world was in disarray. Many of the creatures they thought they were slaying and consuming had, in fact, survived somehow. The Soulless, in their own home, had revealed a great treachery, uncovered too late. Some of the Soulless, giving in to a fiendish temptation for power, betrayed their comrades and allowed certain fiend essences to escape. The traitorous Soulless also conducted great rituals to free the captive souls held by Daemon hunters after their deaths.

Fiends had escaped into the wider world and were possessing the humans of ancient civilization. As Belial went about making plans to seek these monsters out covertly, as his people had not been accepted by 'regular' humans, a great war had begun. Without warning, a tidal flood of water and a great shaking of the earth threatened all they held dear. Somehow, some way, the Bloodstone was aware of it and had created an impenetrable dome around the perimeter of its underground domicile.

The price of survival was almost too much.

A great dome protected his people, but also trapped them in their underground prison. The pyramid knew that there was only one way to keep the essences from escaping out into the wider world, and that was to trap everyone and everything within its confines. Thankfully, it had its Daemon hunters.

The shadows around Belial flared out at the recollection of that day. He could not have known there would be secret ways to eventually escape the prison, and that it would take thousands of years to realize it, yet he still knew it may have doomed his people to a lifetime of being trapped beneath the earth. All at the whim of the Bloodstone.

He tried to remind himself that he and his people were trying to do good. Tried to quell the rioting whispers of the fiends he had trapped in his soul over the years. Tried to vanquish the notion that still, to this day, unquieted Soulless still bartered with the fiends in their hearts for greater power, allowing some essences to escape past the dome.

No where else in the world was there a more diverse and chaotic place than here in the Otherworld.

Which was why Belial still stayed true to the ritual he had done every year for thousands and thousands of years.

Entering his private quarters, he glanced into a small room off to his side, stopping only briefly. There, a lone bed lay empty. Books lined the shelves along the side of it, simple weapons of fiend-bone propped along its edge. Belial shook his head, registering the small room's owner: Sigurd.

He had always been a thorn in Belial's side. Since the time of his Founding where he had faced off with his first devil, Sigurd had thought himself better than his peers. Granted, the child was beyond skilled with the power of the Arts, but his role as Daemon hunter did not afford him the luxury or infamy his heart truly craved. Even now, the dolt was running about the Upperworld, thinking he was to claim some great power or another.

Destiny, Sigurd would claim.

Yes, destiny indeed.

Belial moved towards a wall at the back of the small living area. He did not rest too far from the small room for Sigurd; he having been his apprentice for almost the last ten years. But even Sigurd was unaware of some things Belial had done and still had to do.

Waving his hand across the bare stone, Belial arched his metal-clad gauntlets first thumb to thumb, and pointer finger to pointer finger, before reversing the direction and keeping the digits connected. As his hands turned vertical, a blue glow emanated from the wall in front of him. Spreading slowly to form a door, Belial walked in.

The mass of swirling shadows wavered from the torchlight in the room, which burst to life at his entrance. Though it was in a small cave by itself with no clear entrances or exits, the flame of the torch danced as if a breathing wind was buffeting it about.

Belial sat cross-legged at a small pedestal in the center of this room, which was its only adornment. The pedestal rose only a foot or so from the ground, supporting a small half-globe. Looking much like a snow-globe, the glass of its top was a dark gray and was only large enough to put two hands across.

Belial knew that the time was nigh for him to attempt this ritual again, so he removed his silver gauntlets and stretched his blood-red hands across the globe. Closing his eyes, the shadows about his form seemed to slow in time to his breathing. Concentrating on the globe before him, he funneled what energy he could into the thing.

Slowly, the red mist that seemed to flow out of Belial's palms and fingers coaxed out a scene of some kind in the globe's image.

Almost sensing it, Belial opened his eyes to the images.

Squinting through the misty side of this globe, Belial tried to make out its insides. He knew what to look for but had not seen it in so very long that he sucked in his breath when he did finally discern what he was seeing.

Inside were eleven individuals, all at the outermost edges of the bubble, as if spread out like a clock. Every 'hour' was filled, except for the 11 o'clock position.

This bubble was not big, and the eleven were speaking with each other. Their images were blurry to Belial, but he knew who they were and what they were doing.

All conversation stopped then, as a glow filled the immediate center of their area. They turned as one to greet the shape materializing there. A man, blurred as well, but distinguishable still, appeared before them all, bowing low to the surrounding others, who returned the bow in kind.

He spoke only briefly, his words mumbled as if Belial were underwater. The man in the center of the globe bowed again before disappearing. Then, one by one, the others left as well.

Belial banged on the dome before him in frustration. It had been the same way every year, the eleven arriving to meet. Yet this year, the man in the center had finally returned. Portents and prophecies swirled around the event; many Belial himself had read in his auguries.

Looking up into the darkness, Belial the First, Chosen of the Bloodstone and King of the Otherworld, winced as the realization dawned on him. A look of determination crossed his shadowed face.

"It has begun."

Mason tried to control his excitement. He paced back and forth before the main entrance to the council chambers, reciting the information he had gleaned over the last few days. He knew the Elders would support his decision; he just needed to figure out a way to have them see this the same way he did.

Mason knew too that his master would be present for the summons. Stopping his pacing, he realized that his master might learn this information psychically before he could tell him, which would destroy all his momentum. Mason was not necessarily on good terms with his Dharmapala Avici, who styled himself more a "President" than the leader of the human mystic enclave.

Mason, and many others of his kind, had come to a strange and startling conclusion; the last several Dharmapala's had all been of the same mindset and motivation to steer the all-male enclave of human mystics in certain directions.

Mason did not like being told what to do.

It was bad enough that he and his team had been off in the Olde World stealing children in the night to even consider the implication that his fellow mystics would harbor ill will towards the rest of Atlantis. It had been implicit that all humans were to be 'scanned' regularly by the Enclave to ensure that there were no radical thoughts or fanatic compulsions that would induce them to strike off on their own.

Mason felt that being abducted from your home and brought to a strange world was traumatic enough. Being regularly scanned by your brethren for thought-crimes was going too far.

Mason had only undergone screening once before that. It was random but was unpleasant all the same. He wouldn't allow himself to be stripped down in front of the other Elders. So, it was then he decided to protect not only his own psyche, but that of his companions and the family as well.

Mystic Enclave be damned.

A curtain rustled to the side at the entrance of one of the golem guards.

"Master Clemens, you are formerly presented to the Council. Please follow me."

The golem turned on its heel and walked back through the curtain.

"Well, here goes nothing."

("The High Council Meeting and Qui-Gon's Funeral" from the Star Wars: The Phantom Menace Soundtrack by John Williams)

"The Council now recognizes Master Mason Clemens, leader of Seeker Group Kapha, honorary member of the League of Mysteries and returner of 31 lost souls."

The golem voice echoed in the large chamber. All the lights were dim, but bright enough for Mason to see where he was going. He had been here plenty of times before, though. He knew his way to the central spire, a platform dais in the middle of the concave room where the surrounding Tribal Elders would hear his voice.

He had called for a special summons of the Elders, not done in ages. Reserved for only the most grave and perilous of reasons, Mason knew the Elders would be dissecting every word he would have to say. But he knew that this was the only way.

He had within his midst not only one, but *two* psychic females related by blood. That by itself was not alarming. Mason himself was a very well-known Master Mystic and had met many psychic females in his time in Atlantis.

Those women, though, were all half-breed chimeras. These two women were full-blood human.

"The Council calls to order the matter in which Master Clemens has vaguely described an encounter in the Olde World with a pair of humans that have 'abilities.'"

Mason had left the formal reasoning behind the calling vague. He knew there were some on the council who would not approve of him bringing the women back to Atlantis. If they had been alone, or of slight mystic potential, he would have alerted the council the normal way and let them deal with it.

The way he discovered the women, with the men alongside them, reinforced his motives for bringing them all here.

Already, he could feel the stares coming down to him from on high. Also, he could feel the testing of his mental barrier. He did not want anyone probing his mind without his permission. He also knew that the Elder of his own Tribe would try just such a thing to get a heads up on the information. Mason waved the futile attempt away without a second thought. He did not always see eye-to-eye with his own Elder in matters of Mysticism.

Mason looked up into the darkened shadows above him, determination steeling his resolve.

"Most Revered. Our history tells us that at the founding of this great Empire, ten were chosen to rule alongside the great and mighty High King of Atlantis. Ten, who would parse out the surrounding lands to rule as they saw fit, always with the benefits of the whole in mind."

"Then came war and famine. The great fiend armies came in their natural forms not once, but twice. We fought them back with the joint powers of Atlantis itself. The fiends evolved, using our own intellect and pride against us. Perverting the old protectors into warlocks enslaved to demonic power. We repelled them as well."

"And most recently, in our vast and tumultuous history, the Armies of Man. They, skewed by lust and power stemming from the fiends, made it to our borders to lay waste and destruction. We turned them back, making the most awful of sacrifices."

"I speak to these disastrous times because one thing ties them all together. One thing that rings clearly in the darkness, always showing Atlantis the light. Though I say one thing, I mean four."

"Master Clemens," a male voice in the darkness above him spoke, "we know of our history and can attest to your knowledge of it as well. You speak of the Four Primals. Yes, they have always been present in one incarnation or another. Most recently, as semi-permanent additions to the Soulstone itself. It was they who lent their considerable power to harness the Earth beneath us to move our beloved continent from the Atlantic Ocean to the World Sea."

"Yes, my Lord, but it was also they who said they would return when Atlantis needed them most. Over eleven thousand years have passed since that fateful moment when they stepped into the Soulstone. And then one thousand years of relative peace and tranquility once they mysteriously stepped out and disappeared from our view after 'steering' our home to its present location. Still now, though, the fiends work to tear humankind apart, oblivious to the new location of Atlantis. Possessions are on the rise even as we fight to stem the bloody tide that we know is coming. On top of that, and with no disrespect to the current Elder panel, the original True Elders still slumber!"

"You realize Master Clemens that what you speak of is Prophecy. The True Elders will wake when the time comes to bring Atlantis to bear on our old enemies. Yes, part of the prophecy makes mention of the Four Primals, but it is unknown whether they cause the awakening, or if they are an instrument of the Elders themselves. You speak now as if you have firsthand knowledge of this. Say what you will, Master Clemens, for this panel is growing weary of our history lesson."

"Very well, I apologize my Lords and Ladies. I began my speech with emphasis on the Four Primals because the history we know of them is so fragmented. We know that they each have power over one of the Primal Energies of the world, Earth, air, fire, and water. We also know that they are True Atlanteans, able to enter the Soulstone pyramid like our Great King could. Last, we know they are the yin and yang to each other; two males and two females, the eternal balance.

"In my latest Seeker mission, I tracked an overwhelming power back to a young boy not much older than eleven years. He was powerful beyond all recognition; pyrokinetic and dangerously so. Initially, I thought I would retrieve the child as I had all my earlier missions before, to train and control his powers here on Atlantis. My team, with a high degree of success, infiltrated the home and located the child."

Mason paused to catch his breath. This was the moment that he had dreaded. Mason had always been a powerful mystic. Even his innate abilities astounded many. Subconsciously, he could read the surface thoughts of anyone he could see. At first, it was annoying, always hearing what people were thinking. Over time, though, he learned to harness and control it, like he could with his other abilities.

"While my team made entry into the home, we were amazed to the see the family sleeping defensively in one room, within arm's reach of each other. Because of some... *unforeseen* complications, we entered into combat with the family of four. They all exhibited some minute control over the elements."

Mason stopped talking to take in his audience. Sure enough, there was whispering amongst the Elders. Some grumbling, some excitement. If Mason could see better, he might even get a hint at what they were thinking. But Mason knew better. He knew this council was aware of his powers and had inundated the room with anti-mystic energy to not only quell his abilities but also to keep him honest.

"So, you believe this family of four to be *the* Four Primals?" The scalehide Elder was the first to speak up. Her gravelly and growling nature made it obvious, and Mason knew she would be the first to show support. The scalehide always supported the First King and the Four Primals.

It didn't escape Mason's notice that the possibility of them being the Four Primals was a good thing. Mason knew they were and knew that if that were the sum of the experience, that the Tribal Elders would have nothing to say about it. The Four Primals had been to Atlantis before and would be given the highest accolades.

"Yes, I believe this family to be the incarnation of the Four Primals." Mason replied, bowing his head.

An immediate hush fell over the room. The crowd, all experienced interviewers and sometimes interrogators, fell silent.

"But, you have more to say," came the reply from the elven Tribal Elder, her voice melodic as it floated down to Mason's ears. There was power behind that voice, and Mason knew he would be "invited" to say more. Mason knew his psychic powers were not on the same level as arcane powers. Should the Council use magic, he could not fight off any impulsive thoughts, which would hurt his case.

Mason agreed.

"As I looked into the parent's minds, I saw and felt a telepathic reply."

All was quiet in the room again.

"So, the father is a mystic as well, and you could not locate him as a child?" came the query from the head of his order himself, the human Mystic Elder.

Mason remained quiet for several seconds more. He knew this was the decisive moment. It depended on whether the Elders supported the idea these were the Four Primals or not. The fear that a female mystic would bring about the downfall of Atlantis most was what contested it.

Mason looked up into the darkness toward the voice.

"The telepathic one was the mother."

The room erupted in a cacophony of voices. Some were heated, others were calming. All though, alarmed at the fact that they knew that Mason the Seeker had returned with humans from the Olde World. One of those humans had to have been the human mother. Mason closed his eyes as the verbal onslaught began.

"You dare not approach us with this information first? You put the entire continent at risk for a whim?!"

"These are the Four Primals! They are our heroes! They have saved Atlantis countless times!"

"My Elders..." Mason whispered in the dark and confusion.

"The prophecy rings true! 'And all discover she has a demonheart!' Banish her!"

"She is a Primal! A Primal wouldn't destroy Atlantis!"

"My Elders...." Mason said louder.

"This is treason! They should all be put to the blade!"

"MY ELDERS! I am not finished!" Mason roared above the cacophony, a hint of mystic energy enhancing his voice to quell the arguing.

Silence.

Though the original true Primal Elders were powerful beyond belief and immortal, they had been missing for over a thousand years. They, along with Atlantis' true and rightful High King. These "Elders" that Mason spoke to had been intermediary leaders who held the position but were still only a political talking point that earned their place by popular vote. They were powerful, but not all-knowing. Since they weren't the "true" Elders, people nicknamed them 'Lamps' of Atlantis, because they were nominated to guide their brethren through the darkness.

Mason waited anxiously again to continue his statement. No response from above. No fiery torment of magic or assault of the mind. No blades slung or arrows launched. Steeling his nerves, Mason continued.

"As I am sure you have deduced from my explanation, there is the case for the daughter as well. While the mother has control over the elemental earth, the daughter controls the air. And she is a mystic as well. They all are."

Mason looked up from his eyebrows at the room. They still waited for him to continue.

"My Elders, the Four Primals were capable of amazing things. No one ever stopped to ask them *what* those amazing things were limited to. Yes, they had control over the Primal Energies, but there are stories of them being able to heal the wounded, summon arcane storms and access their inner chi! If only because they were *humans* able to use the elemental powers of the orcs, I would say that in-and-of itself calls for question! And that question is: what *else* were they able to do? I cannot see the saviors of Atlantis also being their downfall."

Silence again. Where Mason had before wanted silence, the sound of it now grew on his nerves. A squeaky voice answered his prayers.

"Yet you say, Master Clemens, that these two are *children*? The Four Primals were grown adults. How can you explain this? How can you explain the fact that you broke protocol and brought them to our home without merit? You knew their location. You could have returned with the Mysteries for further analyzation! Yet you did not."

The accusation was fair enough, and, surprisingly, the Elder of the halflings, known for her patience and knowledge, made the accusation.

"My Lady, as I said before, it was during combat with the family that I had this revelation. For further evidence that these are the Four Primals, the mother and father were not as affected by my sorcerer's magic. They woke at the slightest provocation, even through the effects of both a sleep and silence spell. It was obvious that these four were special and that I needed to get them to you as quickly as possible."

Mason let the last sentence linger for a few seconds as he shifted his feet. The Elders knew he had more to say, and they allowed him to continue. He knew that of all the evidence he had presented to the Elders, these last bits of information were his alone.

"I felt the need to bring them here quickly because I looked into the mind of both parents. What I saw there... I cannot explain. But two things I know for sure."

Hesitation. This could destroy his argument or bring further light to it.

"They have both fought and prevailed against... an incursion of fiends."

Gasps and murmurs again filled the room. An incursion of fiends was not as trivial as he had made it sound. Fiend-possessed humans were one thing. An actual incursion of the creatures was far worse.

"I saw them battling one fiend on a beach. They were both restrained, and the female was approached by the creature. More of the things appeared and fought *with* the male and female against the first fiend. I believe these to be our lost brethren, the Soulless. I cannot explain the fact that they fought one of their own, but both escaped with their lives."

The whispering continued, getting louder.

"Not only had they battled fiends on a beach, but the father had recently battled another while on a plane, who was aided by many more of its kind."

The whispering increased. Mason was not so sure this was aiding his case.

"To emphasize, when I stated we battled *with* the family, I did not mean we battled against them. As we looked to take the child, their home came under attack from the same fiend and his allies that had attacked the father on the plane. We battled together against the fiend, fleeing through a gate back to Atlantis."

Mason knew he had to get this last part out or his voice would be lost. Out of everything... the Four Primals, their mystic connection, or the fighting the fiends; this was the most important thing, even though it was still an unknown to him.

"Last, for my report, I believe that the two parents are the rarest of the rare, which precludes me to think that they were destined to arrive here in Atlantis. I believe they are Soulmates."

CHAPTER NINE

RECOLLECTIONS

Brett paced back and forth inside the waiting room. It had been an hour since Mason left them, and even though the accommodations were nice and they were checked on several times by servitor golems, Brett knew something was up.

"I don't know Kee. Call it my Marine Corps intuition. He said he would just have to go introduce us and he'd be right back. It doesn't take an hour to say our names."

Brett continued his pace, watching the curtains for any newcomers or eavesdroppers.

"I can't tell you what he's doing, love, but we are here now, in a building surrounded by some of the most powerful people in this entire country, and I don't mean politically powerful. You've seen what these people can do! These are their *Elders*."

Ke'eli planted her feet and stood in the middle of Brett's pacing line, hoping to stop him before he wore a hole in the carpet.

He recognized her effort and stopped to face her. Looking at her calm face brought his apprehension down several notches.

"My love, look at that thing out there! It's supposed to be some sort of power source that also instills goodness in you. How can anyone feel negative about anything this close to it?!"

Brett looked out the window that supplied a beautiful view of the Violet Pyramid, which was the source of all Atlantis' power and prestige. He could see to the top of the thing, which gleamed in the sunlight.

("Tala Returns" from the Moana Soundtrack by Mark Mancina)

Brett froze.

There was someone *inside* the pyramid near the top.

As he stared there, his peripheral vision changed. He was outside the Senatus building, surrounded by thousands of people. They all ran about yelling and screaming, weapons at the ready, moving women and children. His family and the Seekers were nowhere to be seen.

He looked around, confusion setting in. Looking back to the top of the pyramid, he could see a young woman there with blond hair floating inside the structure. He looked down at the base of the pyramid and was astounded to see his wife and daughter, but they were not who they were now.

"What the Hell?" Brett exclaimed, noticing his daughter grown up, standing next to a slightly older version of

Ke'eli, yet no less beautiful. As he watched, his wife and daughter entered *into* the pyramid, walking right through the base of it and disappearing.

"It is time, Water-Caller," a voice spoke out to him from behind.

Turning slowly, Brett was shocked to see the woman he thought was in the pyramid standing beside him.

She was young and shapely, blond hair falling straight down to her mid-chest. She looked to be in her 20s, but there was something unnaturally wise about her eyes as they looked into Brett's soul.

"I understand your confusion. You are trying to process memories from your past, your future, and an alternate present. Being this close to the Soulstone is probably not helping."

Brett furrowed his brow, trying to sort through whether or not these images were memories.

"My name is Grace. Well, at least right now it is. But that is not important. Have faith in these people. They are your kin as much as your children are. You will be tried and tested and may feel that all is lost, but do not give in to hate. The enemy is always watching and waiting."

Brett, in a state of obvious confusion, turned back around to try to take in his surroundings and to find his family.

The sound of gunfire made him jump and spin back around towards the woman, hoping to shield her from the barrage. What he saw instead made his eyebrows raise to the top of his head.

A man now stood there, wearing a brown Indiana Jones-like fedora along with a brown half-trench coat. Before Brett could analyze any more of the situation, the man smiled at Brett, yelled out, "Surprise! Time for an alternate-dimension flashback!" before slapping Brett hard in the face.

Brett cringed, closing his eyes from the trivial strike.

When he finally opened them, the shooting sound had dissipated. Arms wrapped around him, hugging him close.

Brett found he could not move his body. He couldn't tell his eyes where to look. He could do nothing but feel the press of bodies around him.

Brett was having another delusion.

He remembered where the gunshots had originated from then. A vision of seeing his son, flying and on fire, get shot down out of the sky by a Terminator-like robot. One of Atlantis's 'golems.'

That was why he didn't like the robots...

But it was not his son. Or was it? The boy was no longer a boy, but a full-grown man of at least 30 years old. And the world he was in was not his own. Or was it the future? The memories flew into his mind, making him weak.

Realization dawned on him suddenly.

The three days he spent lost at sea after the plane crashed remained a mystery. At the time, he did not know what could have happened to him, or why he could not remember the time he was 'dead' underwater. Memories of his body fading like a ghost under the hull of the plane were all he had until now.

The man in the fedora popped back into his mind again.

"Brett, time travel and dimension-hopping always kind of fuddles the memories of those who don't do it often, so be prepared to not remember everything that happened here. Your memories will return, 'in time'."

'This was where I was for those three days. But why can't I remember everything? And where, or when, is here?'

A bright, blinding flash filled Brett's mind as he reeled from a series of images.

'I made it back, didn't I?' he asked his own subconscious, expecting an answer from whoever, or whatever, was opening these doors for him.

But he did not get a response.

In the blink of an eye, he realized that the entire series of memories were coming back to his mind. It was then that he realized two other things.

Every "delusion" he had had his entire life that he could remember were not delusions. They were memories trapped inside his subconscious, fighting to break out. Stressful events and empathetic moments were the key to unlocking them, as well as being in the vicinity to where the memory happened.

Second, he realized what had happened to him that fateful day in the airplane with Andrew.

Andrew, whatever he was, had somehow taken him away from this world to deposit him in another world... another dimension, in fact. It was some odd place that resembled this world, except several hundred years removed.

That world had been destroyed by "Grace", the blond woman in the pyramid; the 'Witch Queen', as he now recalled. And that Witch had helped him for some odd reason and was ingrained in his subconscious.

He hoped the Elders would help him. He knew now that many of those delusional memories were from this place. This... Atlantis. Why or how he had them? He still wasn't sure. But he was gradually putting the pieces of the puzzle together.

Brett blinked his eyes hard, pulling himself from the memory. It didn't hurt him physically, but the emotional backlash of remembering bits and pieces of three days' worth of memories was exhausting.

He opened his eyes, ready to return to whatever was 'real' at the time. He turned from the window, looking out at the Violet Pyramid to make sure he was himself again.

Looking behind him, he realized he was still in the waiting room of the Senatus. His family still sat in their seats and Ke'eli still stood in the middle of the room, blocking his pacing steps.

His concerned face brought Ke'eli closer to him.

"Brett, what's the matter?"

But their conversation would have to wait. Mason had returned, stepping through one of the curtained doorways.

"I am sorry, my friends. It took more... *convincing* than I thought. I did not mean to leave you here alone, though you were never really alone."

Mason waved his hand to the other four Seekers who had stayed by their side. All four smiled and nodded, showing that as much as the family of four were alone, the Seekers were there to protect them.

"You have nothing to fear in this place. The Tribal Elders are not only the most powerful of our people; they are the wisest."

Mason smiled as he took Brett's arm in his.

"Please, allow me to escort you all to the Council chambers. The Elders eagerly await your arrival."

Mason looked back at Ke'eli and the children with a smile on his face.

Keb jumped to his feet and reached out his arm with a toothy grin to Ke'eli, who laughed and accepted it. Xinzang grabbed Drake and threw him on her shoulder, laughing as well. Pwyll hobbled over to Kelly, stuffing a multitude of gadgets he had been fiddling with back into his pockets. Tumidus led the entourage back the way Mason had come.

"Now, there are certain things that the Elders are going to want to see," Mason started. "For instance, that each of you can control one of the four Primal Elements."

Nodding, Brett shrugged his shoulders.

"As long as I don't have to use my spit, which should be doable. What else?"

Mason cringed the slightest bit.

"Well, you will all have to be honest. The room is designed for interviewing people, but also for interrogating them. There is nothing to hide here, though. The Elders have ways of looking into one's soul, and my own Elder can read minds like he is reading the time on his pocket watch. Hide nothing from them. They only wish the best for everyone; especially you."

Mason looked back at Ke'eli. It was true. They had not spoken to anyone about their encounter on the beach, or what had happened to Brett before Ke'eli had saved him all those years ago. More importantly, Brett had not mentioned to them his encounter with 'Andrew'.

"Is this a questioning session? Do they not believe you, Mason? I thought you were one of the head honchos, well-respected by your peers and all that jazz." Brett nudged Mason the slightest bit to make sure he knew he was kidding with him.

"Ah yes, well, this is an incredibly special set of circumstances. As I have mentioned before, human women are not allowed in Atlantis for fear of some ancient prophecy that tells of a human woman mystic who destroys our country. Here, we have not one, but *two* human women right now, only a few hundred yards away from our most celebrated object, the Soulstone Pyramid."

Ke'eli interjected, "But we aren't mystics, Mason, so why do they care?"

Tumidus stopped before a large, ornate door. He looked back at Mason with concern.

"Well, Mrs. Ke'eli. I have news for you. You, all four of you, are indeed Mystics."

Ke'eli looked over to Mason, then to Brett, a questioning look on her face.

"Please, all will be revealed in time. Let us begin with the Elders and we will continue our tour, as well as begin your training!" Mason tried vainly to sound exuberant about the future for the family.

Brett gritted his teeth and looked at the ornate door.

"Screw it. Let's get this over with."

Grace calmly came out of her reverie.

Her blond hair had fallen down around her face to settle near the edges of her thighs it had grown so long. She still sat cross-legged, slowly opening her eyes. It had taken quite a bit of energy to send her thoughts as far away as she was to Brett's mind.

"You done sugar?" a voice whispered to her from not far away.

Grace cringed as other thoughts slowly made their way into her head.

Kill her.

Burn the world.

You've done it before. Do it again.

Grace squinted her eyes and put her hands to her temples.

"Yes, I'm done. Please make it stop."

"Okay, honey, just calm down. Momma's comin'."

A lithe black woman with beautiful black and orange curls for hair slowly tiptoed to sit in front of Grace on the ground.

"I got you, honey. Just breathe." She whispered, holding on to Grace's hands in her own.

Grace could feel the calming energy coming off in waves from the woman in front of her. Not just calming, but numbing.

Grace slowly breathed out as she felt the numbness wash over her. She knew it was something that she should not be embracing, but knew it was this or the fiendish voices in her head vying for control again.

She had not had as much control in this human form as she had when she was a Soulless Daemon hunter. In her tiefling form, she could quell the voices much more easily. As a pitiful human, it felt like trying to quiet the raging inferno of a hurricane.

The woman across from her slowly patted Grace's hands.

"See there, shug, you're just fine. Ain't that right? That's right. Oh, you be fine too, don't you worry. See now? Everybody's just fine."

Grace opened her eyes to take in the woman before her. Sure enough, she was talking to herself once again. Grace understood that this woman, Diana, had some kind of form of schizophrenia. At times, it was endearing. At others, downright insane.

Either way, this woman could somehow quiet the voices in Grace's head, as much as she wasn't able to quiet the voices in her own.

"That's right. She looks hungry, don't she? I bet you she could eat. My boys would eat up everything in the kitchen! All my boys. Where are the boys? You seen 'em there Grace Ann?"

It was the same conversation every time. Grace wasn't sure if the boys were in her head, or if they were real people. Either way, Grace had told her she would help her find them, which had resulted in an immediate liking.

In all honesty, Grace felt bad for the woman. She looked to be in her thirties but had wisdom all about her whenever she was in her right mind, which wasn't often. Little snippets of intellect that would surface at the strangest times. Most often, though, ramblings of scripture or of things she couldn't possibly know. Song lyrics she would sing out of the blue. Movie quotes to films long forgotten. Grace pondered it being much like having fiendish essences inside you, like she did, but not knowing how to quiet them. In time, Grace found the subtle whispers Diana would say more of a challenge in deducing then odd ramblings.

My boys are princes, they are.

He's my morning star; don't judge him by his looks.

When Hades comes, He be coming with him.

If I could save time in a bottle...

She may not look like much, but she's got it where it counts, kid!

Fruit of Life baby. Metatron knows.

Grace had sat with her long enough to know that most of the things she said made no sense. She wrote some of them down, hoping to see some sort of connection between them or some hint as to what voice in her head was saying what.

Sometimes, Grace had to restrain her to keep her from hurting herself.

Rarer than not, Diana would stare off into space and seem to be in another location entirely. She would walk into walls, see things that weren't there, or explain strange occurrences that were actually happening somewhere else in the world. Grace thought that she may had been a mystic telepath like herself, but she dared not try to peer into her mind. The roiling inferno of alternate minds trapped inside her would try to jump from one psyche to another, infiltrating Grace's own consciousness. This much she learned from her mystic predecessor about mental illness.

But sometimes Diana was fully in the here and now, like nothing had ever been bad in the world. They would have conversations about life and their shared journeys. It was at these times that Grace felt a powerful, yet odd, connection to this woman. Almost knowingly, Diana would hint at things going on about them that even Grace, the all-powerful psychic, was unaware of. But even at these times, Diana wouldn't tell her much more about her 'boys', other than that they were lost. Almost like she was purposefully keeping Grace at arm's length until the right time. A fact that Grace found unnerving but reinforced her keeping notes about what Diana said in her more off times.

Yes, Diana was aware of much more than she was letting on.

The fact that she named her right away when they first met added to the speculations.

'Grace Ann', Diana had called her from her neighboring room. Like they were two long-lost relatives.

"You remind me of one of my boys," she had said. "He was so beautiful and big and strong, and he was a hero. If we had had a girl, I would have named her Grace Ann. So, you can be my little girl and I'll be your momma!"

Grace remembered little about what happened when she arrived here in this reality. She remembered jumping into Brett's arms as they left her own crumbling reality, and that was it. She woke in an asylum strapped to a bed, being told by the orderlies that she had struck out at people in the street.

Grace didn't remember that, but she knew it was probably a result of the monsters in her head taking control. Since she had so many monsters to wrangle, they probably fought for dominance. Which, in hindsight, probably made her look pretty insane.

Hence, the asylum.

The voices threatened to take over again until she met Diana. There she was, sitting calmly in her room next door at the asylum, telling Grace that everything was going to be okay, and that an angel sent here her.

Grace laughed at that notion, but noticed the fiends in her mind weren't laughing with her. They were silent. Grace came to understand that just being close to Diana allowed her to quiet the voices. It was only when Grace flexed her considerable mind-powers that the voices came back calling.

Grace would do whatever Diana wanted to keep her close. And that included finding her 'boys'.

Regaining the full measure of her mystic power, Grace and Diana left the asylum on their great journey. Her memories slowly returning to her as well, Grace knew she needed Brett to lead her to the Soulstone. She knew it was under the ice of Antarctica, but wasn't sure how to get there. She would need help.

Grace had Diana as a numbing blockade of consciousness, allowing her to focus on the task at hand. She had a goal in mind and knew that it was still in the South Pole in this reality as well. She just had to figure out a plan of action.

This time, she would not make any mistakes.

Amalzzt had to time this perfectly. One small slip-up, one small inflection spoken the wrong way, and he'd be teleported out into space, or under the sea... under the sea! Darling, it's better, down where it's wetter... oh, sorry. FOCUS!

He flinched and took off the brown fedora to fan away the sweat beading on his upper forehead. One that many people mocked for being so neanderthal. Hey, surprise! That's what happens when you have neanderthal blood in your veins, goofus! You weren't there... you wouldn't know.

Anywho, he practiced the gesture once again. His things were packed. It was time to go. There was a woman standing out by his door. He hated to wake her up to say goodbye. But the dawn was breakin', it was early morn. She was fun, but she had to go. The uber he ordered was blowing his horn.

"So kissssss me and smile for me! Tell me that you'll wait for me! OMG! Stop already! You're distracting me! I have to fuckus!"

Amalzzt growled at no one in particular. It was true; he had found a nice young lass in the taproom last night. He always knew that it was easier to recharge one's magicks the more one partook in... *extracurricular activities.* It just so happened that his were vigorous romps that wore him out physically but recharged him *meta*physically. He gave her the boot pretty rudely this morning, and she had knocked to come back in, but Amalzzt wasn't down for a round two. If you know what I mean... Which you probably don't. Nevermind. Spicy books about Amalzzt inc...

He drew the large circle on the wall of the sparse hotel room he had rented once again. He knew the words, he just had to call on the proper imagery of where he wanted to go. He'd been many places, and many that were very similar in each reality he had visited. Why wouldn't this destination be any different from the other ones he had visited?

He was here now in the *real.* The first reality to rule all other realities. The big honcho. Numero uno. The Alphe Cosmos (Alphe is Atlantean for one, btw. Just wanted you to know that I speak Atlantean. It's a dead language. I know it looks *very* close to Latin, but it's different. Atlantean was here first broski).

"Where do I want to go? Sin City? Asgard? The Capital? Man, so many questions and so few answers! If this were a 'choose your own adventure book', I'd let you all choose for me! Alas, it's not."

Amalzzt huffed as he tried to figure out his options. He knew that wherever he wanted to go wouldn't matter. The Soulstone pyramid had a way of redirecting all portals to a random location within the dome that you could not control.

"I mean, we're still friends, right Big-Violet? You wouldn't send me out over the ocean, wouldya?"

Amalzzt shook his hands vigorously to get the anxiety out. It was time. He had recharged his main invocation, and it was giving him the thumbs up he could teleport. He knew he could because where originally, the Heartstone he had allowed him to go to other realities, it now informed him he was stuck there. It had never been like that before. Normally, Amalzzt would vanquish some foe, bed some maiden, and save the world before the Heartstone would reacquaint itself and let him leave.

Now, though, it just hummed with quiet acceptance.

"Guess I'm sticking around for longer than I expected! Can't wander around here in North Cakalaki. Won't be long before some crazy mage-hunter comes calling. Might as well go there and get this shit rolling!"

Amalzzt looked up and gave you, dear reader, the thumbs up before finally taking his place back before the wall. Closing his eyes, he focused on his destination.

The words to the spell came slowly to his mind. Ancient words of power that resonated deep within his core. A power that could wipe out entire realities. The power of the God-Hunter incarnate. The power...

Knock-knock.

"FUCK BEANS, SON OF A MOTHERLESS GOAT!"

Amalzzt yelled at the interruption at the door. Making a fist and shaking it like mad, Amalzzt relented.

Stomping to the door, he opened it wide.

"What?!"

The sight before him startled him into quiet.

JT, the young man he had saved from the alternate reality where he had also met Brett, stood there before him in a police officer's outfit.

JT stood there, mouth agape as well, as the woman from Amalzzt's earlier escapade pointed at him and started yelling something about him kicking her out before she could get her things. Oblivious, the two men just stood there, staring.

Amalzzt had not seen JT or Jasmine since that fateful day, they all being sent somewhere else. Brett had returned to his own mind. Amalzzt found himself on a dusty roadside and he could only assume that JT and Jasmine had made it back safely.

The man standing before him not only confirmed that but also gave Amalzzt some leeway into *how long* they had been back.

Where the JT in the other reality was in his 20s, this man before him looked to be in his 40s. A small streak of gray was on the sides of his temples and he looked aged, but good.

"Whaaaaaaaaaaaaaaaaaaaaaaattttttt theeeeeee fuuuuuuu-uuuuuuck?" Amalzzt worded out, breathlessly.

"What the fuck is right?! Where the hell have *you* been? It's been like 20 years since we saw you last! You look like you just got here yesterday!" JT put his hands on his belt, scolding Amalzzt like a little kid.

"Well, there now," Amalzzt said, squinting at JT's name tag on his chest, "Officer *Galland*, that's a good question! It just so happens that I arrived here about a month or so ago! As Hootie and the Blowfish would say, 'Tiiiiiime, why you punish me?'"

The woman, tired of waiting for permission to get her things, stormed into the room. Amalzzt just stood there, smiling.

"This is divine, young JT. Or should I say... Jerome... Thompson?" Amalzzt tried guessing at JT's initials again, failing miserably.

JT just nodded his head again.

"My friends call me Gray. Stop calling me JT. That was from another time and another place."

"Awwwwww! Are you saying we're friends?! That's so awesome!"

Amalzzt's eyes went wide as a thought hit him right in the side of the noggin.

"Hey, I'm not kidding. This can't be happenstance. You can't be the one on duty that just so happens to come knocking at my door as I am about to... gooooo somewhere."

Amalzzt skidded his line of thought to a hard brake. He wasn't sure how Gray was going to take his attempt at going to a place that he had just left, that I guess Gray had left 20 years ago, that he was trying to go back to... did you get all that? It made sense in my head...

"What are you planning, Amalzzt? I've seen some crazy stuff here lately, and it's made me think of my time in that other place. A devilish-looking *man* and his entourage came at me and my family not too long ago. It made me think of... *her.*"

Amalzzt knew exactly who *she* was. He had lost track of the Witch Queen as well recently when they both arrived in this reality. He thought he could find her, and occasionally, he would get snippets of her location, but then he would be blocked off suddenly (if you're still confused, read the last section again! Dang dirty Diana! Gotta be making my head trip!).

That made Amalzzt's mind up.

"Listen Gray. She's here in this reality, and I don't know what she's up to. I've been trying to track her, but I keep getting blocked. There's only one thing that she wants: the Violet Pyramid. Remember that thing? It's called the Soulstone, and it's at the center of the secret continent of Atlantis that, yes, *does exist* here in this reality. It's under the ice in Antarctica."

Gray looked forlornly at Amalzzt. He knew where this was going.

"And you need my help to stop her." Gray sighed as he said it.

"Actually, no. I need Jasmine's help." Amalzzt just shrugged, smiling.

"I'm just kidding, bro! Yes, I could use both your help! If she gets her hands all up inside that pyramid, she could do what she did in the other reality we were in. You weren't there for all the craziness when it happened; she basically destroyed the world. If there is anyone here that you care for, your best bet would be to stop her with my help."

Gray just looked at Amalzzt. Whereas a normal person would have laughed the notion of all this away, Gray was not a normal man. He grew up in that alternate reality and saw the devastation she had sowed. He knew that if she could do it again, she probably would.

Taking a deep breath, Gray nodded his head.

"What the fuck are you wackos talking about?" The woman scowled at Gray and Amalzzt as she slinked her way past them both. Looking back at the pair like they were crazy, she made for the elevator. Right before she stepped inside, she looked back at Amalzzt and hesitated, before she put her thumb and pinky to her ear and lips and mouthed the words 'call me'.

"Well, that was interesting! She likes crazy, I can tell."

Gray just shook his head again, before he took out his cellphone.

"What's good Gray? By the way, I have to commend you on your anatomy. (tee hee hee!)"

Gray just looked at him again.

"Get your stuff. You're coming home with me. If we're going to do this, we will need all the help we can get."

"Awesome! Road-trip! We going to get Jasmine so we can save the day together? Three amigos? Or maybe Three Musketeers! Even though she's a girl... we can make it work!"

Gray just nodded again.

"If we're doing this, we're taking everyone. No way I'm leaving my family here."

"Wait-wait-wait... *family?* Gray Galland's gots kids? So, wait, if you see the future and she sees the past... do your kids see... the present? Wtf?"

Gray just stared hard at the strange man, which he now remembered he did often when they were together in their alternate reality.

"Got it. Get my stuff and let's go. Right behind you, Officer sir!"

Amalzzt reached back through the doorway to grab his fedora.

Winking at you, he whispered, "Guess you all will have to read the next series of books to find out more!" before closing the door behind him.

CHAPTER TEN

ILLUMINATIONS

("There are Witches Among us / The Bank / The Niffler from the Fantastic Beasts and Where to Find Them Soundtrack by James Newton Howard)

"The family of Dourdon. Father Brett. Mother Ke'eli. The eldest child, Kelly. Second eldest, Drake. Hailing from California of the United States of America, Olde Earth."

The robotic voice echoed in the air as the family looked around sheepishly.

Brett cringed for the slightest of seconds when the announcer proclaimed their names. Something about the titles and their names stood out as strange to him.

The lights had come up somewhat, enough for the family and the group of Seekers behind them to make out individual silhouettes. Like a clock, there were twelve people surrounding the dais, all on a circular balcony fifteen feet above their heads.

They sat in chairs, some with their hands over the railing to see the recent additions. One was so large they could see his knees.

All sat in silence.

The group remained on the dais in silence as well. While the family stood central to the circle with their backs to the door they came in, the Seekers stood behind them, more to the shadows, but still very much present.

Several moments passed before anything happened at all. Then, a voice.

"My good Master Clemens. Are you protecting the family?"

The voice was that of Mason's Elder.

Mason stepped forward into the greater light of the main dais.

"My Lord, Seeker group Kapha has decided that a just and fair interview of the family should be undertaken. Thus, we have taken steps to protect them from mental, arcane, divine, and spiritual intrusion. We ask that you speak plainly to the family so that the Council all will realize their answers, as opposed to what we who are trained in the Art can decipher without words."

"So, you have enacted a barrier to protect whom, exactly? Them from us? Or us from them?"

Again, Mason's Elder.

Mason looked down at his own feet, then back to the family.

Brett surprised everyone by taking a stand.

"Hey, we're here. No offense sir, but can we get this thing moving along? We're all tired, hungry and dirty and have questions of our own we'd like to ask. So, if you don't mind, sir, grill away."

Mason's worried look turned into a smile.

Shuffling and a slight muffled cough broke the rest of the silence.

"True right! Let's get this ball rolling!" Someone excitedly said, standing on his chair. He leaned forward onto the rail far enough that the light illuminated his features. A smile from ear to ear on a green face that Mason hoped would be contagious to the rest of the watchers on the dais. The goblin had fancy golden studs in his nose and golden hoops in his giant ears. His eyes went from exuberant to super intense in less time than it took to blink.

Mason's Elder continued. "Very well. You will see we have brought out several items. Please, show us your ability with these items."

A plate appeared then, carried by a robotic sentry golem. On it were a pile of sand, a glass of water, a feather, and a piece of coal.

Mason looked back, but the family got the hint.

The children, always excited to show off their talents, leaped at the opportunity.

Drake veritably pushed Kelly back to get to the plate first. Even though he was only eleven years old, he knew what the group wanted him to do. He looked back at his father and mother as he reached the test to make sure they approved.

Brett, with a grin on his face, nodded his head. Ke'eli held her husband's arm tight as she looked on.

Drake stuck his tongue out at his sister as he turned back to the tray, smiling all the bigger. He looked at the four items, aware of which were meant for him. The sense that so many people were watching him, though, made him nervous. Where he was normally a very boisterous and excited child, he had suddenly become very shy.

Ke'eli stepped up beside him. "It's okay, honey. Just relax and do what you like to do. You will be fine. Don't even worry about who's here. Have fun with it!"

Famous last words...

He turned back to the plate; confidence restored. He knew that if he could hang out with a dragon-lady and make awesome fire creatures with his mind, then lighting a stupid piece of coal would be easy. He focused on the piece of coal, hoping to light the thing on fire, but found his eye drifting ever so slightly to the other three items as well.

Have fun with it.

Brett knew that technically, both Kelly and Drake could have manipulated all the items on the tray, so he thought it odd that they would bring out things that were so obvious. Fire was all-consuming, and the air was the opposite. As much as Drake could burn everything up, Kelly could cool everything down. But it was a show all the same.

Brett watched as Drake focused on the coal in front of him.

Suddenly, and all at the same time, the pile of sand melted to glass, the water boiled, the feather burst into flames while the coal ignited and melted through the tray to fall with a 'clunk' to the floor.

The reaction surprised even Drake. He had only meant to burn his sister's feather to mess with her, so he stepped back open-mouthed as well as the coal hissed on the floor, flames sparking.

"You jerk!" Kelly yelled out, pushing him out of the way and raising her hand up.

A blast of wind flew out of her then, pushing the coal across the room and leaving a burning trail of black along the way behind it. Shocked at her own force as well, she turned her hand to blow out the feather, which was still alight.

The coal smacked against the back wall, shattering into several smaller pieces that continued to burn. The feather, which was floating alit in the air, was at the perfect angle to include some Elders with the airy blast that emanated from Kelly's hands.

Immediately, everyone gasped as the gust of wind traveled towards the Elders. The force was not enough to harm but caused the ones that were looking over the railing to fall back into their seats.

The feather itself, though not on fire anymore, settled lightly on top of the short and hairy Elder directly to the front of the group at 12 o'clock. The effect was instantaneous.

"Ah! Iz it on fire?! Get ze zing off me before my beard burns!"

The Elder to his left leaped down from his chair and tried to spray a sort of fire-suppressant on his colleague while others tried to calm the man down.

Some noticed that the feather was not even on fire anymore, but the roaring tumult drowned out any good sense.

Kelly stood there, looking utterly decimated by what she had done. She tried to apologize as Drake stood beside her, saying it wasn't her fault. Though he was typically a prankster, he cared more for his sister than he let on.

Both children tried to tell the Elder that the feather was not on fire anymore, and that he should not have to worry about a small feather, anyway. Their childish innocence came out then, and they laughed at the commotion as the white frothy substance poured all over the man's head.

Brett also tried hard not to laugh, but saw the dilemma brewing. Being the disciplinarian, he gently put his hands on both of his children's shoulders, calming them down instantly. He moved them back behind him to Ke'eli, who brought them close to her side.

The escapade above them was finally dying down as the Elders returned to their seats. There was still some murmuring from above, but all seemed to settle once they saw the older male take the front stage.

He looked over at the glass of boiling water and focused. The remaining water instantly cooled, even though the container's rim had folded over on top of itself from the heat, prohibiting him from getting to its insides.

Looking at the melted pile of sand next to it, Brett remembered his basic chemistry lessons. Melted sand was glass, and if Ke'eli could control the sand, then it would be logical that she could control the glass.

Brett looked back at his wife, who already seemed to understand as she came up beside him, smiling.

Ke'eli closed her eyes and pictured the melted glass of water. Imagining it to be like a closed flower, she tilted her head ever so slightly with a curl from the corner of her lips. Brett knew she was thinking of her beautiful garden back at home. All kinds of flowers grew there, but her favorites had been the roses and tulips.

Her appreciation and understanding of the plants helped her now. She knew not to work too quickly for fear of breaking the glass, but also knew that the cup was still hot.

Slowly, the lips of the glass that had melted inward bent backwards. As beautiful as any real flower, the top of the glass folded and molded itself, using the heat that Drake had supplied to create an object of art. The container did not break; it just came alive and opened the top of the glass so that Brett could get to the water inside. The result imitated a gorgeous flower in full bloom.

Brett saw his opportunity as Ke'eli opened her eyes. Focusing on the now-cooler liquid contents, he made it rise out of the glass to form small floating water bubbles. He slowly made them hover over to the burning pieces of coal, where one by one, he dropped the bubbles on top of them, putting out their fires with slight hisses.

Everyone looked at each other, smiling, and mumbling to themselves as Brett put the finishing touches on the coal. Few were paying attention to him as he finished putting his son's fires out.

Though the back wall was not that far away, Brett still had a small amount of difficulty aiming the bubbles directly on top of each piece of coal. One proved quite difficult, as it was partly behind a pillar holding up the second floor where the Elders sat. Brett stared at the thing in frustration, trying to put it out. He wished it would just be a couple more inches closer!

That last piece of coal suddenly slid several more inches closer to Brett. His eyes widened at the sight, wondering if anyone else had noticed it. As he put out the piece, he looked back to his entourage, but none recognized the feat. He then looked up to the Elders, but if they had noticed, he could not tell.

Brushing it off, he turned and walked back to his family and the Seekers, waiting for the decision of the Elders. All four together again, they stood tall and looked toward Mason's Elder.

"That wasn't exactly how I would have showed them, but hey, it worked." Mason whispered to Brett as he rejoined his wife.

"Eh, I think it was better!" he replied.

Murmuring from the Elders surrounded the family and the Seekers. No one could hear anything much, which was part of the trick of having the Elders in their enclosed space above them. They were all speaking in their normal tones, but the enchantment prohibited the ones below them from hearing them sufficiently.

Finally, the mumbling died down.

Tumidus stepped forward, bowing, as he recognized one Elder who seemed about to speak. It looked as though he wanted to say something but stopped at once as he saw the look on his Elder's face. Slowly, still in a bow, he went back to return to his place.

A tall woman with large, dark eyes and pale gray skin stood at the edge of her rail, motes of dancing light swirling all around her. She leaned out over the rail to address the group, and her face did not appear all that appeased.

"You do indeed seem to be possessed of great power. But you are inexperienced. The Four were powerful as well but could control their abilities. Not to mention, they were much more advanced in their years. Before me, I see two children who should be brought to the Boroughs, and two adults who have somehow slipped past the ever-watchful eye of the Mysteries and their Seekers.

"It has been our discussion now that none in Atlantis are of the ability to properly train this group of newcomers, and it is with fear that we permit them to remain here. None on the council wish to bear the great responsibility of keeping them in check, nor do we have the time or inclination to wait out our seasons to see if these are, indeed, the Four in question."

Tumidus then stepped forward, his smile gone.

"My Lady, we five will take on the responsibility of caring for the family. We will teach them all there is to know about Atlantis and educate them in their abilities."

Tumidus didn't need to look around for his fellows to know that they all felt the same way.

The Elven Elder bowed her head.

"We thought you might respond that way. Unfortunately, even you five, all of considerable power yourselves, are not suited to properly maintain control over what we consider these to be proverbial 'loose cannons.' It has been the Council's decision to remove the memory of this place from the family and to return them to their homes, save a vote from even one Elder to take custody of them instead."

Mason began to step forward to protest, but his own Elder stopped him.

"You would be wise to heed the word of the Elders, Seeker." The bald human began. "The Prophecy states that a female human mystic shall lay waste to the *entire world*, including our very home, if she is not thwarted. Some even speculate that it is at this very Age that it could occur! Before me, I see not one, but *two* human female mystics. In all incarnations of the Four, they have been full-grown adults. I believe this is nothing more than the natural evolution of humankind and some sort of spillage from the elemental planes."

Mason stopped dead in his tracks. Looking back at the family, he could see the defeat in their eyes as well. Something within him though told him not to go down without a fight. But how?

The Elder continued, "We have decreed that the family must be separated, their memories and abilities erased, and for them to be returned to the Olde World with no knowledge of us or our people."

Brett lunged forward suddenly, knocking Mason off the dais and he himself pouncing down to face the human speaker.

"This is bullshit! Tell them Mason! Monsters have attacked us over and over and you want to send us back home defenseless?! We'll be dead before dawn! The only thing that has protected us is our ability!"

Golem robots appeared from the darkness then, weapons leveled Brett's way. Ke'eli grabbed her children and brought them closer to her, a mother's protective instinct overriding her safety.

But she was not alone.

Keb stalked up beside her, blocking her left flank as Xinzang blocked the right flank. Pwyll also came up to supply coverage from behind, his small body covering just enough of the children so that they were all encased in a shield of flesh.

A low rumble echoed from the second floor behind the family as the monstrous brute there rose to its full height, his head inches from the roof. The thing was not a giant, but it well should have been.

"Calm yourselves or I will crush you where you stand." The thing rumbled.

Brett knew they were at a disadvantage. There were nine of them down on the dais, but they were surrounded by robotic killing machines with twelve of the supposedly most powerful beings in the world above them. And two of the nine behind him were his children.

Putting his hands up slowly, Brett lowered his head, looking sidelong at Mason.

"Hey, it's okay. We figured there was a slim chance in Hell that we'd be staying here. After everything you said about this place, it's probably better that we don't cause any civil unrest by poking around. At least we get to go home, right? For as well as that is worth." Brett forced a smile as he clapped Mason on the shoulder.

But the thought did not settle in Mason's head. Something told him to fight. He turned back around to face his Elder.

"My Lord, we respect the council's wishes. It is my request that a formal vote be taken up so that the Four can hear from your own mouths that you do not wish to take them under your charge, and in fact, wish to banish them from this place, which has always held the memory of the Four in high regard."

Mason was heated. The Elder looked down on him and, without even the slightest nod, looked to his brethren.

"My fellow Elders, Master Clemens has requested a verbal vote. We will deliberate the vote and its ramifications amongst ourselves and begin the voting process shortly thereafter." Without even blinking, he nodded to the family and the Seekers, "You are free to speak amongst yourselves while we converse."

The lights dimmed as the muttering speech from the Elders became once again diluted to everyone on the first floor.

Brett spun and returned to his family, hugging them closely.

"It will be okay," he said, but even he couldn't suppress a tear.

("The Return of the King" from the Lord of the Rings: The Return of the King Soundtrack by Howard Shore)

Xinzang looked up around the circular chamber of the Senatus, where the most respected and powerful of her country's leaders worked.

She had never met the other Elders before, but was nominally close to her own draconian Elder, Bao Chányú, who had practiced the same form of Gung-Fu as she. She knew much about the others, as she had been employed by a Seeker team longer than most.

Drake was close to her scaly leg behind her, she protecting him from the golems that had appeared from the shadows. She could feel his hot hand wrapped around her leg, the other wrapped around his mother's. His face peeked out from between their two bodies, curious but ready.

She looked down at him, his eyes wondrous but fearful.

If this were going to be the last time they were to be together, Zang decided it would not be in fear. She kneeled on one knee to be closer to the boy, their faces on level ground.

"Are you afraid hatchling?" she asked, whispering.

"Yes, but no. They are going to erase our memories? Does that mean I won't remember you too?"

She lowered her head, fighting back the tears.

"I know not, young one. Some say that you can fight through the loss of memory to remember the things you hold dear. If you care deeply about someone, then your memory will return in time more quickly."

Drake hugged Zang around her neck, leaning his face against her scaly head.

"Well then, I will remember you pretty quick." he whispered.

Tears rolled down her scales as Zang tried furtively to wipe them away. She needed something else to talk about.

Looking up, she noticed that all the Elders were speaking amongst themselves, except the human Elder, who sat there, staring down at the group.

Something odd about the way he stared at them had her scales bristling.

Looking to the right of the human above her, Zang had an idea. The plane-touched who were blessed by fire could see much better in the darkness, almost endowing them with the ability to see clearly in the dark. Most of the elemental plane-touched were orcs like Keb, but Zang thought it interesting to ask all the same.

"Hatchling, can you see the people up on the second floor?"

"Yeah, some of them. They're kind of shadowy looking, though. Why?"

Drake's attention was at once drawn to the balcony above him, now that Zang had told him to look.

Personally, Zang could not see the shadows that Drake could. The darkness blocked her vision. But it comforted her to know that he would see what she was about to talk to him about.

"Well hatchling, let me tell you about the Elders of our country and who now leads in their stead."

Drake was immediately captivated, fascination etched on his face.

Looking up to the balcony directly in front of them from the door they entered, Zang began the clockwise count of the current Elders, and the True Elders who came before them.

"You see before you now the Elders who have stepped in to take the places of the True Elders before them. The True Elders are not affected by the passage of time and will live forever. They are epitomized as Gods and Goddesses to the rest of the world, and when they entered their temporary slumber, others rose to take their place."

"Many believe, rightfully so, that becoming an Elder gives upon you a certain power that grows as those who are faithful to you grow as well. Many aspire to be an Elder, just at the chance of reaching a sense of immortality. The greed and selfishness of becoming one sometimes outweighs the good of being a respected and cherished leader."

"There are twelve Elders in total, one standing for each racial Tribe. Before us is a dwarf from the Dwervas Tribe. The True Elder is Epimeth, a strong and wise ruler. He is a paladin of the highest order, creator of the Atlantean Guard and ultimate protector of Atlantis. Many attribute him to Odin the All-Father and he is well-respected. In his stead is the current King, Adelhelm. Though he aspires to greatness, he is more concerned with the deep and dark recesses of the Earth and what mysteries there are to be discovered. He believes that there is more of a threat from the Mimics beneath our feet than there are from any fiends beyond our borders."

"Next is a gnome, like Pwyll, from the Tuath Tribe. Their true Elder is Amperes, an intelligent and innovative leader. He created machines and constructs that would eventually lead to the self-aware golems who surround us now. Amperes created the Pioneers, a group of intellects who look to understand the sciences through technology and experimentation. He is commonly associated with Lugh and is an expert craftsman. In his stead is the current Cadeyrn, called Rí. I know little about the machinations of gnomes, but this one seems intent on artificial intelligence and merging the machine with flesh. Can you see his artificial limbs?"

Drake squinted into the darkness, trying to make out the machine-like arms of the gnome, since that was all he could see of the man's torso. Sure enough, Drake smiled, nodding.

Zang looked to the boy as Ke'eli might, indulging in the innocent youth and carefree attitude of the child, even in the face of adversity.

Turning the boy ever so slightly, she made a motion towards the next leader, who she could make out in the darkness as well. A palpable aura of blue energy glowed about the elf, making the shadows a strange pool of swirling darkness.

"Next is an elf, like Tumidus, from the Aelf Tribe. Their True Elder is the magnanimous Elvamon, who delights in the wonder and chaos of magic. He is a powerful sorcerer who can twist reality as easy as twisting a cord of string. Many of the more powerful and innovative magical devices we have now, we owe to him. Not only that, but he also learned to harness the power of the pyramids to control the surrounding weather, earning him the nickname of the Storm Lord. This translated to his being recognized as Zeus in your world. In his place is a female Basilinna by the name of Caelina, who looks to expand the power of Atlantis beyond our borders. She thinks that humankind is ready to receive the benefits, and no doubt the leadership from her, of all people, from the Atlantean Empire. Some believe that she used deceptive magic to gain her seat on the Council, and there is talk of her ejection."

As if she could hear them, the Basilinna looked Drake's way, her eyes glowing. She was more elf than alien-looking, and beautiful in a haunting way. The blue glow made her almost translucent, and Drake thought it would be cool to learn magic.

A flash of fire illuminated the next Elder, as he used a small device to light a large cigar.

"Ah yes, the goblinoids."

This was the one group that Drake had shown the most interest in seeing. Zang caught on quickly that Drake was waiting for her to continue.

"The goblinoids hail from the Vikhura Tribe and are actually three separate species. The one you see there is a true goblin, while there are also kobolds and gremlins as well that make up the bulk of their kind. Each has a specialty that puts them apart from their cousins, but almost all the recent Elders have been goblin because of their True Elder, Mneseus. He is the Master of Secrets, and it is he who we owe for keeping the ultimate secret of Atlantis within our borders. He helped to create the

Inoculators, who specialize in using alchemy to unlock the secrets of the universe. In his place now is the Raja, Mighty-and-Great-is-the-Lineage Prabodh, who claims to be descended from one of Mneseus' own children. I cannot honestly speak to the depredations of the goblinoids, only that they can be both exceptionally reliable, but also extremely dangerous."

Drake looked upon the balcony as the goblin sucked in from his cigar, his face briefly lit up. The gold piercings glowed from the light as the man leaned back and exhaled smoke into the air above him. Right away, a vent opened in the ceiling that sucked in the smoke.

Continuing the lesson, she turned Drake some more.

"And here are the orcs of the Ngoma Tribe. Keb hails from one of the many elemental cities that we have floating around here in our country, and the orcs are generally the most plane-touched out of us all. They have a specific genetic familiarity with other planes, because they speak with our long-dead ancestors the most."

"They can talk to dead people?" Drake asked, eyes wide. He did not know that about Keb.

Zang chuckled. "Yes hatchling. Orcs practice the art of Shamanism and can converse, see, and interact with all kinds of spirits. Keb is also attuned to an earth spirit, which is how he can control the land beneath our feet. This is why you and your family are so important to us; you are not orcs, yet you can 'speak' to the elements and control them."

"Can I talk to dead people?" Drake asked, one eyebrow arched, as if he was not sure he wanted to or not.

Zang tilted her head, pondering.

"I know not, young one," and the thought of him leaving hit her again like a brick in the face. Trying to change the subject, she continued, "the orcs are very skilled in it. Their true Elder is called Autochthone, and he is able to speak to all the spirits of the land, whether they come from our world or another. He also helped to create the Interpreters, which do exactly what they sound like they do. The elements rage in our world, and it is only through their direct communion and control that they do not destroy everything we hold dear. In his place is the incredibly wise and powerful Laman called Njinga. Do you know why he is wise?"

Zang smiled as she nudged Drake, hoping he would get the hint.

Drake looked over at Zang, realization dawning.

"Because he can control fire?" Drake's toothy grin had Zang's fang-filled lips up in a wide smile as well.

Nodding, Zang continued with the next Elder.

"Though not one of the original ten Tribes, some might say that this Tribe is more important than many of the rest. Without their aid, our country would have been lost and the world would be in ruin. They are the aquarians, and they own the sea and its dark depths. They are the ones who came to us from Mu and Lemuria, discovering the magic stone called Deepstone at the bottom of our oceans. With it, we have been able to create the Childe Pyramids at our borders, as well as many other marvels. Though not an original 'Primal' Elder, Elder Menecus was the first to find his 'Soulmate' in the world and is recognized as the official Tribal Elder to the aquarians."

Drake looked up, puzzled.

"Soulmate? Like his wife?"

Zang smiled sadly. Many had aspired to find their Soulmate in the world, which was one reason she considered leaving the role of Seeker behind.

"Yes hatchling, a Soulmate is the genetically and spiritually matched opposite to your own soul and they are the rarest thing in all the world. To find one is to find an everlasting love that transcends space and time. Some say it is another 'gift' from the Soulstone, while others say that it is Fate that steers us to those we are destined to be with."

Drake nodded, trying to absorb the mass of information.

Zang stared off wistfully.

"A Soulmate unlocks your truest potential once you touch, opening your mind to the greatest possibilities and making your bodies almost one entity. Elder Menecus was one of the first, but he was definitely not the last."

Zang looked over at Drake, testing her loyalties. She decided it did not matter, since they would most likely not see each other again after today anyway.

"Can you keep a secret hatchling?" she asked.

Drake, nodding enthusiastically, leaned in closer.

"Do you know why I do not fear for you after today? Why I believe you *will* remember me and this place? Why I think you four are still destined for greatness?" she hesitated before she continued, making sure Drake was paying full attention.

"Your parents are Soulmates."

Zang pulled away to see Drake's exasperated reaction.

"Shhhh, you must keep this a secret from everyone for now. Do you know what this means, though?" she smiled.

Drake shook his head no.

"You are the children of two Soulmates. You have inherited their gifts and their love, which is everlasting. You will never really forget, and you will always find your way back to each other."

Drake hugged Zang close, whispering in her ear.

"I don't want to worry about forgetting you. I don't want to leave. I want to stay here with you and learn from you."

Zang understood. She wanted him to stay, too.

Growling under her breath, she moved on.

"Ah, I must tell you about the Beastlord!"

Turning Drake to face the way they came in, Drake looked up at the monstrosity of a human that stood behind them all.

"There stands an ogre of the beast-born Accala Tribe. The True Elder is also ogrish in size, but is actually a woman."

Drake piqued up at the thought of the first beast-born Elder being an ogre woman.

"Yes, I thought that might make you wonder. She is one of the strongest in the land, a great General of the original Army of Atlantis, and is cunning in her tactics. True Elder Azaes did not stray as far from the original barbarism that gripped our species when we were all once humans. She is known to eat the hearts of her enemies and as the great equalizer of men. She leads the Horde in the South, separating her Tribe into different clans who war against each other to cull the weak. Though they may seem brutish, they have an unbridled rage that comes out when they battle, dimming them to both physical and mental pain. Their current leader is the Tlatoani named Bidziil, who is also an ogre. He is strong at heart, but aspires to sweep through the whole of Atlantis, slaying any who are not pure Atlantean. Unfortunately, that would include the half-bloods, which he sees as misfit mistakes in his eyes."

Zang had heard about the half-elf that Ke'eli had met on the train and expressed her disdain that she was not there to aid her against Tumidus and his choice of words. The family had learned as little since then about the 'chimeras' in Atlantis, but Zang knew Drake thought it sounded cool and that he wanted to see what some of the more exotic mixtures looked like.

"The Dark Knights of the undead are next."

Drake's eyes lit up again. Scanning the darkness, he could see the two pinpricks of blue light that edged out from the encroaching darkness. He knew them to be the creature's eyes from what he had been told earlier, to differentiate them from the evil, uncontrolled undead.

Like the elf's eyes, the undead seemed to sense that Drake was looking at him because he turned his head towards the lower floor.

Drake averted his gaze, not wanting to lock eyes with the thing.

Zang caught the movement and situated her body to block the visage of the undead creature.

"The undead are like the aquarians in that they are not an official Tribe of Atlantis. The True Elder, Arawn, was a gnome in life. Not long after we all were changed into our current forms, Arawn passed away. He was the first of the undead to rise back into un-life. Because he was the first, he acts as the medium between the world of the living, and those others who also came back to join him from the other side. The undead are a special occurrence, in that their existence gives some Atlanteans hope that when they die, they might come back to the world of the living. You see, the undead remain tied to our Earthly plane, if they are remembered. Once the energy of being forgotten coalesces around their necrotic bodies, they lose their mental faculties and 'forget' as well. For this reason, many of the villains we have had in Atlantis have been the undead, as they strive to become a footnote in our history so that none will ever forget. The current Lord is Nadir, a former human who returned after the War of the Old Ones. He is cruel and un-empathetic and would rather the whole of the world resort to necromancy at the school for the dead, called Scholomance, to use both our allies and our enemies who fall in battle to full effect."

Zang snarled her lip up toward the undead, making sure to still block Drake's view of the thing.

"You don't seem to like him very much." Drake said, patting her on the back.

Zang looked back into Drake's eyes.

"Hatchling, the scalehide, who are next on the balcony, abhor the unnatural order. Things live and then things die; this is the way. Scalehide, like myself, strives to find neutrality in all things, whether good or bad. While I cannot say that the undead are not battle-hardened and worthy fighters, I cannot also agree that their presence brings with it the mindless undead, who are as much a scourge as any living, breathing enemy."

"So, if the smart undead weren't around, then the dumb ones wouldn't be either and there wouldn't be anything for them to fight?" Drake asked, the realization dawning on him.

"Precisely. But enough of them. Next are the most important Tribe of all, that of the Xia. We are scalehide, for we are born of the mighty dragon. The True Elder is Basilea, and she was the first to become bonded to a dragon as well."

"What does bonded mean?" Drake asked.

"I am glad you asked hatchling. To be bonded is to have your life intimately shared with that of another creature. Much like a Soulmate, a creature and an Atlantean share a blood-bond that brings their lives together as one. The creature and its rider age much more slowly and they can feel their emotions, even from far away. My Lady Basilea was the first to bond with the King of Dragons, Bahamut himself. They slumber under the mountains of Kunlun now, waiting for when Atlantis needs them, and they awake."

"So only an Atlantean can bond with a dragon?" Drake asked, saddened by the idea.

Zang caught on that the child would love nothing more than to have a dragon by his side.

"Well, none really knows. The only people to have bonded with anything have been from Atlantis, including the Four, of whom I believe you are descended. If there is Atlantean blood in your veins, then you can bond with a dragon, should you want."

"Can I bond with you?" Drake asked, humor in his voice.

"Ah hatchling, I do not think you could take being bonded with as mighty a dragon as I!" she laughed.

"Does this Elder have a real dragon too?"

Zang smiled. She did not agree with her current Elder on many things but could not deny that she was worthy of the post.

"Bao Chányú is many things, but no, she is not bonded. She *is* something else, though; she is a Dragon Princess."

Drake's archetypical one eyebrow rose in curiosity again.

"A Dragon Prince or Princess is one who will receive the energy and essence of an ancient dragon when it is time for it to die."

Zang could see that she had lost Drake. She continued, trying to make it as easy as possible to understand.

"Dragons are not native to this plane or to this Earth. They were some of the first creatures to interact with our early Atlantean Empire, and they were worthy allies. They found out, though, that the creatures did not stop growing. Some of the earliest dragons were the size of mountains and could swallow up entire lakes!"

Drake's eyes were open and paying rapt attention.

"We found early on that when a dragon died, its energy remained behind here on Earth. That energy suffused the ground, causing strange things to happen. Creatures that absorbed the energy became more like dragons; they did not stop growing and were extremely dangerous. So, Elder Basilea discovered a way where an Atlantean could voluntarily share its body with that of a dying dragon, allowing it to be reborn through their own flesh. It is an honor to be chosen, and it is many times at random."

Drake squinted, looking at Zang sidelong.

"So, wait, she's got a dragon *inside* her right now?"

"Yes, hatchling, she shares her body with that of a dragon essence. Though sharing her body prolongs her own lifespan, in time, the dragon will emerge, and she will be no more."

"Sooooo, it's going to eat her?" Drake seemed puzzled.

"No, young one. The draconic essence will take over her mortal form, turning her into a full-fledged dragon once again to repeat the process tens of thousands of years from now."

A growl from up above brought their attention to the very scalehide they had been talking about. The silhouette of the dragon Elder's wings expanded, stretching out into the light. She appeared to be arguing with her neighbor, who Drake could make out had a *lot* of hair on his head.

"Ah, she is arguing with Pharaoh Lycean, the sitting Elder for the Maati Tribe. He is also reportedly descended from the Tribal Elder, Diapepe, the first werewolf."

Zang knew she would have Drake's attention at the mention of werewolves.

"Yes hatchling. Diapepe is an immensely powerful skin-walker, able to take the shape of many animals. His normal form, though, is that of a Lycan, which is half wolf, half human. He is the guardian of nature and the deep recesses of the forests where his people call home. The skinwalkers of the Maati Tribe are some of the most varied of all the Atlanteans. Every kind of combination of animal and human is in West Atlantis, from bull-humans to turtle-humans. Diapepe led them all with a strict viewpoint on what they could and could not do outside Atlantis. It appears his progeny do not agree with his forefather's ideals."

A small shape was standing next to the werewolf, her head barely visible above the railing to the balcony.

Both Zang and Drake squinted in the darkness, trying to make out what was going on.

"It is the Malikah of the halflings, Sarai. She is most beloved of the Eloah Tribe she represents, and the whole of Atlantis."

Zang knew Drake had already had some experience with the halflings, so she kept it short.

"The halflings are led by the True Elder Eloahsippus, a woman of fantastic healing ability. Her clerics are always on the front lines, supplying healing and defense to our fighters. Sarai is a worthy fighter as well, refusing to kneel to an enemy's onslaught. I have seen her battle prowess personally and am glad that she is represented on this council. She appears to be trying to calm Lycean down. She would be better off putting a leash on the creature!"

Zang smiled over at Drake as she said it, getting a smile in return.

The group was in a heated discussion.

All but one.

Zang turned towards the human Elder, Dharmapala Avici. She was going to tell Drake about him and the humans, but she found she was locked in a stare with him. This entire time, he had not moved from his spot nor taken his gaze off the family.

Shaking her head, Zang noted the human stood up straight, looking about the darkened second level of the room. Zang could tell from the corners of her eyes that all motion seemed to slow and stop.

Malikah Sarai returned to her seat as the others began to sit down as well.

"Yeah, who is *that* guy?"

Drake had caught Zang's stare at the human who had done most of the talking before the minor break.

Zang lowered her head, trying to focus. Something buzzed at the back of her skull; something that rang of familiarity.

She could feel an energy then between Drake and her own body. One that filled her with physical warmth, but also mental and spiritual.

She squinted her eyes, trying to remember a memory that did not seem like hers.

An event where she was to bring the child somewhere to someone.

The child, Drake.

Zang looked at Drake as he returned the stare. She knew he could feel something was off with her. He leaned forward and placed his head against hers. As their heads touched, a jolt of heat transferred between the two, clearing away some of the fog of her mind.

"He is Dharmapala Avici, the Elder of the humans. He has taken the place of the True Elder Miestor, the only Elder to have disappeared with no knowledge thousands of years ago. The humans are mystics, their power coming from their minds. Their Tribe is called the Devas Tribe, but there are none now who are alive to say that they are direct descendants of the founders of the Tribe. It is now only a name."

Zang tried to continue but found strange revelations in her mind that she fought to figure out.

"Avici is... Avici is... a human. A human mystic... who wants... what does he want?" Zang asked herself as much as she asked Drake.

But Drake just stood there, not knowing himself.

Zang narrowed her eyes up at the human connecting dots.

She was about to stand back up when Drake tugged on her gi.

"Who is that there?" he asked, pointing into the shadows on the first floor.

Zang, still transfixed by the strange orders she was remembering in her head, looked about, but saw only the golems standing before her.

Drake's question and her dot-connecting would have to wait, though. The human mystic spoke again.

"We are back in session and are prepared to have your vote."

CHAPTER ELEVEN

THE KING RETURNS

Brett stared hard at the twelve "Elders" above him, ready to do violence if he needed to protect his family. He did not entirely trust those around him on the first floor, but he totally didn't trust these supposed benefactors above him.

Brett weighed his options as best he could, relying on first physical brute strength, followed by what he thought was the most powerful 'magic-people' next. He figured the elf was magical and that the gnome had some gadgets or whatnot. The giant behind him, the undead guy and the wolf-thing would be his prime targets.

Take them out, and the rest should be easy, right?

"The vote will be carried out by a majority. In the case of a tie, the adjudication will go to our High Elder for this month, June, which is Xul and belongs to the beast-born as tradition demands, as our High King is not in presence, nor has he been for quite some time."

A chuckle came out behind the family as the ogre of a man crossed his arms across his chest.

Brett looked up at the thing and snarled himself.

Oh, let me at that stupid thing!

"The charge is, majority rule to allow this dangerous family of humans from the Olde World to remain in Atlantis, under the care of the ruling party, for the said ruling party to take these four under their wing, to train as you see fit, taking them as your charges to be responsible for whatever good, or bad, they do, say aye aloud. If not, say nay."

The vote went around the room, starting directly in front of the group.

The surly yet short man stood from his chair, his beard poking out over the rail before him, still covered in white foam. "King Adelhelm of the dwarf Tribe Dwervas votes nay."

Another short man, gears winding as his chair elevated his body up for him, looked down over the group with a pair of what looked like binoculars. "Cadeyrn Rí of the gnome Tribe Tuath votes aye."

Drake brought his fist and elbow down with a loud "yes", drawing glares from everyone else before being ushered back behind Ke'eli.

The glowing woman, who remained standing, bowed her head. She raised her eyes to her companions around the room after several seconds before returning her gaze to the family. "Basilinna Caelina of the elf Tribe Aelf votes aye."

The family turned to each other, smiling. The Seekers, though, stood irresolute. They knew the odds were not in their favor.

The family turned to regard the continuing circle of votes, hearing the next Elder as he plopped back down into his seat, his green and warty face looking excited.

"Raja Prabodh of the goblinoid Tribe Vikhura votes aye."

Three to one so far.

Keb turned to face the next Elder, his eyes looking hard into the darkness. He locked eyes with his Elder then, turning to look back at the family with upraised eyebrows. Just that one move showed that of anyone present, the orcs could handle the elemental powers at hand.

"Laman Njinga of the orc Tribe Ngoma votes aye."

Keb smiled wide, bowing low to his Elder. Four to one.

A woman the others had not noticed before stood next. She leaned into the light, red hair falling over a beautiful blue gown. Her skin had a slight blue tinge to it, and her voice floated through the air. "Lugal Puabi of the aquarians votes nay."

Four to two.

The beast-born was next. With a grunt, the massive body rose from his chair, leaning far out over the railing. His muscles bulged in the meager light, and it seemed as if the railing was ready to be ripped out from the wall.

"If it were my way, I'd have you killed for coming unbidden to Atlantis. Be fortunate you whelplings are being allowed to leave. Tlatoani Bidziil of the beast-born Tribe Accala votes nay."

Four to three.

A clinking of metal on metal greeted the family from the next Elder. A skeletal hand grasped the rail, cold steam billowing out from under the bracers on its forearm. The metal came from the heavy set of plate mail armor the thing wore from head to toe. Blue motes of light burned in the orbitals where the eyes once were as the skull's bottom jaw moved to speak.

"Lord Nadir of the undead votes nay."

Four to four.

It was Xinzang's turn to look into the darkness with hope. Though the scalehide were not elemental masters, they knew how to discipline the mind, body, and spirit. Zang knew she could train the family and admitted to herself that she was sad to see Drake leave.

The female scalehide Elder rose from her seat, her wings whipping around behind her. She wasn't as dark as Zang but was impressively large, with scales the deep color of gold.

"Bao Chányú of the scalehide Tribe Xia votes aye."

Zang smiled from ear to ear, bowing as well. Five to four.

Mason looked back to his Seeker family, as well as the new family he had brought into this world. He knew exactly how the rest would play out. He knew the druids and his own master would refuse while the halfling would agree. The vote would be tied and left to the beast-born, who could very well have them all killed.

'Patience.'

A voice echoed in his head. Was it his own Elder? Was this a ploy to win the favor of the family since his Elder had to go last in the voting?

Another thought occurred to him suddenly, a very frightening one at that. He still had a mental shield around himself and the family. Whoever just whispered in his mind defeated his mind shield, which was almost impossible, even for an Elder.

A growl echoed out into the darkness from the next Elder. Hairy claws gripped the rail, pulling himself to his feet. His posture was bent over, and his coat of hair was silvered in most places. The face that came into the light was that of an old and weary-looking wolf-man.

His answer was more a growl than speech.

"Pharaoh Lycean of the skin-walker Tribe Maati votes nay."

Five to five.

Normally, Mason's Elder would have gone next, but since he was the one that started the vote, his was the last to be counted. So instead, another short and lithe woman stepped up from her seat to the left of the Mystic Elder to lean against the railing. Her face was sad as well, but appeared resolute.

"Malikah Sarai of the halfling Tribe Eloah votes aye."

Six to five.

This was it. If Mason's Elder was waiting for his vote to take guardianship of the family, now was the time.

Mason's Elder still stood at the railing, watching intently as the vote passed from one Elder to the next. As all eyes settled on him then, he looked down at the gathered entourage and smiled.

"I know you think that this family are the Four, but you are mistaken. Dharmapala Avici of the human Tribe Devas votes.... Nay. You see Master Clemens, there is no vote for support."

The room lay silent for a moment longer. The Seekers looked at each other and to the family with long faces, most of them surprised and confused. Their hopes were high coming into the meeting, but the strange way their Elders seemed determined to exile the family shook them to their core.

"Hold up." Brett said as he stepped forward off the dais to approach the Elders.

Mason and the others turned to him, defeat on their faces, yet a kindling of hope that Brett could salvage something. They looked at him now, excitement barely contained. He strode confidently to within a few feet below the Mystic Elder.

"We heard when we first arrived that Atlantis 'welcomed all'. This doesn't seem very welcoming. And no offense, mister, but why are *you* in charge? Do you speak for every Elder here? You get to say what happens, or are you the mouthpiece for the entire group? You guys are like politicians, right? Well, in our world, you don't get to be a politician forever, so I am assuming there are other *retired* Elders still hanging out in Atlantis that are just as wise and all-knowing? Why can't we ask them?"

Brett found he was on a roll. He could see many of the Elders backing down from the fight, looking to each other to make sure all were still in agreeance.

"It seems odd that for as welcoming as Atlantis is, and for how strangely 'gifted' we four are, that you would presume to 'erase our memories' and send us untrained back into the wider world again. Isn't that the whole point of your Seeking thing? To bring powerful people back…"

("I Claim your Sun" from the Transformers: Revenge of the Fallen Soundtrack by Steve Jablonsky)

Brett's voice trailed off as laughter and clapping filled the room.

Brett recognized the sound in an instant.

Andrew.

"Bravo Brett. Bravo. Keep filling their heads with lies about how utterly fantastic you and your cursed family are. I said you would cause the world's destruction, and here you are, starting it earlier than I presumed."

"So, you're the one controlling these puppets, Andrew? Like your other lackeys on the plane? Come out and face me like a man! We have some unfinished business to take care of."

The laughing erupted around him.

Brett could hear another sound but could not make it out, as it was garbled. It surrounded him, though, and caused his senses to flounder.

"Oh, poor Brett. Were you not prepared for this? Whatever will you do now?"

The rattle of chains ground on Brett's subconscious memory. He could feel his body become immobile as the same tightness gripped him as it did on the beach so many years ago. Brett saw Andrew's grinning, devilish face in the shadows now as he inched his way out, one silver claw leading the way.

"Remember this, Brett? How powerless you were to stop me on the beach then? Do you think you are any more powerful now? You are nothing! I could swat you like a bug if I wanted it."

Andrew looked past Brett to his family behind him, smiling.

"And oh, how I look forward to toying with your bride and small children."

That was all Brett needed.

Grinding his teeth against the ever-tightening grip of the chains around his body, he willed himself to become amorphous, pure liquid.

The chains clattered to the floor.

Brett had his hand up at once, imitating the act of gripping Andrew with his innate control over the water, immobilizing him using his blood.

"You will never hurt anyone ever again."

Gasping through the pain, Andrew retorted, "but the blood is on your hands Brett, not mine. You caused the plane to crash. You summoned the tidal wave. You almost killed the gangsters on the beach. What have I done but tried to stop you before you became the monster you are?"

Andrew lifted his clawed hand again, enacting the strange ability he had on the plane. As before, it felt like Brett's essence was being ripped out of him.

Brett looked down at the glowing blue mist coming out of his chest, realizing what he had to do.

There were no people protecting Andrew now. No one to stop Brett from killing him and putting an end to this insanity. Brett knew that if he didn't act, his soul would be torn from his body.

"Don't make me do this, Andrew!" Brett yelled over the pain in his chest.

But Andrew smiled as he grew stronger and stronger in front of Brett's eyes.

"You cannot stop me, Brett. I am inevitable."

Brett closed his eyes. He remembered another vision from the strange flashback he had in the waiting room, not even 15 minutes prior. A strange Terminator-type robot had attacked him in some other sort of reality.

He had destroyed that robot with a flick of his wrist.

Brett reached out to Andrew and closed his eyes. He had hoped that his family would not have to see this, but he knew that if he did not stop Andrew now, the devil would hurt his family after he was done with him.

Brett squeezed his hand tight.

A squish reverberated throughout the room.

Brett felt his mind and body free from the tumult. Painfully, he opened his eyes, afraid of what he might see. He had been a Marine and had seen dead bodies before, but he had never killed anyone, let alone condense every ounce of fluid in someone's body to one point.

The sight surprised him.

"You see my friends? He cannot control his own power!"

The voice was the Mystic Elder's above him.

Brett looked down at where Andrew should have been, but found the destroyed body of the golem who had brought out the tray of items for them to be tested on. The golem's fluids leaked all over the floor, and a small squealing sound came from its servos as they wound down and finally stopped. The lights in its eye sockets went dark.

Though it was a robot, Brett knew that the 'golems' in Atlantis were sentient creatures and that this one was most likely alive in some way. Its death didn't do any less to Brett's psyche than killing a normal human would have.

But where was Andrew?

"This... man... lashed out uncontrolled as a golem sat passively by, no harm to any. He dwells on visions and nightmares of fiends and has no control over his power."

Brett looked back to his family and the Seekers, all wide-eyed at the Elder's words. Mason stepped down off the dais and ushered Brett back to his side.

"You stopped speaking mid-sentence and mumbled something about an 'Andrew' before you destroyed the golem."

Brett felt bewildered.

"I what? No, he was here... he was..."

Mason stopped him.

"I believe I know what happened to you. Stay close to me from now on. Your mind may have been infiltrated when you left my protection."

Mason looked up to his Elder.

"My Elders, this proves my point. They cannot be allowed to return to the old lands. They must be taught here."

The Mystic Elder looked down at the gathered group.

"You are correct, Master Clemens. They cannot be allowed to return to the old lands. My beast-born cousin was right. They are much too dangerous, both for our people and for our distant kin. Thus, I find it in our decree to..."

("Maester" from the Game of Thrones: Season 6 Soundtrack by Ramin Djawadi)

The Mystic Elder looked down at the group and seemed like he was about to say more when his eyes suddenly furrowed, as if he were concentrating on something. Still distant, his eyes darted up into the darkness behind and around the family and the Seekers.

Mason looked at his Elder with eyes wide. Something was happening. He looked back to his other four Seekers, and he knew they could sense it too. Their connection went deeper than just a standard group of adventurers; they were intimately one and could all feel the upwelling of energy in the room.

"There is one more to vote, Sitting Elders."

The voice echoed out all around them.

Brett and his family had caught the hint of what the Mystic Elder was about to mention and had already gone on the defensive, but their anxiety amped up even more as they noted the five Seekers looking about in confusion.

Brett brought his wife and children closer to his side and behind him as they looked for the voice. At first, Brett thought it could be some sort of a ploy by the Elders to take them on aggressively, since they obviously feared them enough to erase their memories, boot them out of the country, or now apparently kill them. But as he looked about the room and onto the balcony, his thoughts changed.

Even the Elders shuffled where they stood. Mason's Elder spoke first.

"This is a closed meeting. I do not know who you are or how you surpassed the wards to enter here, but you violate the sovereign Elder Laws of Atlantis."

Egregious laughter echoed out about the room.

Anxiety now ramped up from the political nay-sayers about them. Ke'eli whispered to Mason, "What is going on? Why are they freaking out? Why are *you* freaking out?"

"This building is secure from all sides." came Mason's reply. "There are arcane and divine wards set about the perimeter, and especially this room that makes it impossible for any outside interference, nor for anyone to enter unbidden. Whoever this is that is speaking has gotten casually into one of the most fortified places in the world. And seeing how as you all are still protected by me, Tumidus and Pwyll, it can't be coming from the Elders as I believe it did a few minutes ago with Brett."

Ke'eli looked back to Brett, who had heard the reply.

"Should we be on guard?" Brett asked, but he knew the reply already.

Why would he be on guard against a man who just said that there was still one vote to count, when six of the "Elders" above him voted no?

The Elder Mystic looked over to Brett's three o'clock, where the alien-looking elf stood. Nodding her head, she peered down into the assembly and yelled out arcane words of power.

"Protegat hunc locum!"

Instantly, the lights rose around the ground floor and a dome of energy erupted around the family and the Seekers on the dais. Another wall of prismatic power came into being along the rails of the balcony, further separating the people down below from the Elders.

Each column that supported the balcony came to life somehow. One erupted lightning from it while another gushed fire. All seemed prepared to attack the first thing they were ordered to. The golems that remained along the edge of the room came rushing back in near the center, weapons bared.

One part of the lower room remained in darkness, the globes of light around it flickering and failing. A hand reached out of the darkness then, touching one column, which was spewing ice in all directions. Suddenly, the ice stopped. The column returned to normal, as did every column around the perimeter. The strange voice spoke out casually.

"Ah, I don't think we have need of such heavily armed troops! Itzul zaitez zure geltokietara."

Immediately, the golems that had come into the room turned around and exited the same way they came.

"How dare you! You openly enter a restricted building to face the combined fury of all 12 Tribal Elders!? This is your last warning; you are not welcome here!"

The thinly veiled threat came from the werewolf-man, who gasped in surprise as the prismatic walls both around the family and around the Elders disappeared as the man in the darkness snapped his fingers. The family could see that this unknown person, who just shut all their defenses down, definitely intimidated the Elders.

"Oh, I think I am welcome," came the reply, as the figure revealed himself by walking into the light on the floor level of the dais.

Brett's eyes at once went wide. This man that walked into the light looked exactly like the man he remembered from his visions of being a child. The one that had kidnapped him from the Garden and whisked him away from Atlantis.

The man sensed Brett's reaction as he looked over at him and gave him a wink.

All the Elder's voices went into an uproar of activity.

The man just looked at them all with a grin on his face. A cane appeared in his hand from behind his back as he slammed it down onto the ground.

"SILENCE!"

The walls shook from the impact, not from the cane, but from the power of his words.

Every single person froze.

The man continued to walk onto the dais. He wore a simple plain robe, and his hair was long and scraggly. He was human, but had much more of a chiseled look about him and walked slowly as he took in his surroundings. As disheveled as he appeared, a tangible air of power flowed with him that had everyone standing in awe, especially after the dramatics.

Coming to the center of the dais to face the family and the Seekers, the man looked to each one present there before him, as if he were reviewing some decision in his mind. He nodded his head yes and turned to address the Elders above him.

"I take custody of this family and requisition the Seekers as my accomplices."

Some Elders, who thought to test the man before them, finally spoke up.

"We are the Tribal Elders of Atlantis," began the large and bestial man behind the group, "and what we say is law. These flesh-bags are to be handed over to me! No matter how powerful you are, you have no say in the matter!"

The man before them laughed at the proclamation.

"You would be wise to not test my power, barbarian. I have wrestled giants to their knees that could fell you with one look!" the man replied, still laughing.

"No matter what you have done old hu-*man*" the elvish Elder said as she glaringly looked up at the mystic Elder human across from her and back down to the crowd, "you are not an Elder and have no right to bargain for these non-Atlanteans. We are the law!"

Again, the man laughed hysterically at the proclamation as he turned to look back at Drake, giving him a wink and a thumbs-up.

"These four behind me are more Atlantean than *any* of you will ever, or could ever, be. You are pale comparisons to the true Standing Elders. Your blood has thinned over these last few thousand years, allowing you to become complacent and uncaring, just as the False Elders were the day of the Reckoning. But that will not remain. It is time for the Awakening."

The response was instant. It was one thing to arrive with an air of power ordering people around; it was another to take aim at the racial pride that came with being one of the first societies to ever bud on the planet Earth. The Elders might not have agreed completely with some matters, but with defending themselves and their homeland, they took it to heart, especially when they were compared to the False Elders of old.

This man saw that and was prepared for it.

Immediately, many of the Elders committed some sort of action. The elf rained arcane fire down at the man while the dwarf summoned radiance from the ceiling to crash down on his head. The goblin threw daggers while the beast-born threw a giant axe with a roar. The gnome fired a massive rifle that appeared to form from his arm and the undead brought soul-sucking ice up from the ground. The werewolf howled as he leaped from his seat down onto the lower floor, changing into an even bigger wolf with spikes coming out of his back. Beside him, the scalehide monk flipped off her railing as well, leading with a clawed foot for the man's shoulder.

The very few that did not act stood by staring word-lessly. The halfling tried to calm everyone down while the orc sat impassively, watching the entire event unfold. The aquarian hid behind her rail as the human Mystic Elder tried in vain to understand what was happening.

It all happened so fast, none on the dais could adequately prepare for the onslaught.

But they found they did not need to.

An explosion rocked the surrounding dais as the man brought his cane down again to the ground. All the magical effects that struck out at him, all the weapons, all the attacks reverberated around the room, returning the way they came. The fire ricocheted back to the elf, as did the radiance raining down upon him to the dwarf. The weapons arced in their trajectory, turning boomerang-like as they sailed back to their owners who dodged out of the way. The surrounding ice shriveled up into nothing while the werewolf and the scalehide were thrown helplessly back the way they came to slam into the wall behind their chairs.

The shockwave rippled out into the room as every other Elder was forced back into their seats or back against the wall. The Elders found they could not move as they looked on in shock and awe. The dais and its occupants around him lay untouched.

"I am Atlas Titanes, once and always High King of Atlantis, and MY word is law!"

The room remained silent as he turned towards his new entourage, leading them out the main doors which opened wide for their returned King.

Chapter Twelve

ICY DESERT

**("The Human Spirit" from the Day After Tomorrow
Soundtrack by Harald Kloser)**

Andrew sloughed through the snowdrifts and the freezing ice plateaus, confident he was on the right trail.

Brigid looked at him with pity. She genuinely cared for him and the rest of her Ring, but she was sure they were on a fool's errand.

The elf they had found back at the human encampment had been a forward scout and scientist, tasked with ensuring the illusion of a secret world beneath their feet. Andrew had teased out as much information as he could from him, before a crystal pendant on the elf's chest began to glow and heat up, eventually causing a minor explosion. The elf's body, as well as that of the other elves in the room, had all disintegrated in a flash.

"A perfect way to cover their tracks." Brigid had told Andrew. "And one we should use caution in pursuing."

But that would not deter the Shadowson. Andrew was determined, dangerously so, to find Brett again.

Brigid watched the tiefling walk, noticing he had started to limp again. Her healing magic had only done so much in fixing his broken body after going out in search of three other 'Soulbound' humans. He had found two of the three other humans, and they had treated him much less kindly than Brett ever had.

One they found in Raleigh, North Carolina. This one could see into the future while his mate could see into the past. That was the shortest adventure, for the man saw the group coming days in advance and was not thrilled when they tried to kidnap his children.

The man with his wife seemed burdened with technology, so much so that he used weapons that seemed not of this world. Knowing what someone was going to do next seemed an applaudable attribute in itself; to have technological advances so profound as to mock all others was another.

Frey took the brunt of that encounter, losing an eye in the process.

None of the Ring ever walked away whole after fighting for Andrew and chasing down his damned 'prophecies'.

The only good that had come from the encounter at the time with this second Soulborn was that the whispered notions of the woman Andrew spoke to in his mind proved correct. Brigid had her reservations, trusting in someone they could not see. But the information had proved correct and though it was frivolous, the Ring still maintained that she was on their side.

After the failure with the second Soulbound, Andrew decided in his wisdom to seek the third. The psychic woman had told him to seek them out in the "halls of Fidelity, Bravery and Integrity", which clued Andrew into the approximate location.

Always answered in riddles, the woman in Andrew's mind was cryptic in her auguries and premonitions, as if she were not entirely sure of the answer herself. On top of that, Andrew had no way to start the mental conversations they would have, so her calling to him always occurred at the most random times.

Regardless, he surmised with his own spells and abilities that the third was a male as well, and one that seemed more accustomed to life in the limelight.

This one wound up in Quantico, Virginia, and was easier to manipulate. Of all the encounters with these mythical Soulbound humans, this one was the most enjoyable and almost successful. An applicant into the prestigious Federal Bureau of Investigation, he was at their academy on the Marine Corps base. His Soulbound mate was there as well, which was amazing for Andrew at the time, but ultimately made it even easier for him to implement his plans.

At one point, the Ring even participated in song and dance. The custom was strange to the group, seeing as they came from a literal Hell. But, strangely, the Ring sensed a much stronger energy coming from the people the third Soulbound knew.

The couple seemed to constantly be surrounded by other powerful individuals; they having their own plans that often went against what Andrew had preferred. Eventually, he gathered some of these powerful people to his side and used them to sway the Soulbound, almost resulting in his success.

The Ring had not expected *other* powerful individuals to interfere with their plans, though.

Much like how Andrew directed Brett to find his Soulmate in Ke'eli, so did he try to come between this other human and his Soulmate as well. Except this time, he used his wits and guile instead of outright violence. He was almost successful.

Some strange and powerful foreign entity had taken an interest in the two human Soulmates, interfering in Andrew's plans. Andrew tried to understand the thing's intentions but was bewildered by its power and plan. It was not of this world, yet seemed to understand and guide things from behind the scenes that even had Andrew wondering at his own inabilities.

In the end, the couple's love had triumphed, causing a disastrous battle to erupt.

Brigid tried to aid the Ring during that battle, but something about the humans had set her back. The couple had fought and sacrificed themselves for each other because of their love. Brigid had known nothing like that. The closest she ever got was the kinship she felt for her friends, whom she considered like brothers and sister.

But their undying passion, the way they looked death in the face and the way they fought for each other, had Brigid wondering about herself and her situation on this surface world.

She never saw the genuine attack coming.

The otherworldly entity that had also taken an interest in this third Soulbound couple came calling. Its power was immense, and it swatted the Ring away like gnats. It had taken control of Andrew as well, using him to further its own gains.

Try as he might, Andrew could not break the spell. At least until he saw his Ringmates almost die. The fey creature that had taken control of Andrew underestimated his resolve and assumed he only wanted power for power's sake. That fact was only half true, and it severely burned Andrew to his core as he broke free.

Brigid herself was seriously injured, as were Pelles and Freyja.

It was only the prompt intervention of Andrew and his power that saved them all. And none more than Brigid.

She had taken a nasty fireball at almost direct range and her body burned beyond all recognition. Her beautiful wings were smoldering, and her armor melted into her body.

Andrew did something amazing then.

Sacrificing the very essence that made him who he was, he divested his energy into Brigid, causing her to heal. She had never seen him do anything of the sort, and it at first caused her such mental pain that it almost caused her to leave their side. In time, though, she realized he divested something of himself in order to keep them by his side. He needed them.

Brigid could still feel the fiendish energy inside her, but her celestial soul kept it at bay. Either way, he had saved her, and all of them, that day.

You are my kin. You are my siblings; he had told them all that day.

Besides, I need your help, he also reminded them.

Brigid laughed to herself at the time of the memory.

She was not laughing now.

They had survived the ordeal against the fey creature who came at them unbidden, and the Soulbound they had tried to control disappeared. None of them could find out where they went or what happened to them, and none of Andrew's spells or the whispers of the woman could tell.

If the drama could have stopped then, Brigid would have been satisfied. But Andrew went right on back to the very beginning, putting plans into motion to find and separate Brett once again.

They still bickered over the mishap on the plane with Brett when Andrew inadvertently said his real last name, as opposed to the one he was raised with. Andrew knew that, but had not realized Brett did not. The wording of the *wish* spell was very intricate. Andrew had instead sent Brett somewhere else, while they dealt with the repercussions.

As the plane made to crash into the ocean, Brigid was able to create a sphere around the group, protecting them from most of the damage.

But the crashing plane was the least of their worries.

They had cast several enormously powerful spells along a major ley line nexus *and* directly confronted Brett. Andrew supposed that the Daemon Hunters who had captured him so many years prior on the beach in Tahiti had placed an abjuration dweomer on Brett to alert them, in case Andrew ever came back to find him.

They found out painfully so that Andrew was right.

A ship arrived not long after the plane had crashed. The Ring was wary of being rescued by any humans, but they need not have worried. The ship was infernal in design, crewed by several of the more powerful Daemon hunters who had splintered off from their dominant faction, intent on still hunting their quarry.

Many of the denizens of their Hell had come to terms with Andrew's power and now followed him. Like any good cult, though, there were many who saw holes in his plans. Belial himself had steeled away with a group of like-minded compatriots, fighting against the leadership that Andrew now commanded. Some of them still looked to bring Andrew back for reckoning, while others flocked to his call.

The battle was long and bloody, but Andrew and his comrades survived the fight, not without penalty though. Freyja was knocked unconscious; Andrew was almost dragged back to Hell and Conall drowned. Brigid was the only rock in that fight, and Andrew knew it.

Her radiant energy was a bane to the fiendish hunters, and they fled from her power. She was also the one to pull Freyja from death's door and bring Conall back from the depths of the sea.

Andrew owed her his life. So, they considered each other even.

Still, the group could not come to terms with the life they left in the Otherworld. Where at once, they were hunted and considered outlaws, now they could come and go as they pleased. The ragtag group of Daemon hunters that found them in the sea were offshoots of Belial's personal retinue, who still were at odds with Andrew and what he planned to do.

Would anything they do ever be enough?

Granted, their hellish home under the earth was chock full of dissenters and had garnered a wicked array of political extremists who scrabbled at any hint of power. None had looked at Andrew that way anymore, or so Brigid thought.

Here was a fiend-blooded Soulless Daemon hunter, very skilled in the warlock Arts, who just so happened to have a celestial-blooded Soulless Daemon hunter in his own personal Ring. The one thing that anyone in the Otherworld needed in order to breach the protective shell around their home: the power of radiance.

Whereas many had come calling to bring Brigid under their fold, none could sway her while the charismatic Sigurd remained in her inner circle. Powerful people beckoned her with gifts of magic and wealth, but all was for naught as Sigurd spun the weave of tales he had learned through study and research.

We are all destined for more, he would tell her.

And she believed him.

The cold bit at her body, even under all the fur she put back on. They had garnered enough information from the elf before he died that showed there was a secret opening around the camp that the people of this hidden world used to get in and out.

Additionally, there were orcs that came out of this exit to 'mend' the ice around the secret place to keep the illusion.

Andrew was determined to find one of these orcs and have it bring them to this secret place.

The six had scoured the ice for miles, though, not finding any sign of life or any hidden entrances.

Brigid had had enough.

"Sigurd! This is madness! We will die out on this frozen rock and your fated 'prophecy' will go unfulfilled!"

Shouting above the howling wind and the thick mask she wore over her face, her voice still echoed out about the landscape.

Andrew turned back to face her, his eyes still scanning the surrounding horizon.

"I saw into the creature's mind. He could not lie to me. There is an entrance out here Brigid, I can feel it."

Brigid laughed. The rest of the Ring had huddled together for warmth and to block the smaller Freyja from the winds.

Her skin still had the scars from the same fireball that had devastated Brigid, and the cold caused it to crack and splinter.

"There is nothing out here, Sigurd. You would have to speak to the ice to find anything resembling a secret entryway, and you do not speak to ice. There is still the fourth Soulbound that we have not found. Let us go in search of him."

It was true. Andrew and his cohorts had found three of the four Soulbound humans, but there was one that had eluded their detection. Andrew had told them they were all connected somehow, and that the fourth should have something in common with the other two and Brett. But it was the biggest piece of the puzzle that Andrew had not figured out, and it grounded against his nerves.

The fourth, by all his reckoning and research, should have been the oldest and most powerful of the group. But wherever he looked, whatever he did to find this oddity, he could not zero in on their location.

He was confident that it was a man and that he was probably in his late 40s or 50s, which should have made the quest easier. Spells and rituals of all kinds were wasted as Andrew called on the powers of his Art to locate this strange piece of the puzzle. Nothing in Andrew's own three decades of life grated on his nerves as much as this damned fruitless search, knowing that as powerful as this man was, he could hide it so easily.

"No! The answer is here. I can feel it! Something is beneath us, and it... it calls to me." Andrew looked about the ice as he said it, imitating that he could almost see through the frozen landscape.

Andrew stopped then, looking back up at Brigid. Neither moved for several seconds, as Brigid deduced the crazed tiefling was scheming under his mask. His sudden movement broke the tension.

"You are correct, Brigid. I cannot speak to the ice, *but I can listen!*"

Andrew took off his gloves and pulled back his hooded jacket, revealing his shock of white hair and devilish horns.

Dropping to all fours, he put his hands flat down on the ice and cocked his head to the side, closing his eyes.

"Sigurd, what are you...."

"Quiet!" Andrew yelled, glaring up at Brigid.

The ice beneath Andrew's hands flared brightly from the heat he emanated, his anger swelling.

Brigid knew Andrew was directing his anger more at himself than at her. She knew he was getting frustrated, blocked at every junction, and stymied at every power grab attempt.

So, she crossed her arms and watched, sad for her distraught friend, who was slowly going insane.

Andrew turned his head side to side, then up, then turned his body in an entirely different direction.

The melted ice had begun to freeze again around Andrew's hands. It did not matter to him, though. He had his answer.

Pulling his hands out of the slush he made and pocketing them in his jacket, he smiled up at Brigid.

"As you are well aware, I siphoned a part of Brett's essence while on the plane. He could tap into that spiritual well of power, which just so happens to be connected to the water element. Though I do not have nearly the control he has, I do have somewhat of a spittle of cognizance of it. And how, pray tell, could that help me right now?"

Andrew looked around at his companions, though none had the answer he sought, as simple as it was.

Brigid was the only one to hazard a guess.

"So, you *can* communicate with the ice? Spit it out Shadowson, I grow weary of not feeling my limbs!"

Andrew tipped his head, tapping one of his temple horns.

Turning to walk back towards Casey Station, Andrew walked with purpose, which was the first time he had since coming out into the icy desert.

The rest of the Ring shuffled to keep up with him, happy at the thought that they were returning to the camp, though they had left no one alive to greet them.

Still, some comfort from the freezing temperature would feel good.

Until Andrew stopped.

Putting his hands on his hips, he stared at a large hole several yards away. They could hear gushing water as it flowed under the ice and into the hole, making a sort of waterfall.

Brigid caught on in a heartbeat.

"No" was all she said.

But Andrew was already walking towards the hole.

"Sigurd, you have lost your mind! That is a hole into oblivion! I will not follow you there!" Brigid lamented, crossing her arms across her chest.

Andrew approached the large hole, which, upon closer inspection, appeared just large enough to allow a body into. He looked about the area before focusing back on the hole.

"Freyja!" he yelled back to his companions without turning to face them.

Like a disciplined child, Freyja waddled up to Andrew, head bent low.

Andrew turned to face her, dropping to one knee.

Before he could even say anything, her brother was there by her side.

"She'll not go into that hole, not knowin' where it might go."

Freyja looked at her twin brother, smiling sadly.

"Aye, I'm the only one around who might not drown."

Andrew looked at the twins and placed his hands on their shoulders. He caught on that they had not rhymed with each other but had only rhymed themselves. He knew he had reached a strange and strained point in their relationship, and what he was about to ask would not help.

"I need you *both* now. You are connected. You can speak to each other through the will of your connected lives. Yes Freyja, I need you to see where that hole goes. I am confident that it leads deeper under the ice to a hollowed-out cave, which is our entrance to the secret world. If it is not, then it will deposit you into an ocean somewhere nearby. You can turn into a penguin and survive long enough for us to find you. You can, can't you?"

Andrew asked the words, but they were more an acknowledgement of her ability than what she could do.

Brigid strolled up.

"And if the waterway leads deeper under the ice and she is killed by the frost and pressure, what then Sigurd? You will have sacrificed Frey's twin for your own arrogance."

Andrew looked up at Brigid.

"It is worth the sacrifice."

Saying nothing further, Andrew stood back up and backed away, extending his hand towards the hole in the ground.

Freyja looked over to her twin, tears freezing on her face already.

"Ye'll be waitin' for me on the other side?"

Frey hugged his sister closely, knowing it could be the last time he would see her.

"No worries now, little sister, just..." but Frey couldn't think of anything else at the time to keep up the rhyming game they had made all their lives.

That broke Brigid more than anything. She moved with a purpose towards Andrew, reaching out to grab him.

"That is enough Sigurd! I will not let our group sacrifice...."

A squeaking chirp came from Freyja then as she dove towards the waterfall hole, turning into a penguin.

Frey went to grab her before she could jump, but her changing form made it impossible to grab anything.

Brigid pushed past Andrew to see if there was something she could do.

Even she noticed Andrew moved forward suddenly, though she could not tell if it was concern over Freyja or to see if she would be successful.

The rest of the Ring closed form tightly around the hole in the ground, not knowing what to expect.

Brigid turned harshly on Andrew.

"You are insane! This whole adventure is insane! You have failed at every turn! You have put us all in peril and, for what, to fulfill a prophecy that only *you* know about and understand? You are my Ring-brother, but I can only support you and bring our allies back from the brink of death for so long before I cannot abide it anymore. I will return to Tartarus and beg for their mercy. I will fight for the right... to... why are you smiling, you fool?!"

Andrew interrupted her with no words or aggression; only a fang-filled smile. He nodded down to Frey, who stood staring down into the hole.

Brigid looked over at him, cocking her head to the side.

Because that was exactly what Frey was doing. Like he was listening to something far away in his head.

Frey brought his hands up to his chest and grabbed them close, as if he were hugging someone.

Smiling himself, Frey looked up at Andrew and Brigid.

"I dinnae know how he knew, but we're in for one helluva ride!"

Frey jumped into the hole.

CHAPTER THIRTEEN

HUNTED

("Tap into your Mind" from A Wrinkle in Time Soundtrack by Ramin Djawadi)

The man who called himself Atlas led the family of four and the five Seekers out into the main promenade in front of the Senate house. He walked faster than one would expect from a man his age.

Sensing that recognition, he looked back at everyone and said sternly, "We must be quick. There are strange things afoot."

Brett stared hard at the man, almost tripping over his own feet. How familiar he seemed, as if he had dreamed him over and over his entire life. Ke'eli reached out to grab her husband's arm to keep him from knocking over his own son, who had to run to keep up.

"Brett, are you okay? You look like you've seen a ghost, and you're trampling over your son, who has been trying to hold your hand since we left."

Coming out of his stupor, Brett's face softened as he looked at his wife and down at his son, who was visibly growing tired. Realizing then he had been failing as a father, he at once grabbed up his son and carried him close to his chest.

"I'm sorry Drake. I love you, bud. I'm just... weirded out a little, you know?" The sincerity was obvious on his face as Drake smiled and shrugged his shoulders.

"Thanks, da-da. I know you would never forget about me." Drake leaned in, squeezing his father, and looking worryingly behind them.

But Brett was again somewhere far away in his mind.

I know you will never forget about me.

Brett had said those words. When he was a young boy, not nearly as young as Drake, but young none-the-less. And he was here, in Atlantis. And he had said them to this man leading them away into a building now.

This man, who Brett had somehow seen before.

As soon as they were all inside the building, Brett took his son and, remembering to be a good father, kissed him on the cheek before carefully handing him over to Ke'eli.

"Who are you?" Brett approached the man quickly, coming face to face with him.

Mason was there as well. His awe was plain as he stood by one of the greatest legends the world had ever seen.

"Brett, this is High King Atlas, first to the Soulstone and...."

"No, I heard that," Brett interrupted. "He knows what I mean."

Brett stood there staring at the man, never backing down.

Atlas did know what he meant. Looking around at the gathered group, Atlas smiled before returning his gaze to Brett.

It was then that somehow everyone in the room recognized it.

The two were both the same height and broad-shouldered. They had the same straight nose and eyes the color of the sea. They both had squared jaws and were almost the same build. Only their slight skin tone color was different.

Even Atlas's smile looked like Brett's.

"It is good to see you too, son."

The gasps could have sucked out all the air in the room if it were any smaller.

Brett furrowed his eyebrows at the man, still trying to piece this all together.

"Please, let us hurry. All will be explained to you in due time. We must not stay in the city for too much longer. Something is wrong with the Elders. They were about to execute you all; Seekers included."

Atlas clapped Brett on the shoulder and continued to lead the way down into a dark basement. After several flights of stairs, they came to the bottom level that had no way out.

Atlas continued walking towards a wall covered in shelving.

Stopping before the wall, he twisted a ring on his finger, muttering something under his breath.

Suddenly, the wall began to hiss and grind.

Slowly, the brick façade lowered into the ground, disappearing. The shelves remained floating in mid-air.

Atlas looked back to the group, smiled again, and walked toward the shelving.

To everyone's surprise, he walked right through the shelves, as though nothing was there. He stopped a short distance through, leaning down to address something that no one could see.

"I think our entrance needs a bit of a dusting."

Standing upright again, Atlas looked back at his entourage.

"Well? Are you all coming? That door won't stay down for long!"

One by one, the group followed Atlas through the door. They found that the shelving was an illusion of some sort, making the appearance that there was something in front of the wall.

As for the "dusting", everyone felt a cool breeze swish by them before looking back to see dust come out of nowhere to cover up their tracks down into the basement. Stair by stair, some invisible thing sprinkled dust over all the footprints.

Tumidus whispered to the family, "A spell called Unseen Servant. Especially useful to clean things up, or in this case, make things dirty!"

As he said it, the wall behind the group started to rise, grating and cracking.

Atlas continued his trek. Now he spoke.

"We are in my secret base of operations. More will be told to you in time, but for now, know that something evil is going on in Atlantis, and has been for some time. We must act now if we are to save our people."

Brett seemed as if he were ready to explode.

"Hey, uh, can we talk or something 'dad'? I know the whole fate of Atlantis thing is pretty important, but I'd say talking to your son who you've never met is pretty freaking important too!"

Atlas stopped dead in his tracks. Turning around, he again had the biggest smile on his face, as opposed to how everyone else thought he might react.

"Son, we have a lot of work to do together, and I promise you I will never lose you again. We *have* met, and I will refresh your memory as we continue this journey together."

As he spoke, Atlas walked slowly to Brett. When he got to within arm's length, Brett could see that Atlas' eyes were tearing up.

"My son, you do not know how much I have missed you. The years we have been apart may not seem like much to you, but they have been an eternity for me, and that's saying a lot for a man who has lived as long as I! Your memory has been affected, and it is partly my doing. But it cannot be undone here and now. I need time to help you remember. I need you to trust me."

Atlas put a hand up to the man's cheek and Brett didn't stop him. He knew deep down in his heart that this really was his father. How? He was not sure. But Brett couldn't hide it. The tears came.

And so did Atlas's.

The two men hugged each other, crying tears of joy.

The feeling was one of the best Brett had ever felt, next to hugging his own children.

There was an immediate bond there, as if Brett knew that this man had done everything in his power to protect him, even going as far as to hide him away so that not even his own father could see him.

"It's so good to see you, my boy. So much to tell. So much..."

The slight cough interrupted the reunion.

Everyone, startled, turned to the sound. Not far ahead stood what looked to be a goblin, wearing dark leather with a sword on one hip and a revolver on the other.

Atlas remained unfazed. He pulled himself away from his son and wiped the tears from his eyes. He looked forward to the goblin introducing him.

"My friends, this is Artaxle the Dark Blade, Grandmaster of the Nizari."

Artaxle gave a slight bow, then looked at Atlas and spoke.

"My King, you were correct. As soon as your group left the Senate, drones were dispatched to follow your every move. My men redirected them to the gardens while you made your exit."

"Good. Now we have a chance to escape the city unseen. Thank you Artaxle, lead the way, my friend."

The goblin turned on his heel and did as he was told, leading the group down another dark hallway to what looked to be an underground railway. There before them was what looked like an old-school railway train that aimed off into the deeper darkness.

"Artaxle is one of my oldest friends, and his father was before that, as was his father's father before him. The Nizari line runs exceptionally long, back to the Founding. He is the direct descendant of Mneseus, one of my closest hunter-brothers. He was there when I found the Soulstone."

The group of Seekers, hinging on every word Atlas said, gasped in amazement. Brett, though, did not find it all that amazing. Mostly because he did not know what he was talking about.

"What are you talking about?"

Ke'eli, ever the psychic connection to Brett that he adored so much, asked for him, winking at her husband.

Atlas, seeming to sense the question coming, waved everyone on board the underground tram. As they sat, he leaned back and closed his eyes, breathing in deeply. The tram moved as Atlas began to speak, first with a sigh.

"I had hoped to catch up more on familial tidings, seeing as I have what appears before me a grandson and a granddaughter, but I understand it must wait. Your memory must be returned to you if you are to aid us in the coming trials! So, let me start at the beginning."

("History of the World" from the Alien vs Predator Soundtrack by Harald Kloser)

"Over 40,000 years ago, my people were the ancient off-shoot race you know of as Neanderthals. We journeyed the land, following the game and living every day together as one tribe: myself and my family."

"One night, a great light lit the sky as we camped together. We did not know what it was at the time, so we did not care. As morning came, I took my hunters out as we did most every day."

"I was the first to see the great pyramid. Being the leader of the tribe, I approached the thing with caution. It sat in a vast crater, smoke still rising from the hole it had left."

"With my hunters by my side, we entered the crater together. What we saw then was not what you see today. The pyramid was cold and lifeless. It did not emanate an overwhelming sense of life and love. It was just... a pyramid. Until I touched it."

"When I placed my hand on its side, the pyramid roared to life. A light inside it grew brighter and brighter. I heard a voice inside my head in a language I could not understand. The light did not stop there. It *physically* flowed outside the pyramid, first enveloping me, and then the rest of my kin. The strength of the light overwhelmed us, and we were brought low by its power."

"When we woke, we found our bodies transformed. No longer were we ape-like beasts. We were tall and strong and... different. Ten of my kin went out with me that day. Ten who woke with me next to this thing that changed us. Adapted us. Made us better, stronger, faster, and, most importantly, smarter."

"That day became known as the Founding. Our people gathered from everywhere, making the pyramid our home. We found that the light had changed everyone on the continent, eradicating the species we once were. We went from a roaming tribe of hunters to a stationary Tribe of philosophers."

"I discovered that I alone could enter the pyramid. Inside, I found things I could not understand. Time slowed for me while inside it, making an hour feel like three. Nowhere was there any sign of what the thing was or how it got here."

"Again, I touched something I did not understand. Images appeared before me then. Images of death and destruction, fiendish creatures that tore up out of the ground to lay waste to the entire world. There were other fiendish creatures as well who fought the first, each seeking dominance. I saw explosions that shook the world, rising in a cloud of disaster and killing people thousands of miles away. Natural disasters that wiped everything man had created off the map."

"I tried to understand what I was seeing, but it was so confusing and scattered. A voice cried out to me from inside the pyramid, aching to make me understand. But I could not. The pyramid sensed that, for suddenly the images concentrated on a singular person, her face flashing over and over around me. A woman whose visage changed constantly, but who I came to understand was the same person."

"She was death and destruction. She appeared as one of the fiends but had a power inside her that echoed out from her mind. Ferocious and nigh unstoppable, her anger and hatred echoed out into the cosmos, drawing the attention of other fiendish creatures. She was the harbinger of Armageddon, and I knew then that it was my duty to stop her."

"One thing I came to understand about her was her power. She could manipulate the very minds of the people she ruled over. With the power of the pyramid, she could rule over an entire world."

"So, you see, the Founding was two things. It was our beginning as Atlanteans, evolving into what you see here now before you. But it was also the founding of our destiny. The pyramid, which we came to call the Soulstone, had tasked us to protect it from the one thing that could destroy all life. We have kept that duty to this day."

"You, being the direct blood son to me, are what we have termed a 'True Atlantean'. I never saw if you could enter the pyramid, but I assume you should be able to. I have had to go into hiding these last many years because of an unnatural feeling I have received from the sentience that is the Soulstone. Something evil is afoot in Atlantis, and I have been trying to discover what it is. You are meant to help me. *All* of you."

Atlas turned to the gathering, who had listened intently to his every word. Somehow, the images he spoke about were vivid in everyone's minds. They felt as if they were there, over 40,000 years ago.

Almost on cue, the railway slowed and stopped. Atlas smiled at the gathering, standing as the doors opened.

"Please, we have so much to do. So much to learn and so much to teach!"

Atlas led the way out of the rail and into another underground building. The air was dank and warm, and Atlas had to light a torch for them to see.

"We are outside the protective radius of the pyramid now, so we must rely on 'natural' energy. Honestly, I prefer it to the hum of electricity, don't you?"

Smiling, Atlas looked at his son and grandson. Drake pipped up excitedly.

"Heck yeah! I love being outdoors! Less stuff to worry about burning!"

Atlas turned his gaze to his son, still smiling from cheek to cheek.

"May I carry my grandson, Brett?"

Brett looked down at Drake to see if he would mind. Before he could even answer, Drake's arms were up, imitating that Atlas should pick him up. He wasn't small for an eleven-year-old, but he also wasn't that big.

"So, you're my real grandpa, huh? What about grumps, though? Isn't he your dad, dad?"

Drake dutifully directed his question to both men, but Brett found he could not answer. A family had indeed raised him from the age of sixteen on, a family that he had grown to love. Unlike Atlas, they were there for him at every turn and were probably worried sick right now, as it dawned on Brett that they had been gone for several days.

"That's a good question 'dad', care to fill in some blanks?"

Brett's tone did not have as much attitude as it had before, and Ke'eli recognized that Brett, as hard-headed as he was, was finally relaxing a little.

Kelly could tell that her dad was curious about Atlas, but also still guarded. Being the most empathetic of the family, Kelly leaned in close to her father and hugged him tight.

Immediately, Brett's heart melted. He looked down at his daughter and smiled.

"Well, it's funny you should say that! How are Frank and Julie? I have known them for so long! They were there for me when I found myself stranded in New York with your mother."

The mention of Brett's mother raised his considerable eyebrows to the top of his head. The thought of his actual mother overwhelmed him, even though he had known love from his stand-in mother for years.

About his father, Atlas, Brett could not remember as much. But somehow, he remembered his mother. The way she loved him and cared for him was imprinted on his soul.

"Where... where is she? My mother?" Brett could barely hold his excitement. He even looked around at the immediate room, dark as it was, expecting her to jump out at him.

Atlas's relentless smile faded.

"Your mother is in the Olde World, somewhere. I will explain more to you soon. Trust me, there is so much to explain. It will take time, and time I am afraid, we have little of. Speaking of time, do not fret about Julie and Frank. They will understand. They are some of the few people in the world who knew who we really were. And since it has now been almost a week since you arrived, they will know that you will not be coming back."

"What? A week? First, how do you know when we got here, and second, it's only been like three days." Brett laughed as he spoke, his nerves still on end from the mention of his mother and how she had been in the 'Olde World' with him the entire time.

By now, Atlas had returned to smiling as he played with Drake. Drake was astounded to see that 'Grandpa Atlas' could also create and control fire, as the pair of them summoned smoky salamanders that twirled around their fingertips.

Grandfather and grandson were enjoying themselves so much, they almost bumped into the stone wall that blocked their path any further.

"Ah, there it is. Brett, as your elven friend explained, the pyramid is like a singularity. Everything within its range, which encompasses the shield across the entire continent, is on its event horizon. For every two days that pass in the Olde World, only one passes in Atlantis. And I knew you had returned because the Soulstone told me so. Now everyone, stand back. With the gifts that my wonderful young grandson just gave me, I will provide us a way out of this dirt hole!"

No one understood what the old man was talking about, but they did as he said.

Raising his arms up to shoulder level, flames licked around his wrists and up and down his arms. Always seeming to stay just off the edge of his clothing, the fire increased in intensity. Atlas finally put his hands together, and giving his grandson a wink, threw his hands open and forward, letting loose a massive ball of fire.

With a crack and a tremendous explosion, the wall before them crumpled into pieces, blasting backwards into an open expanse of land.

Atlas looked back again at Drake.

"My boy, one day, you will be capable of such feats. I only used your gift and enhanced it to its future potential. I have no doubt that you will be a force to be reckoned with!"

Atlas turned to the others and waved them on. Artaxle brought up the rear, looking backwards and around every so often to ensure there were none following them.

"So, I understand you were given a tour of Atlantis when you arrived? We are currently outside the city of Urgyen and will continue on foot until you all can learn to use your abilities. I can't think of a better tour than that!"

Pwyll spoke up at the mention of Urgyen.

"Aye, Milord High King... sir, your Honor... um, did ye say we were outside Urgyen? As in the city that's 150 miles away from Atlantis? We were only on yer tram thing for a few minutes... how?"

Pwyll was both excited and set back. The hover trains could travel faster than anything, but it still took a good amount of time to travel the distance they just had. What kind of ramshackle tram underground could go faster than that?

"Ah, my inquisitive, gnomish friend. The tram was created by Amperes several thousand years ago and needs an extreme power source, to which I am uniquely attuned. They only go back and forth from the principal city, not between the other sister cities. My friends and I have quite a few 'shortcuts' that many other Atlanteans are unaware of. Which is also why I need your help Brett to remedy a bit of a situation I had when I first found you. Speaking of friends,"

Atlas slowed his steady march to address the rest of the group.

"My Seeker friends, I thank you for your help. I have seen inside your hearts and know you to be fair and faithful companions. You do not have to follow us on this quest, though we would surely value your company should you intend to stay."

The Seekers looked at each other, half-smiling already. Mason was the first to speak.

"My King, I believe I speak for the rest of us, that we would like nothing more than to join you on your quest, whatever it may be. We have a personal stake in this family and will fight to protect them. We believe, as you do with your sudden return, that these are the Four. Since they are your family, it makes even more sense that they have returned to us."

Atlas looked at everyone gathered. Faces of determination, confusion, awe, and even fear looked back, but refused to budge.

Atlas nodded his head.

"Eleven it is then, just like in the old days! Very well, I assume you all are interested in this quest I speak of?"

Before Atlas could say anything further, though, a hum resonated from the trees before them and from the mountainous Earth behind them.

From over the trees came an immense tank-like vehicle with no treads, floating in the air. Based all along its sides were heavily armored men with long, golden-colored rifles and who had long swords on their hips.

A man stood atop the vehicle, pointing down to the group as another of the vehicles roared from behind them over the mountainous area they exited from.

"Lay down your arms and prepare to be placed in the custody of the Atlantean Guard!" the voice echoed out.

CHAPTER FOURTEEN

TAINTED CRYSTALS

("War" from the Avatar Soundtrack by James Horner)

"My King! We have been found!" Artaxle yelled out.

Immediately, the five Seekers jumped into action, surrounding the family. Atlas and Artaxle completed the circle with the four inside it, protecting them from whatever threat was about to loom before them.

Atlas looked to each of the gathered soldiers he had about him, confused about how the Guard could have tracked them down.

"Protect my family!" he yelled to them. "They are the future of Atlantis!"

Atlas looked up into the throng of Atlantean Guardsmen, focusing on the leader.

You are wrong in this, Commander. I am High King Atlas, returned to lead Atlantis to a new age. Whatever orders you've received, I remand them.

The Commander's face screwed up in confusion. He grabbed at his head, even resorting to smacking the side of it as if there were water inside his ears.

"He cannot hear my thoughts," Atlas said aloud.

Screams suddenly rent the air. Childish screams.

"No, let me go!"

Drake was being dragged away.

Not by a guard or some invisible assassin. Xinzang was pulling him away with her.

Brett leaped into action, grabbing for his son, but Xinzang kicked him with a roundhouse that sent him stumbling back.

That was when Atlas recognized it. A glow coming from around the scalehide's neck. He looked up at the Commander's neckline as well, recognizing the same thing.

"Take off your crystal shards, now!" he yelled over the tumult.

The Atlantean Guard had rappelled from the sides of the tanks to land in a circle around the family and Seekers.

With no hesitation, the Seekers wrenched off the necklaces they wore around their necks, throwing the crystals everywhere.

Xinzang's focus did not stray as she calmly walked away from the group, still holding on to Drake's arm. Zombie-like, she dragged the poor boy as he wailed at her fist.

"Zang, let me go! You're hurting me!"

A slight hesitation was all Ke'eli needed. She could see that the scalehide was fighting some impulse inside her, but was being dominated by strange magic. A tear slipped down her scaly face as the strange magic forced her to continue.

But Ke'eli was by her side in an instant. The same kick came for her that had hit Brett, but Ke'eli was ready for it.

Steeling her nerves and locking her body tight, Ke'eli became like a block of stone. The kick was tremendous, but the love of a mother was stronger. Ke'eli took the kick full-on in the chest and grunted against the pain.

Seeing the others throwing their crystals away, Ke'eli reached in to grab Xinzang's. But Zang was a scalehide monk and was very experienced. She twisted her body this way and that, blocking Ke'eli's hands away to keep her from touching her body.

Ke'eli saw movement from the corner of her eye and felt her energy flow more smoothly. She recognized the feeling that she always got whenever her husband, her *soulmate*, was near her.

Brett stepped in beside her and took her place as Ke'eli reached out to grab Drake and Xinzang's arm. Zang might have been a powerful monk, but she was not as strong as Ke'eli and could not continue to pull Drake away. Ke'eli veritably wrenched the scalehide's clawed hand off Drake, but not before he received a nasty cut on his arm from her attempt to hold on.

The rest of the Seeker group moved to still be close to the family but found it difficult with how quickly the Guard was approaching.

Brett realized he had little time. He didn't want Zang to walk over to the Guards but knew he couldn't follow her forever.

So, he engaged her in martial arts.

Fists flew and knife hands jabbed. To anyone watching, it would have looked like a duo of ancient kung-fu masters sparring.

Brett wasn't the greatest, and he took some unwelcome pokes to his chest and slaps to the side of his face, but it wasn't the stinging pain that he worried about. He knew he just had to get close enough to rip the jewel off that hung around her neck.

Seeing that the group would not go down quietly, the Commander on the main barge barked out orders to neutralize the group, children included. The rest of the protectors realized that there was no more time to delay.

Artaxle had already splintered off from the main body as soon as the fear of being apprehended became clear. He and Atlas had worked together long enough to understand each other, and Artaxle knew the Commander was also being mentally manipulated to have his troops attack the group.

Artaxle's sole job was to get up to that machine somehow and either disable it or the Commander.

Quickly and with much more stealth than one thought could be possible in broad daylight, the goblin slinked between troops and behind them, creeping along the shadows of the mountainside. To any outside observer who could see him, the obvious benefit of magic was helping him to sneak almost invisibly past the very astute guards.

Tumidus, not wanting to injure the Guards too badly, was not a combat sorcerer and knew only a few offensive spells. One came to mind that would slow or stop at least one flank of the approaching Guards.

Reaching into his pocket, he produced a small crystal vial filled with phosphorescent material, waving it in the area before him. Slowly, that vial took on a life of its own as Tumidus funneled his magical arcane energy into it. The vial grabbed any ambient light in the area and spun it about in magnificent spiraling circles, creating a vortex of light.

The Guards within thirty feet of Tumidus stopped to stare at the hypnotic pattern before them, many dropping their weapons to their sides.

"Do not harm the Guards to my fore!" Tumidus yelled at his companions, though he knew he did not need to.

The Seekers had trained together for many years, which sometimes included combat scenarios. Each had an ability that would combine to aid in the group's survivability. The warning was welcome though to Atlas and the family, who might not had known any better.

Kelly looked about the area, trying in vain to see where she might aid her protectors. She knew she could do something with the air about them if she could focus enough.

When she saw some of the Guard on the floating vessels preparing their rifles, she knew she had to at least try to keep them from shooting at them.

Closing her eyes, she focused on bringing up a small vortex of wind around her parents and protectors. Gradually, the wind picked up, first around her, and then expanding to encompass the entire group.

And just in the nick of time.

The rifles that the Guards were using were non-deadly, but still administered a severe shock if they made contact. Like a 50-foot long taser cable, their weapons shot probes at the group, but the windy whirlpool surrounding the group intercepted them, and none found purchase.

Kelly fought with all her might to maintain the vortex, but she found it was severely taxing to keep her concentration. Slowly, she sank down to the Earth and fought to keep the winds blowing about her and her family.

Xinzang and Brett continued to spar with each other, Brett taking more and more hits. Now that Xinzang did not have a child's arm to hold on to, she was better able to use both her hands to strike at Brett.

Brett's defenses wore down quicker and quicker. Xinzang could strike him five times for his every two, and many times felt his energy sap out from his body from her successful hits. The only way he could fight it off was the initial idea that she would try to steal his son, but now, with him safe with Ke'eli, the initial adrenaline had worn off.

Xinzang continued to punch at Brett, getting past his defenses. Slowing down now, Xinzang, still in her zombie-like state, opened her fists to make a point with her two lead fingers, landing jabs on specific points of Brett's body.

Suddenly, Brett could not move. His entire body went rigid as he fought to keep from falling on his face, but his arms would not obey his commands, and his legs began to shake.

Xinzang turned from him to stalk back towards Drake, reaching for the boy even with Ke'eli standing before him.

The yell from the Guards as they lunged through the howling vortex of wind did not help matters any more. They fought to keep upright as they began their melee assault, and many could get through to put their weapons to bare on the family and Seekers.

Ordered to apprehend and not kill, their weapons were much like the ranged tasers from the Guards still on the tank-vessel, but handheld. They used rifles with long tuning-like forks attached to jab inwards at the group. Several, thinking that Keb was the cause for the wind, struck out at him first, sending bolts of electricity through his body.

But Keb was a proud tribal orc of the Earthmaw Clan. He had prepared for battle and summoned the strength of the stone around him for protection. Though the tasing hurt, Keb's preparation lessened the pain.

Several other tasers found their way towards Atlas, Mason and Pwyll, sending a sizzling sound into the air as their bodies reacted to the assault. To any other group of Atlanteans, it would have meant the end as their bodies caved to the stunning onslaught.

But these were not ordinary Atlanteans, and the wind buffeting the Guards caused them difficulty in keeping in contact with the electrical probes.

Atlas silently thanked his granddaughter as he reached out and grabbed Tumidus.

"Don't mind me son," he said, "you know the Thunderwave spell, yes?"

Nodding quickly, Tumidus backed away to allow Atlas to move to the center.

"That will injure us as well though, my King!" Tumidus tried to warn Atlas over the windy torrent.

Reaching deep within Tumidus' memory, Atlas found the Thunderwave spell and called it to his lips.

"That's why I love metamagic!" Atlas said as he cast the spell.

"*Mutare Locum Fluctus Tonitrui!*"

A blast of energy erupted from Atlas, but almost seemed to flow over the Seekers and family in the middle, to reverberate outside their protective circle. The force of the spell, cast with so much added energy, threw dirt and grass up from the ground, pummeling the Guards closing in.

The shockwave slammed into them, knocking most of them off their feet and sending them flying to the ground. The Guards groaned as they struggled to stand back up.

Tumidus buckled after the theft of some of his power from Atlas. He had heard rumors about the abilities of their High King but had obviously never experienced them firsthand.

Atlas could siphon the abilities of others and then enhance them to their greatest potential. The originator still used the ability in a technical sense but would not impede Atlas. He would act as the conduit for the higher energy, but draining the person he took the power from.

Drake, hiding behind his mother's arms, looked from around them to see Xinzang still stalking in. He had heard

Atlas yell about the crystal shards and saw the device hanging from a chain around her neck.

He wasn't sure what he could do, but he figured he should at least try.

Drake knew from his experience in the Senatus building that if he concentrated enough on something, he could cause it to burn. Was a crystal any different?

Squinting his eyes to stare at the crystal, Drake imagined the thing bursting into flame. He could not have known at the time that it was a creation of magic; a gift from the Soulstone that imparted unique gifts to different people. Because it was a magic item, it would not be burned so easily.

His young and inattentive nature, though, saved his attempt.

Because he could not concentrate so well in the din of battle around him, his gaze ended up including part of the chain that held the crystal to her body. Though the crystal was magic, the chain was not.

Glowing red hot around her neck, Xinzang's reptilian skin did not feel the heat at first. The chain began to melt from around the shard, dropping it lower and lower. Finally, the scalehide stopped to look down at her chest in time to see her shard disconnect from her body.

Instantly, her zombie-like nature cleared up. Tears welled in her eyes as she realized what she had done. She was in her body the entire time, but had found that she could not control her actions.

Anger replaced her sadness as she looked about the battlefield. Looking down to expect returned anger from

Drake, she instead saw a smiling boy who realized he had saved her from herself.

Her anger shifted to a determination to see the boy to safety, no matter what.

She nodded to Pwyll, yelling through the wind.

"The younglings could use some aid there, Father Pwyll! Oh, and Brett too!"

Being a former religious leader in his clan, Pwyll had turned from his studies to taking on a life of adventure and travel. He did not regret it one bit.

Giving the recovered scalehide a big thumbs up, Pwyll took out a long cylinder from his belt before shaking it down. The length of it doubled before the tip expanded sideways, becoming a double-sided hammer. He raised it above his head before pointing towards the children and Brett.

"Chaaaaarge!"

Unbeknownst to them, Pwyll had also chugged a potion he pulled out of his pouch that made his little robotic gnome legs move super-fast. He yanked out one of his grenades, which he threw up in the air like a baseball before whacking it with his newly produced hammer.

The grenade-like device flipped through the air, landing in the middle of a fire team of Guards who ran towards them.

Pwyll knew the device was more fire than shrapnel, so he wasn't worried about killing the guards as much as getting them off their kilter, distracted and heading for him instead of the children.

At that, Pwyll turned with a roar towards the flank of Guards who were still trying to stand and come at him through the wind.

Xinzang ran by Brett, patting him on the shoulder as she passed.

"I am sorry, my friend. The feeling will pass soon enough, and you will continue your fight against our true foes!"

Amazingly, she leaped straight through the windy vortex, side-kicked two other Guards before vaulting over them as well. She saw the large floating vessel above and behind them and knew that they would soon have heavier fire power raining down on their heads unless they disabled the machine.

Brett fought with his nerves to get his body to move again, but found that whatever Xinzang had done to him was not going away anytime soon. He could see out of the corner of his eye the Guards creeping towards him, their long-arm tasers ready.

Thinking it to be some trick, the Guards poked at Brett to see if he would move. When he did not, they prodded him more, the electrical current running throughout his body and making him convulse even more.

But he didn't need to worry.

From the other corner of his eye came his wife, her fury unleashed. Drake was safe with Atlas and Tumidus, and she saw her husband being electrocuted before her eyes.

That day saw a side of Ke'eli that Brett or the children had never seen before.

Ke'eli charged headlong into the two Guards, swatting them away like flies. Her muscles bulged beneath her tight clothes, straining against their confines. Each punch dented the armor, and each parry bent their weapons.

The sight to Brett was beautiful, yet unnerving to behold.

Like a mountain come to life, Ke'eli bore through the Guards, pushing them back into the wind and away at least ten feet. Even after the Guards were far enough away, she still stood her ground, gnashing her teeth and waiting for the next Guard to try to hurt her family.

Keb could feel her rising energy. Being attuned to the elemental Earth as he was, he knew what she was really capable of. He had had little time to teach her, mainly because he was still intimidated because a human could do what the orcs had been doing for thousands of years, but seeing her display of power, he now believed it was right.

Grunting at the repeated punishment of taser probes into his sides and chest, Keb reached out his hand to Mother Earth and whispered through the pain, *"Badili mwamba huu kuwa matope"*.

The ground before him held many Guards, thinking to stop him from bringing on the winds that kept their allies away. They were mistaken to think that the orc was the windcaller though, and the sinking mud at their feet showed them why.

Where there was before solid ground now sucked at the Guard's boots, pulling them deep into the semi-liquid earth. They fought to push through the thick mud, but their heavy armor and weapons kept them from moving but at a snail's pace. The Guards yelled to warn each other, but all who were near to Keb were already stuck.

By now, Artaxle had made it spider-like up through the trees and on to the side of one of the floating tanks. There were Guards stationed along one side of the thing, facing the family and the Seekers, so the far side was vacant.

Silent and deadly, he crawled up the slanted metallic side of the tank-like vehicle. Pulling out a long and serrated dagger, the goblin remained low to not give away his position to anyone else on the other higher-floating tank across the way.

The Commander continued barking orders into a communication device, trying in vain to stage a response to the swirling winds, the non-responsive soldiers standing in a daze, the team stuck in the mud and the few remaining who were still standing against the scalehide and gnome's barrage.

The Commander stood upright taller suddenly, softly muttering to no one as his hand brought the receiver slowly to his mouth. Where before the Guard were to take the family and Seekers into custody without serious harm, the orders that the Commander spoke into the transmitter made Artaxle wince. Robotically and very monotone, the Commander nonchalantly repeated some order he had just received.

"Deadly force is authorized."

But the order never made it to the Guards down below.

Artaxle had deftly swung around and severed the wire connecting the receiver, coming to face the Commander in his turret aboard the tank.

Holding the long blade to the Commander's neck, it would have now been like holding a blade to a blank wall. The Commander stared off into space, giving the order repeatedly while expecting the deaths of the people down below.

Artaxle recognized a charmed person when he saw one. Since most of the crystal shards in Atlantis were equipped to prevent charming, the goblin knew that this was a powerful form of control.

Keeping the blade at his throat, Artaxle reached over and pulled out the chain, keeping the Commander's crystal shard inside his armor like a dog tag. The blade, goblin steel made to vibrate at intense speeds, flashed in the artificial daylight. But there was no blood. Artaxle had cut the shard from its chain and sent it flying down to the ground below them.

Immediately, the Commander's eyes resumed their normal hue as he shook his head in confusion.

"You are assaulting High King Atlas, his escorts, *and his family*. You would do well to not earn his ire."

How Artaxle played the dangerous blade across the man's throat had the Commander wincing from the fear of having his cut ear to ear.

But he was back in his right mind.

"High King Atlas has not been seen for over a thousand years, goblin. We have orders from the Elders to take you all into custody. King Atlas would have to..."

The Commander's speech trailed off into muttering though as his flying tank vehicle began to sharply descend.

Grabbing hold of the surrounding turret, the Commander braced himself for the hard impact, but found he had no need to.

Artaxle had placed his weapon back into its sheath on his belt. Cloyingly, he teased out a question to the Commander.

"Let me ask you Commander; who in all Atlantis has power over the very *gravity* of the place? Who lifted the mountains into the sky and who taught our people to float off their feet? Only one man."

Atlas Titanes.

Standing on the ground surrounded by the Seekers and family, the High King lowered his hand.

He had brought not only the Commander's flying tank down, but the other as well as they both settled onto the ground.

"Commander! I would like a word!" he shouted over the wind, which had finally died down.

Every Guardsman around him stopped what they were doing. All knew the stories about how the Soulstone had taught Atlas how to harness gravity. If he were to have one ability that none other had, it would be that.

With it, Atlas had raised the land and the people from the soft dirt of the earth into the Heavens above. And just as quickly, he could bring it crashing back down.

Artaxle escorted the Commander from his tank cautiously.

The family and the Seekers, all still prepared to continue battle, rearranged themselves to protect the children, but they knew the fight was over.

The Commander walked briskly over to Atlas, who stood standing with his hands on his hips. Already by his side was Artaxle, who supplied the King the Commander's crystal shard.

Atlas took the thing and held it at arm's length, weary to touch the crystal itself.

"You have been compelled to attack us. The order from the Elders did not mention who we were, did it?"

Obviously realizing now who he was standing in front of, the Commander fought to keep his composure.

"Yes, my King, we were ordered... to... *ahem*... bring you back to the Capital."

"By whom? And who gave you the order to use deadly force?"

The Commander was at a loss. The look on his face was clear... that he had no clue.

"My King, I am sorry. I... do not recall who gave the order. And I do not recall getting orders to use deadly force. On children? No..."

The Commander rubbed his head as if he were sore from a beating. Pinching the bridge of his nose, he shook his head as if trying to remember something from a long time ago.

But Atlas already understood what the implications meant.

"You were being controlled."

Turning from the Commander, Atlas looked out to all gathered.

"If you possess an Awoken crystal shard, remove it from your body and bury it."

The statement brought gasps from some men around him.

Brett, finally out of his stunned condition, leaned against his former aggressor Xinzang, who found herself very guilty for beating her ally up.

"What is he talking about? Is that what made you act all crazy?"

Brett unceremoniously looked up and down Xinzang's body. Though she was a scalehide, she still had many of the shapely qualities of a woman.

Catching himself as to what he was doing, Brett nervously turned his head away.

"Sorry about that. I was looking to make sure that shard thing wasn't still hanging from you."

Xinzang chuckled under her breath.

"Crystal shards are farmed in three areas of eminent power around Atlantis and can be 'Awoken' by any pyramid to store unique abilities. Many of the more powerful ones are expensive to purchase, so some Atlanteans find adventure by traveling into those three dangerous territories to gather their own. Some say that a shard can call out to its owner, having some sentience. The shards themselves are supposedly minute connections to the Soulstone itself, so to ask someone to destroy theirs is a tough order to follow."

Brett tried hard to understand but found himself distracted as Atlas set the Commander's chain and shard down on the now-solid ground.

Xinzang looked on in wonder, continuing her explanation of the shards.

"The non-Awoken shards are less powerful and can be used for long-distance communication or to store basic information. Much like your credit cards and cellphones in your Olde World, they allow us some of the basic necessities of life. They do not hold any kind of bond with the wearer, though, and do not require attunement."

As she finished, Atlas cupped his hands over the shard on the ground. Closing his eyes, he buried the thing with dirt, patting it lightly.

Standing to face the Commander, Atlas put on a wide smile.

"Your shard is being cleansed, Commander. I would like you to pass the word to every Atlantean Guardsman to do the same. It is a basic act that allows the natural Earth to wipe any negative energy from the shard. Leave it in the ground for ten minutes and it will be purified."

Patting the Commander on the shoulder, the Guardsman could do nothing but nod at the strangeness of it all.

Other Atlantean Guardsmen around him took off their own shards, doing the same ritual to cleanse them.

"My King, what do we do now?" the Commander asked, turning to face Atlas as he walked to the tree line before him.

Atlas looked back at him and smiled again.

"I forgive you your trespasses, Commander. Spread the word everywhere that Atlas has returned and that he will visit each and every Tribal Capital. He will be accompanied by ten others who will be afforded the same rights and courtesies as I will have."

The Commander nodded, looking over at the ten gathered behind him.

"And last, Commander, and most important of all... do not interfere."

Atlas' jovial mood turned deathly serious as he looked down over his nose at the Commander.

The Commander got the hint.

Turning briskly, he walked away, back towards his tank, which he noticed was hovering again.

CHAPTER FIFTEEN
TREE FLYING

A short rest later, the Atlantean Guard returned to their hovering vehicles wearing dirty crystal shards. All piled into the tanks, looking down at the eleven on the ground with some faces of curiosity and some with awe.

The Commander had to hold off the questions and requests to meet the High King, because he considered it "interfering", and did not want the ire of their newly returned leader. So instead, the Guard loaded into their vehicles and flew back towards the Capital.

Alone again, Atlas looked back at the group.

"Finally! Can we get this train back on its tracks or what?!"

Greeted with enthusiastic nods, Atlas smiled before turning and walking away.

The crowd, all except Artaxle, who followed his King, stood there confused.

Atlas stopped, turning back to them.

"We have a LOT of walking to do and plenty of time to talk on the road. Hop to! Let's go! First stop, close the rift I inadvertently opened when I sent Brett home, and then onward to Shambhala where you will begin, or in your case, Brett, end your training. Everyone get in the sling!"

"Wait, what?" Brett asked, put back on his heels once again.

Atlas smiled back at him.

"From what I hear, you've already run into them. We are heading *back* the way you came when you returned to Atlantis with the Seekers. I need *that*," Atlas pointed at the shard that lay hanging around Ke'eli's neck, "to close the spatial rift I created when I sent Brett home 20 years ago. I 'acquired' Brett while he was training in the Gardens at Shambhala and sent him back to the Olde World with my crystal shard. It's one of the few things capable of being able to teleport *out* of Atlantis, but in doing so, I tore a hole in our reality. That's why you're not supposed to teleport out of Atlantis, even me!"

Atlas turned back around and continued walking towards the tree line.

"The plane-touched." Keb muttered, loud enough for all to hear.

Atlas stopped and turned back to everyone; his head down low.

"Yes, the plane-touched. Only those in that area. I didn't realize until later on that in sending Brett home, I had unwittingly opened a gateway to other realms that no one knew about. And it was a small one too, so it went unnoticed. Some fiends have been able to slip in and cause some chaos. Including the group you ran into."

The group looked back and forth at each other.

Atlas was the reason for the fiends.

Everyone knew he had not meant it. He was saving his son, after all. Wasn't he?

"Look. Rifts open all the time in Atlantis and there are brave Atlanteans there to stop whatever comes through. The Devil's Claw is a rift to the Nine Hells and to the Abyss. Fiends come through all the time there, but I bet you all didn't know that. It's one of the best-kept secrets in Atlantis. Radiant energy permanently kills fiends and their devilish essence. That's how I killed them in France thousands of years ago, and that's how we will kill them here. I need the shard, though, to close the rift I opened, for good."

Atlas stood with his hands on his hips. He had gone from smiling ear to ear, to distraught at his own failure.

Brett walked up with Ke'eli, taking the necklace from around her neck.

"Here you go pop. I understand and would have done the same thing. So, what, 20 years of an open rift in the middle of Atlantis? Let's go kill this thing and shut it down for good."

The surrounding Seekers nodded their ascent that they agreed with Brett.

"10 years for me, but well said, son. I knew you would understand. Now then, are you all ready to fly?"

Atlas turned back to his companions, pointing to a large tree that stood at the edge of a massive forest. They had approached the dense copse of trees and seemed ready to enter before Atlas stopped them.

The excitement of following King Atlas and now fighting with him had stunned the family to the surrounding sights. Brought back to reality, they realized just how tiny they were.

The forest before them was massive. The trees were beautiful and held every odd assortment of species imaginable. Leaves of green, red, gold, and yellow were everywhere, as if the place was in a perpetual state of fall.

"Bohdi Forest," Tumidus began, "home of the Trees of Enlightenment."

Atlas smiled back at the elf.

"And do you know, good elf, *why* they are the Trees of Enlightenment?"

Tumidus' history was impeccable, but in the presence of so great a man, he faltered, not wanting to be incorrect.

"Do not fret, my friend, the feeling will pass. Seriously, all of you, do not look to me as some fleeting figure who will disappear after you have placed so much of your trust in me. Unbelievably, I have been an active part of the goings-on of this country since its start. I know you are aware of the rumors that I tend to come and go as I please, always leaving confusion in my wake..."

"... not to mention death and destruction..." Pwyll mentioned to Mason under his breath.

("Treebeard" from the Lord of the Rings: The Two Towers Soundtrack by Howard Shore)

Atlas erupted into laughter then mid-sentence.

Pwyll shot upright then, realizing that King Atlas was one of the most powerful people on the planet. Surely, he could not have heard him, though!

"Ah, my good gnome. I know of those rumors too. I hope to show you, in time, how false they are. But alas, let me... well, *enlighten* all of you why they call these the Trees of Enlightenment!"

At that, Atlas knocked his knuckles on the side of one tree he had pointed to.

Gradually, the wind seemed to whip up around the tree. The leaves shook, and the branches creaked and moaned.

But it was the only tree to be under this seeming gale-forced wind.

Brett looked at his daughter to see if she was playing any tricks, but she looked up to him, lost as everyone else.

When the tree looked like it could take it no more and the group was on the verge of taking cover, a tremendous roar echoed out across the gully the group stood in.

The roar had come *from* the tree.

There, facing them, was exactly that. A face. In the tree. Smacking its lips from the massive yawn it had just made.

"Oh, I was in such a good deep sleep too! Didn't even hear you all walk up! Must have a bird's nest in my ears again." At that, the tree laughed at his own misfortune as a large limb reached around to pick at the side of the trunk where the face sat.

The tree's eyes were massive, as was the body of the thing. After picking at its ear, it looked down at the assembled crowd, crooning. Until its eyes set on Atlas.

"Oh, well, hello good King! How nice to see you! It has been some time, hasn't it? I see you are in the company of good folk, so I do not believe you will need any of the wisdom from the collective mind?"

Atlas put his hand on the side of the tree and smiled at it.

"No, my old friend, I will not. We need passage northwest, and I could think of no better way than that of the old times. I have some young children here who I am sure would love nothing better than to be in the arms of some of the mightiest entities the Earth has ever created."

Atlas looked back at the family and smiled.

Brett stood there, watching the tree talk and move. He grabbed his wife close.

"An actual talking tree. Probably a thousand years old too, judging by its size. Are we walking to the city with these things, Kee?"

"Well, he said we would be in their arms."

Ke'eli looked more amazed than Brett did. Connected to the Earth, Ke'eli knew some organisms shared their connection with the planet itself. She likened them to the massive forests in California, said to share one system. Roots extending for miles, all interconnected. One giant living thing. That's when she understood the implication of one connected mind of ageless trees, able to communicate, and in this case, enlighten.

"Well then, let me confer with my comrades and we shall have you right off!"

The tree closed its eyes for a moment, nodding and swaying in the invisible wind.

Atlas returned to the group.

"Now, there is a method to my madness, and I need you to not be alarmed at what we are about to do."

"Oh, we get it, the trees are going to carry us!" Drake said, overhearing his father's conversation and thinking that it was going to be easy going.

"Well, you are half right, grandson."

Before Atlas could continue, the tree spoke up, lowering the bulk of its larger branches to the ground.

"We are ready! My comrades are awake and standing by! First up!"

Atlas looked back at the group again and tried to put on his best smile.

"We have little time, but I assure you, this is the quickest, and most importantly quietest, way to get to our destination. You just have to trust me."

Saying that, Atlas walked over to another large tree that had woken up as well. Bowing low to the tree in respect, he reached up to one branch as it lowered to him, plucking off a giant leaf.

"Now, if you would all just do as I do, we will all meet on the eastern edge of Shambhala south of the bay that hugs the city. Do not enter the city!"

Atlas walked casually over to the group of lowered branches and lay down on them, hugging the giant leaf close to his chest.

"Grip the leaf against your chest. When you feel you are ready, raise the leaf above your head and it will aid you. Oh, and I hope you enjoy the view!"

Everyone looked at each other in confusion again, which was a recurring theme with this strange King they had in their midst. Even the Seekers seemed at a loss for words about what exactly they were expected to do.

The result had everyone's jaw dropping.

Without warning, the massive tree pulled its giant branches quickly into the air and slung Atlas off into the distance.

No one else moved.

"Did he really just do that?" Kelly asked the assembled group.

No one could answer.

No one except Artaxle.

"It is safe, girl, as long as you have the leaf. Atlas has a flair for the dramatics and knew you all would be cautious, which is why he went first and left me here. As you soar through the air and begin your descent, lift your leaf. It will act as a glider, slowing your fall tremendously. Another tree will catch you, lower you closer to the ground where you should again grasp your leaf tight against your chest before it too catapults you into the distance. This was the way long-distance travel was many thousands of years ago."

As if proving the idea was sane and sound enough, Artaxle also went to the leaf-giving tree, plucking one off before settling into the lowered branches of the treant.

Atlas had looked confident enough in the means of travel. Artaxle, not so much. He managed a weak smile before clutching the leaf to his chest. Not even a second later, he was soaring through the air.

Everyone who remained looked at each other in concern.

"Are we really going to do this?" Ke'eli asked, a genuine fear in her eyes.

"The children aren't doing it alone, Hell no." Brett replied comically. "We will double up. Ke'eli, you take Drake. I will take Kelly. If anything happens and your leaf or whatever doesn't work, try to use your abilities to slow your fall. Kelly, I'm in your hand's darlin'. If this doesn't work, do you think you can use the wind to slow both our falls?"

Kelly looked at her father and tried to appear confident.

"Yeah dad, I got you." She worked up as big a smile as she could muster.

Brett grabbed her and his wife and son close.

"I know this is crazy, but for some reason, I know it will work. Something seems so stupidly familiar about it; I just can't wrap my head around it. We will be okay. Kee, I know you can already sense the trees, right? You good with this, or do you want to trade?"

Ke'eli nodded her head, smiling.

"Oh yeah, I can feel them all! It's almost smothering, but yeah, if something happens to our leaf, I think I can reach out to somebody to catch us. We're good."

A twang interrupted their huddle.

The group looked over to the Seekers, who had all grabbed leaves and were lining up to launch into the air.

Mason looked over at the family.

"King Atlas has some... *unorthodox* means, but I do not doubt him. These leaves supply a slow fall for a short duration, like a feather. The fronds will dry out within a few hours, though, so best to keep going once you have plucked one. We will all go first to ensure its safety and to set up a perimeter near Shambhala before you arrive."

With that, one by one, the Seekers launched through the air over the trees and away from the family.

"Well, I guess that means we are up!" Brett grabbed his family close again.

"Be safe, don't freak out, and I guess try to enjoy the ride?" Ke'eli told her family.

Brett and Kelly walked up to the frond tree. Bowing low, Brett reached up and plucked a larger looking leaf.

Brett lay down on the branches with Kelly laying on his chest, covered by the giant leaf.

"Hold on tight, honey. I got you." Brett kissed his daughter on the head and hugged her closely.

Brett looked over to his wife, mouthing the words 'I love you', not a second before lifting off the ground and into the air.

("Welcome to the Moors" from the Maleficent Soundtrack by James Newton Howard)

The sudden gush of wind took Brett's breath away. He couldn't see the trajectory his comrades went, so when he opened his eyes and saw that he was hundreds of feet above the trees, he was amazed.

He soared through the air faster than anything he had ever imagined, and as he felt his descent begin, he lifted the giant leaf.

Immediately, the leaf filled with air and slowed his fall, but not his forward momentum. They were speed hang-gliding.

"Kelly! Open your eyes!"

Letting the slightest bit of light into her eyes, Kelly did that. It didn't take her long to open them all the way.

Spread out before her, as far as the eye could see, were gigantic, beautiful trees of all kinds. Water sparkled off a lake not far away while birds fluttered in a flock as they passed.

The trees that most startled them, though, were the ones that rose far above the others. Their trunks were tinged blue, and sparkles seemed to fall from their branches. They were in small groups, but spread out enough where they dotted the landscape.

Even from here, they could see that there were *people* in those trees. They had obviously noted the hang-gliding group and had gone to the edge of the limbs they climbed to see who flew about them so.

Thankfully, the tree-people waved as Brett and Kelly soared by. They could see small villages in and around the blue-tinged trees with some built like treehouses.

Not only was the flight breathtaking, but the scenery was as well.

Both felt as though the natural beauty of the place had far surpassed the artificiality of the cities that had grown up around the pyramids.

Gradually, their descent brought them in line with the tops of some other trees, who reached up their branches to catch them. Lowering down to the ground, the trees once again launched them through the air, continuing their overland flight.

Further ahead, Brett could see some of the Seekers who floated along at the tops of the trees as well and knew they were going in the right direction.

It was not long before he saw the clearing of the forest ahead and felt the 'throwing' of the trees get more directed and less forceful.

The last throw had him only a few hundred feet from the clearing, which Brett found was easy enough to guide his leaf down to.

Getting the hang of the gliding, Brett could steer his leaf toward the small clearing. Landing inside it, the others ran to rejoin their comrades. All had looks of amazement on their faces as they tried to fix their windswept hair.

Atlas strolled away from the wood line as well, waving to another treant as he gave thanks.

"Well, what did you think? Boring hover train, or overland tree-flipping, as I like to call it?"

Everyone wholeheartedly agreed that "tree-flipping" was much more exciting, as exhilarating and scary as it was.

Atlas went from cheery to grim in less time than it took to blink.

"Now, a few miles away is a small encampment of plane-touched halflings and dwarves. I do not know how they have been able to lie under the proverbial radar for so long, which is why I fear that there is something else at work here."

Atlas turned and looked off in the distance to the north.

They could just make out a glistening body of water there. The family and Seekers recognized it as being the same they appeared next to when they fled Brett's home.

"I do not see this encampment High King." Tumidus said, squinting into the distance.

Atlas turned back to the elf, smiling again.

"Yes, good elf, I know. They have hidden it with some form of magic, which adds to their secrecy. I only found it while coming back recently to this place to reminisce about that time 20 years ago when I sent my boy back home. I totally stumbled upon it by accident and was almost laid low myself!"

Atlas turned back around and gathered the group together.

"Now, we must plan a strategy. The area is not excessively big and thankfully, few of my Atlanteans are perverted by the dark energy there. We should split into teams and attack from every flank. Unfortunately, none will give up easily and the battle may become bloody."

Brett looked over at his children, shaking his head no.

"I'm not bringing my kids into battle against anything there 'pop'. We will have to hide them somewhere safe while us grown-ups do all the fighting."

Atlas shrugged his shoulders.

"I agree with you, Brett. Unfortunately, as you all met when you arrived here, there are patrols of these plane-touched. If they find your children unattended, I fear they may take them. I think they would be best suited staying close to their parents or the group at large."

Atlas looked from Brett to Ke'eli, gauging their reaction.

Brett scowled when he looked back at his father. But he also knew that he was right.

Mason interrupted the train of thought.

"Wait, I know where we are! If we are just east of Shambhala, then we are directly south across the lake from where the valixi crashed!"

Atlas looked from Mason to the group.

"It is no small feat for a valixi to crash! Where were you when this happened, and when was it?"

"It was several days ago, my King. We were camped just north of the city of Olam Haba when the ship flew over us in the dark of night. We ascertained they had probably been smugglers, as they flew with no light. They crashed, and we... investigated."

"Why do you say it with apprehension, my mystic friend?" Atlas cocked his head to the side, curious.

"We discovered they were smugglers, and that their cargo was... Myrmidons."

As Atlas' eyebrows rose and he appeared ready to scold the mystic, Mason continued.

"My King! We were unsure at the time but defeated the monsters before they could spread! I apologized then, and do again now, that I brought the family... *your* family, so close to peril."

Atlas tried to maintain his irate visage but knew that the Seekers had done well in protecting his family.

"You are not to blame my folically-challenged friend." Atlas smiled at the quip, hoping it would ease some of the newly made tension. "The Myrmidons most likely sensed the intense emanations of fiendish energy from this gate. They were specifically bred to single fiends out and can enter a state of heightened aggression when they do, even from so far away. That is what most likely caused their escape, and from what I am hearing, the eventual crashing of the valixi."

Brett, patience wearing out, waved the group on.

"Okay, what's the plan? It's going to be getting dark soon and I don't want to be out here with these things again, especially if there's actually an entire camp of them. Flank them and then what?"

Atlas nodded his head, re-affirming his plan.

"We move in from each flank and take out the perimeter guards. We get to the middle of the encampment, and I use the shard to close the gateway. Simple as that."

The Seekers looked at each other nervously. Thankfully, their leader, Mason, was skilled in the arts of subterfuge and secrecy.

"My High King," Mason started, "with all due respect, we may be outmatched if we do not prepare. There are going to be fiends there based on your recollection, and none of us here, except maybe Pwyll, has access to any radiant abilities. If what you say is true and that only radiant power can fully destroy a demon, then how will we ensure each one of them is killed when we attack?"

Atlas continued smiling as Mason spoke. As he finished, he looked at everyone present.

"Have you not heard tales of the 'Four'?" he asked.

The Seekers looked at each other first and then back to the family before them.

They had indeed heard of the Four, as Mason had mentioned back in the Senatus chamber. They knew the Four were possessed of a strange sort of power, and now they also knew that they were descendants of the High King of Atlantis himself.

It was Tumidus who finally put the last piece of the puzzle together.

"They embody each of the five Principles."

"Yes, friend elf, you are correct." Atlas confirmed.

Brett cocked an eyebrow, trying to understand more of the strange Atlantis code-speak, but Atlas was already one step ahead.

Leaning down to the ground, he drew a large circle in the dirt. He then created spokes to each of the four cardinal directions, and then again twice between them. When he was done, the circle looked like a giant clock.

"You believe you are composed of some strange energy that allows you to control the elements. In actuality, you have only uncovered your control of the Spiritual Principle."

Brett still looked at him like he was crazy. Atlas continued.

"There are five Principles in Atlantis. Each race embodies a certain aspect of one of the five. For example, the gnomes, elves and goblinoids embody the Arcane Principle, which allows them to use 'magick'."

Atlas pointed at the 1, 2 and 3 o'clock part of his circular map.

"The orcs, aquarians, beast-born, scalehide and skin-walkers embody the Spiritual Principle, in diverse ways. Where the orcs can manifest elemental energy, the scalehide manifests their inner chi. Either way, it is spiritual in manner."

Atlas then circled the entire southern section of the map.

"The humans embody the Mental Principle, able to use their mystic abilities of the mind. It is this reason that they are so callous and set apart from the rest of Atlantis, because they are singular in their ability."

Atlas circled the 10 o'clock section of his map.

"Last, we have the halflings and dwarves who embody the Divine Principle. They have a connection to the Elders that allows them to channel their power. It is much like magick, but divinely based."

Atlas circled the 11 and 12 o'clock portions of the map.

"Now, there is some blending here and there, as Master Clemens mentioned just now. Gnomes use technology in their devices, and some have gained a divine form of nanobots in their blood as well. I believe Mr. Pwyll has a nominal number of them. Some abilities of other races might appear Arcane or Divine, which is up to their individual interpretation."

"What's the Fifth Principle?" Kelly piped up from the circle, sitting cross-legged on the ground.

Atlas nodded, forgetting that there was one more.

"Yes, my dear granddaughter, I neglected to mention the Fifth. It is the simplest, but most widely used. The Fifth is the Martial Principle, which guides us in combat and is much more closely related to the Spiritual Principle than some give credit. The Dark Knights of the undead embody the Martial Principle, but also parts of the Arcane, Divine and Spiritual as well. They are my perfect example, and thus are you, Kelly."

Kelly perked up her ears.

Brett looked at Atlas again, not understanding.

Atlas waved his hands at the coming questions.

"Back to the history lesson. The 'Four' were the only ones to master all Five Principles. You are all proficient in one type of the Spiritual Principle, signified by the power over a respective element. You have all also come to understand that you are Mystics as well, and I am sure that each of you has knowledge of a specific theme of the Mental Principle that you are better suited for."

Kelly raised her hand before yelling out, "Healing!"

Atlas smiled again, but nodded his head no.

"Actually, my girl, that is why you are my example. All four of you have an aspect of the Divine Principle inside you, but Kelly is the only one to have accessed it so far. It was not your Mystic ability that healed the griffon, it was your Divine. And *each* of you has that in you."

Atlas looked at the rest of the family while Kelly looked down at her own hands.

"So, the plan is, you will each discover a way to tap in to even the most basic part of the Divine Principle, with our aid, so that as we battle the plane-touched, you can dispel them with radiant energy when the time comes."

Again, Atlas just smiled.

Brett had found that his smile got them into more trouble than he thought it was worth.

CHAPTER SIXTEEN

BANISHING DEMONS

("Hero's Theme" from the Justice League Soundtrack by Danny Elfman)

The family marched north towards the distant body of water they remembered was Lake Apsu. They knew they would have several hours to prepare, so each went to work with a tutor to get to where they could summon even the most basic radiant cantrip.

Atlas walked up and down the line, tapping into the family's powers occasionally. He alone knew when the individual family member had achieved success, because he could amplify their ability and feel it himself.

Mason helped by trying to aid the family mentally while being *inside* their minds. At first, they did not like the idea of Mason snooping around inside their heads, but with the promise that he would only help them focus, they finally relented.

Brett worked with Tumidus, who taught him to focus on summoning divine energy to his hand. They discovered, humorously, that Brett was very adept at creating holy water. In the end, Atlas believed it sufficient to destroy the escaping essences of fiends. Tumidus, having several empty potion containers, bottled as much of the fluid as he could.

Ke'eli worked with Keb, who taught her to think of the Living Earth as a deity in and of itself. The orcs worshipped Mother Nature and knew that the elements were at her disposal. Keb taught Ke'eli how to manifest the power of the Earth in each of her physical strikes, not only lending strength to the blow itself but also allowing it to radiate divine energy.

Kelly stayed with Pwyll, who showed her how to imbue herbs into an essence that allowed the final concoction to heal wounds and bring allies back from the brink of death. Kelly's divine ability ended up being exactly what she thought: healing. She could use that healing aspect with Pwyll to draw any fiendish essence out of a possessed person. The better for them to be put down for good.

And last, Drake learned to subtly twist his fire evocation to be less flame-like, and more flaming radiance. As a combat-themed change, his was also extremely easy to manipulate. In short order, Drake had learned how to call down a pillar of radiant flaming energy that would be the most reliable in the coming battle.

With the original crystal shard in hand, Atlas decided that he, Artaxle, and Mason would stalk invisibly to the middle of the encampment. Atlas could slow most of the other occupants of the camp down mentally from that one crucial point to make it easier to dispatch their foes for the rest of the team. He would need Mason by his side to do that and Artaxle to also protect him when it came time to mend the rift.

So as the groups crept closer to the encampment, at first, all they could see was a slight shimmer off the coast of the Lake.

"It is there," Atlas assured them. "Brett, come in from the waterside to the north. Ke'eli, from the south. Kelly from the east and Drake from the west."

The four groups hugged each other before splitting off their separate ways.

They all had a signal to attack, one that would be easy to spot.

Atlas was going to bring the illusion of the camp down. Once they could see where they were going, the rest of the groups would converge on the camp and attack.

Atlas looked over at Mason and then at Artaxle.

"Gentlemen, shall we begin?"

Mason faced Atlas and Artaxle, placing his hands on their shoulders. Closing his eyes, he imagined all three of them were no longer visible to the unaided eye. They did not disappear in the invisible sense, but Mason assured them they could not be seen.

Trusting in his ability, Atlas led the group straight towards where he knew the camp to be. It did not take them long to enter the camp properly.

Pushing through what seemed like an airy bubble, the trio paused as the entire camp came into view.

There was much more activity going on here than Atlas thought.

Plane-touched dwarves were everywhere, building weapons, armor, and vehicles. The plane-touched halflings were endowing their magicks into scrolls and gearing up.

Atlas knew Mason could hear his thoughts.

They are aware and are preparing for battle. Some ally of theirs must have alerted them to their discovery.

Atlas saw Mason nod his head.

Looking over to his goblin friend, Atlas nodded his head to him as well.

Almost like a trick of the eye, Artaxle splintered off from the duo, blending in with the shadows.

Atlas and Mason continued towards the center of the encampment. They could now see a large scaffold with metal columns on either side of a glowing red rift. A red rift that flowed with fiendish energy resembling a massive eye.

In front of the rift sat a crystal ball set into a smaller column. It seemed specifically made to enhance the rift's power. Even now, the two could see a glowing tendril of energy flow from the rift to the crystal ball, and then out to the edges of the camp.

There it is. Once I disable the orb in front of the rift, the illusion will fade.

Mason furrowed his brow. Atlas could sense that the man was afraid but knew that he was confident with the King of the entire country by his side.

It was good to be back in the thick of things.

For too long, Atlas had been stagnant. He had several particularly important tasks he led he knew would aid the country in the battle to come, but he also knew that it took away from the time he could have spent with this family. The High King had many secrets, though only a select few knew of them.

Thinking about his secrets, Atlas looked over to the side where Artaxle mirrored their pace, keeping close enough to launch an attack if necessary on anyone who might discover their invisible presence. Atlas nodded to Artaxle, giving him a certain sign in the air with his hand.

Artaxle paused for the slightest of moments, his eyes going wide. But he was also a Nizari Hashashin and was one of the most skilled in the entire world. He had promised Atlas his aid with a blood-bond, and he would not back down from that promise now.

Artaxle nodded to the High King, giving a quick salute.

Atlas and Mason approached the crystal ball.

Looking back to Mason, Atlas indicated he should prepare for combat. Mason turned his back on Atlas, who at once went to work.

Reaching out with both hands, Atlas hovered over each end of the crystal ball device without touching it. He could sense the evil inside it, using the open rift to power much of the encampment.

"Do you like my little toy, High King?"

The voice came not from the crystal ball, but from the human who strode out of a tent not far away from the rift.

Atlas barely lifted open his eyes, instead deciding to focus on the instrument before him. The human was a mystic, trained to see through the illusionary invisibility that Mason had created.

And Atlas knew Mason was by his side.

Atlas could sense the mental battle that ensued between Mason and this other strange plane-touched human.

Atlas delved deeper into the depths of the crystal ball, trusting in Mason to protect him from the Mystic, and for Artaxle to protect him from any other threat.

Spending as much time as he would dare, Atlas fueled the mystic energy he 'borrowed' from Mason into himself, enhancing it to its full potential. With the already considerable power that Mason had, Atlas found it jokingly easy to disable the connection between the crystal ball, the rift, and the encampment.

The illusion around the camp dwindled away to nothing.

Atlas could hear the battle begin on the outskirts of the camp. He knew the dwarves and halflings had been caught unawares. He hoped to expel the fiendish essences from enough of them and spare their bodies from death, but knew that nothing was certain.

Atlas felt a slight tug of mental insinuation from the human battling Mason. The human knew Atlas had disabled his camp's defenses and tried to instruct the High King to re-erect them.

Atlas laughed at the prospect.

No, I think not. He 'thought' aloud.

A growl responded in his mind to his mental statement.

Atlas focused on that growl, realizing that it came not from the human, but from the crystal ball.

This thing was more dangerous than he thought.

Risking a glance to see how the battle was unfolding, Atlas saw Mason was wearing the other human Mystic down. Where most humans wore robes of plain brown or white, this one wore black robes and had very carnal tattoos on his bald head and neck. Both Mystics fought with only their hands, using their mental energies to stun, throw things and compel others to fight for them.

Looking beyond them, Atlas could see Brett and Tumidus coming in from the north. Atlas smiled at the pride he felt for his son, who he had not seen in so long; much longer than he had let on. Brett swatted the enemy combatants away, using their very own blood before splashing them with the holy water. Tumidus resorted to evocation magic, using frost and fire to carve a line through the encampment to its center.

To the east, Atlas could see his granddaughter coming in with Pwyll. The gnome blasted the enemy with his explosive bombs to keep them off balance, while Kelly healed those whose bodies had been purged of the vile essences. The divine healing caused pain to the fiends, disintegrating them on sight.

To the west, divine fury rained down on many an unfortunate foe while draconic flame toasted many others. Atlas admired his grandson more than the boy could imagine, knowing how much pain and torture the boy was going to have to go through in his life before he could finally find peace.

As for his beautiful and loving daughter-in-law, Atlas could feel the force of her energy coming up behind him. Between her Gods-send strength and that of Keb's, the duo paved a way through the scattered troops, swatting them like bugs. Atlas could very well imagine Ke'eli hitting someone so hard that the essence of the fiend would be left behind as the body would be sent sailing.

Atlas closed his eyes again to focus on the task at hand. He had already sent a tumultuous wave out through the camp, causing their foes to be distracted and disorganized. But he knew that there were two more things he would have to do.

Reaching down to the crystal shard he wore around his neck, Atlas brought it up before him towards the red-glowing rift. Focusing on channeling the energy from his body through the crystal and into the rift, he imagined pulling back that energy from the rift, back into the crystal.

Slowly, the rift began to close.

As if fighting him, the crystal ball flashed as the swirling depths of darkness inside it coalesced into shape. The ball itself began to vibrate and spin in its metal brace, the sound grating on the ears.

Atlas held on to the power of shutting down the rift. Piece by painful piece, the tear in reality grew smaller and smaller as the globe before him spun faster and faster. Sparks flew from the edges of the crystal ball as the thing heated.

Atlas furrowed his brow, sweat trickling from the edge of his head. He pushed on though, knowing the rift to almost be closed.

With a flash, the rift sealed in on itself just as the globe before Atlas shattered. Sparks flew in all directions as a reddish puff of smoke appeared in the place where the ball formerly stood.

A massive sword shot out from the reddish mist then, piercing Atlas' chest.

Lifting the High King off the ground impaled on its sword was a massive devil, the epitome of all the horror stories of the Bible, or any other book of religion. Its skin was blood red, and its muscles rippled as the thing effortlessly lifted the human man at the end of its blade. Massive wings spread behind it, open before a fanged mouth with temple horns that erupted high into the air.

The thing wore nothing but a belt and a metal skirt of some kind, wielding only the giant sword.

It laughed in the face of Atlas as blood bubbled from the High King's mouth.

"You are defeated, puny human."

The thing looked Atlas up and down, deciding on how best to eat the mortal.

Atlas hung there, coughing as he gripped the edges of the blade.

"Do it," he murmured.

Suddenly, Artaxle was upon the back of the fiend, driving his serrated blade deep into the back flesh of the devil.

Letting out a tremendous roar, the devil tried to spin to dislodge the blade in its back, but found that the weapon coveted his blood and would not be easily removed.

("My Watch had Ended" from the Game of Thrones: Season 6 Soundtrack by Ramin Djawadi)

Atlas' body dropped back down to the ground, still impaled on the sword. The devilish fiend tried to pull the weapon free, but Atlas held on tight to the blade, keeping it in his body.

Atlas could see the rest of his family coming to aid him. He could see the looks on their faces as they saw in terror what had happened. They would be angry and would fight to save him. He knew, though, that they were too late.

Brett willed the remaining enemies away from him with a wave of his hand, causing them to flip away like rag dolls.

He let out the most desperate scream as he watched the father he just found and finally remembered start to close his eyes as his body went limp.

But Atlas could still see his son. He could sense his daughter-in-law storming up behind him, using her powers to have the Earth grip the devil's feet, wrenching it down tight. He could feel the heat as Drake called down his divine fury on top of the devil, its skin burning and sizzling away. He could feel the warming glow from Kelly as she tried to use her power to heal him.

Atlas looked over at his granddaughter and smiled that same smile once again. He fought to keep concentration, as he knew he would not have long to say what he needed to say, once this fiendish devil was no more.

The joint fury of all ten of his new comrades came down upon the devil, who could do nothing but accept the strikes. It did not take long before the sword dropped lower and lower to the ground, depositing the body of Atlas with it. With a resounding *whoosh*, the devil's body disintegrated into nothing as the successive radiant attacks destroyed it.

Dropping to his knees, Atlas fought to keep his eyes open. He knew that if he closed them, he would fall.

Brett rushed up to his father, clutching him.

"Dad! Don't... don't go. We got you. Kelly can heal you. We just... need to get this out of you."

Atlas held his son's hand as Ke'eli came up on his other side, supporting his body so that the blade, still impaled through his chest, did not cut any wider.

The rest of the Seekers converged on the family, picking off several of the remaining plane-touched who remained.

Artaxle came up beside his King.

"Nizari. Keep the Oath. Take them to Stheno. She will know what to do. Promise me this." Atlas gurgled out the last few words, focusing his gaze on the goblin.

Artaxle nodded before bowing low. "I will do as you instructed, my High King."

"No no no... we just got here!" Brett was beside himself, looking around for something, anything, to use to help.

Kelly and Drake were by his side only seconds later.

Kelly looked down at her grandfather and cried.

"Dad, I don't know what to do!"

Drake began crying too, holding on to his own father tightly.

"My family... it will be alright.... You Four were destined long ago... to return to Atlantis to save us all. Learn the ways of our people. Go to the Tribal Sanctuaries. Hone your abilities. Awaken the Tribal Elders. Promise me."

Atlas reached out his hand to Brett, who grasped it.

Brett cried more than he ever had in his entire life.

He had just found his father, and now he was losing him again. Like a tease of Fate.

"I promise, dad."

"I love you, son. You've made me proud."

"I love you too dad..."

Atlas' body started to dematerialize in Brett's hands. Flesh turned in to sparkling motes of energy as the wind came through and scattered those motes like dust. One thing slowly settled into Brett's supporting hand: his father's crystal shard necklace.

The family gathered around Brett, hugging him tight. Clattering to the ground, the fiendish sword released Atlas' body, the last remnants of energy twinkling off into the dusky light. The Seekers surrounded the family, protecting them from any other threats, but also shedding a tear for their new friends.

"Why Kee? I don't... I don't understand. He's supposed to be all powerful or whatever. This isn't fair!"

Brett yelled, a force of energy enveloping the group. It was not physically painful, but mental. Everyone could feel the anguish deep inside his soul.

Artaxle walked up to the kneeling group, closing Brett's hand over the crystal. Brett growled as he looked up at the goblin. Wasn't he supposed to be his protector?

As if sensing the thought, Artaxle looked Brett in the eye.

"There might still be a way to save your father."

EPILOGUE

Thousands of miles away, Andrew scowled at the creature before him. He knew it was unavoidable, but had hoped that the going would be quicker. His entourage never took their eyes off the creature as well, their trust in Andrew's judgment overriding their own concerns.

The creature they poked and prodded before them was an elderly female orc, its skin tinged a light blue with icicles clinging precariously to the blond hair on its head. It moved slowly, as if walking hurt. In reality, the ground on which the creature walked was slick with ice, and one wrong move would send it tumbling.

"Yes, Ysbouer bring you. Bring to home. Dan sal die land jou kry." The orc giggled as she finished her sentence, looking back at the ones who followed it with pearly blue eyes and tusks that looked like jagged ice.

"Speak common pig, or we will skewer you and roast you alive!"

Andrew looked back at the speaker, his clear look of disdain quieting the upstart Conall at once. Conall scowled at the look, lowering his gaze to the ground. He adjusted his weapons and armor under the layers of thick clothing that he had donned to protect him from the cold.

The twins Frey and Freyja glanced at each other, smiling in the dim light provided by Brigid's glowing weapon. Both stayed closed to each other, the male fixing his bow and arrows over his shoulder while the female looked around at the ice, amazement obvious on her face. The winged woman Brigid stayed close to the middle, supplying the natural light they needed to see their way through the ice caverns.

Pelles the rogue was the only one obviously not present, as he was no doubt covering their rear. His unnatural form, mutated as it was, gave him a sense of stealth that was unsurpassed, providing him the ability to remain hidden both from the visual eye and the mental.

The group was in a small tunnel made entirely of ice and hard-packed snow. They followed the lead of the orc, though none appeared thrilled with the situation. The group had entered the tunnel only recently after having slid down the water shoot that deposited them in a large chamber.

The water there was heated, so it was easy enough for the Ring to dry themselves off and explore the naturally formed cavern. As they did so, they learned they were not alone.

And so, the group waylaid this solitary "ice-shaper", as she had named herself. One creature whose sole job it was to keep up the illusion that Antarctica was nothing but a giant block of ice resting upon a slab of land. She appeared down one tunnel and went to work, reinforcing the ice above and around her that was gradually melting away into the surrounding seas.

("Specter of the Goblin" from the Spider-Man Soundtrack by Peter Anthony)

Global warming had caused an issue with the secret that was Atlantis, melting the edges of the continent at an exponential rate. Orcs, being the most attuned to the elements, volunteered their services to rebuild the ice wall around their protective shield, if only to delay the inevitable.

And so, with a mixture of deception, interrogation and magic, Andrew had convinced the orc woman to lead them through the ancient tunnels back to the under-ice land of her home. She had led them over bottomless crevasses, over lakes of crystallized water polished to a mirror-like sheen, and through cave-ins and avalanches of powdered snow.

Ysbouer, as she had called herself, had escaped once. Sliding into the ice like a snowman melting in lava, she waved sheepishly at the group as her form coincided with their frozen surroundings. She had not realized that Andrew was a powerful warlock, but also owned some abilities of Brett the Water-Caller. Though Brett had not come to full terms with his abilities, Andrew wasted no time in testing his limits.

Immediately, Andrew reached within himself and combined the fel energies of his homeland with that of the surrounding ice, which, in essence was frozen water. He could feel Ysbouer gliding through the ground like a warm current compared to the surrounding frost. Reaching out with his mind and his own magic, he whispered the words to the ice beneath his fingers.

"Tamen Habere Personam."

Ysbouer's momentum froze in line with her frozen surroundings, black chains of ice gripping her body.

"I know you can hear me. I also know that you cannot stay in that form forever and will change back into your normal form soon enough. I will hold you here and entomb you in the unforgiving ice. Unless..."

Andrew embraced his more charismatic side. It was this that had compelled the orc to lead them in the end, more so than the intimidation or magic. He continued, caressing his words.

"Return to me. Lead me and my fellows onward to the shield. I have seen your mind. You are adamant that we cannot pass. If that is so, you still have my word that we will free you."

Andrew waited a few seconds more to let the words sink in. He also realized that the ice-shaper had little time left before she did indeed return to her normal self. With a flourish, he released his hold on her beneath the ice.

Sure enough, a puddle formed before them, coalescing into the form of the elderly orc. She furrowed her brow and puckered her lips at the group. But she did not flee again, and that had been many hours prior.

So, she continued. Andrew had chosen a side of the continent well, knowing from his memories somehow that one side was closer to the outer edge than any other. What could have taken weeks of traveling only took the group hours.

Soon enough, the light before them grew brighter. The blue reflections in the surrounding ice sparkled with the radiant energy of sunlight as opposed to Brigid's glowing weapon. The ice remained perfectly compact and slick, but further up ahead, the group could see what looked to be a sea lapping in the sunlight.

They were surprised as they realized that the chill from the pervading ice dome around them seemed to stop suddenly, giving way to what looked like water. A small sea was before them, but so was a massive series of ice floes that bobbed and ebbed up against an unseen barrier. Still inside the frozen tunnels, none dared to step any closer. They feared the stories Ysbouer had told them of what would happen to an outsider who touched their invisible shield. In addition, they worried that their first step in would cause their frozen drowning death.

Ysbouer looked back at the group and then forward at the rippling sea.

"You fear? Ah. Look. No fear. Land close by."

She smiled, pointing to the left of the opening in the wall.

Cautiously, Andrew approached the wall where she stood. He could see the drastic difference in both ice and wall where he assumed the 'shield' lay. Though he could not physically see this shield, he could feel it. The light covered him, making him wince as the brightness surprised him. Growing accustomed to this strange sight, Andrew opened his eyes wide and scanned the horizon.

Sure enough, there was a large body of land near to their current location. The water warmed considerably as it got further and further from the edge of the icy shield. Andrew could even see large-masted ships riding the waves and what looked to be a magnificent city in the distance.

Ysbouer, still smiling, continued walking.

Andrew, distracted by the sight of the city, did not realize she was gone until his comrades started yelling for him to wake up.

When he did so, he realized she stood on one of the ice floes, bobbing gently in the water away from their ice tunnel. She sat down, waving at the group, as she whispered something to the ice beneath her.

Slowly at first, but then gaining speed, the ice floe she was on moved toward the nearest land.

Andrew cursed himself for being distracted.

His entourage crept up beside him, worrying that they might inadvertently touch the magic shield that protected this place from all outsiders. They had heard legends of an old place that was protected from their 'kind' that would burn them to a crisp or cause them to suffer incurable bouts of madness.

Pelles, finally reuniting with the group, looked up to his master, one eye grotesquely larger than the other. He, of all the group, seemed the most hesitant to approach.

"What now, my Lord?"

Andrew looked on again at the city. Just being this near to the secret place sent his mind reeling. Memories that were not his flooded into his mind.

"Alaka" he murmured. That was the name of the city before him. They were all to the east of the continent; at least the east that it was before it became the South Pole.

Andrew looked back at his comrades. A feeling warmed his insides, making the strange demonic-looking creature smile. He could not explain it, but somehow, he knew the shield would let him pass.

Looking back over to the sea and the departing orc, he realized it would not matter soon if they didn't act fast.

Without a second thought, Andrew walked through the shield.

Immediately, a strange rippling spiraled out from the place his body had touched on the shield, as if he had walked through water. The shield did not slow or stop him in any way, nor did it disintegrate him. He slid down a short embankment of ice to the edge of the sea.

A loud humming sound emanated from the shield then, as if a gong had gone off across the whole of the continent. It pulsated with light, becoming visible, then opaque, then clear again. Ice fell in places the shield had before held back. The frozen piece of land that Andrew was on began to break apart from the chunks of frozen debris that cascaded all around it.

Andrew could see the inside of the tunnel that his comrades were in starting to collapse as well.

"Move through the barrier!" he yelled, but he knew they could not hear him.

The reply surprised him.

"The shield... destroy us! Better... inside and take our... with the tunnel!"

Brigid had heard him. And more importantly, he could hear her.

"The shield is fluctuating! Move quickly before it repairs itself!"

Andrew made a motion with his hand, showing they should move toward him. He also realized he did not have long to wait, as the surrounding sea was getting very rough. Larger chunks of ice were breaking off in the distance, and Andrew knew that when a sizeable chunk of ice hit the water, an enormous wave would be the result.

Wasting no more time, Brigid leaped through. Of all the group, she was the most confident that the shield would not deter her. Her Chosen form was that of a celestial, as opposed to her brethren the fiend. Inherently good-natured, her knowledge of the protective nature of the shield showed it would keep out evil creatures and fiends. She was neither; at least she thought so.

Sure enough, her wings spread wide and caught the wind that was building up near the inner edge of the shield. She floated down beside Andrew, fear and excitement on her face.

The twins came on next. Holding hands, Frey and Freyja got a running start and leaped from the edge of where they thought the shield would be, sliding down a slight snowy incline to plop into the edge of the icy sea. The cold did not phase them in the least though. They looked at each other and saw that they were in one piece, which was all that mattered to them.

Conall, normally the bravest of the group, with his powerful armor and weapons, waited anxiously. He tried to time the phasing of the shield, but found that it was random. He noticed that the phasing was speeding up, which to him meant he had little time left. Looking back at Pelles, he put on as confident a face as he could.

"Let's go creature!" he yelled to his diminutive friend.

Grabbing hold of the rogue, Conall dragged him along, running for the shield. Pelles, always the first to run and hide, dragged his feet behind him, not wanting to press his luck against the destructive shield.

Conall's greater strength brought him along anyway, the small rogue powerless against the bigger warrior. Conall lifted the creature up, flinging him through the shield with enough force that had the shield been up, the throw would probably have broken the rogue's neck.

But Pelles was through and sliding face-first down the snowy decline.

Conall, the brashest of the group, was also the most caring.

He took one more look at the shield, then lowered his head as he charged with a defiant roar. At the last second, he lifted off the ground with a loud grunt, sailing through the air.

The shield sensed him then, as a red aura glowed out and around where his body pierced its protective layer. Conall stopped in mid-jump, as a painful force of energy enveloped him, keeping him held aloft in the air.

("Hinx" from the Spectre Soundtrack by Thomas Newman)

The shield reformed around him, cutting into his body, where the shield met between his left shoulder blade and his right hip. An agonizing scream rent the air as Conall began to be cut in half.

Andrew looked on in as much pain as his comrade. Without thinking, he ran up the snowy slope back to the inside edge of the shield, if anything, to be there for his friend as he died.

But another thought came to Andrew then as he approached the shield.

'*It shut down for* me,' he thought. '*What if it did again? What if it only did, though, because I have part of Brett's essence inside me?*'

Pressing his luck, Andrew raised a hand to the red-glowing shield that was cutting his friend in half. Tentatively, he laid his fingers on the inside.

A cold numbing sensation flowed into his hand, followed by an immense energy that cascaded into the rest of his body. The power almost stopped his heart, but Andrew knew he had to control it, or he would certainly lose his life, besides Conall's.

The energy slowed, as did the disastrous aura that was cutting Conall in half. Andrew could sense Brigid by his side and knew that the shield was hesitantly letting Conall go. Andrew could hear him screaming still as the aura razed the rest of his body as Brigid pulled him through.

Even after Conall was freed from his painful prison, Andrew held on to the inside of the shield. The energy had ebbed its flow and was now exhilarating. Brigid was back by his side, though, yanking him back away from the wall as the sea roiled from the earlier onslaught of ice.

Andrew's eyes grew wide before he passed out from the sudden severing of the energy flow. But three words remained with him as he lost consciousness. Three words that the Soulstone pyramid had imparted to him before being cut off.

"Welcome home, Master."

ABOUT THE AUTHOR

Tony harkens from the southern reaches of Florida, where the blazing sun and the lapping waves at the beach lulled him into this imaginative world. Daydreaming of worlds beyond worlds, Tony began playing 2nd Edition Dungeons & Dragons in 1992, followed by games from the Palladium Universe like Heroes Unlimited and Rifts.

Being a game/dungeon master fueled the blazing fire inside his mind, delving deeper and deeper into different realities. Never satisfied with only one genre, Tony has sought out inspiration from all over the world for his games. It was in 2000 that his "main" character, Amalzzt, started to take shape. It wasn't until he returned from Iraq with the U.S. Marine Corps that he began to take notes of this enigmatic character.

More than 20 years later and Amalzzt is still romping around the multiverse. It's only now that he and his companions are starting to get the limelight they so richly deserve. Music had always been a gateway into these other universes for Tony, and it was the soundtracks he created that drove him to finally put his many ideas to paper.

Tony currently lives in Virginia with his amazing wife and two children who definitely did not fall far from the proverbial tree. They play Warhammer 40k, Age of Sigmar, Magic the Gathering, Marvel 616, Heroes Unlimited/Nightbane, and of course, plenty of Dungeons & Dragons when they aren't playing all kinds of other board games.